Blood of Vengeance

A Feral Breed: Desert Hellions MC Novel

Ellis Leigh

kinship press

To the woman who got hit on at her local gas station by a man who said "if you had a man, you wouldn't be at the gas station because your man would be handling that for you" and posted a TikTok about the experience. That one minute spawned 100,000 words of paranormal romance with a hero named Flinch.

BLOOD
OF
VENGEANCE

Copyright © Blood of Vengeance by Ellis Leigh

All rights reserved.

No part of this book may be reproduced in any form or by any electronic or mechanical means, including information storage and retrieval systems, without written permission from the author, except for the use of brief quotations in a book review.

Blood of Vengeance is a work of fiction. Names, characters, places, and incidents are either the products of the author's imagination or are used fictitiously, and any resemblances to actual persons, living or dead, business establishments, events, or locales is coincidental.

EBook: 978-1-954702-63-9
Paperback: 978-1-954702-64-6
Hardcover: 978-1-954702-65-3
Large Print Hardcover: 978-1-954702-66-0

Edited by Lisa Hollett of Silently Correcting Your Grammar, LLC
Ebook Cover by Natasha Snow Design
Print Cover by Selena Blake

For inquiries, contact ellis@ellisleigh.com

ONE

LOCKLYN

Being hit on sucked donkey balls. Being hit on at four in the morning while pumping gas in the freezing cold after working all night at a dive bar was some sort of sixty-ninth level of hell bullshit.

"Yo, baby. Let me get your number."

I rolled my eyes and prayed to the gas pump gods that the numbers would scroll faster, doing my best to ignore the man approaching from the other side of the lot.

"C'mon," I whispered, keeping an eye on the person and clinging to the coat that wasn't anywhere near warm enough for a Detroit winter. "Let's go, let's go."

In a moment of luck the likes of which I had never experienced, the digital screen flipped to show twenty dollars, and the pump clicked off. Thanking the universe for the bit of fortune I'd been shown, I returned the nozzle to the holder, screwed the cap on my tank, and rushed around the front of the car right as the man reached my trunk.

"Hey, beautiful. I'm not going to hurt you. I just want to know your name."

Sure you do. "I got a man. I don't need another."

"If you got a man, what're you doing out here pumping gas so late? If you had a man, he'd be taking care of that for you."

I hopped into the driver's seat and slammed the door, locking it behind me. I didn't know what men he knew, but none of the ones I'd ever dated would have given two shits about how much gas I had in my tank, let alone would have made sure to fill it for me. Someone lived in fairy-tale land, and that person sure as hell wasn't me.

The old beater I drove coughed and sputtered, but she started, granting me the escape I so desperately needed, though not before I heard the man scream out an insult and bang on the hood of my trunk. Typical—he called me baby and beautiful until he didn't get what he wanted, then he spewed some C-U-Next-Tuesday attitude and aggression. But he was a man who'd fill my gas tank for me? *Right.*

I drove to the apartment I shared with my best friend, parking two blocks away in the only free spot I could find. I would need to wake up by nine to move my car or risk getting another ticket I couldn't afford to pay. Not fun but normal. Sleeping in short shifts because of the parking rules in my neighborhood had become my lifestyle.

"That you, Locklyn?"

I sighed and closed the door behind me, exhaustion making my bones hurt but the scent of something warm and yummy keeping my attention. "Yeah, it's me. What are you doing up?"

Zella—all five-foot-two of my favorite person on earth—peeked around the corner, a tired smile tugging up her pale lips. "I'm pulling a double shift at the hospital because they're offering overtime this week."

"Don't wear yourself out."

She gave me a quick hug as I passed, tucking her head against my shoulder for just a second before moving toward the stove. "I need the money, and the work is easy. Way easier than being on my feet all night like you."

The woman didn't lie. Zella had waitressed at a white-table-cloth restaurant in Grosse Pointe Shores when I'd met her, earning sweet tips and rubbing elbows with the richest of the rich on the daily. Unfortunately, an autoimmune condition had made that sort of job impossible, so she'd been forced to quit and take a job a little less physically demanding. Working at the hospital didn't always fill her wallet the same way a good week at the restaurant had, but her pain level had dropped since quitting. Having access to health insurance had been another pro in her book, especially with the health issues that seemed to be piling up for her.

"Come," Zella said as she headed for the counter, her near-constant limp barely noticeable. "Let's eat. I haven't seen you in days and need my Locklyn time."

That right there—the simple gift of wanting to spend time with me. That's what made Zella so special in my world. I would have given anything to that woman. "You didn't have to cook to spend time with me."

"I know I didn't have to, but I wanted to. Breakfast for me, dinner for you." She slid onto the barstool, setting my plate in front of my spot. I took my seat and dug in, the need for food overriding my need for sleep. At least for a little bit.

"Have you talked to your father?" Zella asked out of the blue. Or maybe not so out of the blue.

"Have I been saying his name in my sleep again?"

"Sometimes." She kept her eyes on her food, pushing and yet not overstepping any boundaries I may have had in regard to my fucked-up family situation. "I know you were worried about him."

Not past tense—I worried daily about the man. Or shifter. Because the guy everyone knew as Chiggy wasn't human. At least, not all the time. But even Zella didn't know that, which made talking to her about the current lack of communication that much harder.

"He hasn't answered my calls, and I keep having these dreams about him. In the desert." I sighed and stared at my plate, no longer hungry. "They're creeping me out."

Zella nodded, setting her fork down gently before pushing away from the counter. "Think it's time to take a trip?"

A trip. To the desert. To check in on the man who had sent me away and told me to never come back there again. "I don't think so."

"You're going to keep worrying."

"He's not exactly the most stable man in the world."

"No, but he answers your calls, doesn't he?"

Always. Even if he was busy, he would at least send me a text to let me know when he would call me back. He hadn't wanted me to stay in Mesa, but he hadn't kicked me out of his life. Just his town and his shifter world.

"Can you call the club?"

The motorcycle club he ran. The one filled with other wolf shifters like him. The one I had never been allowed to be involved with. "I already did."

Zella turned, one delicate black eyebrow raised. "And?"

"No dice. They won't return my messages."

"Damn." She rinsed off our plates and set them in the sink, wiping her hands on a hand towel that read "Don't Be a Cuntosaurus Rex" above a drawing of a rainbow-colored dinosaur, before turning my way once more. "So, what's the plan?"

"I wait...it's the only thing I can do."

She didn't look convinced, but she also didn't know the

whole story. Couldn't. I loved Zella like a sister, but my dad's life had to be off-limits. His secret was not mine to tell.

"Okay, then," Zella said, clapping her hands once and sighing. "I need to get this ass of mine to work, and you look ready to pass out."

"Yeah. Sleep has been...difficult."

"Those duffel bags under your eyes make that more than obvious." She grabbed her work bag from the floor and her coat from the rack, wincing as she shrugged into the calf-length black puffy thing that seemed to be a uniform of urban Midwesterners in winter. "Get some sleep. We can try to call your dad again once I get home. I'll bring wine."

"Perfect." I rose to my feet and stretched, yawning loudly. "Have a great day. Don't kill anyone with paperwork."

"I make no promises." With that, Zella swept into the hall and closed the door behind her, leaving me to myself for the day. I quickly cleaned up the mess from our dinner/breakfast and double-checked all the locks, craving the dark of my room and the softness of my bed.

But first...

With more than a little trepidation in my bones, I pulled my phone from my pocket. It was early in Mesa...or late, really. Two thirty in the morning would be late for my dad. He wouldn't be sleeping, though. The lifestyle he lived made him a bit of a night owl. Holding my breath, I scrolled through my contacts to his name and pressed the green button to connect. Hoping against hope to hear the deep rumble of his voice.

The line never even rang—just went straight to voice mail.

"You've reached Chiggy. Tell me what I need to know."

I sighed again, half tempted to throw the phone across the room, but biting back my ire and hitting the end button instead.

"Where are you, Dad?"

I didn't receive an answer, so I headed for the bathroom to

get ready for bed, then curled up under my blanket and stared at my silent phone until sleep finally took me.

The dream came quickly—the desert, the sound of motorcycles in the distance, the wolf howls ringing through the night air. The acrid smell of land scorched by the sun, highlighted by a slight floral note I recognized but couldn't name. An intensifying sense of dread and an eerie feeling of being watched that blanketed me as the valley came into full view. As the dream showed me her truth. All the other times I'd witnessed the scene before me, my dad had been standing in front of his truck, backlit by the headlights, my placement all wrong to spot details. I'd never even seen his face, but I'd known it was him. Had recognized the shape of him.

This time, I had been dropped in a different spot. This time, I saw his face.

"You're making a mistake," my dad called out, looking fierce and ready to fight even as he put his hands on his head. "My brothers won't let you get away with this."

A laugh came from behind him, from a pocket of shadows I couldn't see into because of the brightness of the headlights. I didn't need to see to feel the menace in the air, though. The malevolence. I stared at my dad, my heart racing and my stomach churning. Terrified for him. Knowing what was coming without ever having seen it.

"Daddy," I whispered, unable to hold my tongue. His head jerked up, his eyes meeting mine for just a moment. A look of shock rolled across his aged face, as if he hadn't expected to see me. That expression quickly turned to one of fear. Something I had never seen him wear.

"Locklyn." My name came from behind my dad, came from the deepest, darkest shadows. Came from where the energy had turned cold and hard and dangerous. From a voice I had never heard before and said in a way that sounded like a threat. Like a challenge.

And then a gun fired.

I woke with a start, screaming into the dark room. Wanting to go back, to travel through space and time so I could do something to stop whatever had just happened. Without thought, I grabbed my phone and scrolled to my dad's name. Chanting prayers and wishing for miracles as the line connected.

Curling over in horror as it clicked into nothing.

Not even connecting to his voice mail.

"He's dead," I whispered to myself. Feeling the weight of truth in the words. Shaking with the knowledge that I had seen his death from almost two thousand miles away. Certain of it.

There would be no space or time travel for me. No chance to save the man I called Dad.

I had only one choice left.

I needed to go to Mesa to find him.

Two

FLINCH

Death had been a part of my job for too many decades to count. I was good at killing—a natural. And when it came to getting rid of threats to my club brothers, I actually enjoyed it a little. But cleaning up the mess after one of my brothers got a little too excited during a fight had become the bane of my existence.

"Get the hydrogen peroxide." I tossed the shovels into the back of my truck, making sure they landed in the tarp I'd laid down. "You need to wash your hands and boots."

"Why?"

I slammed the tailgate closed and turned to glare at the man we called Rush. "Because I fucking said so."

"Yeah. Okay." Rush shook his head but followed my directions, grabbing the bottle of hydrogen peroxide and pouring it over his hands. As he dealt with his boots, I took one last look around the patch of desert where I'd decided to plant our friend. Nothing stood out, not a single thing attracted my eyes to that random stretch of sand, and yet something felt off. Felt missed. I couldn't pin the feeling down, couldn't find where it was coming from, and that left me and my wolf on edge.

Once all the blood had been cleaned by the shifter who was about to become my personal punching bag and I'd made sure to remove every trace that we'd ever been on that plot of scorched earth, we hopped into my truck and headed for the clubhouse. I kept my speed just above the limit, kept my stops complete. The idiot beside me likely had blood or something on his clothes that would delight the local crime scene investigators, so I made sure to keep any cops hiding along the highway from taking an interest in us. I stayed fucking invisible, because if someone noticed me, they'd have to be the next one in a shallow grave in the desert. And I wasn't in the mood for a round two.

When I finally hit the clubhouse lot, I pulled into my spot and threw the truck into park before turning toward my passenger. Shit like this only ever went sideways for two reasons: being unprepared or being an idiot. Rush's behavior since the moment he'd gone berserk on the now-dead human made me think we were going to have trouble with both.

"The only way this stays between us is if you keep your mouth closed."

Rush huffed, not looking all that agreeable. "The fucker shouldn't have started talking about the girls like that."

The girls, meaning the females—shifters and human—who liked hanging around the club and getting railed by my brothers. But Rush hadn't been worried about the *girls*. He'd been worried about *one* girl. A certain human who did business at the club, selling us a few of the custom spirits she brewed every month. A female he'd denied having any interest in since the moment he'd caught sight of her tight jeans and red cowboy boots. The one he lied about on the daily.

Mated wolves would be the death of me.

"I don't care if some blowhard hanger-on starts fucking her

on the bar—you don't kill a human without making preparations. The mess attracts the cops."

"There's no mess."

"Because of me," I spat, the growl of my wolf making my words rumble through the night. "You gonna listen to me now and keep that fucking trap shut?"

He flinched. The tic likely would have been unseen by most, but not me. I saw it; I knew he didn't like being talked to like a little punk. Knew it and didn't give a flying fuck about his feelings. My wolf reveled in knowing we had the upper hand.

"Well?" I growled out, letting my inner beast come out to play a little more. Feeling my canines descend and my face lengthen. Making sure the man beside me knew who ranked higher than him on every scale and who wouldn't take his shit.

Rush twitched a lip again, his own wolf likely making an appearance, but neither the man nor the beast took the bait to fight. Smart move on both their parts.

"Yeah," he finally said before letting out an irritated huff. "My trap stays fucking shut."

"Good. Now get the fuck out of my truck." I threw open my door and stepped out, freezing into place the second the wind hit me. The second I recognized the scent being carried on it.

"You smell roses?"

Rush looked at me as if I'd just asked him to eat a dick. "No. You do?"

I did, but I didn't give him the gift of a reply, assuming the scent of roses on the wind—one that was already fading away—was some sort of response to all the shit flying at me lately. Instead, I slammed the truck door closed behind me and headed for the bar. I needed a stiff drink and some club pussy to give me her mouth in order for me to get my brain to unwind. Nothing about the night had gone the way I'd wanted it to, mostly because of Rush, but also because of the buzz I'd felt in the desert. The sort of buzz that my wolf and I knew could only mean one thing. Trouble was on the horizon.

"Yo, Flinch," Preacher, the enforcer of the club, hollered from his seat at the bar the second I walked inside, looking as serious as ever. "The old man wants you."

I nodded once before heading for the back. The boys all looked to be having a grand old time—drinking, fucking, and fighting a little bit. Nothing serious, nothing out of hand. Just a normal Friday night with the Desert Riders. As normal as it could be, considering how fucked up things seemed lately.

I popped a knuckle against the doorjamb, giving the vice president of the club, a wolf named Cutter, the chance to tell me to fuck off. Not that he would if he'd been looking for me.

"You rang?"

Cutter waved me in, keeping his eyes locked on the papers before him. "Where you been?"

"Cleaning up Rush's mess."

My VP looked up, one gray eyebrow cocked. "Anything we need to be worried about?"

"We? No. Me?" I shrugged before taking a seat in the chair across from him. "I'll take care of whatever blowback comes our way."

"You always do." He rocked back in his leather office chair, his ice-blue eyes locking on mine. He had his long silver hair tied back tonight, a black tee making him appear more stone-cold than ever. The man tended to scare the humans who hung around the club, though none of them could have explained why. I could have. He exuded predator energy from the top of his head to the bottom of his boots. Everyone outside of his circle of brothers was a bag of flesh to him—nothing more, nothing less. Even a few of the brothers didn't get to be viewed as more than an organ donor. The man just couldn't be bothered to give a single fuck for the majority.

He held my gaze, likely waiting for me to break. Playing some fucked-up power game our wolves found fun. I kept my face flat, my eyes steady. Didn't even fucking blink.

Finally, his lips twitched into his version of a smile, and he shook his head. "Do you even know how to back down?"

"No."

One word—full sentence.

His grunt of acceptance came with a head nod. "Chiggy's missing."

Chiggy. Club president. Longtime member. Badass older wolf who definitely knew how to handle himself.

"Leads?"

"None. I sent Mule and Zed over to his place, but they got nothing so far. I'm still waiting on them to come back after doing a bit more looking around."

"His ride there?"

"His bike, yeah. Zed said his truck wasn't in the garage."

"Think he ditched?" I didn't. The man would no sooner run from us than he would suck a cock on the pool table in the club. He'd always been as steady and loyal as they came.

Cutter seemed to agree with me. "I doubt it, but at this point, what the fuck do I know? The guy's in the wind."

"What do you want me to do?"

"Wait for Mule and Zed to get back, then go out to Chiggy's house. Take Banger—that old bastard hung with Chiggy the most. With his knowledge and your...skills" —he quirked an eyebrow at my snort— "maybe you can piece together something. A possibility. We need a place to start."

"Understood. That it?"

"Yeah." He went back to reading over the papers before him as I rose to my feet and headed for the door, stopping me with a barked, "Flinch."

I turned, waiting. And waiting some more. "Yeah?"

"Keep this quiet."

"Not a problem." I headed down the hall and into the club room, hunting for Banger. The old wolf shifter could usually be found flirting with the club pussy. He didn't fuck in the club like the younger guys, but he liked showing the younger boys up. Had fun getting the females to give him their attention over the buffer, more ego-driven brothers before slipping away with them for a little privacy. The man had entertained me pulling his shit for years, but tonight, he wasn't entertaining the ladies. He wasn't even in the bar area of the clubhouse. That fact didn't help the sense of dread slowly building in my gut.

"Yo, Preach." I slid in beside the shifter at the bar, keeping my voice low. "Where's Banger?"

"Don't know. Why you looking for him?"

Before I could answer, someone hollered from the other side of the room. "We've got a live one."

I turned right as the door slammed closed, the heavy thump of the music playing overhead matching the sudden pounding of my heart. A woman stood just inside the door—a dark-haired beauty with high tits, hips made for grabbing, and way more worry in her eyes than any female should have been living with. She seemed to be chatting with the prospect on door duty, and while he looked to be enjoying the interaction, she did not. But that wasn't what kept me staring. Wasn't what had me heading in her direction without any intention on my part.

My wolf wanted to be closer to her, and I never ignored my beast.

I caught the end of her side of the conversation as I moved in behind her.

"...he's not answering my calls, and no one seems to be able to tell me what's happening."

"Yeah, I..." The prospect spotted me as I came to a stop. Gave me one look before the wolf within him peeked through, recognizing my status as the bigger predator between us. I wasn't looking to pull rank, though. He didn't matter.

"I've got this one, prospect."

The kid—no clue of his actual name—gave me a nod then got the fuck out of the way. The woman turned all slow and calm, her scent slamming into me just as her eyes met mine. I had three impressions in those first seconds. One, the girl had green eyes, the shape more familiar than I would have liked. Two, those tits were even more fucking amazing than I had thought from across the room. And three, I was fucked. Absolutely fucked.

My fated mate had just walked into the club.

Three

LOCKLYN

The Hellions clubhouse sat deep in the desert outside of Mesa, a shabby, low-slung building with concrete walls and blacked-out windows. The type of place no sane, single woman would walk into alone. I was both sane and single, but I was going to have to cross that threshold. Once I got myself ready. There was no place for me to pop into, no gas station or store with a restroom I could use to freshen up, so I crouched behind a pickup truck on the outskirts of the lot and unzipped my backpack.

"Whore bath it is," I whispered, my heart breaking a little at the colloquialism I'd picked up from my dad. I tugged a face-cleansing wipe from my toiletries bag and gave myself a quick wipe-down to remove the worst of the dirt and smell. Three days on a bus was no picnic, but I didn't have the time, energy, or money to rent a hotel room and rest. I needed to find my dad, which meant I needed to head inside his club and ask a few questions. I had a feeling that was going to go over like a lead balloon, but it wouldn't be the first time I'd faced down angry bikers.

Once relatively clean, I grabbed my makeup bag and went to work beating my face into some semblance of normal. My eyes were red-rimmed, with large, dark bags under them from the whole not-sleeping thing I had going on, which made the job a little harder. Between the noises of the bus itself, the creeper passengers, and the fact that the nightmare of my dad's murder refused to stop replaying in my head, I could have probably counted the hours slept on my journey across the country on one hand. But I needed the men of the club to talk to me, and the easiest way to get those jaws moving was to appeal to their base needs. Sex being the first one that came to mind.

"Wing the eye and rouge the cheeks. It's showtime." I blew myself a kiss in the compact mirror and tucked everything into my backpack. Without giving myself a second to think twice about my plan, I headed for the door to the club, wanting so badly to get this over with but doubting I'd get what I needed.

The pounding beat of some sort of heavy metal music made the parking lot practically vibrate, and the smell of smoke and weed slammed into me as I pulled open the door. It took a moment for my eyes to adjust to the darkness inside, but once they did, I got a good hard look at the place that had always meant so much to my dad. That I had been sent away from and told never to return to.

Sorry I couldn't follow your directions, Dad.

"We got a live one," someone yelled from deeper in the club, reminding me to pay attention. This wasn't a place to get lost in memories. I had been Chiggy's daughter all those years ago—without his protection, I was nothing more than fresh meat. I took a deep breath and let the door close behind me, locking myself inside with men who were either my family...or my enemies.

A big man sat just inside the door—a prospect, or wannabe

member of the club, if the rules were what I remembered—and gave me a solid perusing before grunting.

"Business or pleasure, sweetheart?"

I kept my chin up, kept my voice firm and without a bit of waver from the nerves building up in me as I said, "Business, then pleasure if things work out."

His slow grin sent a chill up my spine, but I didn't shiver. Not even when he reached forward and grabbed a lock of my hair, pulling it over my shoulder and staring at the dark strands as if examining them. "What kind of business does a woman like you have in a place like this?"

"I'm looking for my dad."

"Got a lot of men in here willing to play the daddy role for you."

The eye roll I shot his way was something I couldn't have held back if I'd wanted to. "Not into that particular kink, but I really am looking for my dad. Maybe you know him—goes by Chiggy."

The guy darted a look down at me, and something in his expression made my stomach drop. Something that looked way too much like fear to calm me down.

"Have you seen him?" I asked. "Because he's not answering my calls, and that's not normal."

"Yeah, I..." The guy looked past me right as the scent of sage and leather caught my attention, his eyes locking on something over my shoulder.

Before I could turn, a warm, gravelly voice came from behind me. "I've got this one, prospect."

The prospect nodded once then rose from his stool and walked away. Mr. Gravel-Voice stepped around me, staring in a way that seemed more hunter than inquisitor, his broad shoulders and ridiculous height dwarfing me in ways that both terrified and intrigued. His light eyes captured every breath I took, every flick of my own eyes taking him in. And his slow grin as I lifted my chin seemed more sarcastic than happy.

"What do we have here?"

I breathed slow and deep, forcing myself not to respond to the way his presence rocked my confidence. Trying my best not to tremble in fear before him. He stared at my lips, something like a growl rumbling in the space between us. Something like heat there, too. The way he looked at me should have been illegal, how he devoured me with his eyes. The man was sex on wheels and—if I had to guess—as dangerous as they came, a deadly combination to a gal's thought processes.

But I had no time to make bad decisions with Mr. Tall-Dark-and-Murderous. I had to find Chiggy.

"My dad's not answering my calls, so I came to look for him," I said, keeping my voice calm and neutral. Fighting not to tremble as he ran that intense gaze down my body. "I'm Chiggy's daughter."

The man's light eyes darted to mine, his heated expression slamming closed and switching to a dangerous blankness that chilled me to my bones. "How the fuck could Chiggy have a kid?"

That question, I could handle. "Well, when a man and a woman really like each other—"

He huffed a startled laugh, his blank expression cracking.

"All right, smartass. I know how fucking works." He inched closer, throwing a deep shadow over my entire body. "You got proof you're Chiggy's?"

I wasn't prepared for that question, but I knew who my dad's friends were. Who would remember the days when I'd sat at the bar with a Barbie and a kiddie cocktail. "Is Banger around?"

The guy stared for an extended moment, keeping his eyes locked on mine for far longer than was comfortable. I didn't look away, though. Didn't even blink. His expression stayed stonelike, his entire body still. He gave nothing away.

Finally, he opened his mouth. "I might be able to wrangle him up."

"Then wrangle," I said, something close to relief settling in my chest. "He'll vouch for me."

He didn't wait this time, just barked a single word. "Prospect."

The man who'd been watching the door appeared beside me. "Yeah?"

"Watch her. Anyone steps out of line, they'll be dealing with me."

I had no idea if his threat applied more to if I stepped out of line or if any of the other brothers did, but I didn't care because in the next second, he was gone. Disappearing deeper into the bar, hopefully on his trek to find Banger.

"Sit," the prospect said, moving to stand on the other side of his stool. I did as I'd been told, rising up on the ball of my foot to slide my hip onto the seat before taking a good look around. The club had changed a lot over the years, and yet some things had stayed the same. There were still neon beer signs on the walls and motorcycle parts hanging from the ceiling like some sort of modern art display. Gone were the brown leather bar chairs I remembered sitting and spinning in as a kid, replaced by sleek, black leather stools with chrome legs. The liquor bottles still sat in front of an ancient, dirty mirror, but the bar itself looked new and clean, the shape different from the pictures in my hazy memories. The people had changed, too, the men who had made up this club likely moving on or retiring and getting replaced with younger ones. The women were the same, though—faceless, generic-looking blondes with big tits and wearing almost nothing sitting with random men who looked to care about as much for them as they did their beer. Those women would likely be fucked on the pool table or in a back hallway, used by one and then handed off to the next in line. And they loved it.

At least, they did for a while. My mom had until she'd met Chiggy. She'd loved him hard, desperately wanting to become his old lady and work the bar at the clubhouse. But things hadn't worked out that way.

I had just spotted Mr. Gravel-Voice with the light-blue eyes that seemed to look right through me, had just gotten yanked out of my memories by the reality of my present once more, when the door burst open. A different man stormed inside—one I remembered—followed by a man with arms the size of tree trunks and a jaw that could cut glass who happened to be wearing sunglasses. At night. Something I didn't have time to ponder.

"Where's Cutter?" the man I knew—Mule, a longtime friend of my dad—yelled, pushing past me without even glancing my way. "Where the fuck is Cutter?"

Mr. Gravel-Voice stalked over, looking from me and back to Sunglasses before focusing on Mule. "He's in the back. What's up?"

"I think Chiggy's gone."

The words landed like a punch, pain exploding from the point of contact.

Mr. Gravel-Voice didn't react. Didn't twitch a single muscle at the news. "Not possible."

"Yeah, it is." I slipped in beside Mule, looking up into his face. Giving him a sad sort of half smile when recognition lit. Everyone always said I had my dad's eyes. "I've seen his death. That's why I'm here."

The world went still, the loud music stopping within a beat as the attention of every nonhuman in the room turned our way.

Mr. Gravel-Voice spoke first. "What do you mean, you've seen it?"

I shrugged, suddenly fighting the urge to cry. Grief growing dark and heavy within me, tendrils of pure sadness slipping between my bones. "I kept seeing him die in my dreams. My nightmares wouldn't let me be, so I came to check. To see who killed him."

"What the fuck are you talking about?" Sunglasses grabbed my arm and yanked me almost off my feet, looking ready to fight. Ready to shift. "What did you do to Chiggy?"

Mr. Gravel-Voice growled low and deep, shoving his big body between us. Pushing me back and wrapping one arm around my waist from behind as he practically snarled at the other man. His touch sent flames shooting through my chest, but I didn't have time to figure out what that meant because his snarl turned into a deep, threatening growl as he took one single step closer to Sunglasses.

"Don't ever fucking touch her, Zed."

The larger brother—Zed—didn't back down. "Fuck you, Flinch. How 'bout asking her what she means. Are you saying someone did something to Chiggy?"

I nodded, catching the ice-blue eyes of the man they called Flinch as he turned to watch me. "If my dreams are right, yes. Someone murdered him."

The growls that filled the room sent the hairs on my neck rising, but I held my ground. I couldn't show fear around shifters. My dad had definitely taught me that rule. Along with a couple others.

Never come unannounced.

Never trust a shifter.

And never show them you're afraid.

With my dad dead, his lessons were all I had to keep me safe. That, and the beast named Flinch, who stood between me and his brothers. For the moment, at least. Because one other thing about motorcycle clubs and shifters my dad had taught me sang loud and clear in my memories.

Riders will always choose their brothers over everything else.

Which meant, eventually...I'd be expendable.

I needed to figure out what had happened to my dad before that came true.

FOUR

FLINCH

I'd cleaned up a murder that hadn't been thought through or planned out, the fates had decided to fuck me over by tossing my mate—a woman who had shown up at the club with nothing more than a backpack and a little hope to figure out what had happened to her father—right in my lap, and we had a motorcycle club with a dead president.

This fucking day.

"That's it," I said, giving each one of my brothers a dead-eyed stare to make sure they knew I meant business. "Executive team meeting. Now."

The men who ran the club nodded and began heading for the war room, while the regular members grumbled. Everyone would eventually have to be involved with what needed to happen next, but too many mouths fighting for words would create a fucking mess instead of a plan. We needed to keep things small.

And I needed to keep an eye on my new mate.

"You're coming with me." I grabbed her arm and pulled her along beside me, not giving her the chance to argue. Her skin burned under my touch, soft and pliable and delicate even as it set me on fire. Super-soft. I felt like a damn monster gripping her like I was, so I relaxed my hold. All that did was give her the opportunity to pull away. To stop following me.

"Stop dragging me around." She stood Peter-Pan-style with her hands on the swell of her hips. Inviting me to look. To feel. To take a bite. She also looked about ready to try to kick my ass. A motherfucking bunny rabbit trying to look like a pit bull. "I just came to figure out what happened to Chiggy."

"And that's what we're going to discuss." I grabbed her again —gentler this time, because fuck me, my inner wolf might lose his shit if I hurt her—and led her through the bar area and into the back of the club. The darkness of the hallway only made me think about all the naughty things I could do to her in the shadows. Not that I would—not in the club. Plenty of brothers enjoyed putting on a show for the others, but not me. Especially not with my mate. The only person seeing her taking my cock would be me and her.

Fuck, that made me realize I should buy one of those big floor mirrors for my bedroom. For later. Much later. I didn't have time to think of that at the moment.

"In here." I directed her through a doorway before following and closing the door behind me. Past the president's office sat a large conference room with a long table, some really uncomfortable office chairs on wheels, and a couple of recliners. I plopped her thick ass in one of the latter and pulled an office chair beside it, pretty much blocking her from the rest of the men around the table. Cutter raised an eyebrow in my direction when he walked in, but I didn't budge. I simply stared back at the man, letting my wolf creep to the surface.

Making sure he and everyone else knew she was under my protection.

"Change in plans?" he asked as he took a seat near me, keeping his voice low and a little distance between us. Cutter wasn't one to back down, but he had enough sense to leave me to whatever I had going on. He'd have questions, though. Later. And since he was the current head man in the club, I might actually have to answer them.

"Seems like it," I said, still watching the door.

The VP let out a sigh and rubbed his temples, eyeing each brother until the last man entered. Until that door had been closed and locked.

"Let's get to skinning this cat." Cutter sat a little deeper in his chair, his gaze hard and his energy one of fuck-around-and-find-out. The entire eight-member executive committee wasn't currently at the bar, so only five men were in the room with Chiggy's daughter. The five of us could make decisions, though. We had to. "What the fuck do we do about Chiggy?"

Zed, our warlord and the one who led any sort of operation that could end up with dead men on either side, grunted his way into the conversation. "*If* he's actually dead, we figure out who killed him and return the favor."

Preacher, our enforcer, nodded. Our treasurer, Mule, kept his mouth shut—which wasn't surprising—though I had a feeling he'd pony up some serious resources, both cash and otherwise, if the call was made for it.

Cutter turned my way. "You're the cleanup man. You got this?"

"We find the fucker who did this, and I'll make sure no blowback hits the crew."

"Good."

Zed took control of the conversation next, focusing on my mate. "*What's your story?*"

I didn't turn to look at her, didn't dare lose focus on the four men all staring her way. Three, actually, because when I checked in on Cutter, that man had his gaze locked right on me instead.

"What's her name, Flinch?" Cutter asked. He knew... How and when he picked up on the fact that the woman sitting behind me had been fated to be mine, I had no idea, but the bastard knew. His deferring to me instead of speaking directly to her told me so.

But fuck if I could answer him. "Don't know."

One eyebrow flew up. Just one. Fucker had a skill. "You planning on asking her?"

"It's Locklyn," the girl said, her voice strong and clear and seemingly unafraid. "My name is Locklyn."

Cutter glanced my way once more before focusing on her. "And you're Chiggy's daughter. Whom none of us knew about."

"Banger knows me. He'd vouch for me."

"Banger ain't here," Zed said. "What else you got?"

The girl—Locklyn—went silent for a minute. I noticed her look toward Mule, who sat with his mouth closed and his eyes on her. I had a feeling the old man knew something, but he wasn't telling anyone shit. Typical. I could feel her anxiety, though— sense her stress. My wolf whined inside my head, wanting to jump in front of her. To protect her. And what my wolf wanted, he got.

"She's got Chiggy's eyes," I said.

Zed huffed. "Not enough."

He wasn't wrong, but his attitude still made me want to show my teeth. Instead, I pulled my phone from my pocket and tapped through to Banger's number, setting it on the table and putting it on speakerphone. My eyes locked on Zed's as the device sounded a ringing tone before a familiar voice answered.

"I'm busy. Make it quick."

I could do that. "Chiggy got a daughter?"

"What the fuck?" He mumbled a few other words, the sound of a hand pressing against the microphone causing something like static on the call before he came back. "Try me again with that one."

"Chiggy. Got. A. Daughter. Ain't that hard, old man."

"Don't you think you should be asking Chiggy that?"

Cutter jumped in, adding his VP weight. "We believe Chiggy's dead, and there's a girl here claiming she's his kin. So, what say you—did the man have a kid or what?"

"Fuck me." Banger sighed, his voice growing harder as he said, "I'll be there in five. Don't fucking touch that girl until I say so."

No wolf liked being told what to do—especially mine—but the man laying down the law like that soothed something in me. I'd fight every brother to keep Locklyn safe, and it sounded like Banger might be willing to as well. Always good to have backup, even when you didn't need it.

We sat in silence for what ended up being about three minutes and thirty seconds. Where Banger had been holed up, I had no idea, but my guess was in a rig in the yard and with a woman, because he smelled like weed and sex when he came storming in.

"Where is she?"

Locklyn rose to her feet, which meant I did, too. Banger shot me a glare before focusing on the woman behind me, his face falling into something like sadness and fear and rage all at once.

"Motherfucker, you are here. So then it's true—Chiggy's dead?"

Locklyn stepped around me. I moved to block her, but she locked eyes with me, something in her pretty green ones calming my wolf enough to let her pass. I followed her, though. Kept real close to that ass as she crept over to Banger.

"The nightmares wouldn't let up, so I knew I had to come. Mule said he was gone too—"

"I meant missing, girl. Not dead." Mule moved as if to rise but froze when I growled low and rough. I had no doubt every man in the room understood the warning that sound represented, though the human wouldn't have even heard it. Make that shouldn't have, because her body stiffened just like the shifters', the threat definitely received.

I had too much to deal with to wonder how an at-most half shifter had even recognized that sound, and I needed to start with Mule.

"Why did you think Chiggy was missing?"

Dark eyes met mine. He raised his hand and ticked off each response on a finger. "Bike, home. Truck, gone. Phone, off. House, ransacked. A fucking red rose lying on his porch like some sort of gift. Not a goddamned word to anyone about cutting town for a bit."

Zed huffed. "No Hellions member would cut out like that. Especially not the prez."

He wasn't wrong—our club was strong and loyal, filled with shifters who had become family. Chiggy especially wouldn't have abandoned us without a word.

"Where's the body?" Mule asked, our usually silent treasurer asking the question that needed to be asked. "You said you saw the murder in your dreams, so where's the body?"

Locklyn shook her head. "I don't know—the desert."

"There's a lot of that around here," Zed said, leaning forward over the table. "We're going to need to know all the details."

Locklyn nodded but yawned at the same time. Something about that act, about her acquiescing when she obviously needed rest, riled up my wolf. The way her shirt pulled tight across those tits of hers did the same to the human side of me. It was time to give the girl a break.

"In the morning." I grabbed Locklyn by the arm once more and tugged her behind me. "We start all that shit in the morning."

Cutter glared my way. "Flinch, maybe—"

"Maybe nothing. The girl's tired, it's late, and we need clear heads if we're going to handle an investigation into Chiggy's possible murder without fucking it up and getting caught in some useless cop's radar. We start tomorrow."

Everyone in the room stared at me, all waiting for someone to tell me no. Not that it would happen—the only one with the balls or rank was Cutter, and he seemed to know exactly why I was pulling Locklyn out of that room with me.

"Fine," the VP finally said. "But I want everyone here by ten. And you—" he pointed at Locklyn "—you have any more dreams, you write that shit down. Every detail—sounds, smells, terrain. Anything at all."

"Sure, I just..." She stopped, forcing me to pause and turn. "I had been planning on staying at my dad's place, but if it's ra—"

"You're staying with me."

Her eyes could not have gotten any bigger. "Excuse me?"

Cutter chuckled, sitting deeper and tilting back in the chair. Looking as if he enjoyed the show. "You heard the man. You're under our watch, and that means we make the rules. If our tail gunner thinks you're safest with him, that's where you're going. Right, Banger?"

The old man looked me up and down, his expression hard. He didn't like this one bit, but no asshole would keep me from my mate. Not today, not ever. If he tried to stop me, he'd be eating his own dick.

"Yeah. Seems fine," he finally said, shooting me with a hard glare that made my wolf perk up. Made us both ready to fight. "But she comes in with one mark on that body, and you're dealing with me. That's Chiggy's kid—the man used to change her diapers in this club."

Warning heard. I nodded once, offering him the respect he deserved as an old man in the club. Before Locklyn could part those pretty lips again, I grabbed her backpack from where she'd dropped it, tugged on her arm, and hurried her through the door, slipping out the back instead of dealing with the guys in the bar. Within seconds, I had her beside my bike, pausing only long enough to pull my keys from my pocket. I swung a leg over, handed her the backpack, then patted the seat behind me.

"Your ass goes here."

"My ass goes where I say it does." She slipped her arms into the bag straps then crossed them, making her tits practically pop out of her skimpy top. The woman was trying to kill me.

"Then tell your ass it needs to go to my house. Or would you rather I leave you in the club and let my brothers decide what to do with you?"

Her face flashed with horror at that idea for just a second before it cleared, but I'd seen her flinch. I knew her fear. No way would I ever let anyone—brother or not—touch her, but if scaring her meant I got her to spread her legs around my hips and hang on for a ride, so be it.

With a sigh, Locklyn did just as I'd wanted. She mounted my bike behind me, crawled up nice and close, and wrapped her arms around my waist.

"Anyone ever told you this seat's uncomfortable?" she asked.

"Not a one."

"You must date women with hard asses."

I chuckled and started the bike, revving the engine until it purred just right, and then knocking back the stand. "You trying to insult me?"

"Maybe."

"You're going to have to try harder to rile me up, short

stack." I rolled slowly to the end of the driveway, ready to turn onto the highway. Before I did, I turned and grabbed her thigh. Making sure I had her full fucking attention. "No one's ever complained about that seat because no bitch has ever ridden this beast with me. Now, sit back and hang on. I'll give you a good ride."

FIVE

LOCKLYN

Flinch's place wasn't anything to write home about—a single-story stucco home in the desert with a deep porch, a cheap couch in the living room, and what seemed like nothing else. No pictures on the walls, no decorations, not a bit of softness or color anywhere. The entire place smelled like him, though. A mixture of sage and leather that made me want to curl up in his blankets and breathe deeply. Which could actually happen, considering the man had a huge bed. Just one, though.

"You'll sleep in here." Flinch tossed my bag on the corner of the mattress then slipped into the hall, staying close but not too close. "Bathroom's through the door over there. Don't open the other one. Don't touch my shit."

"Where are you going to sleep?"

That got his attention. I would have sworn his blue eyes darkened as the expression on his face went from nothing to...everything. "Why? You planning on inviting me into my own bed with you?"

I felt a moment of something close to shame, to guilt. Some sort of misplaced need to be nice and tell the huge, scary man—who could probably pick me up with one hand and looked like he would if I pissed him off—that there was plenty of room and we could share the bed.

But my mom hadn't raised a nice girl. She'd raised one who knew to listen to her intuition to keep herself safe.

"No. But I do want to know where you'll be in case I get up for water or something."

His expression shifted back to the nothing of before. His face like stone, his body locked into place. Taking up the entire doorway without even trying to. *Intimidating, thy name is Flinch.*

But I was not one to be intimidated. "So? Where will you be?"

He almost smiled, if that was what the tightening around his lips meant.

"There's a glass in the bathroom for water, plenty of snacks in the kitchen, and beer's in the fridge. I'll be on the back porch." He turned to walk down the hall, not even pausing as he hollered, "And don't touch my shit."

I shut the door behind him—a little harder than I probably needed to—and crossed to the bed, falling onto the mattress with a groan. I was relieved to be rid of Flinch for the moment, but also so tired. Between the nightmares, the bus ride, and the stress of the night, I'd had enough. And as much as it felt silly to grieve the loss of my dad, I did. The man had left us when I'd been a kid, and I hadn't seen too much of him in the years since. A yearly visit to wherever I was living at the time seemed to be about all the traveling he had been up to. But he'd always answered when I'd called. He'd always sent money when I'd needed it. He'd always tried to teach me lessons about his kind and the world he came from, even though I seemed to have skipped any sort of shifter genetics. One of those lessons being that I should never trust a shifter, yet there I was, lying in one's bed. Alone. Just Flinch and me in the desert.

If I woke up dead, I was going to be really pissed off.

As if she could sense I was finally alone, my phone rang, and Zella's name appeared on the screen. I tapped to open the video app and accept the call, rolling over as her face appeared. Her slightly unhappy face.

"Where the hell have you been?"

"You don't want to know." I sighed and frowned. "Well, maybe you do."

"I do. How was the clubhouse? Did you figure out where your dad is yet? Where are you now?"

"Slow down." I rolled over again and sat up, sliding to the head of the mattress so I could lean against the wall. No headboard for Mr. Scary. "The clubhouse was...well, it was a motorcycle clubhouse."

"Lots of tits and ass?"

"And drinking and general debauchery."

"Sounds like fun."

"Not at all. And the men...they didn't want to let me in, but I proved who I was, so they sort of had to, I guess."

"Did they tell you anything about your dad?"

"He's missing."

"Missing or..."

"I think he's dead. I really do." I looked up at the ceiling, blinking against the tears burning my eyes. "One of the club guys came in, saying his place had been ransacked, and I knew. I just knew."

"I'm so sorry, Lock."

The sincerity in her voice ate at me, weakened my defenses. And my first tears began to burn a path down my cheeks. "We're going to start looking for his body in the morning."

"You'll find him, and then you can honor him the way he deserves."

"Yeah." I frowned and wiped my eyes, then adjusted the height of the screen to get a better look. "Where are you?"

"Work. I picked up an extra shift."

"Don't wear yourself out."

"Okay, Mom." She rolled her eyes, but there was no hiding how tired she looked. "Now answer the same—where are you? A hotel?"

I fought the instinctual urge to lie. To tell her, yes, I was in a hotel room. That I was alone and safe and completely locked up in some sort of official place. But I had never lied to Zella about anything, and I wasn't about to start.

"One of the guys at the club brought me home to stay at his place."

Her expression went dark, and her tone dropped as she said a simple, "Locklyn."

"It's fine. He gave me the bedroom, there's a private bath, and he's hanging outside. It's fine."

"You said it's fine twice. Where's his girl?"

"What do you mean?"

"That looks like an actual headboard behind you. Looks like something from this decade and everything, being all creamy taupe. So where's the girl who picked it out?"

I looked over my shoulder, eyeing the oatmeal-colored wall. "No headboard—just a wall."

"You sure?"

My eye roll nearly gave me a headache.

"I'm leaning against it. Trust me, it's a wall." I raised a fist and tapped against said wall. "See? Wall. And there's nothing here—a couch, a table, this bed. That's pretty much it. No sign of a woman ever having been here."

She huffed a defeated laugh. "Check for tampons in the bathroom."

"Zella."

"Locklyn." She glared at me through the screen for a long moment, not backing down. I didn't either, though, and eventually, it was Zella who broke the contest. "Fine. No woman to worry about, but he's still a stranger. A dangerous one. Just...be careful."

"I will. I promise."

"And know that I'm tracking your location. You don't text me every few hours? I'm coming."

"You don't need to be here."

"Need is a qualitative word. I'll decide what I need for my peace of mind. You just make sure you keep me up to date on what's happening. Otherwise, expect a knock on that door."

My heart broke, my grief swelling even more as my best friend in the world berated me. "I love you, Zel."

She frowned, watching me fight back tears again. "That's it. I'm getting on a plane tomorrow."

"Don't you dare." I wiped away the single tear that had escaped and pasted a wobbly smile on my face. "I'm fine...see? It's all good. I'm just really tired and need to go to sleep."

Zella sighed. "Fine. But I'm not kidding—"

"Text every few hours. Got it. Go back to work, but don't you dare wear yourself down. Do I need to send you food or anything?"

"I should be asking you that."

"I'm fine." My stomach chose that moment to growl, the fact that I hadn't eaten all day making itself known. Thankfully, Zella didn't seem to notice.

"You're always fine. I don't think you even know what that means."

"I'm fine—as in I'm about to go grab a snack, have a beer, and go to bed. Is that a good enough definition for you?"

"Depends. You going to bed alone?"

"I already told you I was."

"Then yeah, that's fine. Get some sleep."

"I will. Don't work too hard." I ended the call and slipped out of bed, completely focused on the snack I needed. Flinch had mentioned food, so he wouldn't mind. At least, I hoped not. The man certainly had a presence that could scare the paint off a car, but there was something about him that seemed... Okay, it seemed dangerous and deadly. But I hadn't felt the energy focused in my direction, which made me think grabbing an apple or a piece of bread wouldn't be too big of a deal.

I crept through the silent house, finding the kitchen in the back. I didn't bother looking for a light switch because enough light was pouring in from the string lights outside. Flinch sat in a hammock at the edge of a deep, covered porch, an in-ground pool with lights glowing just beyond the awning, swinging back and forth with a bottle in his hand. He looked to be watching something on his phone, a totally normal thing to do. And yet somehow, the relaxed nature of the moment didn't fit him. I couldn't put my finger on it, but something about him belonged in the wild. Not in a hammock with string lights hanging over-head and a damn pool. An in-ground one, at that.

"Snack and bed, Locklyn. Snack and bed." I caught sight of a fruit bowl on the counter, eyeing what looked like green apples. A box of crackers sat on a shelf above it, a perfect combination for me. I grabbed an apple, a sleeve of crackers, and opened the refrigerator to find the beers he'd mentioned. What caught my eye instead was a row of flavored sparkling waters, bougie brand ones. The kind that cost more than a sandwich at the corner store. My mouth watered at the thought, so I grabbed one of them—coconut-lime flavored—and hurried back to the bedroom, shutting the door behind me. My heart raced, fear of getting caught making me want to hide. Why, I had no idea, but Flinch made me nervous, and there likely would be no changing that.

I settled onto the floor next to the bed, opened the fancy water, and took a sip. "Tastes like money."

A fact that didn't quite fit the reclusive wolf shifter in the hammock outside. Who was Flinch, and why had he been so adamant I stay with him?

FLINCH

It didn't surprise me when Cutter showed up to my house that night. What did surprise me were the number of grocery bags he carried with him.

"What's all this?" I asked, not moving out of the hammock I had found myself taking up residence in.

"She'll be hungry, and you probably have no food. So, this is food." He huffed and set them down by the back door before turning and looking me over. His brow furrowed deep, and his scowl grew. "What the fuck is all this?"

All this likely meaning the hammock and the string lights hanging overhead. "It's my oasis."

He didn't look convinced. "Christmas lights mean oasis to you?"

"No, fucker. They're string lights. See the big bulbs hanging? String lights, not Christmas lights."

"So you're telling me you like big...bulbs." The silence weighed heavy between us for a good five seconds before he broke into a laugh. "I'm just fucking with you."

"Yeah, I figured that out." I turned as a noise from inside caught my attention, dropping my voice into something quiet and hiss-like. "Step back. She's moving around inside."

Cutter slipped around the side of the house, keeping an eye on the back door as if afraid Locklyn would bust right through it. I lay back in the hammock, knowing she'd be able to see me through the kitchen window. I kept my phone in my hand and scrolled a social media feed for a minute or two, listening to her move around. To her opening the refrigerator. My mate was hungry. I had to fight the urge to rush inside with all the groceries Cutter had brought and make her something for dinner. Had to fight to stay still in that hammock. She'd just gotten here, and she didn't know me yet. I didn't want to invade the space she seemed to need, even though I hated not being in there to help her.

"We good?" Cutter whispered after the snick of the bedroom door closing reached our ears.

I nodded and sat up, tossing my phone toward where my feet had been. "Sounds like she's gone to bed."

"You only have the one bedroom."

His low growl incited my own, though I fought to keep it quiet as I replied, "And it's hers for now."

A single nod from the VP and the growl cut off. He and his wolf were satisfied with that response. "So what's the plan?"

"Regarding?"

"The fact that your fated mate just came strolling into your life. What is your plan with Locklyn?"

I sighed and ran a hand over my face as my thoughts swirled. My plans involved a lot of getting to know her with my dick— fingers and tongue, too—but I had a feeling that wasn't the sort of answer he was looking for.

"I don't fucking know—take care of her, find Chiggy's body, avenge his murder, prove I'm a quality mate for her. That's all I've got so far."

He froze, staring at me for a long moment, before settling onto a chair beside the pool. He even kicked his boots up on a side table near it. "Seems like a good start."

"Yeah." I lay back in my hammock and looked up at the sky, spotting a few constellations I recognized but mostly seeing a bunch of fucking stars that littered the darkness above. "How long you staying?"

"Not sure. At least until you put the fucking groceries I bought for you away and maybe offer me a drink."

I rolled off the hammock, shaking my head. "Asshole."

"Asshole who brought your mate snacks."

No lies detected there, though he was still an asshole for the way he had reminded me about them. I snuck inside, creeping like a thief in the dark in my own damn house so I didn't wake up Locklyn or scare her. I took a quick inventory of what I had known to be on the shelves so I could determine what she'd eaten, which wasn't much. Seemed like she'd taken an apple and some crackers to my room. No protein, no healthy fats to keep her feeling full. Not even one of the little peanut butter packs I kept around. Damn it.

I quickly put away the groceries Cutter had brought—snacks, for sure, but also eggs, avocados, tomatoes, and other good things that would make breakfast more substantial for my girl. That was all I could think about—making sure she had a solid meal in the morning since she definitely hadn't tonight. I'd make her a feast.

Once finished, I grabbed two sparkling waters and headed back outside to find Cutter sprawled out in my hammock.

"Comfy, old man?"

"Sure am," he said, not even bothering to turn his head my way. "This is quite the oasis."

I set his water on the little table tucked under the head of the hammock. "Thought you didn't like the lights."

"Oh, I like them. They just don't seem like something you'd care about."

He wasn't wrong. "The previous owner installed them."

"You could have taken them down."

I sighed and looked across my backyard, letting my gaze wander to the desert that stretched out behind my property. This place—this little house with almost no neighbors—had originally been a hotel room. A place to sleep in between visits to the clubhouse. It had become more over the years. The pool, the patio, the hammock—those had become a spot of respite for me and my old wolf. The inside might have been bare bones, but out here, I kept it comfy.

"I like how the light reflects off the water," I admitted, keeping the rest to myself. That my wolf loved the way the hammock swayed and how nice it was to dive into the pool—with its salty water instead of nasty chlorine crap—after a long, hot day on my bike. How I slept out here most nights just to feel the breeze roll through. That I really hoped Locklyn enjoyed swimming because we would be spending a lot of time out there. Hopefully with her in a bikini...or nothing at all. The no-neighbors thing was a huge plus in that regard.

"You've got a right peaceful place." He rose from the hammock and stretched, looking out into the desert just as I had done. "But that openness is a weak spot. We'll need to get you some cameras or motion detectors for that property line."

I nodded, thinking the same thing. "I don't want anyone sneaking up on Locklyn when she's out here, especially if I'm not home."

"Exactly." He grabbed his water then offered his fist for a bump before heading for the driveway, leaving my little oasis just as he'd arrived. "Keep your ass outside tonight and feed that girl in the morning. I don't like the idea of a brother's daughter starving when we can easily take care of that."

"I got this."

He stopped before disappearing around the corner of the house, giving me a strong glare. Letting his wolf come through.

My own bristled, not liking another beast trying to intimidate him, but this was Cutter. My VP. I knew how to take orders from the man.

And an order was exactly what the man laid down. "Take care of her. For Chiggy."

Six

Locklyn

Wind blowing across a desert landscape.
Wolf howls.
My name on my dad's lips.
A single gunshot.

I awoke with a start, sitting straight up in bed. It took me a full ten seconds to calm my heart enough to recognize I had been dreaming, that no gun had gone off in the house. That I wasn't in immediate danger. My stomach churned and my mouth watered from the need to be sick, but I held it back. I didn't want to lose the apple and crackers I'd eaten before I'd crawled into Flinch's bed.

A knock sounded on the door just as I got myself pulled together enough to not feel nauseated.

"Yeah?"

"Breakfast. Let's go."

I took a deep breath and stretched, then threw off the blanket and rose to my feet, still a little wobbly but better than ten seconds before. Instead of hurrying out the door, I grabbed my phone and tapped into a new note, typing out all the details I could remember from my dream. The shadows, the stars, the few sights I could make out beyond the lights from my dad's truck. Everything. I was still typing when Flinch yelled my name from beyond the door, so I rushed out into the hallway while continuing to type. Not giving any thought to the fact that I had slept in nothing but a T-shirt.

A T-shirt that barely covered my ass.

"Good morn—" Flinch turned and froze mid-word, his cool eyes sliding all the way down my body as I became fully aware of how little the shirt covered. I ran one foot up the other leg, sort of crossing them while standing, as his weighted gaze raised goose bumps from one end of me to the other.

"Sorry," I said, tugging on the hem of the shirt as if I could magically make it longer. "I can get dressed."

"No need." He nodded toward the table in the corner, keeping his eyes decidedly off my legs. "Sit and eat. We've got to head for the club soon."

I did as I'd been told, settling onto a chair at the table. Happy to be covered by the furniture itself. Flinch set a plate in front of me piled high with eggs, bacon, fruit, and a biscuit. He then set down a glass of water right next to the coffee cup filled with dark brew.

I had no idea where to start. "This is all...too much."

"You didn't eat last night."

"I grabbed an apple."

"And some crackers. That's not a meal."

I shrugged. "It was for me."

"I told you there were snacks. I thought you'd eat more."

"I didn't have much of an appetite." I picked up the biscuit and tore off a piece. "Plus, I didn't want to be a bother."

"How about you be a bother instead of starving to death under my roof?" He plopped onto the seat across from me. "Now, eat."

Since I'd already set the precedent of following his directions, I kept that up, diving into my breakfast with gusto. I hadn't even realized or thought about how hungry I had been until the smell of all that food surrounded me. I didn't speak, barely came up for air, as I devoured everything he'd put on my plate. And when I finished, I looked up to find Flinch staring at me with more heat in his eyes than I had been prepared for.

"What?" I asked, wiping around my mouth with a napkin in case I had made a mess. "You said to eat."

"I did. And you ate." His lips kicked up into what I had a feeling was supposed to be a smile but looked more like the man had just won something I wouldn't have wanted to put up for a bet. "Good girl."

I shivered. Unable not to as some sort of electricity burned its way from my heart to between my legs and back at those two words. His smile ratcheted up a notch, which only made him look like more of a threat.

"I need to finish getting ready." I rose from my seat and grabbed my plate, shaky and uncomfortable but also wanting to throw myself at Flinch and see if I could wipe that expression from his mouth. Punch it off or kiss it off, didn't really matter at that moment. I just wanted it gone.

He grabbed my plate, stepping way closer than needed. Moving into my space and brushing my arm with his. "I've got this. Go get ready. Do you need to shower?"

"No. I did that last night."

"Good. I want to be on the road in fifteen."

I nodded and hurried down the hall, escaping to the quiet of

Flinch's bedroom. It took me a few minutes of deep breathing and a quick makeup session to settle my nerves and be ready to return to the living area of the house. The empty house. I followed the rumble of his motorcycle engine out the back door to where he sat, waiting for me.

"Hey," I said, pointing over my shoulder. "How do I lock up?"

"You don't." He held up his phone. "The locks will set once I leave the property. Now get your ass on my bike."

I shut the door behind me and headed over, swinging my leg up and over the back of the seat. Like the night before, Flinch gave me a moment to find my balance and settle in. And like the night before, I wrapped my arms around his waist and curved my body against his back.

"Ready?"

I nodded, knowing he could feel it against his shoulder, and tightened my grip. The man revved the engine and took off, heading back to the clubhouse. Ready to start a hunt to find the body of my dead father.

We arrived within minutes, pulling into the lot where ten other bikes and bikers sat ready to go. Flinch rolled up beside Cutter and killed the engine.

"Got anything?" Cutter asked, looking right at me. His gaze one that sent my heart skittering on a journey to tachycardia. The man had a way about him—an air of pure malice that filled the space between us I'd been too tired to notice the night before. But I had Flinch in front of me, and I had a feeling that meant I was safe. At least a little bit.

"I dreamed about his death again," I said. "One gunshot, wolves howling, in the desert."

Cutter smirked. "That's about anywhere out here. Thankfully, Banger called in a favor with some trackers he knows. We've got an idea of where to go and can meet up with them later to refine the location if we don't find anything." He turned his predator eyes on Flinch. "Females are inside."

My stomach dropped. They weren't going to let me go with them, even though it was *my* dad they were looking for. Even though I was the one who had told them I thought he'd been murdered. I was about to argue, to try to present my case to be included, when Flinch laid a hand on my thigh.

"She rides with me."

Every man around us turned and stared, the entire crew going silent. I had no idea what Flinch had just done, had no clue why even Cutter seemed to be gobsmacked over those four words, but I didn't need to know. I rode with Flinch, which meant I got to help find my dad's body.

Eventually, Cutter nodded. "Understood, though we'll need to have a discussion later."

Flinch nodded once, a stiff and almost subtle movement. Then he took his hand away, restarted his bike, and leaned back to murmur only to me.

"Hold on. This is going to be rough."

FLINCH

Riding to the club with a fucking hard-on might have been the worst idea in the history of man or beast, especially after not sleeping. Fucking Locklyn, being all gorgeous and distracting. Pretty sure my dick would fall off from how hard it got just being around the woman. And the fact that she had been sleeping in *my* bed? Impossible to get over. I'd ended up having to come inside to be closer to her, though I hadn't invaded her space. She'd shut the bedroom door, and I'd respected that. Even if I had been fucking miserable.

And then she came out in that tiny tee this morning, showing me her goodies. Not that she'd meant to, but I saw them. I motherfucking memorized them. Especially the panties she'd worn under that shirt, the ones that had cupped her ass cheeks and clung to her hips like the straps might break at any moment. Pink fabric hugging all that warm skin. Like the color her pussy lips would be once I got them all plump and juicy with my—

My dick was going to fall off for real if I didn't start thinking of baseball or some shit.

The crew rode with us as we headed for the desert, the rumble of motorcycle engines music to my ears. I liked having Locklyn on the back of my bike—liked knowing she was safe and feeling her body against mine. No fucking way would I have left her at the bar with the club pussy. Cutter should have known better than to even suggest such shit.

A tug from Locklyn at a stoplight had me turning my head to give her my attention. She leaned forward, hand on my shoulder, surrounding me in her scent and making my wolf positively salivate.

"Can we swing by my dad's place? I want to see it."

Right. Dead father. My wolf and my dick were going to have to wait. I gave her a single head nod and motioned to the brothers that I would be taking the lead. I made a left once the light changed in my favor, heading north instead of east. The team followed behind me, likely knowing where we were headed.

Chiggy had lived in a trailer he'd dropped on a piece of scrubland close to the club. There wasn't much to see there—the house, a garage he'd built to store and work on his bikes, and a lot of dirt that led up to some mountains. Typical Mesa outskirts. Every Desert Hellion had been to Chiggy's place at one time or another—whether to help the brother out, for a party, or just to shoot the shit on a Tuesday night. The man had an open-door policy, and we had all taken advantage of his hospitality.

He would be fucking missed.

I pulled to a stop out front of the trailer, already knowing the place sat empty. Sensing the lack of life within. My brothers rolled in behind me but kept their distance. Seemed like they all understood this wasn't an investigatory visit.

Locklyn swung her leg over and climbed off my bike, standing beside me and staring off at the place her dad had called home for as many years as I'd known him. Which hadn't been all that long—I'd rolled into Mesa just over a decade before. Long after the woman beside me had been born.

"It's dirtier than I remember," she said, her voice small and quiet. Something in my chest burned, the heat creating this weird tightness. Like a pulled muscle or something.

"You lived here as a kid?"

"Yeah. My mom and I. Not for long." She turned my way, those pain-filled green eyes making the tightness in my chest increase. "He kicked us out right after my sixth birthday."

If Chiggy hadn't been dead, I would have killed him with my bare hands for putting that expression on my girl's face. "He ever give you a reason?"

"To get us away from all of you." She turned back to look at the house, taking away my access to those eyes. To her emotions. "You can't trust a shifter."

The one good thing about such cutting words was they absolutely deflated my poor dick finally. I sat perfectly still on my bike, that tightness in my chest growing hotter and deeper. I had a mate who would never trust me, which meant... Fuck, I didn't even know what it meant. But it wasn't good.

"You done here?" The tone of my voice—the harshness— grated at my wolf, but there was no pulling the words back. I nodded toward Locklyn's seat when she turned my way, completely ignoring the surprise on her pretty face. The wariness. "We can come back so you can go inside, but only once our team gets out here to look for evidence of what happened to him. Just in case. Even though you can't trust us."

Her brow grew tight, the scrunch of her nose hitting me like a punch in the gut. Irritation caused by both my lack of fucking emotional regulation and her pained response to my carelessness made my chest tighten. I wasn't going to win today, not with her. Not with my head filled with her words. With the fact that she would never trust me.

Time for a change of scenery.

"Well?" I finally said, the word coming out harder and meaner than I'd intended it to. The pain growing in my chest distracting me. "Get that ass on my bike. We've got places to be."

She did as I'd told her, hopping onto the back of my bike like a good little girl. But this time, she didn't shift forward or wrap her arms around my waist. She kept space between us and held on to the sides of my cut. I caught Cutter looking my way as I maneuvered the bike to head toward the road, his frown like a spotlight on my messed-up response to my mate. I had somehow managed to stick my foot all the way up my own ass in less than three minutes, and I had no idea how to remove the offending appendage.

SEVEN

FLINCH

The last thing I wanted was my new mate out in the desert searching for the dead body of her father—my club prez—but that was exactly where we ended up, along with all my brothers from the club. Chiggy had been a popular president. His death would leave a scar for both the club and Locklyn. We needed to find his body, to offer him the same respect in death that we gave him in life. And I needed to focus on the club to accomplish that.

"The trackers said we'd find trails and evidence starting here. They did not track the body themselves, so finding him is on us," Banger said once all engines had been quieted. The hard earth spread around us, the road we'd followed for a solid mile to find this spot really what could only have been called a path through the desert. A path that had tossed sand and rocks into our faces the entire way. I would be spitting grit for hours.

"I can't see shit because my eyes are full of sand." I rubbed a hand over my face, turning slightly and setting a hand on Locklyn's thigh. "You good back there?"

"Fine," she said. "I hid behind your back once we turned off the highway."

Smart girl.

"I see tire tracks," Cutter called, pointing up a slight rise in the distance. One that would require us to leave our bikes behind and hunt on foot. Or rather, paws.

"Let's get ready to shift." Zed swung a leg over his seat, rising to his full height. He spotted Locklyn on the back of my bike as he did. "Eyes to yourself, little girl."

Locklyn stiffened behind me. On an instinct driven almost solely by my wolf, I rose to my feet and stepped directly between her and my brother. Keeping my eyes locked on his. Warning him. Zed's expression stayed neutral, his wolf wary behind his human expression. Eventually, he gave me a chin bob and turned away. Backing down from the fight neither of us wanted to enter into. I would have, though. Would have pounded his ass into the dirt for Locklyn. For my mate. Even if she didn't trust me yet.

"I'll leave someone with you," I said, that chest burn from earlier back and more irritating than ever.

Locklyn nodded, not looking at me. "Okay."

She didn't sound okay, though.

"You good?"

"I'm...probably not." She finally met my gaze, her green eyes so much like Chiggy's practically searing into mine. "But I want my dad found, so go ahead. Do the thing. I'll be fine."

The woman lied like I played golf. Badly.

"You *will* be fine. I'll make damn sure of it." I leaned in, dropping my voice to barely more than a whisper, the ache in my chest pulling taut. "I may be a shifter, but you can trust me. Only me."

She didn't respond, but the look on her face said everything she didn't—it would be a long, hard road to get her to believe that. One I was going to have to traverse if I wanted her in my life.

I turned and headed for my brothers, something dark and twisty sitting deep in my gut. Something more uncomfortable than the burn in my chest. "Just keep an eye on our clothes for us once we're gone."

Zed caught me before I reached the rest of the guys, keeping his voice down as he asked, "What's up with bringing tits along?"

I growled under my breath, not answering him. Keeping my eyes on the horizon as I fought the urge to shift and claw him a new orifice.

"Call her tits again, and the brothers will be out here looking for *your* body."

He fell back, leaving me to walk alone. Swallowing down the anger that practically oozed from his body. His wolf didn't like being talked to like that, and mine picked up on the beast's irritation. They would both settle the fuck down once Zed learned about my mating. They'd understand. Any male shifter would.

But it wasn't the time to tell anyone yet.

Cutter came next, the VP more of a smart shifter than a brash one, which was why the man was the most dangerous of the group. He didn't ask a single question. Instead, he gave me four words of advice in a quiet voice no one else would have been able to hear.

"Keep your mate safe."

No questions, no options. A direct order. One I fully intended to follow.

I gave the man a nod and kept walking, not stopping until I had reached one of the largest and most volatile brothers on our team. The one who owed me big. The closest thing I had to a man I could trust. More because I had dirt to hold over his head than any sort of expected loyalty. And definitely not just a prospect.

"Rush." I bumped fists with the man I had gotten bloody for just the night before. "You're babysitting."

The big shifter glanced over my shoulder to where Locklyn still sat on my bike. I could see the tension in his jaw, knew he wanted to complain, but he had more of a brain than to do so, considering I had helped him avoid a charge. I also knew he had a mate of his own, not that he had admitted that fact yet. But he would get it. Even without knowing how Locklyn and I were connected, he would protect the woman for me. I knew it.

Thankfully, Rush bit back his irritation and kept shit simple. "Anything I need to know?"

"Yeah. Don't touch her, keep the chatter to a minimum, and don't fuck this up."

He grunted his acknowledgment then walked past me, heading straight for Locklyn. Her worried eyes met mine, bouncing to the approaching man and back. I waited until he had arrived at her side and spoken a few words to her, until I saw her visibly relax a little, before I continued on to my team.

"We're here to hunt for Chiggy's body," Cutter said, giving me a solid beat of attention before moving on to the others. "The trackers have seen evidence of tire tracks out this way, so this is where we start. We need to figure out what happened so we can track down whoever did this. Be cautious in your travel. I don't want to be comparing paw prints for days on end because you got too excited to watch where you stepped. Now shift, and let's get this shit over with."

My brothers all moved out to strip, folding and setting clothes in neat piles on the rocks around us. Shifting destroyed anything we wore, and running around the desert as a naked human was never a good idea. Being conscious of the need to care for our clothes came almost on an instinctual level for us. Shifters in other parts of the country didn't seem to worry as much, but they'd likely never been stung by a scorpion on their nutsacks. Only took once for a man to figure out he needed his jeans to stay in one piece.

I glanced over my shoulder as I folded my pants, catching Locklyn looking at me. I kept my back to her, letting her see all she wanted to. Letting her get an eyeful. A certain sort of pride came with knowing she watched me. That was my mate; this body now belonged to her. Scars, ink, muscles...all of it. Hers and only hers. She just didn't know it yet. She'd figure that out and see the rest eventually.

Once naked, I shifted into my wolf form. My brothers all did the same, making their shifts on their own time. No one rushing. This wasn't a rescue mission—we were looking for a body. We had time. I even took a moment to run back to my bike and give Locklyn a good view of this side of me. Wanting her not to be afraid. The thought of leaving her behind and out of my watchful eye didn't sit well with me, but I also didn't want her traipsing around the desert or coming upon anything that she maybe shouldn't see.

Thankfully, she seemed distracted and almost intrigued by me.

"Your fur is darker than I would have expected, what with you being more blond than brunette." She reached over slowly, letting her fingers lightly touch the top of my head. Taking a moment to familiarize herself with my fur before moving to scratch around my ears as if I were a dog. Not that I minded. That shit felt good. "Do I really have to stay here and wait?"

I growled low and laid my head on her thigh, holding her in place. She sighed and looked away.

"Fine. I'll stay here."

Her acceptance was about all I could hope for. I gave her one last nuzzle, earning another ear scratch, before turning and running back to my brothers. They had all shifted by that point, and Cutter looked ready to lead us on our trek. Not that he needed to do much more than point us in the right direction. We'd created search parties before—we had that shit on lock.

Searching took a good few hours. We stopped twice for water breaks and even sent Zed back to where we'd started to make sure Rush and Locklyn were okay. They had shade, food, and water so the rest weren't too worried, but I couldn't stop thinking about her. Was the heat too much? Was she hungry? Did she need protection from something other than the elements? The need to spin around and race back to her sat heavy on my shoulders, the pull in my chest growing worse as the hours passed. But I resisted the urge to turn around. I had a job to do—find her father's body. That was how I needed to take care of her.

Three hours and some change into the day, I did exactly that. The scent of decay came at me first, leading my wolf down a sandy rise and around a patch of baby brittlebush. The body lay in what looked like a dry creek bed, facedown and fully clothed. The sight of Chiggy like that—the vision of weakness in a man who was anything but—hit me square in the gut. I couldn't move, couldn't signal my brothers who had yet to find their way to me. All I could do was stare.

Stare and take in everything—the tire tracks, the footprints, the casing left behind from some sort of gun. I crept closer, not wanting to disturb anything but needing a better look. So I could take full inventory of his perfect position, the way his clothes had yet to be shredded. His wholeness in death. Scavengers looked to have gotten a hold of him if the amount of open flesh around his neck was any indication. Food was food to animals, and a dead body was a lot of food. Because that was how they had treated Chiggy in the end—as nothing more than some random dead body.

The very idea of one of my brothers being left for a snack in the desert filled me with the sort of rage that usually ended with me killing something or someone.

But I would need to figure out where to direct that anger before I got to that point. And to do that, I needed my team. I howled long and deep, letting my voice rise up. Letting my brothers know where I was and that I needed them. We would work this scene as a group, as a family. As a crew. We would make sure Chiggy got better than being left as a coyote snack.

I held back the furious heat growing within me and sniffed around the body once done howling, hunting for any scents that didn't belong as I waited for my brothers to get to me. There wasn't much, just an unusual floral odor whispering across the air. The scent of decomposition hit harder and almost covered it, but I caught a bit. I couldn't identify it, though.

Preacher came over the hill first, running slow and careful. A man who had experience in crime scenes and tracking. I yipped to him as he approached, watching as his nose worked overtime. The man was a good scenter. Better than me, for sure. If I had caught that floral scent, he would as well. There would be two of us searching it out, logging it in to our brains to identify later. Preacher took a long moment to sniff all around the body and the air of the area then gave me a quiet huff. Scents logged. Time to move on to other evidence-gathering.

The rest of the team arrived shortly after Preacher. Cutter and Zed shifted human to examine the body, while the rest of us scented and circled outward to look for anything to give us an idea of who or how or why. Everyone acting responsibly and precisely, being extremely careful where we placed our feet. No one giving in to their rage just yet, though the feelings we shared were almost palpable. There was an energy to our group, a flavor on the air that we all tasted. We were ready to go to war against whoever had killed our brother. And we would.

Eventually, Preacher found a second bullet casing, alerting with a quiet yip-like sound and staying close to it so as not to lose the location. Eyes hard and body tight. Ready to rip someone's throat out, it seemed.

I found remnants of tire tracks—not super-detailed but at least enough to get an idea on tire size. The find fueled my anger—the killer wasn't even smart enough to cover his fucking tracks? How had he been able to get a jump on someone like Chiggy and then fuck up to the point of even a human cop finding evidence? The crime scene made no sense.

It was Cutter who finally rose to his feet and whistled for our attention, his own rage leaving him partially shifted, fur and claws standing out on his more human form.

"Brother Chiggy was shot at close range in the chest. The bullet looks to have been a hollow-point by the amount of damage done, though why he bled out so quickly isn't immediately obvious. Either the assailant got lucky and just happened to be carrying that sort of ammunition that edged around Chiggy's natural ability to regenerate, or they knew his physiology and came prepared with something that could kill even a strong shifter like our brother. Either way, the club has suffered a horrible loss, and we will grieve that loss before finding out the how, the why, and making sure the who never gets a second chance at taking out a Hellion."

He bowed his head and placed his hand over his heart, holding space in silence for a long moment, the rage on the air cooling into something like grief. Like mourning. Every wolf watched him, giving the respect of silence to our fallen brother. Standing quiet in the desert and allowing our group rage to move in another direction.

It was Zed who finally broke the silence, shifting to his wolf form and rolling right into a soulful howl. The rest of us joined in, singing to the sky above. Calling out our sadness and loss and respect for the man who lay dead beside us. The one who had been a true brother to each and every Hellion member. We sang our grief to the sky above, letting the gods of Fate know this fallen brother had been respected. He had been loved. He had been a packman who would truly be missed.

When the howling ended, I shifted human and caught Cutter's eye, rubbing at the ache in my chest. I knew Locklyn would likely hear our call—the Hellion with her definitely would —and she would worry what it meant. I needed to get back to her.

"Tire tracks are here," I said. "I'll get the war wagon and bring it over so we can take Chiggy's body back with us. Collect the evidence and make sure I don't fuck up the tracks when I drive in."

Cutter nodded, eyeing me hard. Likely knowing why I had just volunteered to retrieve the van we used as a war wagon. I needed to be the one to tell Locklyn about her dad. Needed to be there to make sure she had support when the truth of her situation was revealed.

I needed to take care of my mate, so I shifted once more, and I ran.

EIGHT

LOCKLYN

My dad was dead.

I'd already known that—had seen him die in my dreams—but to have his death confirmed felt different. When Flinch's wolf had finally come over the rise, when he'd frozen across the sand from me and his wolf eyes had met mine, my entire body had gone cold. They hadn't been empty eyes. They'd been filled with a rage that could have singed the desert floor. Chiggy's murder had gone from assumption to fact without a word from the team who'd been looking for him, and I had no idea how to handle that.

"I'll take him to Popper's." Zed walked around the van, taking the keys from the prospect who'd driven it back to the clubhouse from the desert. My father's body lay in the back. I hadn't seen it—Flinch had made sure of that. I didn't want to, either. Not really. Then again...

"Did you find any evidence on him?" I asked, keeping my voice low. Flinch turned my way along with Cutter, both men looking at me with the same anger smoldering under the surface. I couldn't be distracted by them, though. By their rage. I would eventually need to deal with my own. "You know...fibers or hair or stuff on his clothes? Anything that seemed unusual or out of place?"

"Other than the bullet hole?" Cutter asked, eyes blazing but face blank.

I swallowed, holding on tight to the food I had in my belly as I tried my hardest to avoid that visual. "Yeah. Other than the bullet hole. Any markings or signs of struggle or handprints on his truck or...I don't know. The stuff they look for on that CSI show."

"The blue one or the red one?" asked Rush, his brow furrowing in an almost adorable manner. If a man his size could be considered adorable.

But his words hadn't quite made sense to me. "The what?"

"The blue one or the red one. Vegas or Miami?"

"There's a gray one, too." The man—patched in as Ridge if I read his cut right—dismounted his bike and sidled over. "New York. That one's gray."

Realization hit me hard in the chest. "You're right—red, blue, gray. They color-code the shows."

"Gives them ambiance," said Cutter. "Vegas was blue because they were the night crew. Miami's red because it's fucking hot there—"

"Like it isn't in Vegas?" Rush interjected.

"Apparently the producers think Miami is hotter." Cutter shrugged with his wide, thick shoulders, looking like a mountain in motion. "*CSI* was the shit."

Rush scoffed. "Not the gray one."

That riled up Ridge. "Don't fuck with the New York show. That shit rocked."

"Nothing beats Vegas—Gil Grissom? No contest." Zed

stepped into the circle that had formed, staring down at his phone as he tapped on the screen and stealing everyone's attention. He eventually grunted then tucked his phone into his pocket. "Popper's got a guy who can take a look for all that CSI shit."

"Good," I said, crossing my arms and wishing I had a sweater or sweatshirt to wrap myself up in. Cold from the inside as the sun blazed down on me. "I just wanted... I mean, I need to know..."

But there was no way to finish that sentence. I needed to know what exactly? If my dad had put up a fight? If he had left a clue? Someone or something had made sure I saw his murder in my dreams. I had to assume I had all the clues I needed. What I was supposed to do with them was a whole other question. One I had no idea how to answer.

A warm hand landed on my hip, and the scent of sage and leather surrounded me. Flinch. He leaned down, practically covering me with his big body. Instantly warming me with just his presence.

His lips brushed against my ear as he whispered, "Anything in particular you think we should be looking for?"

I shook my head, my brain spinning in three different directions at once. As sad as I was to know my dad truly had been murdered and as ready as I was to jump into a mystery investigation to find out who had killed him, Flinch being so close to me created a massive distraction. The man oozed danger and excitement, sex appeal practically running through his blood and smelling like some sort of pheromone created by fate to do nothing but attract the females in the area. A lethal combination to my lady bits, while also being a totally inappropriate distraction in the moment.

Focus, Locklyn.

"I just..." I started, sighing when finding words became too hard. "I need to know."

Flinch held me in place for a moment, staring down at me from behind a pair of mirrored sunglasses. Or at least, that's what I assumed since the glasses covered his eyes. I felt his gaze, though, so the assumption felt safe.

Finally, he gave my hip a smack and focused on Zed. "I'm riding behind you and Chiggy."

Zed nodded once. "Daylight's burning."

Flinch herded me toward where he'd parked his bike, still talking to Zed. "Give me twenty to get her back to my place. I'll need a prospect to babysit."

"You'll have one," Cutter said.

Before I could even be insulted by the whole babysit term, Flinch picked me up and set me on the back of his bike. He leaned in close, caging me with his arms.

"Keep that pretty ass right there."

He strode across the gravel lot to where Cutter stood, both men obviously involved in what looked like a serious conversation. Flinch shook his head twice before finally giving Cutter a nod. Something had been decided.

Flinch returned without delay, those mirrored glasses still blocking his eyes from me. I felt his attention, though. Knew he had me locked in his view from the second he'd turned around. The man had a stare that carried weight, and I felt it for sure.

"What was that about?" I asked once he reached his bike.

He grunted a non-answer and slipped a leg over his bike, settling in front of me on the seat. "Making sure you're safe while I'm busy, is all."

"Had to get the right babysitter?"

He laid his big hand on my thigh, giving it a squeeze. "Exactly. Now hang on."

I did as I'd been told, hanging on as he drove me back to his place. Once parked, he helped me off the bike and led me inside. He seemed rushed, as if he really wanted to be somewhere else. Which I guess he did. He had to ride along with my father's body.

"Shower," he said as he walked right past me through the living room. "Sand can irritate your skin—best to wash it off."

"You trying to take the place of my father now?"

He turned, pulling off his sunglasses, those ice-blue eyes practically setting me on fire with the intensity of his stare. "No, but I'll be your daddy anytime you want, so long as you'll be my good girl."

Well fuck, I'd walked right into that one. I swallowed hard, fighting to keep my hands from trembling. To keep myself calm and collected. To not jump the man right there in his living room. That comment wasn't fair—I hadn't been ready for it. That wouldn't happen again.

With a huff and an eye roll to hide how much his words had affected me, I headed for the bedroom to shower and change. My dad's warning—*never trust a shifter*—was practically a chant in my mind.

Ten minutes and a clean pair of shorts with a tank top later, I walked out of the bedroom to find the house empty. No sign of the man who owned the place other than the lingering of his scent. I simply couldn't escape that, it seemed.

I walked through the entire house and even checked the back porch, not noticing the empty driveway until I'd circled back to the living room. He'd taken the truck and left. Just as I'd told him to do, but still.

My chest ached, and my stomach turned for inexplicable reasons.

"He could have at least said bye," I whispered to the empty house.

I had just walked back into the kitchen—hoping to find some

sort of snack—when the rumble of a truck pulling into the drive made me stop. I was almost too afraid to look, knowing it could very well be my babysitter and not Flinch. But then the man I had wanted to see opened the front door and strode into his house.

"You good?"

A simple question leading to what could have been a complicated answer from me, but just knowing he hadn't left without saying goodbye settled something inside me enough to nod in the affirmative. Was I good? No, but I was better knowing he had come back.

"Truck is yours," he said, handing me his keys. "Give me your phone."

"What?"

"Your phone." He held out his hand. "Unlock it and give it."

I did as he'd instructed, still somewhat confused as to the demand. He tapped something onto the screen then held my phone close to his. Oddly enough, the lock on the front door beeped.

"Done. My number's in there, and you've been added to the locks. If you leave the property, they'll lock. Just hold your phone up by the door when you get back, and they'll unlock."

I took my phone back when he handed it to me, staring down at the screen as if it was something I had never seen before. "Oh."

"The prospect will be out front and will follow you if you go anywhere—that's it, though. He's a fucking shadow. If he bugs you, tell him to fuck off. If he hits on you, text me and I'll handle it. There's food in the fridge." He pulled out his wallet and tugged two fifties from inside it. "The taco place on the corner is good, but if you go half a mile past, you'll see a yellow van in the parking lot of what was once a gas station. No signs, no tables. Buy from him, and you'll have the best tacos of your life."

My stomach practically rumbled at the thought. I could go for tacos. But then... "What will you do for dinner?"

He looked up at me, seeming surprised by my question, a slow smile forming as he cocked his head. "You worried about me, short stack?"

I huffed, the nickname grating. "I'm not short, and no. Not worried. More curious."

He set the money and keys on the side table, moving in closer. Invading my space with his big body and his annoying scent. "Don't worry about me, short stack. I'll grab something while I'm out."

I wanted to clap back at the nickname, but the reality of the situation hit me right in that moment. I nodded, staring down at the fifties and keys. Shifting my weight from one foot to the other as the anxiety of having to watch him walk out the door settled in deep. As the knowledge that I would be spending the evening alone enveloped me.

Crap, why did that make me feel so sad?

"You good?" he asked, his voice a little lower than before. A little quieter, yet deeper. Inching a little closer.

I shivered, cold settling deep inside me, just like it had at the clubhouse. "I'm fine."

He grunted, pulling me into his thick arms and against the wall of his chest. There was no way to resist him, not that I wanted to. He simply absorbed me into his frame. Making me feel small and protected. I felt safe with him, which seemed ridiculous. He was both a wolf shifter and a biker. There was no safe place in either world for me, and yet...

"Do you have to go?"

My question came out as barely more than a sigh, one I knew he'd heard when he tensed. I tried to pull out of his hold, but he squeezed me tighter and curled his body over mine, dropping his head to once again brush his lips against my ear as he whispered to me.

"I want to make sure your dad gets the respect he deserves in his final journey, but I don't think you need to see him like he is. That's the only reason I'm leaving you here."

I nodded against him, clinging to his biceps.

"Fuck, short stack. You're shivering."

"I'm fine. It's just been...a lot. Today has been a lot."

He sighed and rested his head on top of mine for a moment. Hanging on tightly. Not allowing even a breath of space between us. "It's going to get worse before it gets better, but it will get better. I promise."

"Okay." I took a deep breath and pulled out of his hold, trying my best to give him a solid smile. "Go. You told Zed you needed twenty to deal with me, and it's been longer than that."

"That fucker can wait."

"Go." I pushed him—not that I had anywhere near enough strength to move him. Thankfully, he went along with my ridiculous shove and started backing toward the door. "Go do what you need to. I'm looking forward to tacos for dinner and some cop shows to entertain me."

"Red, blue, or gray?"

I grinned, unable not to. "Blue. Blue is the best."

"Good to know." He stepped out the door just as a bike pulled into the front yard. The prospect from the front door of the club sat astride a motorcycle, dark sunglasses in place, face firmly not looking in our direction. "You don't need to entertain him."

I returned my gaze to Flinch, giving him a nod. "I know."

"And make sure you lock the doors."

"I know."

"You've got a full tank of gas—"

"Enough." I smacked at his arm. "Would you go? I am an adult, you know. I can take care of myself."

"Yeah. Well, maybe you shouldn't have to."

With that, he turned and jogged to his bike. Settling those damned sunglasses on his face once more and hiding that intense gaze from me. I still felt it, though. Knew he was giving me one last look over before he started his bike and walked it backward out of the driveway. He nodded once to the prospect before turning onto the street and riding away. Leaving me alone. In his house. With a babysitter.

Nine

FLINCH

Popper owned a crematorium so far out in the desert, no one really bothered him with things like inspections and business license review. The man offered a service—he cremated loved ones and the ones not so loved for dirt cheap, while still honoring and respecting the lives and traditions of the deceased. If they deserved either.

Chiggy deserved every bit of respect.

"I'll have my assistant check him over for any evidence of the responsible party. That will push back his service—" Popper flipped a page in his notebook, frowning as he looked over what he had written there. "Three days. Evening. Will you be sending people to witness?"

"Yes." Zed never glanced my way, taking lead with a contractor I normally dealt with. As tail gunner, I cleaned up the messes club members made, like making sure the bodies wouldn't be discovered. As warlord, Zed kept the brothers safe and made sure they got home at night. He would be leading the charge to send Chiggy home. "He's a brother, Pops. We'll all be here."

The old man with the beady eyes who had burned more bodies for me than I could even remember nodded solemnly. "Again, I'm very sorry for your loss. You Hellions have been good to me—I'll be sure to be good to your brother."

"We appreciate that," I said. "Got a time for his service? The club will want to know when to roll up."

"Eight thirty. I'll make sure he's the first of the night."

So his ashes wouldn't mix with anyone else's. He didn't need to tell me—I'd been there for burnings before. Hell, I'd watched him toss ten bodies in a pile and fire it up. I'd been the one who'd told him to do it. Chiggy would get better. The best.

Once finished with Popper, Zed and I headed back to our rides. We had to check in at the clubhouse and let Cutter know the situation. We also needed to start spreading the word about the vigil we would hold for Chiggy while he burned. But first, I needed a little time alone with the club warlord so no unwelcome ears overheard.

"Thoughts on Chiggy's murder?" I asked once we made it to the van.

Zed grunted, slipping off his ever-present sunglasses and looking around the empty lot as if expecting someone to be hidden in a pocket of scrub grass. The man took caution to an extreme.

"I think a normal gunshot—even a hollow-point—shouldn't have been able to drop the old man. I think everything about this situation feels off. I think we've got a shitstorm headed toward us." He looked my way, those black eyes locking on mine and making my inner wolf tense. "And I think your new girl's sitting square in the middle of all of it."

My new girl. He had no fucking clue.

"She's his daughter—she's definitely in the middle of it."

"How come we never knew he had a daughter?"

I shrugged, pondering the same thing. "Would you want a young girl around the brothers? At the clubhouse?"

"Fuck no."

"Then there's your answer." I took a moment to rub a dirt spot off my odometer, sinking into thoughts about Locklyn and Chiggy. "He told her to never trust shifters."

"Smart man. Humans should stay the fuck away."

"She's half shifter."

"Still more human, though." He leaned closer as I jerked back, giving me an exaggerated sniff. "There's not a bit of shifter in her smell. Just that human perfume...and you."

I growled low, making sure he knew he was coming close to crossing lines. Making sure he knew nothing had changed with me—he still wouldn't want to go claws out against me. Thankfully, Zed was a good brother and a smart fucking wolf. He didn't press the issue, didn't open his mouth and spout off. Instead, he slid into the van and rolled down the window, looking out toward the horizon where the sun had started to dip behind a rise. Darkness would arrive soon, the shadows already deepening and growing longer. It was time to get home, but my wolf wasn't ready to back down, and Zed wasn't done quite yet.

"I checked your scent to prove a point," he said. "Not to start a fight."

"And what point is that?"

"This one: That girl is pure human, the only shifter scent being the one tying you two together as mates." He started the van, looking my way once more. Deep, dead eyes meeting mine and locking on hard. Not showing dominance, showing how much he knew. How much he hadn't been saying. How fucking stupid I had been to assume my connection with Locklyn could be kept a secret. "Most of the brothers won't recognize the scent, but some will. Their wolves will. Some of the dumber ones might try to challenge you for pack hierarchy if they do. They might try to steal her from you. And those are the people you think of as brothers. Our adversaries? They'll kill her just for the fun of it."

Rage unlike any I'd ever experienced blazed through me, making my entire body burn with the hatred of my wolf. "The fuck they will. I'll lay them out before they ever even get close."

"Good, because you're going to need that energy." Zed nodded and threw the van into gear. "Keep your eyes open and your circle tight. We lost Chiggy—it would be disrespectful to his memory to lose his daughter, too. Especially to an internal."

With that, he rolled off, heading for the driveway leading back onto the highway. Leaving me to stew for a second in my own internal thoughts. Someone in my own club might try to take my mate? Fuck and no. Not the Hellions. Maybe other clubs, other groups of shifters, but our team was solid. If a newbie or young one even joked about doing something so stupid, the older crew would beat the fuck out of them.

But if an older brother decided to take a chance...

"Never fucking happening," I said into the gloaming, tired of being in my head already. I started my bike and followed the van, my brain still spinning. No way would any of my brothers get near Locklyn. I'd rip their fucking arms off if they even thought about it. And take her? Not happening. I may not have claimed her yet, but the woman was mine. All mine. And I would do anything to keep her.

And anything included taking out one of my own if necessary.

———

Zed and I hadn't made it ten feet through the clubhouse door when Preacher yelled that Cutter wanted to see us. We both headed straight back to the office, Zed tapping on the doorframe before walking in.

"What's up, boss man?"

Cutter scowled. "I'm not the boss...yet. How'd it go with Popper?"

I settled in a seat across from his desk. Zed stayed on his feet, leaning against a file cabinet closer to the door that he had closed.

"His assistant is going to CSI the body tomorrow," Zed said, keeping his voice quiet and low. "The burn will happen two nights later."

"We got a time?"

"Eight thirty," I said. "We'll need to get the word out."

Cutter nodded. "Let's start that tonight. I want every man there—no excuses. They show up to honor Chiggy, or they get the fuck out."

"Good call," Zed said with a nod. "You planning on taking over for the old man?"

"I'm planning on letting the brothers vote—either they choose me, or they choose to start a hunt for a new prez." Cutter sighed and sat back, his light eyes holding mine, looking downright mean and ready to fight. "They have to want me in this seat to follow me. I either earn it, or I don't."

And that was what would make the man such a good leader for our crew.

"When's the vote?" I asked.

"After we figure out who killed Chiggy." Cutter stabbed Zed with a hard look. "Any ideas yet?"

"Not random, not internal, and likely not another shifter."

"So who, then?"

"Don't know." He glanced my way. "But we'll figure it out."

"You'd better," Cutter said. "I don't want the brothers out there with someone hunting them, but I also don't want the cops involved in Hellions business. Clean it up, but don't leave a trace."

"I've got it covered," I said, confident I could hold off any police action if they ended up with their sights on us. Paying off the cops was the easy part—actually hunting down a killer who knew how to take down a wolf shifter in cold blood would be harder.

"Good." Cutter nodded once, giving Zed a look that spoke volumes. "Go start letting the boys know about Chiggy's service. All there, or they're out."

Zed pushed off the file cabinet. "Understood."

As soon as Zed closed the door behind himself, Cutter turned that steely gaze my way. "How's your mate?"

"She's..." But how could I answer that? Adorable. Sexy as sin. Making me hard as a rock from memories of those pink panties hugging her hips. I didn't know enough about her to know if she needed anything, and I had barely spoken to her so far. She was my mate, and already I hadn't figured out a thing about her.

"So the talking and getting to know each other is going well," Cutter said with a smirk.

"Fuck you."

He shrugged, looking quite pleased with himself. "You're not the first to find their mate, you know."

"No one in the club is mated."

"Not officially, but we both know that's not true."

Facts. "No one in the club is out as being mated."

"No, because most choose to leave. They pick their mate over their brothers." His smile fell, his face growing more serious. "You're allowed to choose her."

I said nothing, just sat and stared and waited him out. Mostly because I already knew I could choose her. But also because...I had no fucking clue what would happen if I did.

Cutter eventually grunted once, pinning me with his stare. "Your wolf wants her, so that's it. Mating bond or not. The wolf will get what the wolf wants."

My wolf agreed, the prick growling his approval to our soon-to-be prez. The man in me had a commitment to honor, though. "I won't leave the club unless I have to."

"That decision is a long time off at this point," Cutter said. "For right now, you need to worry about getting to know your human mate because she likely doesn't have any wolf instincts when it comes to this mating—"

"Fuck, I hadn't thought about—"

"—and then you need to claim her. Full mating bites exchanged." His gaze grew harder, eyes darkening and voice dropping lower. "The fuckers around here won't accept anything less."

My temper snapped, and a throaty growl escaped me. "You think they would try to take her from me?"

"I think there will be some who will use her as a way to challenge you. None smart enough to keep their dick out of a fire ant hill, but some. To claim another wolf's woman? To be powerful enough to entice a fated partner into rejecting her mate? That's like candy to some of these fuckers."

My mind spun, thoughts of Locklyn with one of my brothers making my chest burn again. The bastards in the club would never get the chance. Not with my girl. Not with my mate.

"She's mine."

Cutter shot me another smirk. "Then claim her."

But there was one hole leaking air out of my confidence balloon. "Chiggy taught her well. She won't trust a shifter."

"So don't be just any shifter. That's your mate—be better than the rest for her. Earn her."

Those words played on repeat as I finished my conversation with Cutter, as I popped into the clubhouse to make sure the boys didn't need me, as I pushed past the club pussy and out the door. They repeated loudly in my skull all the way home. I didn't even bother giving the prospect at the door my attention—just a curt, "You can leave" before entering my home and locking the door behind me.

I hunted Locklyn down, my animal side more dominant with my thoughts taken up by the idea of earning her. I found her where I had expected to—in my bed. Alone. She had wrapped herself in my blankets like some sort of burrito, only the top of her head and all that dark hair visible outside of her cotton capsule. I stood and stared for a long moment, my wolf begging me to enter our room. The man in me knowing that crossed a line I couldn't uncross even if she did leave the door open.

Earn her.

I sighed and stripped right there in the doorway, listening to the little murmurs and sighs coming from the bed. Locklyn talked in her sleep. Not anything understandable—at least not at the moment—but definitely words and phrases that meant something to her subconscious. I couldn't wait for the day she would invite me into her bed so I could stay up and listen to her.

I also couldn't wait until I could feel her naked body pressed against mine, but that was another thought. One that woke up my dick and had me extra annoyed.

"Flinch."

"Fuck." I nearly stumbled, nearly fell right into the room as my name left Locklyn's lips on a breathy sigh that had me harder than I'd ever been. She hadn't woken up, but she'd said my name. Clearly. Was she dreaming about me?

"Mmm, Flinch." Locklyn rolled over, her burrito enclosure

slipping off her. Exposing her backside to me right there. The moonlight coming through the windows played into the hands of fate, practically shining right on those ass cheeks I wanted to bite. Her panties weren't pink this time but green. Emerald green —her ass encased in silky fabric like a jewel. That fact didn't make me want to bite it, smack it, or lick it any less.

I wanted her more. Needed her. Needed something.

"Yeah, beautiful. I'm here." Here but not invited, so I kept my ass outside the room. Stood like a statue in the fucking doorframe. Still, the need grew with every second, the desire burning as I stared at that tempting ass. I couldn't resist, couldn't stop myself from getting a little release.

I couldn't pass up the chance to come with that ass in view.

Without another thought, I dropped my hand to my jeans, freeing myself. I immediately sought my dick, grabbing it to pull it out, rubbing my thumb over the tip as I squeezed. Giving myself attention without stroking. Not yet. I had a war going on in my head. The wolf in me wanted to jump into that bed with her and rut her through the mattress. The man knew better, knew an invitation had to be offered first if we were to keep respecting our mate. So I locked my knees and gripped the doorframe with my one available hand to hold myself in place as I squeezed my dick almost to the point of pain. If I didn't, I would break. I would end up in that bed. I would—

A low groan sounded from across the room, and my mate rocked her hips once. Twice. Green satin practically glowing in the moonlight. The scent of her desire whispering on the air around me for the first time. She smelled like cherries and sin, like something that would ruin my life in the best possible way. Her need smelled like coming home, and I wanted to fucking bathe myself in it.

"Fuck, Locklyn." I breathed deep and moved my hand on my

dick. Had to. Not a full stroke, just enough to give me a little shiver. To make the hair on my legs stand up.

The third time my mate whispered my name in her sleep—the time when her hand slipped underneath her hips and I assumed into those green panties—I broke. With a growl and more self-restraint than I thought possible, I lunged across the hall, keeping my hand on my dick as I slammed into the wall and dropped to the floor. My feet pressed into the wall opposite me, my dick throbbing as I began stroking. And of course, because I was a sick son of a bitch, I ended up with enough of a view of Locklyn's ass to make me lose all control. Ended up still smelling that cherry-coated goodness between her thighs and wanting to devour it. I growled and humped my hand, tugging hard and squeezing tight on the entire four strokes it took me to get off. Coming into my fist in seconds like some sort of pup during his first game of beating the bishop.

"Fuck," I groaned, stretching my orgasm out as much as possible, thumbing over the head of my cock and pushing off the wall as the trembles took over my legs. As the feeling of euphoria faded slowly. Still keeping my eyes on that ass as I nudged my thumb tip into my slit for a little bite of pain to go along with the pleasure.

Locklyn had fallen back into a deeper sleep, no more words being whispered, her hand tucked somewhere underneath her. I wanted to think of her with her hand in her pussy, her fingers growing wet and sticky as she slipped them inside herself. Her skin growing hot under her own touch.

"Enough," I hissed, pushing off the wall and stumbling into the half bath. I washed my hands, staring at the wild wolf eyes looking back at me in the mirror. Both disgusted and proud of myself for resisting the call to invade my mate's space. Just the thought of Locklyn—of those fucking emerald-green panties—

had my dick growing hard again. The need to touch and taste and feel my mate underneath me a powerful drug.

One I had to resist.

Earn her.

"I will." I reached down to grab my dick again, unable not to. Knowing it was going to be a long night of me and my hand and the image of those panties burned into my brain. "Fuck, I totally will."

Ten

LOCKLYN

I didn't get to see Flinch for long the next morning, not that I needed to. Or should have wanted to. But I'd had some intense dreams starring him, and I had an urge to stay close to him. Something that he had made clear would be impossible from the moment I woke up. The man had plans.

"Eat," he said, his energy high and his movements rushed. "I have to meet Zed in fifteen."

"Then go." I picked up a fork to dive into the spread he'd made—eggs, sliced tomatoes, bacon, toast. The man knew how to eat, and he made sure I didn't starve. Even if I had missed breakfast and rolled right into lunchtime.

"You eat, then I'll go." He cussed under his breath and ran out the back door, reentering the kitchen with what looked like a stack of money in his hands. "What did you spend yesterday?"

My mouth felt glued shut, and my body went cold. "Uh... what?"

He counted the cash, not paying attention to me whatsoever. "What did you spend? Was it enough? Do you need—"

He glanced up, and his face went blank. Serial-killer blank. First night at the clubhouse blank. He stared at me with no emotion, those light eyes a physical force against my skin. Making goose bumps rise on my flesh.

"Why are you scared?" he finally asked.

I swallowed back the fear creeping up my throat, unsure where it had come from. Not knowing if there was a right answer to his question. "I didn't spend much. And I left the extra—"

He dropped the money on the table—all of it. Three good inches of what looked like twenty-dollar bills.

"That money is yours. This money is also yours. Spend it how you like." He waited for me to nod before coming around the table and leaning down so he could make sure he had my attention. So his face was the only thing I could see. "And you don't ever have to be afraid of me, short stack."

Something inside me relaxed at that comment, but my neck still felt tight and my stomach remained clenched. "I don't like feeling like I owe someone."

"I get that, but you don't owe me shit. Your dad would have wanted you taken care of, and as his club brother, I will make sure to honor that. Got it?" He waited for me to nod, then dropped a kiss to my forehead. "Good. Now, eat your brunch. I have to go, and I won't feel right leaving you unless I know you're not going to starve."

"I won't starve," I said, even as I resumed digging into the food on my plate. "I know where that taco truck is."

"The good one?"

"Yeah."

"You liked it?" he asked, sounding almost excited about it. As if my liking his recommendation for dinner made him happy.

"Loved it. Thanks for telling me about it." I took a drink of my coffee as his phone beeped. Watching as he frowned when he looked at the screen. "You can go. I'll be okay."

He didn't look up from his phone as he said, "You deserve more than just okay."

I froze again, fork halfway to my mouth. "Are you all right?"

He finally tucked his phone away, still looking harried. "Yeah. I really have to get going. We were supposed to meet at ten, but the morning got away from me. This fucking club stuff has to get done before nightfall."

Club stuff that I wasn't privy to. "So, go. I'm fine."

"Your guard isn't here yet."

Ah, so that was his holdup. "I can be alone for however long it takes him to get here. I am a functioning adult, you know. I'm alone a lot."

"Not anymore." He darted a look my way, frowning as he headed for the front window. "He's here."

My stomach sank, but I held myself together. Knowing he had to go and that it made no sense for me to be afraid of him doing so. I pulled myself together and kept my voice flat as I asked, "So, you're leaving?"

"Yeah. Hang on." He stepped outside, obviously talking to someone else, though I couldn't make out the words. He came back inside as I was washing my dish. "You good?"

I looked his way and gave him a smile, still in turmoil inside but fighting through it. "Yeah. I'm good."

He hurried over, taking the dish from my hands to dry it. "Money's there, and it's yours. Spend what you want. Make sure you get a good dinner because I don't know if I'll be back in time to feed you. Truck's yours, too."

"I know—the prospect will follow me. Text you if he hits on me."

"He won't," he said. Not making eye contact. "It's not a prospect this time."

"No?"

"No. I brought in a full brother. One who knows better than to look at you twice." He stopped, looking me over from top to bottom. "You look really pretty today, by the way. Stay the fuck away from other men."

I had no answer for him, though he didn't wait for one. He simply turned and walked out of the house, calling out a curt, "Text me if you need me" before shutting the front door behind himself. Leaving me alone.

And distracted. "What other men?"

Four hours and way more time spent on my hair than should have been necessary, I headed out to Flinch's truck. The sun shone bright from the western sky, a sign that night would be falling soon. I had plenty of time to get out and do something before it got dark. While ridiculous, considering how late I tended to be out in Detroit, I didn't want to be outside after dark in Mesa. I had a feeling it wouldn't be good for me.

The brother—sporting a shock of bright-red hair and the lovely road name of Rooster—rose when I walked past him.

"Where we going?"

I shrugged. "Out. I can't sit in this house anymore."

"Shopping?"

I scowled. "God, no. I want to be out, not in. Outdoors. Maybe take a hike or something."

He stared at me for a solid ten seconds in silence, his face blank and his light eyes just sort of locked into place on mine. They were the most uncomfortable ten seconds of my recent memory.

Finally, he nodded. "There's a solid drive up into the mountains that I know of. You avoid the traffic of the national forest but get some good views."

"Perfect." I grinned, gripping Flinch's keys tighter. "Should I follow you, then?"

He nodded again then headed for his bike, his lack of conversation skills easily ignored at the thought of getting out into the desert for a bit. I hopped into the truck and started the engine, frowning when I looked at the dash. A single red rose lay directly in front of the steering wheel against the window. That hadn't been there the day before, so it must have come from Flinch. He didn't really seem like the roses sort of guy, but I had been wrong before about men. I reached for the rose and brought it to my nose, sniffing the overtly floral scent from a good two inches away.

"Pretty." But then something else caught my attention, and I set the rose on the seat beside me. The truck had a full tank of gas. I hadn't driven all over Mesa the day before, but I had driven around quite a bit. Enough to have used at least a few gallons of gas.

But obviously not.

"Must have fantastic gas mileage," I said to no one right as I heard a slight honk from the bike waiting for me. Rooster had grown impatient. Without another thought, I threw the truck into reverse and backed out of the driveway, my excitement making me practically bounce in my seat. Desert mountain views awaited, and I was ready for them. Sure, I'd spent yesterday in the desert, but that hadn't been fun. At all. I needed a little hike and some fresh air away from the stress of the Hellions and what had happened to Chiggy. I needed space. Something hard to find back in Detroit.

I followed Rooster to the highway, both of us speeding up once we made it to the concrete road. He signaled well in advance and always seemed to wait for me to make a turn, being a good leader. Other than that, we had no interactions. One truck and one bike, alone and yet together. I followed him for a solid hour, enjoying the ride and singing along to the radio as the houses grew farther apart.

But as the desert grew more desertlike, the land becoming more hostile, my thoughts slipped to my dad. What had he been doing out in the middle of nowhere? Who had he been meeting? He'd said he'd done what he was supposed to—what could that be? I didn't know my dad like his Hellion Riders did, but nothing about that moment fit into what I *did* know of him. He wasn't a dumb man—he wouldn't have fallen victim to some scheme. And he certainly wouldn't have worked with any sort of government agency or other group against his own crew. So why had he been out there alone? And who had killed him?

As my thoughts spun, my phone rang. I glanced down to see Zella's face on the screen and immediately swiped to answer her call.

"Yo, where are you?" she asked first thing.

"I'm driving out to the mountains. Where are you?"

"On my way home from work. Why are you in the mountains?"

"I needed to get out of the house. Flinch is busy with the club, and sitting around isn't my thing."

"You don't say," she said, her tone sarcastic. "Never would have thought that about you."

"Brat."

"You love me."

"I do." I sighed, slowing down as the bike's brake lights flashed. He turned onto a dirt strip that was far less road than path through some brushy, hilly land. I would never have been willing to drive on the rutted two-track alone, but Rooster was leading so I followed. Albeit a little less happily.

"Why do you sound like that?" Zella asked, her voice harsher than before. "What's happening?"

"Uh, I think Flinch's friend may be taking me out to the desert to kill me." I tried to smile to smooth the edges of my words, but I happened to hit a big rut at that moment and ended up cursing under my breath instead.

"What the hell, Lock." Zella no longer sounded sarcastic. "Where are you, and what are you talking about?"

"Sorry—I was kidding." Mostly. Because the hills were getting hillier and the brush thicker. "I'm following the man who's babysitting me since Flinch can't be here, and he just turned onto a dirt road that barely looks like a road."

"Do you trust him?"

Never trust a shifter.

"Not completely."

"Text Flinch."

"What?" I frowned as the motorcycle sped up and made a turn along the dirt that took him out of my line of sight. "What are you talking about?"

"Text Flinch and share your location with him. Just in case."

"Zella, he's not—"

"Someone murdered your dad, Lock. You dreamed of that murder...a lot. Text Flinch."

I slowed down, the shadows and desolation of the place getting to me. The remembrance of the murder that continued to haunt me in my sleep sending a chill of fear down my spine. No more than Zella's worried voice, though.

"Fine." I swiped up and tapped through to my settings, giving Flinch the ability to see my location then texting him a quick message.

> Your friend promised me beautiful mountain views, but I'm in the middle of nowhere and getting uncomfortable. If I don't make it home, avenge me. Or at least come find my body.

I had barely hit send when my phone rang, the screen

lighting up with Flinch's name and options to ignore, hang up on Zella and answer Flinch, or bring Flinch into the conversation with Zella. I chose the latter.

He answered simply. "Where the fuck are you?"

"That's no way to answer the phone," Zella said. "But since we're short on time, she's in the mountains with your friend and afraid she's going to get murdered."

"That may be an exaggeration," I said, rolling slowly toward where the motorcycle had turned. "He said we were going to see some mountain views."

"Locklyn," Flinch said, sounded madder than anyone I had ever heard before. "Tell me where you are."

I sighed, looking out over the desert and wondering just how dumb I could be. Dumb enough to follow strange men into the desert, apparently. "I sent you my location."

He grunted. "I don't know—"

"How old are you?" Zella asked, sounding really annoyed. "Go to your Find My app then scroll to her name. It'll show you that she's in some patch of nothing right off highway 12, northeast of the city."

"Who the fuck is this?" Flinch asked, the growl in his voice growing more pronounced with every syllable.

A fact that didn't slow Zella down in the least. "I'm Zella, and Lock is my best friend. So, are you going to make sure your guy doesn't murder her, or do I need to get my ass on a plane?"

"I've got her. Locklyn, stay put."

He disconnected, leaving only Zella and me on the phone.

"Uh," I started, unsure what to do next. "I guess he's handling things."

"Are you still following your murderer?"

"He's probably not my murderer."

"We don't know that yet."

"You're ridiculous, and yes, I'm still following him. I just need to make it around this turn—"

But that was when I dropped the phone.

FLINCH

There was no rage in the world like what burned inside me. My mate was scared, possibly in trouble, and I had no idea how to get to her. "Locklyn, tell me where you are."

Cutter and Zed walked closer, both of them having pulled over on the side of the road when I had. We'd been riding when Locklyn's text had come in, the flat, computerized voice reading it to me through my headphones making me want to throw my bike into the desert and shift right there. But I had to know how to find her first, had to figure out a direction to go before I could take off.

Cutter mouthed "She good?" at me, but I shook my head, still holding my phone to my ear. Waiting.

The device pinged, and then I heard Locklyn say, "I sent you my location."

I pulled the phone away from my face and tapped through to put it on speaker, my hands trembling in both fear that someone would hurt her and fury that someone had dared to attempt it. I tried to figure out what she meant, even looking in my texts for something from her, but my brain could not focus on the frustrating little rectangle in my hand, plus the rate of her breathing, and forcing my wolf not to explode into being on the side of the highway.

I sighed and shook my head. "I don't know—"

"How old are you?" someone—a voice I had never heard—asked, making me nearly drop my phone. "Go to your Find My app then scroll to her name. It'll show you that she's in some patch of nothing right off highway 12, northeast of the city."

Cutter lunged and nearly took the phone from my hands, his growl and mine melding into a cacophony of predator instinct. Thankfully, I held on as I shoulder-blocked him, tapping the app the voice had instructed me to even as I snapped back at them.

"Who the fuck is this?"

The unknown woman didn't lessen her tone or volume a single bit. "I'm Zella, and Lock is my best friend. So, are you going to make sure your guy doesn't murder her, or do I need to get my ass on a plane?"

I did as she said, focused solely on the little blue dot right where she had said it would be. Locklyn—my mate—would be there. I looked up, eyes meeting those of my VP before holding up my phone so he could see the screen with that blue dot. He glanced at the phone in my hand, his face set in a scowl I had never seen him wear before, and nodded before jogging back to his bike. Location determined and leader notified. We were riding out.

"I've got her. Locklyn, stay put."

I ended the call and pocketed the phone, revving my bike to life. I tended to ride at the back of the line—the tail gunner rode last in our club—but not this time. I rolled to the very front, settling in beside Cutter.

"You good?" he asked over the engine noise. I wasn't—not in the least. My girl needed me, which meant the only thing I could focus on was finding her and killing Rooster for scaring her. Killing was a nice word—I was going to rip his fucking arms off and use his own fingers to disembowel him.

But that would have to wait, seeing as how I needed to get to her first.

So instead of going full berserker on some stupid motherfucker, I nodded, skipping words.

Thankfully, Cutter seemed almost as rage-filled as I did. He accepted the nod and held up one arm before yelling, "Let's roll."

With that, the club took off, everyone gunning it hard and following Cutter and me down the highway. Thankfully, we were only about ten miles from Locklyn's location if what she had sent to my phone had been right. It needed to be because I was barely hanging on to my wolf. If we got to the little blue dot on the map and my mate wasn't there? There would be no controlling him.

And there would be nothing left of whoever had taken my girl from me.

Eleven

LOCKLYN

I dropped the phone, unable to speak and think and observe what had just appeared before me all at the same time. Rooster sat on his bike on the far right of the road, but he didn't matter because before me lay a valley filled with desert wildflowers and tall cacti. On the horizon sat a mountain I couldn't have named even if I *had* known more about the region, its hillsides draped in shadows as the sun began to descend behind it. The oncoming night had turned the sky shades of orange and pink much deeper than I saw in Detroit, colors bleeding into darkness, all with a sliver of moon peeking out from the depth. The beauty left me speechless for a good fifteen seconds as I looked out across what appeared to be a painting of a desert sunset.

"Zella," I whispered, still stunned by the image before me. "You need to see this."

"Lock? Are you okay?"

I reached down and grabbed my phone, rolling to a stop close to where the biker sat on his motorcycle. A smile broke out involuntarily when her face appeared on my screen, our audio call switching smoothly to video after a couple of taps. But I wanted her to see more than just me. "Hang on—let me flip the camera."

I tore my eyes away from hers to find the icon I needed, barely noticing her worried expression before changing to the back camera and holding up my phone as I approached the edge of the road.

"Look at this." I threw the truck into park and hopped out, still unable to take my eyes off the vista ahead. "Seriously, Zella. Look at how pretty this is."

"Told you," Rooster said as he lounged on his bike. "It's a great view out here."

"It really is."

"And no tourists." He turned my way, looking at me with a gentle smile and a knowing sort of expression. "I'm surprised Flinch hasn't brought you out here. You're worth the drive."

I cringed as Zella laughed, the sound of her giggle reminding me that she was watching and listening to everything.

"What's so funny?" I switched the camera back to front-facing, creeping toward the truck and away from Rooster. Wanting a little space from his assumption because that's what it had to be, right? He was assuming Flinch and I were...something. At least, it felt as if he was.

Zella shook her head and huffed. "That was a dig."

"It was not," Rooster yelled, voice filled with laughter. "I was just stating facts. Don't go getting me in trouble."

"It totally was a dig, sir." Zella grinned, her eyes locked on mine. "And one meant to uncover your relationship with Flinch."

The biker smiled again, raising his eyebrows as if actually wanting to know that bit of information.

I rolled my eyes and sighed. "I don't have a relationship with Flinch."

But Zella could be a bulldog when she wanted to. "You sleep in his bed."

I opened my mouth to respond, but no words came out. She wasn't wrong—I did sleep in his bed. Alone.

"Told you," Zella said. "How long do you think it's going to be before Flinch shows up?"

"Flinch is coming?" Rooster rolled up to a sitting position, suddenly looking a lot less comfortable.

"Uh...yes?" Because I had told him I thought I might be murdered. "Oh hell."

The sound of engines suddenly filled the quiet of the gloaming. Rooster rose to his feet, his face going hard and mean. My stomach dropped as the noise grew louder, the sounds of motorcycles approaching at top speeds undeniable. Flinch had arrived, and though his protection didn't seem necessary, I was undoubtedly happy to see the man.

Even if he did look ready to commit murder.

"I am so sorry," I said to Rooster before running past the truck, hoping to cut off Flinch before he reached the poor guy. Five bikes crested the hill and came to a stop, practically forming a circle around me. I recognized a few of the riders from the first night at the club, but the only one holding my attention was Flinch.

"You good?" he asked as he swung one long leg over his parked bike and rose to his full height. His eyes catalogued me from head to toe and back again before turning icy cold and sliding over my shoulder to where I knew Rooster to be. Flinch went from big, bad biker to predator in a split second, expression changing and—impossibly—facial features shifting more wolflike. Absolutely terrifying...but not to me.

If I were honest with myself, I would have to admit that the protection thing was hot. I'd never had a man look ready to kill for me. I'd never had a man who would have defended me at all.

Flinch coming to my rescue—no questions asked—cracked something open within me, a feeling of wanting to be protected by him. Of liking the look of pure fury on the man's face all because I had been afraid. That seemed like some antifeminist shit right there, but I couldn't help it. I had taken care of myself for a long time and was quite capable of doing so. But it was kind of nice to know someone else might be there to help you out when you needed it. That you had backup. That in moments of pure fear, there was someone who would protect you.

Unfortunately, Flinch was about to protect me from someone who didn't deserve the wrath aimed his way.

"I'm fine." I stepped in front of him, using my body as a barrier to keep him away from Rooster. Shivering slightly as he pressed into me, as his hand slipped around to hold on to my hip as if anchoring me to him. "I was nervous, but everything's fine."

"What's happening here?" Rooster asked, looking as confused as he should have been. "What did I do?"

"You fucking scared her," Flinch said, moving as if to push past me but allowing me to stop him. I held on to his cut and refused to move, keeping my body pressed to his. Keeping us still in that moment. We both knew he could have shoved me aside, but I wasn't letting him slip by, and he wasn't manhandling me out of the way. Instead, he held on to my hip tighter, keeping us close. Connected. And fuck if protective and grabby-handed Flinch wasn't even hotter. His hands felt right on my body, even if the timing was all sorts of wrong.

"She wanted to get out of the house," Rooster said with his hands up as if trying to show he had no weapons, forcing my attention back to him. Breaking through the haze that had seemed to settle around me since Flinch had arrived. "I honestly just thought she might like the view."

"I do," I said, trying to get Flinch's attention. Trying to make my point clear. "I think with my dad's death and the isolation out here, I got a little nervous. I shouldn't have called you."

Flinch looked down at me, his brow furrowed. Those ice-blue eyes stabbing me in place even as they made my heart race faster.

"You absolutely should have called me if you felt nervous." He ran a single finger down my cheek, lowering his head and his voice. Making me feel as if we were having a private conversation. "I'll always come to help you."

Dead. I was dead. Right there on the hill, murdered by simple words from Flinch's lips. How had this happened? And why did I suddenly want to kiss the man more than breathe?

"Sounds like a miscommunication," Cutter said, walking past us to look out over the valley. Shattering the moment into a thousand pieces.

Flinch kept his eyes locked on mine, kept our bodies tight together with his arm around my back while his thumb rubbed against my rib cage. "You good?"

I nodded, leaning my forehead against his chest. Relaxing into his embrace.

"This is an incredible view Rooster found." Cutter stood on a slight rise, staring off into the distance. "I had no idea you could see the valley from out here. And no tourists."

"Exactly," Rooster said, coming to stand to the side so he could address Flinch, catching my eye for just a second before focusing on the man who had turned me just enough to put his shoulder between me and the redhead. "I'm sorry if bringing Locklyn here was a bad idea—I wasn't thinking about how being so far out might bother her because of Chiggy."

This time, the growl came from a different Hellion member. From a giant of a man who had risen to his feet and dismounted to stand a few steps behind Flinch. The man they called Rush, who happened to have one hell of a growl. "She's a woman alone with a man she doesn't know in a secluded area—it's about more than Chiggy, you dumbfuck."

And damn if he wasn't right. But Rush's addition to the moment only made Flinch more tense, which was the wrong direction to go in. "I'm fine. Really."

"She's fine," Zella said, her voice carrying across the quiet from the phone I still clutched in my hand. "But I really was about to haul ass down there. You can't leave her alone and not expect her to get into trouble, Flinch."

Cutter cocked his head, staring at the phone in my hand as if he had no idea what it was. "Who is that?"

"Zella. My best friend."

"She's a little sassy," Rooster said. "And she'll get a man in trouble with that mouth."

Zella huffed audibly. "Not my fault you were digging."

Cutter kept staring at my phone, his expression dark and unreadable. Which only made me more uncomfortable, so I lifted the phone, my finger over the end call button.

"I'll call you later, Zee." And then I hung up, not missing the flash of anger that danced across Cutter's face. "Uh... Sorry."

"Nothing to be sorry about—she's right." Flinch sighed and pulled me in tighter before turning us so we stood side by side. Still holding on to me, though. Still teasing me with his thumb, too. "Next time you want to take her somewhere, check in with me."

Rooster nodded once in a way that screamed respect. It also screamed he was never taking on babysitting duties again. "Understood."

"So, we good here?" Cutter asked, grunting softly when Flinch nodded. "Then let's get back on the road. We have a few more brothers to find before the wake at the clubhouse."

It was my turn to frown. "There's a wake?"

"Hellions only," Banger said, piping up from where he sat on his bike. "Your dad wouldn't want you there."

I stiffened, unable not to, and immediately looked to Flinch. I had no idea what he saw on my face that made him react, but he growled low and garnered the attention of everyone on his team.

"Rooster can take my spot on the team for the night. I'm staying with Locklyn."

Cutter didn't seem to like that idea. "Flinch, we need—"

"We need to remember that it's her father who's gone. She gets to mourn, too."

Cutter didn't look happy—looked downright furious, to be honest—but he eventually nodded his agreement. "Fine...this time. Rooster, you're with us. Let's roll."

The redhead nodded once, mouthing a "Sorry, kid" at me before heading for his bike. Rush gave Flinch a long look, some sort of communication happening in that moment, before retreating to his bike once more. The motorcycles began to rumble, all the men turning and riding back down the dirt road, Rooster taking the spot at the end as he followed them out to the highway. Flinch stood right by my side, never looking away from me. Never even glancing back at his brothers as they left. Standing his ground...with me.

"You didn't have to stay," I said once the motorcycles had made it far enough away to be nothing more than a buzzing in the distance.

"Of course I did." He grabbed my hand and pulled me along behind him, stopping at the top of the hill and moving me to stand in front of him. "Look at that sunset. Don't see this view every day."

"You could if you wanted to." I shivered, the warmth of his hands on me raising my own internal temperature. Making the world seem too cold to be away from his touch. "I don't have anything like this in Detroit."

"True enough." He stood behind me, hands running from my shoulders down to my wrists and back up. Slowly, so very slowly. Leaning over to speak into my ear. Body close but not close enough as he said, "The sunrise over Lake Erie is pretty good, though."

That statement took me by surprise. "You've been to Michigan?"

"More than a few times. I rode with a club out there for a while." His hands dropped to my hips, and he tugged me closer. Not harshly or demanding—more of a question. A slight pull that gave me the option to follow or ignore. A suggestion.

I settled back against him, unable not to. Needing to touch and feel in that moment. To connect. "What brought you out here?"

"I wanted to ride with the Hellions."

"Really?"

"Yeah. I'd been with the Feral Breed for a few decades when I heard about the Hellions, so I started making my way west and south from club to club."

"My dad talked about the Feral Breed occasionally," I said, my heart breaking a little as I remembered his last few visits to Detroit. "When he would come to visit me, he would always stop to see the local guys."

"I'm not surprised." He slipped his thumbs over the waistband of my shorts, tucking them against my skin. Subtle and stealthy but unbearably hot. "We're actually part of them—Feral Breed Desert Riders or some shit—but we keep to ourselves a bit more. We keep our Hellions branding and don't go to the national meetings or Gathering shit."

I refused to be distracted by his thumbs, the ones that moved back and forth against the skin of my stomach. Little digits of restraint destruction, those two. "What's a gathering?"

"A fuckfest for shifters looking for their fated mates."

I...well, that was something I hadn't been prepared for. "You've been?"

He stayed silent for a long time—thumbs stilling against my skin—as my stomach fell all the way to my knees.

Voice calm and quiet, energy buzzing in a way that screamed he didn't want to go down this path, he answered with just one word. "Once."

"Not a big enough fuckfest for you?" I asked, my voice tight even to my own ears.

Thankfully, Flinch didn't acknowledge the sound of—was that jealousy? Couldn't have been, and yet it sure seemed like it. And the way my stomach clenched at the thought of him bouncing from woman to woman... He had been a single man, still was. He had the right.

But man, I hated the thought of it.

"No women worth spending time with there," he finally said.

"I highly doubt that."

He leaned over my shoulder again, keeping his lips close to my ear as he grumbled a low, "You weren't there."

I shivered, unable not to. The man had played that particular hazard well, reassuring me without actually acknowledging how unfair my jealousy would have been. I took a deep breath and fought to regain my senses, to recenter myself in the moment.

"So...what now? Do you have to go to the clubhouse tonight?"

"Nah. I'm sticking with you, short stack." He pulled his hands from my body and hopped onto the hood of the truck, tugging me with him until I had a seat on his lap. My back to his front. My body wrapped up in his. "Let's watch this sunset, then we can head home. Maybe grab some tacos on the way."

"Sounds perfect." And it did. It also sounded much like a date. "Though, I'm still out in the middle of nowhere with a strange man who could kill me at any moment."

He chuckled all low and dark. "I'm not going to kill you."

"How do I know that?"

"Guess you just have to trust me."

"I'm not supposed to trust shifters." But the words felt wrong in my mouth, and I gave them no energy to exist. As much as I hated to say it, my dad could have been wrong. He could have taught me strict, black-and-white rules but never refined them for the gray of the world around me. He could have said them without knowing the connection I would feel to Flinch.

The man in question slipped his hands over my hips and down my thighs, breathing me in as he grabbed at my flesh. As he pushed us over the edge from possible friends into...something else. Because friends didn't run their fingers over my inner thighs or pull my legs apart. Friends didn't growl into my ear and tickle the seam between my leg and my ass. Friends didn't make me want to get naked right there in the desert.

"I know you're not supposed to trust me," he said, hands still roaming, voice dark and deep and growly as he kept teasing my body. "But you can. And we're going to work on that. You and me."

I swallowed hard, giving in to the desire I felt. Turning to straddle him. To bring us closer together and look into those ice-blue eyes that seemed to see straight into my soul. "I feel like I can trust you, Flinch."

He kept his face stiff, kept his emotions hidden. His body, though, gave him away. The way he slipped his hands down my thighs, letting his fingertips dance across my skin. The way his breaths became slower and deeper as he stared at me. The way he grew hard underneath me, not moving to try to hide it. The man felt the same attraction I did.

But then he opened his mouth. "Maybe you shouldn't."

Trust him. I shouldn't trust him. But I wanted to... And if I were honest with myself, I did. I already did. "My instincts are good—I'm not afraid of you."

Flinch didn't respond, though he did grab me by the hips and tug me closer. Ran his hands over my ass and up my back to press me against his chest. He even leaned in, growling all low and soft, and making me shiver as he scented up my neck. Kissing me there. Teasing me. I moaned softly and arched my back when his teeth brushed against my skin, wanting so much more. Needing it.

"Locklyn," he whispered against my skin, kissing over my jaw and grabbing me by the neck. Holding me in place with his thumb right over my pulse point. "I'm going to fucking ruin you."

I leaned forward, letting the pressure on my neck guide me. Loving how his grip tightened just a bit as I nipped at his lip.

"Good."

His kiss came violent and strong, lips and teeth and tongue devouring me in a flash. I couldn't hold back, couldn't pull away. All I could do was ride out his attack, hoping and praying he couldn't feel how wet I was becoming. How I couldn't hold my body still and instead had to rock over where he had grown so hard for me.

"Fuck me," he whispered when he finally broke the kiss to drag his lips down my neck, bringing us even closer as his entire body seemed to envelop mine in a writhing sort of hug. Growling steadily under his breath when he whispered, "You're going to be such a good girl for me, aren't you?"

Died. I almost died right there. I was pretty sure I actually whimpered as he grabbed me by the back of the neck and pulled me closer again. This man—this beast who had me pinned against him—would destroy me. I knew it. He knew it. And it seemed we were both perfectly willing to head down that path of destruction. Together.

I couldn't wait.

He had just unsnapped my shorts with one hand, had just growled my name and nearly made me come with that one word as his fingers began delving into my panties, when both our phones started ringing.

"Fuck," he whispered, letting go of my neck and dropping his hand to my thigh as he panted like a marathon runner. "Looks like someone's trying to get in touch with us."

Breathing hard and fighting to come back from the edge of whatever emotional wasteland had taken over my brain, I pulled my phone from my pocket. "I don't know this number."

"It's local—don't answer it." Flinch tapped to answer his, making sure the call would come through the speaker. "Yeah?"

"It's Zed. Popper's CSI guy came through. Cutter needs you at the clubhouse. Bring the girl. He's got questions."

TWELVE

FLINCH

I could hear the bass from the music inside the clubhouse before we even rolled onto the lot. Sounded like my brothers were celebrating Chiggy's life instead of mourning his death. Typical and not unexpected, but I had a feeling Locklyn was about to see exactly why her dad hadn't wanted her around the brothers. Considering the way her arms hugged her little body tighter to mine once her human ears caught the noise, I'd have taken bets that she knew it, too.

"Stay close," I said as soon as I dismounted my bike. Locklyn's eyebrows tightened over her pretty eyes, the green flashing at me.

"Why?"

I grabbed her hand, pulling her into me. Looming over her before dropping a soft, gentle kiss on the lips that owned my soul. "Because I like the feel of you against me, and I make no excuses for what my brothers are likely doing in there."

With that, I headed for the front door, still holding Locklyn's hand and making sure to keep my body directly in front of hers. I wanted to block her as much as possible, to keep her from capturing the attention of any of the brothers who might have had a little too much to drink. Or worse.

"Flinch." The prospect at the door nodded in respect. "Cutter's waiting for you in the meeting room."

"Thanks."

I moved to walk by, but he leaned to look past me. To look right at Locklyn.

"Hey, beautiful. Why don't you set that ass on my chair tonight and let the big dogs handle their business?"

My wolf—already on edge from our little dry hump on the ridge—snapped. We growled loud and long, stepping closer to the prospect, making sure his wolf understood how outmatched he would be in a fight. "Don't ever fucking talk to her."

Locklyn grabbed my arm, hanging on to me with both hands as she inched closer. "It's fine. Just keep moving."

It wasn't fine, but I wasn't about to argue with her. I also wasn't going to make her spend one extra minute in the club-house with all the brothers watching her, because every eye in the place seemed to be minding our business instead of its own. Nosy fuckers.

But I couldn't just let it go.

"You ever talk about her ass again, and I'll break your spine so you can eat your own." And without another moment of atten-tion wasted on the prospect, I headed deeper into the club, keeping Locklyn as close as possible. Holding on to her hand and reining her in tight against me. But that closeness didn't block out as much as I had hoped, and eventually, she stopped in the middle of the floor. When I felt the tug and turned, the nervous expression she wore as she took in the chaos didn't surprise me, but I hated it anyway. This woman was not ready for my world. Not yet anyway.

I stepped into her body, blocking out most of the scene around us. Using physical contact to regain her attention. Or as much of it as I could, considering how distracted she seemed to be. Once I had at least a good amount of her gaze on me, I leaned in close, rubbing my cheek against hers as I brought my lips to her ear. "What's up, short stack?"

"Are they always so—" she looked around, gaze landing on mine every few seconds before flitting off to take in the club, brow tightening with every return "—outgoing?"

That question stumped me. Outgoing? I looked past her, investigating more of the room and trying to see it through her perception. Watching my brothers being themselves—drinking, laughing, playing darts. Nothing too crazy. Nothing outgoing.

"I don't know what you mean."

She nodded toward the opposite corner—one not in my visual field—so I moved to step behind her, pressing my body against hers and grabbing her by the hips. Making my claim well-known and taking in the sight of about ten brothers all playing pool. We had four tables, and three had some standard games playing out on them. The fourth, well...*that* was a different story.

"That table slants," I said, assuming her "outgoing" comment from earlier was in regard to the fourth table. I slid my hand up her ribs and pulled her body against mine. Enjoying the feel of every inch pressed against me as I leaned over her to keep my mouth near her ear. "No one uses it for pool."

"Are they..." For the first time, Locklyn seemed dumbfounded. Unable to finish her words.

I pulled her tighter against me, making sure to seat her ass firmly against my dick. "Fucking? Yes. They are definitely fucking."

She breathed out in a huff, her entire body going through a quick shiver in my arms. "All of them?"

Because there had to be ten brothers around the table and

who knew how many of the club pussy had chosen to join in. Legs and arms and hair abounded, the pile of people in various states of undress too chaotic to make heads or tails of exactly who was where and with which partner. Not really all that unusual, to be honest. With shifters, sex was a no-holds-barred experience.

"Whoever wants to participate can." I growled low and soft, making sure I had every ounce of her attention. Pulling my lips back over my teeth when I saw the hair rise on her skin. "What's got you all tangled, short stack?"

She shivered again then turned, keeping her body pressed against mine even as my hands found themselves climbing up her rib cage. "Have you ever fucked women on that table?"

Every muscle locked down as my brain went completely sideways. Fuck, I had a feeling she wouldn't like my answer.

But I would never lie to her.

"Yes."

Those green eyes darted up to meet mine. "Really?"

Time to get really fucking honest. I crouched a bit, getting right into her face to block out the rest of the club. Making sure I held her gaze. Making sure she heard every word. "Have I fucked club pussy on that pool table in the past? Yes, I have. Years ago, when I was new here and figuring out the culture of the club. I swung my dick around this bar just like the rest of them. Will I ever again? Fuck no."

"Why not?"

I wanted to tell her the truth. To tell her she was the only woman I wanted on my dick, and the only man who should be privileged enough to see her come was me. That I wanted every hot, breathy moment with her to be mine and mine alone. I was a cleanup man—I would clean up her sexual history so only I would know her juicy secrets. Kill every man—or woman—who had been gifted access to the sweet cherry-scented place I longed to be. Grind up their bodies, destroy all evidence, and walk away happy, knowing I would be the only man left alive who had ever felt, seen, smelled, or tasted her sweet pussy. I would do it all without a second fucking thought.

But she wasn't ready for all that just yet, so instead, I growled again, running my nose up her cheek. "Why? You feel like joining in?"

Her green eyes flashed, her neck growing darker. Redder. I could practically smell the arousal on her skin, and I liked it. Craved that cherry scent like no other.

"Locklyn," I singsonged when she didn't answer, sliding my hand down. Using it to press her hips even harder against me while letting my fingers tease her cunt through her jean shorts. "Is that what you want? To be fucked by three or four wolf shifters right here in front of everyone?"

A thought that made my wolf want to jump through my skin and immediately go on the attack to keep the idea from coming to fruition. Not that I needed to worry about that.

Locklyn turned in my arms again, rising onto the balls of her feet to bring her mouth to my ear. A feat I had to crouch down to help her accomplish. But when we were lined up, when those plush pink lips opened and I felt them brush against my skin, when her words skimmed across my flesh on the warm air of her breath, she gave me the gift of the right answer.

"I'm more of a one-man type of woman."

And no fucking way was anyone else going to be that man.

"Good." I glanced back at the table for just a moment before smacking her ass to make sure I had her full attention. "Happy to put in my application to be that man whenever the opportunity arises."

With that, I started us moving again, keeping her hand in mine and our bodies close. Making a path so she didn't have to bump into any of the brothers along the way. She kept hold of both my hand and my arm as she followed me down the hallway and into the meeting room, practically clinging to me. Making me feel like the protective force I wanted her to see me as. The woman had me all riled up, but I liked it.

"You called?" I said as soon as we walked into the meeting room. Cutter looked up from where he had been sitting at the head of the table, neatening the papers he'd been reviewing as he scowled my way.

"About fucking time you got here."

I pointed a thumb at Locklyn. "The short stack held me up."

The way her mouth opened and her expression changed to one so affronted had me chuckling. "How is you being late my fault?"

"You're the one who wanted to stop and watch the brothers fucking on the pool table."

Her cheeks went tomato red, and she snapped her jaw closed. "You asshole."

Cutter huffed a sarcastic sort of laugh. "They had better not break another pool table out there."

"They're sticking to the bad one so far."

"Good." He gave Locklyn what constituted a smile for him, the corners of his mouth twitching up just slightly. "Sorry about that. The boys needed to burn off some steam after today."

She shrugged, still clinging to me but obviously much more relaxed than out in the actual bar. "It's fine. This jackass didn't prepare me for what I was about to see, is all."

"If I had known you liked watching people fuck—" I jumped back and let out an exaggerated hiss when she smacked my arm, as if she had actually hurt me with the little tap. "Let's not get abusive. Not my fault the old man here lets the brothers run wild in the club."

"I'm not the one who has let those brothers do shit." Cutter moved to settle back down at the table, waving toward the open seats. "Locklyn, you will learn that the shifters of the Desert

Hellions are all assholes with too much testosterone running through their veins. There's always some sort of drama out there, and usually it revolves around fucking or fighting."

"Sounds like most bars."

The old shifter huffed another laugh. "So then, you're used to it. Good. Because you're always welcome in the bar known as the Devil's Lounge."

"Is that what this place is called?" I asked, having had no idea of any official name.

Cutter shrugged. "Technically. We needed a business name to file the paperwork, and that's what was chosen. I wasn't with the club then, so I have no idea how they arrived at that."

"My mom," Locklyn said. She gave my hand a squeeze before letting go and stepping around the table, finding a seat along the wall to drop into. "Chiggy set this place up as a business to make it easier for the shifters to have legal records when needed—jobs, income, all that stuff. Once credit scores became a thing, hiding from the government became harder, you know? My mom and he had met in some sleazy lounge in Vegas where she'd been a waitress, so she said he should call it Devil's Lounge. As a reminder of their past but with a hint of Hellions in it."

Cutter glanced my way, looking as surprised as I felt. "That's sort of...sweet."

Locklyn snorted a sarcastic laugh. "My dad wasn't sweet, but he cared for my mom. That's one of the reasons he sent us packing."

I settled in beside her, reaching under the table to rest my hand on her leg. Cassidy—the sole waitress for the club—walked in at that moment carrying a tray with drinks.

"For you," she said, smiling at Cutter and handing him what I had to assume was his normal bourbon. "And I saw you come in, so I grabbed one of your waters."

She set a glass down in front of me and turned her smile to Locklyn. "Hey, girl. I'm Cassidy. What can I get you?"

Locklyn glanced my way before lifting a shoulder. "I'll have one of his fancy waters."

"Perfect." Cassidy hurried out the door just as Zed walked in and started a conversation with Cutter. That gave me a chance to lean over Locklyn and reclaim her attention.

"Why are you always in my space?" she asked, not sounding at all perturbed by my presence.

I leaned in even closer, letting my lips brush her cheek. "Do you mind me being in your space?"

She froze, breath catching. For a long moment, she stayed perfectly still. Like prey that had just realized the big, bad wolf had them in their grasp. Trying to hide in plain sight.

Finally, she took a breath and said a simple, "No."

Question answered, I squeezed her thigh and moved my hand up a little higher. Teasing her under the table. Keeping enough attention on the others in the room to know they had no fucking idea what was happening with us. "Good. And did you really call my sparkling water fancy?"

She sat back, smiling at me. Our noses almost touching. "I did, and they are. That's some bougie water you drink."

"It's just water."

"There's one in your refrigerator that's coconut açai. I don't even know what açai is."

"It's a superfruit. Great antioxidant content."

"You're worried about antioxidants?"

"Worried, no. But I like to make sure I get some in my diet, considering my age."

She tilted her head, her brow furrowing as if confused. "How old are you?"

Now that was a question, and one I wasn't willing to answer just yet. Thankfully, Cassidy came in at that moment with

Locklyn's *fancy* water on a tray. As soon as she left the room—shutting the door behind her this time—Cutter coughed and reclaimed our attention. Question avoided.

"Sorry to interrupt," he said, looking more at me than Locklyn. "Zed and I were going over notes from Locklyn's dreams, Popper's findings, and the crime scene, and we have a few questions."

"Okay." Locklyn adjusted her chair to turn toward them while also pushing it closer to mine. I grabbed the arms and yanked it between my legs, surrounding her because what she wanted, she got. And right then, it sure seemed like she wanted my presence to protect her.

"Popper's guy didn't get much—some dirt, some gunshot residue, a waxy substance on one hand he wasn't sure about. The damage to his neck was a mix of pre- and post-mortem, but the guy couldn't identify what creature had caused it. Could be a coyote, could be a werewolf, could be a vampire, could be some sort of demon—"

"Jesus," Locklyn said, looking horrified. "Those are the options?"

"Welcome to the world of the supernatural. Try not to piss off a demon." Cutter looked back over his notes, shaking his head. "There's nothing here to really point us in the direction of the killer, so we need to go back to what you kept seeing in your dreams."

Cutter spent the next ten minutes peppering Locklyn with questions—sounds, sights, smells, feelings. Anything to get the girl to expound on what she'd already told them. I sat back and let her speak. Just there as a bodyguard in that moment.

"Where's your mom?" Zed asked out of the blue, definitely catching my attention. Locklyn stiffened immediately, the energy around her shifting. Growing darker.

"Dead. Cancer, two years ago."

"Fuck, I'm sorry." Cutter glared at Zed before continuing. "We should have been a bit gentler with that question."

"It's fine." Locklyn shrugged, her shoulders tighter than usual. "No harm done."

But she'd started bouncing one leg and looked stiff as a board. Obviously, asking about her mother had been about as far from fine as a question could be.

"Let's wrap this up," I said. "What else you got?"

Cutter shot a glance at Zed before bringing his attention back to my girl. "You mentioned Chiggy's truck in your dream."

"Right," she said with a nod. "The headlights lit the scene."

He nodded, scribbling something on the notebook before him with his pen. "And at the time of his death, the headlights from his truck backlit him. Right?"

"Yes."

"So your dad's truck was there in the desert when he was shot?"

"Absolutely."

Cutter nodded and looked right at her, seemingly not convinced. "You sure it was Chiggy's?"

Locklyn paused, obviously thinking. "Yeah. Well... I'm 90% sure."

"Only ninety?" Zed leaned across the table, dark eyes locked on her. "Why not a hundred?"

"Because I hadn't seen my dad's truck in a few years. He didn't want me coming out here, so he would visit me in Detroit instead. The last few times, he flew there."

"But you think it was his?" Cutter asked.

"Yeah. The horns sort of gave it away."

The horns—Chiggy had driven a truck with longhorn antlers since I'd known him. Only man in the club to do so. Shit, only man in northeast Arizona to do so that I could tell. That seemed more like a Texas adornment, but Chiggy had loved those fuckers.

"You saw the longhorns?" I asked.

Locklyn nodded. "Definitely, that's why I assumed it was his truck."

I looked up at the two men across the table. "Sounds like Chiggy's truck."

Zed sat deeper in his chair, blowing breath out of his nose as his entire face tightened. "So where the fuck is it?"

"That's what we need to find out." Cutter rose to his feet and nodded our way. "Thanks, Locklyn. We appreciate you coming down here."

"Anything to help you find out who killed my dad." She rose to her feet, and I followed, still sticking close to her.

Cutter seemed to notice because he looked my way, frowning. "We hunt tonight. Get her settled."

Locklyn glanced up at me, eyes wide. I could practically smell the fear rolling off her, but I didn't address it. Not yet.

"Ready to go home?"

She nodded and automatically reached for my hand, weaving our fingers together as if she always had. I liked it—the comfort with which she reached for me, the trust she put in me. Earn her, Cutter had said. I was earning.

We reached my house without incident, but my mind hadn't stopped spinning since I'd seen the expression on Locklyn's face when Cutter had told me to get her settled. She didn't want to be alone, and I didn't want to leave her. Tonight would be hard, so I sent a quick text to Cutter and Zed before walking inside the house. One that simply said *I need an hour*. They would have to deal with my delay.

"You hungry?" I asked as soon as I closed the door behind me. Locklyn shook her head, silent. Arms crossed over herself as if in protection mode. That just wouldn't fucking do. "Want to watch something? I've got all the streaming shit."

"No thanks." Soft voice. No emotion. Fuck. Time to be bluntly honest with her.

"I have to go hunt for your dad's truck with the club."

"I know."

"I can't leave you here like this."

"Like what?"

"Half dead and looking afraid. What do you need?"

She shook her head, silent once more. Fuck that noise. Without another word, I growled and lunged at her, picking her up and wrapping her legs around me before carrying her down the hallway. I kicked open the door to my bedroom, the room that now smelled like Locklyn and got me hard just walking inside it, and headed across the threshold. She may not have invited me in, but she certainly wasn't trying to stop me. I took that as some sort of consent. I hadn't earned her yet, so there would be a hard stop ahead, but for the moment, I basked in all things Locklyn because she needed me to.

I didn't stop until I reached my bed, basically throwing myself down on the mattress with Locklyn still wrapped around me.

"Flinch," she yelped, though not as an admonishment. No, the woman had a solid hold on me and wasn't letting go. There was also a softness to her body, a willingness. She liked this. Even if my name in that tone sounded like a warning.

One I wasn't about to listen to.

"My bed, my rules." I wrapped myself around her and tugged her almost underneath me, letting my weight rest partially on her. Turning myself into her shifter weighted blanket and hoping I worked to soothe her anxiety. I even let my wolf growl nice and low and continuously. Vibrating against her like a goddamned massaging recliner.

All my tricks eventually worked. Locklyn relaxed beneath me, her body going pliant. Her hands burying themselves in my hair as my head rested on her chest. Her touch felt good. Too good. I was either going to fall asleep or fuck her through the mattress if we didn't get up soon. And once I got inside her, I had a feeling I would never want to leave. Brothers and their need to hunt for Chiggy's killer be damned.

Which meant I needed to stay on task.

"Better?" I asked, fighting the urge to bite her soft skin and taste her sweet blood.

"Yes."

"What got to you?"

"Everything. It's all...crazy."

My phone vibrated in my pocket. I knew it had to be a brother, but I had a mate who needed me. One who took priority in that moment. The boys would have to wait.

"It is crazy, but I've got you. I'll be the calm inside the chaos for you." I growled louder, letting the sound massage her one last time. "Ready for some food now?"

Locklyn sighed and squeezed me tighter for just a moment. "Maybe a little something."

My girl was hungry, which meant I had a job to do. But she also needed my physical contact. I knew that as well as I knew my own name, could tell by the way she clung to my side that she wasn't ready to be away from me just yet. Which was fine by me —I would give her what she wanted while making sure she had what she needed. That was my job.

I held her tightly as I sat up, pulling her with me so we didn't break contact. Once I had myself in a seated position with her on my lap, she wrapped herself around me. Fuck, what I would have given to have been naked in that moment. To have had my girl bouncing on my dick. Such an impossible thought in that moment, and yet one I couldn't help but want to sink into. I knew she had to feel how hard I was under her, knew she noticed the fucking tree trunk pressed against her. She didn't seem to mind, though. She might have even wiggled her hips a little as if to line me up with her pussy.

Something that would definitely break my control if I didn't get my ass in gear.

"Food. Gotta make some food," I said, practically to myself. Reminding my wolf what we needed to do to distract him from ripping off her clothes and sliding deep. *Not tonight, friend.*

Thankfully, Locklyn didn't put up a fight as I grabbed her ass, rose to my feet, and carried her to the kitchen. I set her down on the table so I could keep touching her, so she could reach me if she needed to. So the connection between us didn't break while I cooked for her. My kitchen wasn't anything out of some designer magazine—it wasn't open concept and huge. I had a typical small 1960s kitchen with a little round table in one corner. I could almost keep a hand on Locklyn's knee and cook her entire meal. Almost.

I pulled some steak strips from the freezer and collected the rest of the ingredients I would need, mostly from the cabinets. I didn't keep a lot of fresh stuff around because I usually wasn't home enough, but I had the basics for street tacos.

Within minutes, the kitchen filled with the aroma of warm spices and meat. I was about to head out to my patio to grab one last thing when I had to stop.

"You like cilantro?"

Locklyn nodded. "I do, yes."

I grunted and continued outside, grabbing a few sprigs from one of my cilantro plants before returning to the kitchen. Locklyn looked up when I came through the door and smiled, nearly punching me in the gut with the power of her attention. Fuck, this girl had me spinning in circles.

I had to focus on the food. "Some humans say this stuff tastes like soap."

She tilted her head. "Shifters don't?"

"None that I've ever met, and I'm old as fuck."

"How old?"

The same question as back at the club, and I'd walked right into her asking it. I would eventually have to answer, but we didn't have the time for that particular discussion, so I put her tacos together instead and headed her way, holding out the plate like a peace offering. "Old enough to know you might not be comfortable with that discussion."

Locklyn took a taco and bit into it, chewing with a contemplative look on her face before swallowing and attacking my restraint once more. "Older than my dad?"

"Yes."

"By a lot?"

"Yes."

"You don't look as old as him."

"It's the antioxidants in my bougie water, I wear sunscreen religiously, and my skincare regimen is on point. Self-Care fucking Sunday is my jam."

She choked out a laugh, and I smiled, unable not to. This woman had me wrapped. Two days, and there was nothing I wouldn't do for her. Nothing I wouldn't give up. And someday, I would tell her that.

Lights suddenly shone through the window, and the sound of multiple motorcycle engines rolling down my driveway broke the moment. My smile immediately fell, and Locklyn looked up, her expression turning fearful.

I lifted a finger to her chin and turned her face my way, regaining her focus. "It's the club coming to get me."

"Why wouldn't they just call?"

"They did."

She frowned, that brow furrowing adorably. "You ignored them?"

"Yes."

"Why?"

"You needed to calm down so you could eat."

My mate did not seem convinced. "Pretty sure my dad never once ignored the guys for my mom."

"Then she didn't matter as much to him as the club."

Locklyn scoffed. "Yeah, seems that way."

Her irritation intrigued me. "Were they mated?"

"Who?"

"Chiggy and your mom."

A simple lift of her shoulder was all the answer I needed, but she followed it up with a quiet, "I don't know."

But I did. "Then no."

"Why? Does being mated matter?"

There was no way to answer that without giving myself away. No way to explain the whole fated mates ephemera in what little time I had. So I leaned in close, taking up space once more. Inserting my hips between her thighs and running my hands down her back as I whispered to her.

"A mated wolf would have never let their mate walk away. He would have chased her down and given up the world for her. He would have done anything to make her happy." I backed away, sighing. "Are you going to be okay if I go?"

"Do you have a choice?"

I glanced at the front door as Cutter's voice came from the other side. My likely new club president yelling for me. He needed me, but so did my mate.

"When it comes to you, I will always have a choice." I leaned in closer, wanting so badly to kiss her but holding back. "We're hunting for your dad's truck, not partying. If it were anything else, I'd tell them to fuck off. But I want to know who killed

Chiggy so I can return the favor. Your dad deserved that much. You do, too."

She stared up at me for a long moment, contemplative. Anxiety gone and eyes once again fierce. "Then go find my dad's truck. And whoever killed him."

Decision made. I leaned in and dropped a kiss to her lips, unable not to. Keeping my tongue in my mouth like a fucking gentleman even as I pressed my hard dick against her.

"I'll find it for you. You still got the money I gave you?" I murmured when we broke apart, stealing one more taste before taking a step back, grunting softly when she nodded. "Good. Get some rest—I'll likely be gone most of the night, but there'll be a man outside."

I turned on my heel and headed for the front door, knowing I had only one shot at leaving. If she called my name, if I paused for even a second, I'd have her naked and underneath me for the night. There would be no hunt for Chiggy's truck, no club business, that could take me from her. Not if I surrendered the way I wanted to.

But soon. Very soon.

"You finally ready?" Cutter asked when I opened the front door, sounding pissed. Not that I gave a fuck. I had my eyes on the prospect who would be guarding Locklyn for me. The same prospect who had tried chatting her up at the clubhouse. The same one who needed to learn a motherfucking lesson.

I stalked over to the shifter and punched him squarely in the face, knocking him right off the porch and into the dirt. Not a single brother moved to protect him, though Banger did back his bike away so the shifter didn't roll into it. Priorities.

I followed after the prospect, yanking him back to his feet and pulling him right up into my face. "You step out of line with her for one fucking second, and I'll dismember you and feed your intestines to the coyotes myself. After you've eaten your own ass for our entertainment."

"What the fuck did I do?" he asked, his voice filled with an attitude that would certainly get him killed.

It was Rush who answered from his seat on his bike, though. "You talked about her ass, my dude. That's like basic sexist bull-shit right there."

The prospect huffed and avoided looking at me. "It was just a joke."

That got Rush to rise to his feet. Got the man stalking closer. I stood back and let him come, let him take control of this conversation. He looked like a man with an axe to grind, and I had no interest in getting in his way.

Thankfully, Rush kept his voice low when he stepped onto the porch, addressing the prospect in a growling hiss that had the bastard's hairs standing on end.

"Your joke wasn't funny, and Locklyn is Flinch's bitch, motherfucker. His girl, his rules."

The prospect didn't say a word, showing at least an inkling of smarts as he kept his eyes on my shoulder and simply nodded. Point made, I shoved him toward Rush and stormed to my bike, catching Locklyn looking through the front window as I mounted up. Knowing she had seen that. Not regretting the punch for a second. No one hit on my girl.

Rush pushed the prospect into the chair on the porch then headed for his own bike, giving me a fist bump as he passed. Simple, easy, no words necessary. I hadn't needed the backup, but he'd still stepped in to support Locklyn. I could appreciate that.

"Let's go find the fucking truck," Zed called from his spot in the pack, obviously done with the bullshit.

I barked my agreement along with the rest of the brothers, all of us seemingly ready to roll. We would find the truck and Chiggy's killer. I would make damn sure of it because the little human staring at me from inside my house needed answers. And I needed her.

Earn her.

Getting revenge on Chiggy's killer would earn a lot. Maybe not all of her, but some. The rest, I would have to figure out as I went.

Thirteen

LOCKLYN

Sleep didn't come easily after Flinch left. In a way, I waited up for him. Listening for any sign of his bike rolling back onto the driveway. None came, and when the sun finally rose, I felt worse than when I had gone to bed.

"I need coffee," I said to the empty room as I stretched. Coffee would make everything better. Or at least the things I could control.

Once vertical, I got ready and headed for the front door, phone in hand and my maps app searching for local coffee places. I would take a chain if necessary, but I would eventually like to find a little local place to visit. Daily coffee runs could really help a small business.

I pulled up short with my hand on the doorknob, completely frozen in place as that thought echoed in my head. Daily coffee runs...in Mesa. How long would I be in Arizona? I would eventually go back to Detroit...right? But returning to Detroit meant a life without Flinch, something I wasn't ready to think about. I'd only known the man for a handful of days, and yet I couldn't imagine a future without him somehow. Which made no sense.

"Coffee. You just really need coffee." I grabbed the handle and yanked open the front door, practically stumbling when the man on the porch looked up at me from his seat. The prospect from the door of the club. The one Flinch had punched in the face.

Well, this was awkward.

"Morning," I said, suddenly unsure what to do.

"Where are you off to?"

"Uh...I was going to run and grab a coffee."

He grunted some sort of sound of acceptance and slowly rose to his feet, a mountain unfurling before my eyes. Flinch and his shifter brothers were huge. "I know a place."

I nodded and headed for the truck, freezing once more when he opened the passenger door and hopped inside.

He must have noticed my surprise because he gave me a smirky sort of smile and said, "This is easier."

I had a feeling Flinch wouldn't like him being in the truck with me, more because it made me a bit uncomfortable than anything else, but I kept my mouth shut and slipped into the driver's seat. We didn't need another Hellion getting into trouble because I felt intimidated by them.

When I turned the key and the dash lit up, though, I frowned.

"What's up?"

"This gauge has to be broken," I said, tapping on the computer-like dash that likely wasn't broken but couldn't be showing what it was. "The tank always reads the same. It's always full, even if I drove around town and know I used gas."

The prospect huffed a laugh. "It's not broken. Flinch takes it every night to fill it up for you."

I whipped my head in his direction so fast, I almost wobbled in my seat. "He does?"

"Yup. He rode in about two last night and took it before heading back out with the crew."

That made no sense. "Why?"

The leer that man sent me had me refocusing on how uncomfortable it felt to be confined to such a small space with him.

"You tell me. What do you have going on that would make a man simp out like that?"

I had no answer to that, and the stare he pinned me with only kept me feeling more uncomfortable by the minute, so I chose to ignore him.

I stared straight ahead, not giving him my attention for another second, and threw the truck in gear. "Where am I going?"

Thankfully, the prospect turned in his seat and stopped trying to see right through me as I began to drive. He even cracked a few jokes as he gave me directions to a small coffee shop in a strip of shops in town. The place looked clean but outdated, likely a perfect local joint to grab a cup of something well brewed. Inside, the menu was relatively simple—coffee, tea, and espresso-based drinks with different milk options and some standard syrups. Nothing crazy. They weren't a coffee shop trying to get Instagram-famous or have the biggest menu in town. They seemed like a place that made a good cup of coffee all day. I liked it immediately.

"Best espresso in town," he said before nodding toward the menu. "What will you have? My treat."

"Oh no. I can—"

"Flinch would kill me." He turned to look in the pastry case. "Let me buy you a coffee so I can keep breathing."

Well, when he put it that way...

"Cappuccino. Nothing fancy."

The prospect bought us our drinks—Americano for him and the frothiest cappuccino I'd ever seen for me—and chose a couple of Danishes as well. I wasn't actually hungry, but I acquiesced to the idea of at least picking at one. Once we had our food and drinks, I led the way to the front of the shop and settled into an armchair by the front window.

"This place is nice," I said, hoping to shrug off the sense of unease that had seemed to settle like a yoke around my neck. "Local favorite?"

"Yeah. The owner supports about every local charity and kids sports team in town, so most people come here instead of hitting up the chain out by the highway. You can't get one of those shaken upside-down frappe-happy things, but the coffee's good, the espresso is strong, and the prices are right."

I shrugged, sitting deeper in the chair, sipping on my mug of delicious, foamy goodness. "He's got the equipment to do the same drinks as any chain shop. It's all just espresso and milk, you know? The variances are in what order things go in and how you treat the milk."

"You work at a coffee place?"

"No, but I used to. I'm a bartender back home."

"Where's home?"

"Detroit."

He frowned, looking as if he didn't believe me. "No one who says they're from Detroit is actually from the city."

I laughed, curling over myself and practically guffawing. "I'm a transplant, but I actually do live in the city."

He grunted and sat a little deeper, taking a sip of his Americano before pulling out his next question. "Where are you from originally?"

I shrugged, taking a deep sip of my own drink before answering. "Here, technically. At least, I was born in Mesa. Chiggy kicked us out when I was six, so my mom just sort of started making her way east. Oklahoma, Texas, Arkansas, Missouri, Illinois, Michigan—she kept moving us around until we ended up in Philly."

"The fuck-around-and-find-out town."

I raised my cup as if in a toast. "The very one. She died there, and I didn't want to be there without her, so I turned around and went back to where I had felt the most at home. Ended up in Detroit."

"And you like it there?"

"I do—most of the time. Winters are hard." At that moment, a chill not due to the temperature around me skated up my spine. The weight of someone watching me settled firmly on my shoulders, and I darted a look outside. Unable not to. Needing to find whoever seemed to have taken an interest in me.

It took me far longer than I had hoped, but eventually, I noticed a man standing in the shadows across the street. He wore casual clothes—generic, not standing out—and sported mirrored sunglasses, but there was no doubt in my mind that he was staring right at me. As I watched, he removed the sunglasses, holding my gaze the entire time. Unblinking. Deep, dark eyes locked on mine in a way that made my blood run cold. And his hands—such long, thin fingers. Something about his hands didn't sit right with me. Made me wonder if he was even human, which would have been an odd thought to have except for the fact that I was sitting across from a man who could shift into a wolf.

"You okay?" the prospect asked, concern laced through his voice.

I shook my head, unable to stop staring at the man across the street. Almost enthralled into doing so, even though I wanted nothing more than to stop. "No. I'm not. I need to go home."

The prospect did something that made him leave his chair—

likely dealing with our garbage and dirty plates—before he came and grabbed my arm. It was only his touch and tug that made me vacate my seat, only his constant pressure to move that had my feet stepping in the direction of the door. It was almost as if I had little to no control of my body, and I didn't like it.

"What the fuck is happening?" The prospect turned me toward him, breaking my stare-off with the man across the street and sounding downright angry. "What's got you all zombie-like?"

I swallowed and licked my lips, my mouth suddenly too dry. "Did you see that guy?"

"What guy?"

"The one in front of the restaurant across the street." I looked over his shoulder, but the man was gone. I even stepped around the prospect to look up and down the street, but the man with the weird hands and the dark eyes was nowhere to be found. "He was right there."

"We're going back to Flinch's," he said, pulling me to the truck. A single red rose lay on the ground in front of it, half dead and covered in ants. So completely out of place that I couldn't tear my eyes away from the thing. Not even when the prospect stepped on it as he pulled me to the passenger side. I finally had to look away as the prospect—I still didn't even know his name —shoved me bodily into the truck, not letting me go until he had me settled on the seat and even buckled in. "You sit right there. I'm driving."

Which seemed like a good idea, seeing as how I still felt oddly shaky and out of control. And all I could think about was that weird red rose.

The drive home helped, the distance between me and the strange man likely working in ways nothing else could. Once the prospect pulled into Flinch's driveway, I headed directly into the house, locking the door behind me and walking straight into

Flinch's main bathroom. His soaps were there, his scent deeply embedded in the space. I stepped right into his shower and sat for a long moment just breathing him in, trying to re-center myself. Trying to shake off the feeling of being completely out of control, of the loss of agency that man had instilled in me. It took more time than I would have liked, but I eventually began to feel more like myself. Mostly.

"You need some exercise," I said to myself, still reeling from my morning. "Clear away the cobwebs."

I slipped into my swimsuit and headed out back, knowing a swim would cool me off in the best way possible. I had just dived in when the prospect came around the corner. The second his eyes locked on me, another shiver raced up my spine. This one different from the one the man in the shadows had initiated. That man had seemed to want to control me. The prospect wanted to...well, I wasn't totally sure, but I had a feeling my being in so little clothing played into his hands just fine. A thought that had me doubting myself. He had been nothing but kind when we'd been in the truck. Just the initial weird staring, which could have been my perception of something being off. Just like his being around me in the pool—he could have shown up without any sort of untoward intentions. I might have been a little too overstimulated by the day's events.

"I'm okay," I said, wishing he would go back to the front porch and hating myself a little bit for feeling so anxious. "You don't need to babysit me back here."

He shrugged his boulder of a shoulder. "Flinch said watch you, so I'm watching."

That answer only made me feel more awkward. I swam back and forth for a few minutes, entirely too aware of how high cut my bikini bottoms were and how much of my ass cheeks likely showed, before I no longer felt comfortable. The swim wouldn't clear any of the cobwebs in my head or calm me down, so I exited the pool at the far side, grabbing the towel I had brought out and wiping myself down. I was just about to wrap the towel around my body to cover up when I heard my name called in the most comforting voice in the world.

"Flinch!" I hurried toward him, towel still in hand. Awkwardness of being in my bikini forgotten.

Flinch stepped around the corner of the house, and all my worries disappeared. All the stress flew off my shoulders. And the way he looked at me—those light eyes catalogued every detail from the tips of my toes to the top of my head. He ran that gaze over me multiple times, taking in every inch. Eyes growing darker with each pass. Unlike the prospect's, Flinch's gaze didn't make me want to hide. At all. I liked him watching me.

"Having fun, short stack?" he asked. Before I could answer, he darted a look over my shoulder, and his entire face changed. He suddenly looked pissed as hell and ready to fight, which meant he had noticed the prospect who was likely still staring at my ass.

"Flinch."

He growled, the sound deepening quickly and becoming more like a snarl as he tugged my towel to cover me. With one move, he grabbed me by my ass and lifted, settling me in his arms as I wrapped my legs around his waist. His hands stayed covering my ass cheeks, and he looked over my shoulder, that growling snarl growing deeper and more menacing.

"Get the fuck out of here, prospect. I can take care of my girl."

The growling continued, so I ran my hands up over his shoulders and neck and into his hair. Trying to soothe him. Relaxing into his hold to give him the same comfort he gave me. It didn't take too long, likely just enough time for the prospect to bug out, but eventually, Flinch stopped growling.

"Feel better?" I asked, still tugging on his hair.

He squeezed my ass and sighed. "He always look at you like that?"

"Like he wants me to be wearing even fewer clothes than I already am?"

The growl came back as he said, "Yeah."

"Occasionally."

"I'll fucking kill him."

I gripped him tighter, unwilling to let him go. Needing the feel of his body against mine to relax. "Don't. He's not worth it."

"But you are." He dropped his head and kissed my shoulder, sighing. "Fuck, short stack. I thought this bikini was going to kill me when I first saw you in it."

I giggled, still clinging to him. "You like it?"

"Like isn't the right word." He pulled back, those light eyes locking on mine. "Can I show you how much?"

I had no idea what he meant or was about to do, but I knew whatever it was, he wouldn't hurt me. So I nodded my consent. Flinch dropped a quick kiss on my chin, and then we were in motion. For a second, I had no idea what had happened, but then water enveloped me. I held my breath and waited, inhaling and laughing as I came back to the surface. Still in Flinch's arms.

"You're still dressed!" I released him, laughing as he kept his hands on me. As he refused to let me go. "You probably ruined your phone."

"It's on the table." He grinned and disappeared under the surface, rubbing a hand over his face when he reappeared. "Fuck, this feels good."

"It does." I leaned back, still with my legs around him, my upper body floating in the warm water. "Does the water get too hot in the summer to swim?"

"Sometimes. Some people have coolers to keep the water chilled."

"That's amazing. There're only a few good months for

outdoor swimming in Detroit—or really anywhere up north. It gets too cold when it's not summer."

He hummed some sort of agreement, bringing his fingers to my neck and running them down my body. Between my breasts. Over my stomach. All the way to the top of my bikini bottoms. I floated and reveled in his touch, wanting more. Letting myself surrender to the haze being around him caused. So much more pleasurable than the one the creepy man had made me feel.

"You're so fucking beautiful," Flinch said, his voice rough, his cock growing hard against me. "Do I get to touch, short stack?"

I nodded, moaning his name softly when he moved us to where he could lean against the side of the pool. I felt the rough wall on my toes, the feeling in such contrast to his skin and the water that I shivered when it made contact.

"That's my good girl," he said in a voice growing progressively deeper. One hand dropped to my thigh, tugging me until I let the leg drop. For a split second, I worried about slipping under the water, but then he slid that hand up my back. Supporting me. Holding me up as he let his other explore. As the heat of his fingers left sparks along my skin. I floated and I breathed and I surrendered to him.

"Fucking strings." He tugged on the ties holding my bikini together, the ones at my hips. "You're putting a lot of faith in these fucking strings, assuming they're strong enough to keep all that ass covered."

"They haven't failed me yet."

He grunted then tugged, my bottoms releasing against my skin. I felt a rush of coolness then the heat from Flinch's hand. Under my top. On my skin. Slowly moving lower. I kept hold of him with one leg, the other dropping, and opening myself to him. Ready for whatever he had planned. Needing it.

But floating was becoming impossible. "You're going to drown me."

Flinch grunted then moved us again, turning and lifting me so I could rest against the side of the pool. Grabbing my discarded towel from the ground and bunching it up to protect my head from the hard concrete.

"Better?" he asked. I nodded, reaching for him. Wanting to return to the haze of him. And he was going to take me there. That hand of his was right there on my thigh, climbing higher. About to be where I so wanted it...and yet...

"Flinch, I—"

"You know why I want to kill that prospect?" he asked, distracting me from the progression of his hand. Not completely; I still felt those fingers dipping between my legs. But my focus was split.

"Why?"

"Because he covets." He leaned forward and bit my bikini top, tugging it down before kissing my breast. Licking a trail over my nipple as his fingers danced right over the folds covering my clit. "He covets what's going to be mine. You're not yet—I haven't earned you—but he'd take my place in a heartbeat if he could."

One finger pressed harder between my legs, sliding over my clit and making me jerk. I wanted to grab his shoulders and feel his weight on me, wanted to know the warmth of his naked body against mine, but I floated in salty water instead. Teased with the feel of his hand under my back, his lips on my breast, and his hand between my legs. Anchored in place by the concrete at my neck and under my head. Such a cacophony of sensation.

"I wouldn't want him to take your place," I said, grabbing his bicep with one hand. Wanting so much to feel even more. To overwhelm my senses with him. "You're the only one."

"Good. That's my good girl." He refocused on my breast,

suckling my nipple as he moved the hand between my legs lower. As he gently pushed a finger inside me. The water wasn't actually helping anything, and our skin stuck together in ways that weren't perfect, but I couldn't ask him to stop. Didn't want to.

Wanting to bury myself in sensation, I pushed off the wall and let my head drop into the water. I kept one arm raised to hold myself up, but I let my head drop until the water covered my ears. Until I couldn't hear the white noise of the day around me. All I could hear was the sound of Flinch moving through the water, my heartbeat, and a wall of pressure that intensified every-thing else. I closed my eyes and shut down two of my senses. All I wanted in that moment was to feel. To give my body over to him. I wanted to be owned by him.

And he somehow knew that.

"Just keep floating, beautiful," he said, his voice a muffled murmur underwater. "I'll take care of you. I'll make this pretty pussy happy."

And he did. He started slow and smooth, just one finger teasing its way in and out until he had me slippery. Then he added a second. And a third. Pressing his thumb on my clit and increasing the sensation. Something about the dichotomy of the coolness of the water and the heat of his hand stole all my focus, allowing me to drop into a space of pure pleasure and sensation instead of worrying about things like staying afloat or if someone might come into the backyard. I had no worries with Flinch—he would make sure I stayed above the water. He would keep me safe from other people. He would pleasure me right there in his pool, and all I needed to do was let him.

"More," I cried and popped my ears above water. Unable not to arch my entire body as those three fingers sat deep, as they bent and curved and touched spots inside me that made me jump. As he pressed that thumb relentlessly against my clit, causing explosions of sensation all over my body. "Flinch, I need more."

"Fuck, your pussy is a greedy bitch, isn't it? Sucking my fingers in like this. I can't wait to get my cock inside her." He growled low and returned to my nipple, sucking hard. Biting. Laving the pool water from my skin. The hand under my back flexed and clung, still holding me up but obviously wanting more, just like me. We needed a flat, dry surface, fewer clothes, and time. Lots of time to explore each other. We had none of that, though.

"Flinch," I said again, reaching for him. Losing myself to the sensations he wrought. The man didn't answer. Instead, he relaxed the hand under my back. Letting me fall slightly deeper into the water. Letting the coolness cover my ears. Sounds both disappeared and surrounded me, the world outside the two of us gone. But under there, I could hear his hand moving. Could tell every time he pushed inside my body, not from the feel but the waves he caused. The vibrations. Flinch had dropped me into a sensation chamber where nothing mattered but what that hand was doing between my legs, and I loved it. Sank into it. Gave myself over to it.

Surrendered.

With a long, hard press of his thumb and one last thrust inside me with his fingers, Flinch growled. Not low or quiet—he practically roared. The sound made the vibrations in the water explode, made my entire body feel the power behind it. I sat on the precipice of coming to his voice, to the sound of his wolf. My pussy squeezing his fingers and every muscle locking into place. Held there on the edge, not falling, not surrendering. Knowing my release was right there but edging slightly as I waited to be pushed over.

"That's my good fucking girl," Flinch said, his voice distorted and his words hard to hear, but hear them, I did. I crashed at the sound, coming around his fingers. Coming while surrounded by him—his body, his voice, his wolf's growl. All of it. I couldn't have escaped him if I'd wanted to, but I didn't want to. I wanted to stay right there, wrapped in pleasure. Falling apart and letting him put me back together again.

As everything came back online—as my body relaxed and reality began to intrude on my thoughts—Flinch grabbed me and lifted me. Tugging me into his arms as he moved us through the water. Pressing me against the side of the pool and grinding his cock between my legs as he growled into my neck. As he bit down, his body tense as if holding back.

I didn't want him holding back.

"I want you," I whispered, clinging to him. Rocking my hips against his. "Take me inside, and let me make you feel good."

He huffed a sound like a laugh, collapsing against me. Biting a little harder before kissing my neck. Licking me slow and long as if savoring the taste on his tongue.

"If I take you inside, we're not coming out for days." He pulled back, staring down at me, those light eyes much darker and hotter than I'd ever seen them as he brought his hand to his mouth. The same one that had been between my legs. The one likely covered in my juices. He kept eye contact as he licked his fingers, growling low. His stomach vibrating against me and making me squirm. "Cherries. Just like I thought. Fuck, short stack—a man could live on the taste of you."

I laughed, unable not to. "Flinch—"

"When I take you to bed for the first time, I'm not doing it with a clock ticking on us. The club's not done hunting, and I have to get back out there soon." He leaned closer, letting his lips brush against my cheek. "When I get you naked and alone, I'm not going to be able to think about anything but that sweet pussy and making you scream my name a hundred times. Right now, I don't have that luxury."

I sighed, understanding but still annoyed. "Fine, but I owe you."

He chuckled, grabbing my hand and kissing the palm of it. "You don't owe me shit, short stack. I'm a two-for-one type of guy. Two for you, one for me. I still owe you one before I let you touch me."

I kissed him, unable not to. Tangling my tongue with his as he pressed me harder into the wall. As his cock teased me through his jeans. Nothing about the moment felt super comfortable, but I wouldn't have traded it for anything. Wouldn't have let that man out of my hold just because the concrete scratched my back or the denim felt rough. He *was* rough—and I liked him that way.

"Okay," he said, pulling away. Taking a deep breath before refocusing on me. "We need to get out of this pool, and you need to get dressed before my dick takes over the thinking."

I slipped a hand between us, smiling up at him. "Maybe I want your dick to be the one thinking."

He grabbed my wrist, raising an eyebrow at me as he dragged my hand up his body to kiss my palm once again. "When it's my turn, I want those dick-sucking lips, not your fingers." He leaned in for a kiss before pushing off the wall and walking toward the steps out of the pool. "Though I'll definitely take what I can get."

"You can get it all."

He groaned, his hands gripping me tighter. "Bad fucking timing, short stack. We've got some bad fucking timing."

He set me down then grabbed a dry towel from a stack by the back door, bringing me one and drying me off with it before wrapping it around me like a blanket. He took another and rubbed it roughly over his head and face, not even bothering with attempting to dry his sodden clothes.

"You going to strip out here, or are you taking the show

inside?" I asked, grinning up at him as I grabbed the waistband of his jeans and pulled.

"Smartass," he said with a laugh. "You take yourself inside and hop in the shower. I don't need you getting all dickmatized when I strip off these jeans."

I found his arrogance far more charming than I probably should have. "You think what you've got will dickmatize me?"

He growled again, the sound making my clit throb, goose bumps rising all over my body. Fuck, I remembered that sound. In the pool. Ears under water. With his hand...

"That's what I thought," he said, cocky enough to make me want to punch him. "Now get your ass inside. I need to clean up and get back out on the road."

A sad, horrible, miserable thought. "Fine. But someday..."

I headed for the door, leaving the threat hanging. Smiling as Flinch laughed behind me.

"Someday, I'm going to fuck the sass right out of you, Locklyn."

And I couldn't wait for that.

FOURTEEN

FLINCH

I washed off in the outdoor shower while Locklyn ran inside to take command of the bathroom. I needed the cool water to calm me the fuck down after that escapade in the pool. My girl had been so beautiful—so sexy and giving as she'd come on my fingers. I'd wanted to pin her down and fuck her right there on the concrete, but I couldn't. She deserved better than for me to behave like an animal for her first time with me.

But after that? After I gave her a full night of my mouth, my fingers, and my dick? After I made sure I knew every single sound of pleasure I could wring from her and exactly how to make her come? All bets were off. I'd be fucking her wherever and whenever she let me as hard and wild as she could take.

Thinking about fucking her on the hood of my truck at that spot we had watched the sunset wasn't helping my situation any, so I adjusted myself over my clean, dry jeans and refocused on my phone. The brothers were hunting hard and needed my help. I needed to be out there with them so we could find Chiggy's truck, but I had to deal with Locklyn first. She was my priority.

"Hey."

I smiled on instinct at the sound of her voice, finishing my text to the brothers before looking up. The sight of her stole my breath. Locklyn stood in the kitchen entry wearing what looked like the softest, shortest pajamas I had ever seen. The girl showed so much skin, and yet the pastel color and fuzzy fabric made her seem extra innocent. A vixen and a virgin, all wrapped up in one hot-as-fuck package. And all mine.

"You look..." I shook my head, a low rumble coming from my chest as my wolf made his interest known. As I lost a little control over him. Her lips slid up into a slow, almost taunting smile, and she crossed one ankle over the other as she leaned against the wall.

"I look...?"

Fuck her and that teasing tone. I snarled full out and leaped toward her, catching her in my arms and picking her up. Those legs wrapped around my waist as my lips caught hers in a ferocious kiss. Lost. The smell, taste, and feel of Locklyn had me lost in my own house. The place I had lived for years. The building where I had slept but that had never been my home. Not until I had looked up and seen her standing right there in the middle of it. Fuck, I was lost to her. I would do anything for her. Apparently that including dry humping her against the wall like the damned animal I was.

"Sorry," I said on a gasp as I wrenched my mouth away from hers. My dick...well, he wasn't leaving the warmth of being shoved up against her sweet pussy. Not yet, so I kept her pinned to the wall as I fought to control myself. "Just give me a minute."

Locklyn chuckled softly, running her fingers up my neck and through my hair like the goddamned tease she was. "I'll give you ten if you keep kissing me like that."

"Another day. I have to hunt with the brothers tonight." I dropped one more kiss on those plump lips then pulled away, hanging on to her hand to keep my wolf happy. To keep us connected. "You'll have a different man on the door."

"No more creepy prospect?"

That caught my attention. "Has he been bothering you?"

She lifted a single shoulder in a weak sort of shrug and—key to what was really going on—looked away. "No. Not really."

Fuck that. I leaned in closer, getting in her face. Refusing to let up until those green eyes locked on mine once more. "No, or not really?"

She didn't answer, just stood and stared at me. Back straight, eyes hard. Brave. She wasn't going to tell me how much the prospect I'd forced on her had bothered her, but he had. And that was my fault and my problem.

"Thought so," I finally said. I rose to my full height and pulled my wallet from my pocket, grabbing all the bills. "This is in case you need anything."

Locklyn looked at the cash then at me, her eyes wide. "No, no. That's too much. I still have—"

A knock at the door interrupted her, the sound of engines growing louder in the background telling me all I needed to know. The brothers had arrived.

"Take it," I said, pushing the cash into her hand. "I won't be able to focus if I think you need something and can't get it."

She glared at me, obviously unhappy. Still not gripping the money but instead holding it out as if to give it back. Challenging me. I stood and stared right back, refusing to take it. Needing her to accept my care so my wolf didn't try to eat his way out of our shared body. But my mate was stubborn.

Too stubborn.

Finally, I sighed and grabbed her shoulders. Massaging her. Trying to get her to release a little of the tension she seemed to be carrying right along with the cash. And then I said the only thing I could think of. The only word that might allow her to relax a little.

"Please."

That seemed to be the magic word. She still looked annoyed that I had given her money, but she took it and shoved it all into her pocket. Not saying a word and definitely glaring my way, which was fine by me. I would take any win I could get, but I would also make sure she knew how much I liked it when she let me get away with taking care of her.

I ran my hand up under her shirt, using my position to move her back until I had her pressed against the wall once more. Her breathing became deeper, faster, and her eyes locked right on mine. My girl was independent as fuck, but she liked me being demanding with her body. Good, because I had a preference.

Once I had my hand all the way up, her shirt pulled taut and showing off the bottoms of her breasts, I slipped my fingers around her throat and leaned in close. Tightening my grip just enough for her to feel it. Growling softly under my breath as I whispered, "That's my good girl."

She whimpered, and I smiled before kissing her again. Long and deep, sweeping my tongue across hers and biding my time. Letting my other hand reach around to grab her ass and pull her closer. This girl was going to destroy me from the get-go, and I couldn't help but race for that starting line.

"Flinch," she gasped when I finally pulled away. Hanging on to my shirt with both hands. "You have to go."

By the way she pulled me closer, she didn't want me to go. Hell, I didn't, either. I had her by the throat with a solid grip on her ass and the taste of her mouth on my tongue. Seemed like the start to one hell of a good night for the two of us. Instead, it was the end to one.

"Come on," I said, pulling my hands off her. Resettling her

shirt into place so no one got to see her goodies. No one but me. "Come say goodbye to me."

I grabbed her hand and tugged her behind me, walking into and through the house. Taking her with me out the front. My new man on the door—Rush, the brother who still owed me big for killing a human without an exit strategy—glanced up from his spot on my porch. He'd be guarding Locklyn tonight.

"Brother," I said, giving him a head nod. He returned the gesture, no words necessary, then looked away. This job was both a punishment and a way to earn back my trust. He knew it; I knew it. The whole fucking crew knew it.

Locklyn settled in beside me, keeping her body almost behind my arm. Clinging to me. "Hi."

Rush glanced to me before locking eyes with Locklyn. He even gave the woman a small smile. "Hi. I've got you tonight, so you have nothing to worry about."

And then he looked away. Motherfucking respectful, that man.

"We ready to go?" Cutter yelled from the driveway where he sat with the rest of the guys who would be hunting for Chiggy's truck tonight.

I grabbed Locklyn's hand and squeezed. "Yeah. We're ready."

"Be careful," Locklyn said, her voice tight and small. Quiet. Worried.

"I will." I tugged her closer, turning my back to my team. Hiding her from them. "Make sure you eat a good dinner."

She finally smiled. "I plan on it."

"What's that look for?"

She rose onto the balls of her feet for a second before dropping back down, looking like a kid about to get a new toy or some shit. "I found an Italian place that delivers here. I've been craving pasta."

Craving pasta...something I had missed. Fuck, I had been

directing her to taco stands, and she had been wanting pasta. I was going to have to work a little harder to figure out what she wanted. Though, if she wanted Italian, I had put the right guy on the door. Rush was about as Italian as you could get in this state.

"Yo, Rush." I waited until I saw his head pop up from the corner of my eye. "Locklyn is getting dinner from an Italian place tonight."

"Which Italian place?" Rush asked, his brow furrowed. "There aren't a lot around here."

Locklyn glanced at me then pulled her phone from her pocket. "Uh... It's called Sorrento's. Any good?"

Rush scowled and shook his head, pulling out his own phone. "No. I'll get you Giacomo's."

It was my turn to interrupt just so he didn't write a check his ass couldn't cash. "They don't deliver out here."

Rush grinned my way, looking cocky as fuck. "They will for me."

I snorted a laugh. "Okay, brother. Feed her well."

He looked past me, catching Locklyn's attention again. "You want something specific?"

"Do they have cacio e pepe?" Locklyn glanced at me, definitely excited by the thought of good Italian food coming her way. "That's my favorite."

Rush grunted. "Classic. If they don't have it on the menu tonight, they'll make it for you."

"Thanks." She looked up at me, smile soft and eyes slightly sad. "I'm all set. Time for you to go."

It was, and that sucked more than she could have known. The last thing I wanted was to leave her, but I had to deal with her father's murder. Had to find out who did it and why. So I gave her a hug and patted her ass before kissing the top of her head.

"Be safe while I'm gone."

She chuckled and gripped my arms tighter for just a second before letting me go. "I'll do my best."

And with that, I walked off the porch and toward my crew, hating leaving her behind but knowing I had work to do. Work that would help solve what had happened to her father. A priority for me.

"You good?" Cutter asked as I passed him, keeping his voice low so only those of us closest to him could hear. I gave him a nod then headed right for my bike, swinging a leg over to mount up as soon as I reached her.

"Where we headed?"

Ridge, our road captain, answered that one. "Last ping on Chiggy's cell phone came from an area nowhere near where he was killed. My guess is he left it in the truck."

Some men might have wondered how a quiet, bearded biker like Ridge had possibly gotten his hands on information like cell phone pings. Those of us who knew the guy chose not to—what Ridge could do with a computer was a little scary and a whole lot illegal. We didn't ask, he never told, and information kept flowing our way.

"Good guess," I said with a slight nod and a glance at Cutter. "Let's ride."

I started the engine, looking up to see my girl one last time before I had to go. She stared out at me from the porch, looking like a fucking angel under the lights. An angel with a demon guarding her. Rush hunkered in a chair at her side, looking like the guard dog he was. Taking up more space than any normal human had a right to. He had his eyes on the brothers, had his shoulders set and squared. Ready for battle. Which was good. I needed him to keep his head in the game.

I needed him to keep my mate safe.

———

LOCKLYN

I had been sitting on Flinch's bed, contemplating how my life had ended up the way it had while staring at the ceiling, when a knock sounded from the front. I jumped up and rushed to the living room, throwing open the door.

"Hi," I said, trying to smile. "What's up?"

Rush didn't smile. He didn't even wear an expressionless face. He glared at me.

"You always open the door like that?"

The anger in his voice took me by surprise. "I...what?"

Rush glanced past me. "I have food. Can I come in?"

From scolding to polite requests for access—the man was giving me conversational whiplash. "Yeah. Of course. But what about the door?"

He walked past me, carrying bags and completely surrounded by the smell of amazing food. "You shouldn't just yank open the door like that. You never know who could be on the other side."

"I knew you were on the other side."

"Just because I'm a brother doesn't mean I'm safe." He shot me a hard look. "You always check who's there and what the situation is before you open that door, you hear me?"

I nodded, feeling rightfully chastened. Rush left my scolding at that, though. He held his tongue while setting the bags down and peeking inside them, moving containers of food from one to another and placing some on the table itself.

"There you go," he finally said. "Cacio e pepe, the best you'll ever have. I went ahead and ordered an appetizer sampler for you and some focaccia. There's good olive oil in the bowl container, and the smaller ones are fresh parm."

I couldn't stop staring at the containers on the table. The multiple containers. "This is a lot of food."

"Giacomo's doesn't fuck around on portions. Not for me."

I tore my gaze from the table to catch his. "You related to them or something?"

He stared hard, silent. I thought he wasn't going to answer and had begun to rack my brain for what to say next when he finally opened his mouth.

"My twin sister owns it."

"Oh." His reply felt heavy, as if he had just admitted something he hadn't wanted to. As if he had chosen to trust me. I couldn't ignore that sensation. "Thanks for telling me. I won't mention it."

Rush huffed, grabbing a bag from the table and taking a step back. "Flinch knows. He and Cutter both. Your dad knew, too. Chiggy liked the calamari from the appetizer sampler best."

I smiled, thinking about my dad sitting down with Rush and having a meal. "Last time he visited me, he took me to three different restaurants just to try their calamari. It was his favorite dish."

"Sounds about right—I brought him calamari from Giacamo's every week. We would sit out on his porch and shoot the shit after dinner. He taught me what biker life was really like, and I made sure to let him know how fucking old he was as much as possible." Rush shifted his weight from one foot to the other, looking uncomfortable, then made a sound like a sigh. "He was a good man."

I nodded, heart breaking a little and yet happy to hear Chiggy had impacted a brother in that way. "Yeah, he was."

Rush nodded once and moved as if to collect the extra bags—plural—of food. "Well, I'm going to—"

"Do you want to join me?"

The man balked, taking a visible step back. I would have been offended had he not looked almost terrified in that moment.

"No offense, Locklyn, but Flinch would fucking kill me if I sat at his table and ate dinner with his woman."

"Right." I pasted on a smile once more, pushing the irritation at being controlled by Flinch even when the man wasn't with me to the side. I knew it was for my own good; it was just...new. "I hope you got something for yourself."

He held up his bag, already moving toward the front door. "Definitely. No way would I pass up my sister's food. It's the best."

I followed him to the door, trying to be polite. "Thank you for making this happen. I'm excited to try it."

"Anything for Flinch's woman. Now, lock the door, and don't ever throw it open like that again."

"Yes, sir."

I did as I'd been told—locking the door behind him—then rushed into the kitchen. The scent of garlic and onions hung in the air, making my mouth practically water. I set about opening containers and making myself a plate, picking appetizers that wouldn't reheat as well to eat first since there was no way I could finish everything in one meal. As I munched on calamari, bread, and pasta, I called Zella. She had worked in fancy restaurants. She would understand my bliss at the food before me. Unfortunately, she didn't answer. She could have been working or out for the night, but it still stung that I couldn't reach her. I wasn't used to being so alone—no Zella to come home to, no Flinch, no one to chat with. I was sitting in a house I didn't live in that was owned by a man I barely knew and with a man I didn't know outside guarding me. Flinch would be home eventually, but even then, he wouldn't be with me. He would leave me in his bed and go sleep outside in the hammock. He was respectful like that.

I was really tired of respectful and alone.

Once I finished dinner and had cleaned up—making sure to package all the leftover food to share with Flinch later—I grabbed a pillow and blanket before heading out back. I settled into the hammock, my phone in hand in case Zella called, and got comfortable. The desert wind danced across the pool, making small ripples appear, ending in a gentle breeze that cooled me. That wind carried a slight floral scent to it, which seemed both natural and out of place. I would have expected the acrid scent of the desert—the smell of baked earth and slight sweetness of desert vegetation. Instead, I got...

"Roses," I whispered into the night, curling up in the hammock and looking out at the darkness. The night sounds of the world beyond Flinch's house calmed me like white noise, and the blanket of inky night sky enveloped and soothed. I felt safe and at home, which made no sense. Not really. Maybe another day it would.

Maybe...but first...the night pulled me down. Deeper, darker. Until...the sound of motorcycles in the distance, the wolf howls ringing through the night air. The smell of land scorched by the sun and highlighted by a slight floral note I now recognized as the scent of roses. An intensifying sense of dread and an eerie feeling of being watched that chilled me as the valley came into full view. As the dream showed me her truth.

"Daddy."

FIFTEEN

FLINCH

There weren't a ton of people who chose to live out in the desert. Those who did tended to do so to put a little space between them and their neighbors. They also had a propensity for lifestyles considered outside the norm. Sort of like the shifters who bought land to roam, or the gun nuts who built concrete bunkers as armories. Or the chaos demons who ran junkyards to get off on the residual energy from things like car crashes and stolen vehicles.

"How sideways is this going to go?" Zed asked as soon as we came to a stop at the gate. The sun had long set, the shadows caused by the floodlights along the fence of the lot growing deep and dark. Nighttime wouldn't have been my choice to come talk to a demon, but we needed to find Chiggy's truck and fast. That meant doing things we didn't want to do.

Like talking to demons at night.

I sighed. "Real fucking sideways if we don't mind our manners."

Because while the chaos demon looked and acted human, he wasn't. Far from it. If he decided to go all destruction on us, we'd be in for a fight. That was why I only allowed Zed to come with me—I couldn't risk a younger wolf reacting to the stench of death that emanated from the man. The scent our wolves had a hard time staying docile around.

"Here he comes." Zed sat up a little straighter, looking through the gate as what appeared to be a short but fit fortysomething man jogged our way in sweat pants and dad sneakers. The image didn't match the malevolent energy vibrating through the air, though. The demon had arrived.

"Adam," I said as soon as he had reached the gate, offering a head nod. "You know my brother Zed."

The demon with the generic name looked Zed up and down then refocused on me, sizing me up. "What is this energy you have surrounding you, Wolf Flinch? It's delicious in its chaotic nature."

"No idea, man. I'm just here to ask about a missing vehicle."

Adam stared at me in silence, the intensity of his gaze inciting my need to growl. I bit that back, though. No need to throw this meeting into destruction before we'd even really started talking.

After a long, hard staredown, Adam grunted and stepped to the side to open the mechanical gate. Zed and I stayed put, not rolling onto his property. Not putting ourselves in a situation where he could close that gate with us on the wrong side. This wasn't my first rodeo.

"Wolf Zed." Adam kept his eyes on me but stood closer to my brother. "What's changed in Wolf Flinch's life? What is this energy around him? I've sensed it before on others but can't quite place it."

Zed never wavered, never even looked my way, as he answered, "Fuck if I know. I'm just here to find a truck."

"What kind of truck?"

My turn. "The kind with longhorn antlers on the front."

"I've seen one recently. Red truck, older, smooth engine." He smiled slowly, the grin creeping across his face and making my wolf even more uncomfortable. "Delicious death energy radiating from it."

Zed shifted his weight on his bike, the only sign of how uncomfortable he'd grown, though enough of one to attract Adam's attention.

"Your wolf doesn't like me," Adam said, staring at Zed. "Does he want to come out and play?"

I held my tongue, keeping my eyes on the demon. Knowing Zed wasn't stupid enough to fall into his hands but still on edge. Adam had a way of getting what he wanted, and if he wanted to play with Zed's wolf...

"Nope," Zed finally replied, sitting just a little deeper in his seat. "We're just fine where we are."

"Too bad. I could use the exercise." Adam returned his intense gaze to me. "The truck you're looking for was brought in to be junked. I turned them away."

"Who brought it?"

"Vampires. I recognized the stench before they even made it to the gate. I don't fuck with their kind."

Fucking vampires. I hated those creepy bastards. "Happen to know where the truck is now?"

Adam shrugged. "Find the vamp nest, you'll find the truck."

Which translated to he didn't know shit.

"Thanks." I adjusted in my seat, popping up the stand and steering as I inched the old girl backward. "I appreciate your time. You see that truck again, let me know."

"Will do." Adam pulled his face into an expression that likely should have been a wide grin but instead showed more teeth than a human would and made his eyes look positively unearthly. The demon peeking out. "Come play sometime, Zed. I haven't had a good fight in too many years."

Zed said nothing, just backed his bike up and followed me down the road. We made it about halfway to the highway before we stopped, both of us cutting engines right there in the middle of nowhere.

"So," Zed started with a slow, repeating head nod. Looking like one of those dashboard critters people bought. "We're dealing with vampires."

I laughed. It was all I could do. The man looked ready to explode with that knowledge in his brain but still nodded his head as if it were on a spring.

"You okay over there?" I asked, still chuckling.

The nodding stopped, and he released a heavy sigh as he ran a hand over his face. "Fucking vampires."

Yeah, I felt that one. The world of supernaturals tended not to overlap too much—barring the occasional demon or witch who ended up in the same area as shifters—and we fully avoided vamps. Death sacks with teeth didn't get along with our wolf sides. Not a whole lot could kill us in a fair fight, but vamps could, for sure. Which meant Chiggy's death had just gotten a lot easier to understand in regard to the how.

"Call Cutter." Zed looked my way, eyes dark and wolf growl present as he spoke. The man was spooked. "This changes everything."

I pulled my phone from my pocket and tapped to dial, knowing the words Zed had spoken were as true as could be. Vamps changed every rule and required much more skill and finesse to deal with.

"Flinch," Cutter answered.

"Vamps have the truck. Don't know where, but Adam at the yard confirmed."

Cutter stayed quiet for about thirty solid seconds. I didn't push or assume the phone had disconnected us; I knew he had to be thinking. Examining every angle and working every possibility.

Finally, he cursed under his breath. "Go home. We'll start again after the wake tomorrow."

I ended the call and looked up at Zed, who had taken to staring right back at me. "The hunt's over for now."

"I heard. You'd better get your ass home. If these fuckers figure out who Locklyn is, they may decide Chiggy wasn't enough."

The thought had my blood running cold. A human was no match for a vampire. I had left Rush with her as a guard, but that wasn't enough. I didn't want the bloodsuckers anywhere near my mate, but if they dared come for her, I wanted to be the one to protect her. Needed to be. And if the way I felt my teeth descend and the long fur sprouting on my arms were any indication, my wolf agreed.

"Thanks, brother."

"Let me know if you need me." He nodded my way once, his eyes on the horizon. "No wolf should have to bury their mate."

Fuck me, he wasn't wrong. I revved the engine and took off for home, hauling ass on the rural desert roads with his words bouncing around my head. Bury Locklyn? Not fucking happening. I'd go down long before anyone got a chance to take her out.

My bike rode smooth and hot, hugging curves and screaming down the straights. I had her pushed wide open at times to gobble up the miles between us and Locklyn, though by the way my fingers kept slipping into claws, it didn't seem to be enough to appease my beast. My wolf wanted to shift and run, to have control over our travel, but the bike would be faster in this instance. I just had to keep him under my control a little longer to prove that point.

"She's good," I muttered under my breath, more to my wolf

than to myself. "She's home and safe. Rush has got her back until we get there."

Yeah, that wasn't nearly enough, so I rode the throttle a little harder.

I rolled into the driveway what seemed like hours later—even though it could only have been ten minutes or so—at a speed that would have definitely made a less confident rider wipe out. Rush stood on the edge of the porch, obviously having heard the engine moving closer at high speeds. He looked big and bad and ready to fight the world, which was good. That was what Locklyn needed. A man to kill for her.

But I needed to be that man.

"What's up?" Rush asked once I turned off the engine.

"It's vamps. They took out Chiggy."

Rush didn't speak for a long moment, didn't even seem to register what I'd said. At least not until he hissed out a low, "Shit."

"Yeah." I pushed past him, needing to see Locklyn for myself. My wolf not as anxious as before but still present. Still wanting me to shift so he could see for himself what was happening with our mate. Fuck, I just needed to get my hands on her for a second, then we could calm down. I needed—

Rush stopped me with a hand to the chest, ignoring the snarl I released at the contact. "She's out back."

That was enough to resettle my human mind. Mostly. "Why?"

"Don't know, but she fell asleep in the hammock. I've been looping back and forth to keep an eye on her."

In the hammock. My hammock. Where I had been sleeping. My girl had gone to my spot and waited for me. She'd needed me tonight and had found comfort where I rested. She could have been inside in my nice fluffy bed, but she'd never actually seen me sleeping there.

Locklyn had gone to what she knew as my bed to find her peace for the night.

Fuck, I loved that.

I breathed a sigh of relief as my wolf finally receded and then held out my fist, bumping his when he offered it. "Thanks, brother."

"No worries. I'll hang out in the neighborhood in case you need me." He stepped off the porch, heading for his own bike. Pausing to look back at me one last time. "She's a good one."

Didn't I know it.

With Rush handled, I hurried around the house and into the backyard. There, in the hammock, lay a sleeping Locklyn. She had likely once been covered by the light blanket I kept on the porch, but that sat on the ground, probably having been kicked off. Her long legs were twisted together, her ass peeking at me from the pulled-up hem of her little sleep shorts. She looked sweet and innocent and sexy as fuck, a juxtaposition I didn't know how to deal with. She also looked unprotected right there on my back porch with no walls around her. Locklyn may have been a strong woman, but she was still just a delicate human. Against a shifter or a vamp? She'd go down before she even knew what was coming at her. And I couldn't let that happen.

I gently extricated her from her hammock bed, lifting her into my arms and striding for the glass doors that would lead me inside. Locklyn immediately cuddled into my chest, gripping my shirt in her sleep. Making my knees bobble for just one step. Fuck, this girl had me in knots. Her snuggling close? Choosing to want me closer? Killer. I knew I was strong as fuck, but she could knock me over with a feather if she just gave me one of her smiles.

"Fucking goner," I whispered to myself as I stepped inside, taking a moment to kick off my boots. I even locked the door behind me. Did it matter if a supernatural wanted inside? No.

Was I still going to do it so meth head Timmy down the road didn't come walking inside? Of course. No-brainer.

I carried Locklyn into what had become her room, a low growl rumbling through my chest. The whole room smelled of her. Deep and sensual and with an almost fruity tinge to it. The scent rocked me, making my wolf wake up once more. Making my growl grow louder. I needed to get the fuck out of there before I stripped her naked and had her riding my cock. Needed to jack off ten times before I dared to try to sleep. Needed—

"Flinch."

My girl whispered my name in her sleep, and my heart melted. "Yeah, short stack?"

"Stay." She gripped me tightly, pulling herself closer to my chest. I carefully set her down on the bed and dropped to my knees. Hanging on to her as she continued to grip my arm.

"I can't stay," I said, literally shaking with restraint. "If I crawl into that bed with you, I won't be able to control myself."

Locklyn opened her eyes, staring straight into mine. "That's what I want."

"Baby, I—"

"I need you here." She rolled forward, grabbing me behind the neck, and I lost my fucking mind. Nothing could have held me back from her in that moment. Not a goddamned thing. I quickly stripped myself bare, growling the entire time, and climbed onto the bed. Running my nose along her cheek, I practically rolled over her, avoiding laying my weight on her, to end up on the mattress behind her. She turned immediately, facing me. Curling her body into mine the second I had settled.

"Better," she whispered, though my neglected cock and anxious wolf would have argued with her. This wasn't better. Having my mate in my house—in my bed—while keeping a physical distance from her had been bad enough. Lying with her, feeling her body heat against mine as I drowned in her scent? Fucking torture.

And then those wicked hands started running over my skin. Not widely at first, just a small patch of my chest. Her fingers seemed to like to curl into the hair there. My cock grew heavy and weepy between my thighs, and I locked every muscle down to keep him on a fucking leash. Locklyn didn't make it easy. The hands on my chest weren't enough, apparently. She also scooted closer and hiked one of her long legs over my hip. Opening herself to me.

The scent around us deepened, her need and desire growing more apparent.

"Locklyn," I growled, no longer able to control the wolf within me. No longer able to keep my hands off her body, though forcing myself to stop at gripping her hips. Hard. My mate would have bruises in the morning that I would want to kiss better.

She didn't heed my warning, though. Instead, she curled even closer, sighing as our bodies met. As she pressed her breasts against me in an act of overt aggression.

"Mate." The word came out choked and indistinguishable, my growl deepening to the point of pain. Once again, Locklyn didn't heed the warning. She invited me closer, letting those wandering hands and curious fingers slide over my hips and around. Gripping my ass tightly and tugging me between her thighs.

The second I felt the warmth of her pussy against my needy cock, I broke. Surrendered to the wants and needs of my basest desires when it came to her. At least partially, because my desire was to watch my girl bounce on my cock for an hour or so, but we weren't there yet. Two-for-one...I still owed her. And I always paid my debts.

Without a word, I rolled us over so she ended up straddling

my waist. Her weight on me called up something from deep within me, something more animalistic than I had ever felt before. The want and need to bite into her flesh, to join with my mate while she screamed out her pleasure rocked me right down to my toes. I had to resist, though. Had to do right by her. Had to give instead of receive.

"Flinch," she whimpered, rocking her hips against me. Breaking through a handful of threads of my control.

Fuck, I just needed a taste.

With a roar from the depths of my soul, I ripped her pajamas from her body, slicing right through the flimsy fabric of her panties in the same go. Thankfully not catching any skin. I had a feeling if I had scratched her—if the scent of her blood had dared to greet me—I would have buried my teeth in her neck and said fuck the giving. I would have given her my cock and nothing else. But I still had some control, which meant I was going to get my taste of her. Just not her blood.

Gripping her hips, I tugged and lifted until she followed my directions. Dragged her body up mine until her knees were on either side of my head and her swollen pussy hovered directly above my face. Until that sweet cherry scent enveloped me and had my cock leaking at the thought of getting inside her juicy heaven.

This was going to be a long night.

"You want me, you've got me," I said, every word rolling with the snarl of my inner beast. "Now sit on my face and ride my tongue. I need to taste you come."

Sixteen

LOCKLYN

Flinch was going to kill me. Absolutely kill me dead with nothing more than his rough hands and dirty mouth.

"Now," he said and smacked my ass a lot harder than I would have expected. I did as I'd been told, lowering my weight so he had access to me. "I said sit."

"I am sitting."

With a growl that likely should have scared me but instead had me dripping at the sound of it, Flinch grabbed me and began manhandling me again. He pulled me straight down, forcing me to practically fall right on his face. I gasped and tried to raise up, somehow afraid I would hurt him, but he kept a strong hold and refused to release me for even a breath.

"That's it," he said, his voice slightly muffled by my being in the way. His lips brushing against me making my entire body break out in goose bumps. "When I say sit on my face, I mean sit. None of this hovering bullshit."

I laughed, the sound transforming into a moan when he

licked right into me. The pleasure hit so hard and so fast, I couldn't contain myself. I slammed my hands against the wall and arched my back. Ready for more, and yet...

"If I sit, I might suffocate you," I said, struggling really hard to focus on things like syllables and vowels. Words. Who could possibly think of such things when a man had you quite literally sitting on his face. Flinch owned me in that moment, his fingers digging into my thighs and his tongue laving me from top to bottom. Teasing me and yet giving me everything all at once.

"I'm the one responsible for figuring out how to breathe," he said, groaning deep as he pulled me down even tighter. "You just need to give me that pussy."

And give him, I did. I let my weight rest on his face as he began to slowly torture me with his inconsistent movements and refusal to focus. The man licked me all over, teasing me hard, while what I really wanted was his tongue on my clit. But it was as if he purposely avoided that particular area, making me shake and curse and start to writhe over him. Searching out the friction I needed.

The bastard knew what he was doing, too.

"Flinch," I moaned, growing absolutely irritated when the man chuckled. "Please."

"I like hearing you beg, short stack." He lifted his head and pressed deeper into my flesh, making me shake from head to toe. "Fucking cherries. I knew you'd taste like cherries. Be a good girl and fuck my tongue."

I moaned again, using both hands on the wall to push back, to hold me up as I moved. As I rolled my hips as much as I could, considering the man had me in a vise grip. Finally, with a growl that vibrated all the way through my body, he gave me what I so desperately wanted. He licked right across my clit with enough pressure to make my toes curl.

"Yes, Flinch. Yes."

That damn chuckle returned. "I've got you, mate."

It was the mate that did me in. Being called short stack was cute and all, but mate? From a man like Flinch? That rocked my world all the way down to the depths of my soul. It wasn't the first time I'd ever heard that word, but it was the first that really resonated. That had me surrendering in the way he had wanted. I sat right down and began to move in earnest, chasing his tongue as he worked it over my flesh. Demanding my pleasure from the man so intent on giving it to me. Every touch to my overstimulated clit pushing me toward a finish I needed. One I wanted so badly. One Flinch seemed intent on bringing me to.

And bring me, he did. Hands in his hair to direct him and body curled over his, I came with a groan that should have embarrassed me, but without enough focus to truly care. I had never exploded in pleasure the way Flinch made me, had never given in to the sensations coursing through my body the way I did with him. I rocked and writhed and demanded he keep me riding my orgasm, chanting his name as my entire body shook.

Eventually the pleasure turned to pain, my oversensitized clit throbbing, so I lifted off Flinch's face. Almost embarrassed as I caught him staring up at me.

"You okay down there?"

He chuckled and grabbed me, rolling and tugging me down the mattress until he had me on my back with his hips nestled between my thighs.

"You're a little sassy for someone about to beg me to fuck them."

Oh. Oh, the overconfidence of this man. It intrigued me. "I'm not begging for anything."

He curled over, taking my nipple into his mouth. Keeping his eyes on mine as he bit the small bud just to the point of pain before releasing it. "Not yet, but you will be."

I actually had no doubt the man could make me beg. None

whatsoever. After what he'd already done to me, I could totally see him working some simple finger magic and having me at his mercy in less than a minute. Which was why I didn't even try to resist him. Instead, I pulled him in close, pressing a kiss to his lips and wrapping one leg around his hips. Wanting him there. Needing it. I tasted myself on his tongue, the flavor sparking something dirty and wild within me. Something that had me wanting to claim him in some way. This was my man. Mine. And every wolf in his club, every female shifter who walked into their bar, would know it simply by the way my scent mingled with his. I'd make sure of it.

"Mate," Flinch whispered as he began to rock his hips, slowly pressing against where I was already so soaked for him. "Are you sure you're ready for me?"

I nodded, tugging him closer. Opening myself to him. That word again—mate. He'd talked about *fated* mates once—how they would always choose their other half over anything else. How they would have never been able to let their partner walk away. But he wasn't using both words, so just *mate*. Something I would need to think about later. Or not. It was just a word after all. Just a word.

One I stopped being able to think about the second the man's cock slipped into place between my legs. I gasped and froze, my pussy practically trembling as he pressed against me. So very ready for this. With a pained sort of groan, he nudged his way just inside, dragging his heavy cock out slowly before pushing in again a little farther than the first time. Inching his way deeper and deeper into me. Slowing down on every forward thrust and making me understand why he was so certain I would beg. Because I would. Right then, I would have begged for more.

"Flinch." I clawed at his back, planting my feet firmly on the mattress and lifting my hips into him. Moaning as he slid deeper. Biting back the please on the tip of my tongue. "Quit playing."

That chuckle returned, sounding far more pained than earlier. "Trust me, mate. There's no playing happening here."

"Then why are you teasing me like this?"

He froze, staring down at me. Those light eyes meeting mine. Something grew between us, some sort of emotional connection I felt all the way in my heart. Something deep and meaningful and inexplicable.

"I don't want to hurt you," he said, his voice softer. His words a confession.

Oh, my sweet wolf shifter.

"You won't." I ran my hands over his head, digging my fingers into his hair as I shook my head subtly. "I promise, you won't hurt me. I want you inside me."

He growled long and deep, leaning in to kiss me one more time before he began to move in earnest. Before he filled me over and over again, the girth of his cock forcing its way inside and stretching me to the max as it drove deeper. I had known the man was big, but nothing could have prepared me for the feeling of being overwhelmed by his size. Of the stretch and burn of him that kept me on a razor's edge between coming and crying. Filling me to the point of pleasure that could easily tilt into pain. I lost myself to him, becoming a part of him instead of my own entity. Both of us joined in a way that was far more than physical as he buried himself inside me.

"So wet," he mumbled as he thrust harder and faster than before. Groaning and growling through every push and pull. On a retreat, he paused just long enough to grab my hips, lifting me off the bed as he rose onto his knees. Changing the angle to power down into me. Making me twist and gasp and scream into his pillow as he hit places inside me I hadn't known could feel so good. As he punched deeper than I'd have thought possible while I fought to hang on to this reality. "You're so fucking wet, mate.

Downright sloppy for me. Do you hear how good this pussy is taking me?"

I did. I heard the wet, slapping sounds as he fucked me. Felt the moisture sliding out of me and down my skin. I couldn't focus on those, though, because Flinch had me lifted, filled, and completely feral. He'd set every nerve ending aflame, had teased me to the edge and brought me back from it. Had fucked me almost senseless. I needed to come, and I needed him to be the one to make me.

"Flinch," I moaned, reaching for him as I untwisted myself. Settling my upper back against the mattress and gripping his arms. Wanting his weight and his heat when I finally broke. "I'm so close."

The man groaned and dropped onto me as if he understood the want I hadn't vocalized, pinning me to the mattress under his big body. He grabbed one leg and pulled it over his shoulder, opening me wide for him. Making me yelp as an entire wave of new sensations rocked my foundation. His hips snapped harder and faster as he growled continuously. As he thrust deep then ground the base of his cock against my clit, sending sparkles shooting all over my body.

As he pushed me right over the edge and had me screaming his name while I came around him. Finally begging him for more. Pleading with him as my entire body gave itself over to the sensations he wrought.

Flinch growled longer and deeper than ever, his thrusts losing their rhythm. His entire body clenching on top of me as he came. As he filled me while I still pulsed around him. Finishing inside me like...

Fuck, we hadn't grabbed a condom.

"Oh no," I said, pushing him off me before he had even relaxed. Likely before he had completely finished.

"What's wrong?" He rolled off me, breathing hard and looking completely frazzled. "Did I hurt you?"

"No. I just..." I hopped out of bed, heading for the bathroom. "We forgot the condom."

Before I could reach the door, Flinch grabbed me around the waist and picked me up off my feet, burying his head in my neck as he softly said, "You're not fertile right now."

I froze. "Huh?"

He kissed my neck, running one hand up from where he held me to my breast and teasing my nipple. "I could smell if you were. You're not, so a condom wasn't necessary."

"Oh." Something akin to embarrassment washed over me, but I pushed it away. He was a wolf shifter—the fact that he could smell my cycle changes shouldn't have been a surprise. It was, but it shouldn't have been. "I didn't know—"

He growled and spun, dropping me back onto the mattress and falling on top of me. "There's a lot of things you don't know about wolf shifters. But I'll teach you." He leaned in to plant a long, deep kiss on me, tangling his tongue with mine before pulling away once more. "Give me time, and I'll teach you, mate."

Mate, but not fated. And to be honest, I didn't know if I had time—I would eventually have to go back to Detroit. To cold winters and drunks at the bar hitting on me. To dirty streets and dangerous corners without Flinch watching over me. But that time wasn't now, and the last thing I wanted to think about was walking away from the man who had just made my entire body his own.

So I ignored the itch of impending endings and curled into his side. Stealing his warmth while I could.

SEVENTEEN

Waking up with Locklyn in my arms was a dream come true. Waking up with my cock weeping because her thick ass was pushed up against me was a tease impossible to resist.

"What are you trying to do here, short stack?" I dragged my hand over her hip and down, not stopping until I had her pussy cupped. Until I was in a position to slip a finger or two inside. "You wake up hungry?"

She giggled and pushed back with her hips, opening herself up to me. Giving me the most perfect gift ever—access to her luscious body. Something I would never turn down.

I hooked her leg over mine and pulled, spreading her wider as I plunged a third finger inside my mate's sweet pussy. She felt soaked and puffy, her soft groans and deep breathing adding to her pussy's response to guide me on my quest to make her come. I needed to feel it, needed to know she'd gotten hers before I dared to get my cock involved. The girl was a drug to me—one I was definitely already addicted to. My cock couldn't resist her. I would be ready to spill the second I felt that heat surround me.

"Flinch," she whined, grabbing my wrist and pushing my hand deeper inside her. "Want you."

Two words I could have never even dreamed I'd hear from a woman like her.

"Fuck." I curled over her, my wolf pushing forward and taking more control of my mind. The beast digging our teeth into her neck. Not breaking the skin—not yet—but wanting to. Feeling the instinctual need to close the deal on our mating and permanently bond us. I didn't know how I'd resisted last night, how I'd kept myself from biting into the thigh that had enveloped my head as I'd had her ride my tongue. And today wasn't going to be any easier, which meant I needed to keep my teeth to myself. So I pulled myself away from her neck and pressed my fingers deeper, letting my thumb join the party on her clit. Knowing what would get her there. Knowing as soon as she came, I was going to fuck her like a beast.

The second I felt the telltale clench of her pussy around my fingers, the moment she finally came on my hand, I rolled her over and pinned her facedown to the mattress. Climbed on top of my gorgeous girl and got to work. It took one drive of my hips to slip inside her, one small motion for me to find myself home again. To be back in the heaven of her body.

But I wasn't an angel—I couldn't be sweet with her. I plunged in deep and hard, feeling the bed hit the wall on every push. Relishing her gasps and grunts as I let my wolf run the show this time. As I took her like an animal right there on my bed. Holding her hip in my hand, claws pushing through just enough to poke into her soft flesh. To leave a few marks. I'd lick them later, lick her all over to make sure I hadn't hurt her. But right then, I needed to see evidence of me owning her. Needed to know signs of me would be left behind.

My wolf and I needed to know that our mate would be marked.

"Sloppiest fucking pussy," I said on a growl, rolling my entire body into hers as I held her down by the back of the neck. Keeping her pinned and far enough away so my wolf wouldn't take over and lunge in, teeth first. Fighting the pull of his need to sink our teeth into her smooth shoulder and claim her as I fucked her from behind. "You were made for me, mate. Made to drive me mad with wanting this pussy."

"Oh god." She gripped the pillow beneath her, burying her forehead in it as she pushed back against me. Writhing in my hold like prey to my predator. Making it that much harder to resist. "Flinch, I'm going to—"

She didn't finish her sentence because that pussy clamped down on me in an orgasm that just about sucked my soul from my body, let alone hers. I fell upon her, bunny-humping her ass like a chump as I followed right behind her. As I came inside her sweet heat again, wanting so much to bite the delicate skin of her neck and just fucking claim her. As my wolf howled in my mind and tried so hard to push through so he could finish the bonding.

Not yet. Not yet.

When I had full control of my wolf side, I rolled off my mate and grabbed her arm, keeping us close. Slipping out of her on a squelch that had me feeling far prouder than I would ever admit. Yeah, I'd filled her up. "Fuck, Locklyn. You've spoiled me."

She chuckled against me, body draped across mine. "How have I spoiled you?"

"That pussy." I smacked her ass, grabbing one cheek and wiggling it. "That ass. They're fucking perfect for me."

Her laugh brought more sunshine to the world than the fucking orb in the sky ever could. "You're ridiculous."

"Nah, I'm just pussy-whipped." I pulled her in tighter,

kissing the top of her head. "It's almost noon. I see two options for our day."

"What're those?"

"You can climb up here, let me stick my dick in you to keep my cock warm while we take a nap, or we get cleaned up and I'll take you for lunch." Because either option was a win in my book.

But Locklyn didn't smile or laugh as I'd expected her to. Instead, she stared up at me with a serious expression as she asked, "No club business today?"

I froze, knowing tonight would be the burning for her dad. The ceremony to honor his death and return his body to the earth. It would be an emotional night for her. I didn't want to ignore that fact but also knew mentioning it would change the entire mood for the day, so I went with the simplest response I could think of.

"Not until tonight."

She sighed and looked away, clinging a little tighter to me before rolling toward the edge of the mattress. The flash of sadness in her eyes was the only clue I had that she knew what I was doing—that she remembered what tonight would bring. Apparently we were both avoiding the topic because all she said was, "I could eat."

Not wanting to end our morning in bed on a sad note, I grabbed her thigh before she could get away, letting my fingers tease her pussy lips as I growled at her. "I'm always up for eating."

"You're obsessed," she said with a laugh before slipping out of the bed and heading for the bathroom. Leaving me alone, in a bed that still held her warmth, covered in her smell.

"No shit."

———

Forty minutes and one dry hump in the shower later, I opened the passenger door to the truck I'd just parked outside a steak house. I held out my hand for Locklyn to take, liking the way her body rubbed against mine as she found her footing.

"Thank you," she said, her voice soft but her eyes sparkling. "Though I can open my own doors."

"You can. Or I could be a man worthy of your attention and do it for you."

She hummed, grabbing the hand I offered her and walking beside me across the lot. "What is this place?"

"Steak house. You like steak?"

"I do."

"This place does them right, though he's also got a pork chop that will make you cry."

"He...as in the chef?"

"The owner. You'll meet him for sure—he's always here."

I opened the door and let her walk into the dark and moody interior in front of me, following that ass into the darkness. The place had a total 70's vibe—mood lighting, fake leather banquettes with high backs for privacy, and good ol' Frank crooning softly through the speakers. It was a favorite with the brothers when they were trying to impress a chick. Me...well, I liked a good steak. And impressing Locklyn even a little bit might not be a bad idea.

"Flinch, my old friend." Dean, the owner of the place, strode across the dining room from the bar, martini in hand and hair slicked back as always. "It's so good to see you. Who's the lucky lady?"

Locklyn practically cowered into my side, so I grabbed her hip and leaned forward a bit, keeping her tucked just enough behind me to make sure she knew I had her covered. No one would be getting near her if she didn't want them there.

"This is Locklyn," I said, eyeing him hard. Making sure Dean knew his place. "She's in from Detroit and likes a good steak."

Dean looked her up and down, appraising but not coveting. Keeping a good foot between himself and her. He then shot me a look that was pure wolf. "Congrats, old man. If the lovely lady wants a steak, she'll get the best from me. Come. I have a perfect booth for a little afternoon delight."

Locklyn's eyebrows flew up, but I just chuckled and led her across the restaurant. When we reached the banquette, Dean stood at one side to assist Locklyn into her seat while I slid in from the other. The man kept his eyes off my mate while he directed the waiter to set down our glasses of water, kept his actions respectable. Being a wolf shifter in the restaurant business might have been tricky, but being a male wolf shifter around mated couples definitely seemed more difficult because I was ready to claw out his neck just for standing within ten feet of my girl. Not that I needed to. The man handled himself with class, respectful to the ladies at all times. And obviously aware of the need to keep Locklyn at arm's length so as not to upset my wolf.

"I've got a few bottles of pinot in the cellar that are absolutely —" Dean kissed the tips of his fingers, still primarily addressing only me. "I'll bring one up for you. Will you need a menu, or will you trust your old friend Dean to feed you the best steak of your life?"

Locklyn glanced at me, lifting one shoulder in a move I took as acquiescence. "Take it away, Dean."

"Excellent." Dean leaned a little closer to Locklyn, his smile glued in place. "And how do you prefer your steak cooked, my lovely?"

For the first time, Dean directed his full attention to Locklyn. Brought his gaze right to her and held her with it. I watched as she stiffened in her seat, likely the realization that a predator had her in her sights kicking off some human survival instinct. A normal response, but not something I wanted my mate to experience. Especially not yet—she wasn't used to so many wolves around her yet. So I growled low, making sure Dean heard me. Directing him without words to ease off.

Locklyn darted a look my way, obviously calming. Likely having heard me. "Medium rare, please."

Dean nodded once, taking a step away from the table and shooting me a wink. "Perfect. I'll alert the chef." He started to walk away then turned back, giving us a very well-rehearsed, almost confused look. "You want some antipasto? A little snack before the meal? I'll get you one."

And as I expected, he disappeared into the back, never needing us to confirm or deny his offer of a starter course.

"He's...something."

I shot a smile at Locklyn, who looked about as shell-shocked as I had expected. "He's a legend. Been here for decades. Claims to have some serious mob connections, which brings all the old Vegasophiles here. They love the kitschy, 70's feel of his place, and he loves the act."

"Think he was really in the mob?"

"Nope." I leaned closer, sliding across the booth to reduce the space between us. "He's an old wolf shifter who grew up in the high desert outside of Reno, not Vegas."

Locklyn practically jerked backward, immediately looking off in the direction Dean had gone. "*He's* a shifter?"

"Yeah. You find that surprising?" I grabbed my water glass, raising it to my lips to take a sip. Keeping my eyes on her over the rim.

"He's just so...little."

Water...everywhere. I laughed so hard I nearly dropped the entire glass in my own damn lap. "Jesus, Locklyn."

"What?" She shrugged, smiling my way. "My only experience with shifters has been my dad and the men of the Hellions.

You're all—" she waved her hand at me and scrunched her nose in the most adorable way I had ever seen someone do "—huge. You're huge. He's not."

"We come in all shapes and sizes."

"Huh. Would have never guessed."

And that was how our amazingly long and luxurious lunch started. Dean did not disappoint—five courses, all delicious, all comprised of items not on the menu. And when I let it slip that my girl liked something as classic and simple as cacio e pepe? The man might as well have been in heaven. Unlike Rush, I didn't think Dean was Italian by heritage, but his love for the food and culture shone.

"I am going to die from too much food," Locklyn said as we hobbled our way back to my truck. "That was intense."

"Yeah, but we might not have time for much of a dinner. I thought this would be a good alternative."

"You thought correctly. Oh, a rose." She grabbed the stem of a long red rose from the hood of my truck and brought it to her nose. "Did you put this here?"

I shook my head, absolutely enraptured by the joy on her face as she let the delicate flower dance across her skin. "No, but Dean might have. He's romantic like that."

"I should probably thank him, but..." She rose onto the balls of her feet and placed the simplest, sweetest kiss on my lips that I had ever experienced. I had been balls deep inside this woman just hours before, but that kiss held more intimacy than anything we'd done in the bedroom. That kiss was filled with a power the woman didn't even realize she held over me, and I loved it.

"What was that for?" I asked when she dropped down and tucked herself under my arm.

"Just wanted to say thank you for today. You've been a wonderful distraction."

I huffed, reaching past her to open the door. "I'm more than a distraction."

"You are." She hopped inside, stabbing me with her gaze once her ass had settled onto my seat. Still letting those deep red petals tease her cheek and jaw. "But I needed you to be a distraction today, and you came through with flying colors."

I leaned in, pinning her against the seat and kissing her in a much less sweet, much more aggressive way. I practically devoured her lips, tangling my tongue with hers and slipping my hand under her shirt to grab her breast. Needing to touch her, taste her, feel her. Wanting to bury myself inside her right there in the parking lot. Not that I would.

"I like being a distraction," I whispered as I pulled away.

Locklyn gazed at me all unfocused, her pink tongue appearing to subtly lick at her bottom lip. Jesus, I wanted those lips wrapped around my cock so bad, but I couldn't. We were burning her old man tonight. I needed to focus on her needs, her pleasure. Her distractions.

With that in mind, I stepped back and closed her door, adjusting myself through my jeans before rushing around the truck to the driver's seat. I hopped in and started the engine, immediately grabbing my girl's thigh.

"Ready?"

She stared out the window and nodded, looking distracted, though not by me. "Yeah."

"You okay?" Because she had been just seconds before. What had changed?

"I think so." Another nose scrunch. "You ever get the feeling someone's watching you?"

My wolf immediately reacted, slamming through my human consciousness to assess our situation. We looked all around, eyeing every shadow. Peering over every roofline. Just in case. We found nothing.

"I have. You feel that way now?"

"I feel that way whenever I'm outside. Ever since the guy..."

"What guy?" Those words came out on more of a growl than I had intended, the tone attracting Locklyn's attention. She turned in her seat to stare at me, green eyes focused and clear.

"There was a guy watching me outside of the coffee shop I went to with the prospect the other day. Nothing happened, he didn't interact. He just..." She turned, looking out the front window again. "He stared."

I was going to need to have a serious chat with that fucking prospect. "I find a fucker staring, I'll dig his eyes out."

Locklyn huffed as I put the truck into drive and headed for the road. "People stare. You can't dig their eyes out for that."

"Watch me."

"You're ridiculous."

"And you're mine. It's my job to keep you safe." I squeezed her thigh, keeping my grip strong. "I refuse to fail at that."

The closer we got to my little house, the quieter Locklyn became. Not that she'd been excessively chatty that day, but the tension in the air and the lack of words coming from her mouth stood out. She would say goodbye to her father tonight surrounded by a bunch of men she really didn't know. Even me —her mate—she barely knew. That fact had irked me from the moment we'd locked in the date and time with Popper.

Thankfully, I was a nosy son of a bitch with a fat bankroll and some questionable morals when it came to things like cell phone access.

"Who's that?" Locklyn asked as we pulled onto my street. I kept my motherfucking mouth closed, knowing exactly who stood on my porch. The two whos—one Hellion and one support person for Locklyn.

"Oh my god." Locklyn was in motion before I put the truck in park, swinging her door open wide and jumping down from the seat. The woman on the porch rushed toward her, both coming together in squeals and hugs and pure happiness. Reunited and obviously very excited about it.

Rush moseyed over to my side of the truck, both of us watching them.

"You flew her best friend out?"

I shrugged as if it wasn't the best thing I'd ever thought of. "Seemed like a good idea."

He nodded. "Good job, man. Good job."

"I can't believe you did this," Locklyn said, smiling my way with her friend Zella still in her arms. "How did you know?"

"I made an assumption that you might need extra support today."

Zella—short, waifish, with big eyes and a cunning gaze—smiled my way. "Good assumption. I didn't want to miss this."

Locklyn wiped a tear from under her eyes and pulled Zella toward the house, both women disappearing inside. I waited by the truck until they were gone so I could address Rush in private.

"Everything good?"

He shrugged. "Mostly. She smells sick."

"Sick, how?"

"Deep sick—she said something about arthritis on the ride over. Might want to see if there's any old witchy women in the hills who could take a look at her."

I grunted, knowing those women had more knowledge in their pinkies than most doctors in the human world, but recognizing that Zella might not trust us enough to let us take her to one.

"Get Mule on it—he's been known to visit a witch or two." I turned my back to the house, keeping my voice low. Not wanting Locklyn or her friend to hear me as I walked, "What's this about a man watching Locklyn? Something about a coffee shop with the prospect."

My brother frowned. "No idea. She mention it?"

"Yeah. Said it wasn't a big deal—no interaction—but it made her uncomfortable. She couldn't stop looking outside, as if she expected him to still be around, watching her. And she said she keeps feeling eyes on her when she's outside."

Rush grunted. "Never heard a fucking word about it, but I'll inquire for you."

"Thanks. I'd do it, but—"

"You've got more important things to worry about today. Take care of her—I've got the rest."

I reached out to bump a fist with the man. "I appreciate it, brother."

"You'd do the same for me."

"Every time." I headed inside, surprised to find Zella alone in the living room. Almost as if she had been lying in wait for me. "Everything good?"

"She's in the bathroom." The little human stepped toward me, pinning me in place with her light-brown eyes. The scent of her definitely tinged with something deep and old and...sick. "I appreciate you setting all this up."

I locked myself into place, readying for a fight for some reason. Feeling under attack from the spry human. "She needed a friend here. I made that happen."

Zella nodded, not looking convinced. "She says she's been fine, but that's bullshit. How has she really been?"

Finally relaxing from the nonexistent threat, I took a moment to formulate a response, knowing this woman knew Locklyn in a way I didn't. Knowing she would sense if something was wrong likely before I would. The only answer I could come up with was a simple one.

"Distracted."

She huffed and looked away, releasing me from the prison of her stare. "I can't imagine how hard this is on her. Chiggy was the last of her family—no siblings, no aunts or uncles, no one left."

I had nothing to say to that. My only interpersonal connections were the ones I had made with the Hellions, so I couldn't relate to the human notion of family. Not really. I mean, I had a sister, but we went decades without contact. Totally different from weekly or even monthly interactions. But Zella seemed to feel strongly that not having family was a big deal, so I went with it.

Eventually, Locklyn appeared. Heading directly for Zella and wrapping her arms around her friend even as her glowing green eyes met mine. Good god, the woman practically radiated happiness. If I had known how her eyes would light up this way, I would have flown Zella out to the desert on day one.

"You have no idea how happy I am that you're here," Locklyn said, her voice muffled but strong.

"You're my best friend," Zella said, catching my gaze over Locklyn's shoulder. Her stare full of something that set even my wolf on edge. "I wouldn't have missed tonight for the world."

Eighteen

LOCKLYN

I had never attended the burning of a wolf shifter. To be honest, I had never attended the burning of a human either, but I had to assume the shifter version was more unusual than that.

"You okay?" Zella gripped my hand, sticking to my side like glue. She'd been physically and emotionally supporting me since she'd arrived, keeping herself available as I greeted people and was introduced to every biker of the club by Cutter. They all shook my hand or offered a fist bump, showing their respect to Chiggy's daughter even though they hadn't known I existed. A few had even offered hugs, but it seemed a hard glare from Flinch put an end to that. Thank goodness—I wasn't up for so much physical affection from strangers.

"Hey," Zella said, giving my hand a squeeze. "Are you okay?"

"I'm fine." The answer came automatically, but I couldn't leave it at that. "Sorry—I'm lost in my thoughts, I guess."

"Understandable." She stood at the edge of the lot with me, both of us looking over the crowd of bikers waiting for the creepiest-looking man I had ever met—Popper the mortician, according to Flinch—to begin the actual burning. My dad's body lay draped in black on a slab that would eventually be pushed into a furnace-like thing. I didn't know the name, but I had to assume it was the same setup as a crematorium. Except maybe in the human world, they didn't allow parking-lot access so people could watch the actual burning. Again, first time—I had no idea what "normal" was.

"Have you ever been to a service like this?" I asked, curious if my small family had simply left me unprepared for such things.

"No. I don't think any human has ever been to a service like this."

Her wording caught my attention, and I slid a sly gaze in her direction. "Human?"

Zella looked my way, not backing down. "Locklyn."

I sighed. The woman had a way of pulling truths out of me. I had kept Chiggy's secret for him, had done what he'd asked, but Chiggy was dead. And I had somehow managed to get my best friend involved in his world without her knowing about him. That seemed wrong.

"My dad...he wasn't human."

"Okay."

I swallowed hard, knowing the words would sound absolutely ridiculous. Wondering if she was going to try to send me on a grippy-sock vacation when I admitted the truth. No way to know but to do it.

"He was a wolf shifter."

Zella nodded, looking out across the crowd. "I know."

That had me spinning on the spot. "You *know*?"

"I do. Your dad told me last time he visited. He knew you would keep his secret, but he wanted me to know just in case something happened to you. Or to him." She squeezed my hand again, looking out across the crowd and seeming to smile softly at the small group of men that had stayed the closest to us—Flinch, Rush, Cutter, and Mule. Our guards for the event, it seemed. "He loved you so much. He didn't know how to be a dad, but he loved you in his own way, and he tried for you. He tried so hard."

I broke. Tears trickled down my face as I fought for air. As the weight of the grief pulled me under and stole all the oxygen from my lungs. Flinch appeared almost immediately, wrapping me in his big, thick arms and pulling me into his chest.

"It's okay, short stack. I've got you."

And he did. He had me. I curled into his hold and surrendered to the pain losing my dad had wrought. No pretense, no fear of social acceptance, I simply let go and sobbed against Flinch as a hundred or so bikers looked on. As my best friend grabbed my hand and held it, watching over the service right along with me.

And when the furnace started burning, when my dad's body was pulled into the flames, I cried even harder. Singing my grief through tears as Cutter made a speech I couldn't listen to and the rest of the Hellions howled to the night sky. I cried and howled and mourned right along with them.

———

"Ladies." Cutter slid into our circle, looking over me and then Zella almost apprehensively. "I hope the service for Chiggy was seen as respectful."

I nodded, tears dry but still clinging to Flinch. Completely drained from my emotional outburst the night had brought.

Thankfully, Zella knew to speak for me. "It was a heart-warming display of your crew's grief. While Locklyn lost a dad, you and your brothers certainly seemed to have lost someone very special to you."

Cutter nodded, again looking almost shy or anxious. Not at

all how I had seen the man act before. "We have. For sure." He coughed and took a deep breath, visually re-centering himself. "There will be a celebration of Chiggy's life at the clubhouse after this. I would like to invite you two ladies to the event and personally guarantee your safety there."

I looked up at Flinch, who stood frowning at Cutter. Zella also caught my eye, giving me a small shrug with one shoulder as if to say "Up to you."

"I think that would be nice," I said, ignoring the way Flinch grabbed my hip tighter at my words. "I appreciate the invitation."

Cutter nodded, shooting a look at Zella. "Do you need a lift?"

"On your bike?"

"Yeah," he said with a smile that seemed so out of place on his usually hardened face. "It's the only way to ride."

Zella's smile fell. "Thanks, but I should probably—"

"I've got her," Flinch interrupted, his deep voice a balm on my soul. "Locklyn will be fine with me."

Zella stared at the man for a long minute, obviously taking his measure. She broke the stare to glance my way for a moment before turning back to Cutter.

"Just give me a minute." She grabbed my arm and pulled me away, her voice halfway to a whisper as she asked, "Are you okay?"

"I'm fine." I sighed when she gave me an exasperated glare. "I'm good—sad and waterlogged, but good."

"So you don't mind if I go with Mr. Tall, Gray, and Sexy AF?"

I coughed a laugh. "No. Feel free. Ride off into the sunset."

Her eye roll could only be described as epic. "None of that. I've just never been on the back of a motorcycle before. If I've only got one chance, I'm glad it's with someone I don't mind holding on to."

"Flinch would have given you a ride—"

I couldn't even finish the sentence before her eyebrow winged up. "You think I'm going to get all up close and personal with my best friend's man?"

I didn't quite know what to say to that, because no, I didn't think that, but also, I knew I could trust her and Flinch together. I knew Flinch wouldn't cross a line, and Zella would have murdered him if he had even tried. All thoughts that felt out of place, considering the moment.

I sighed, my head swimming a bit. "Just go ride. We'll meet you there."

She paused, eyes heavy with concern. "Are you sure you're okay?"

Was I? No, probably not. But also, yes. My dad hadn't been a daily part of my life...ever. Yes, we talked on the phone often enough and he visited yearly, but there were no good-morning or good-night texts, no calls in the middle of the day just because. No real sense of stability I had a feeling more traditional parent-child relationships offered. I would be okay on my own because I had always been okay on my own. But knowing I no longer had any sort of older relatives—no grandparents, aunts, uncles, parents, or even cousins—left me feeling slightly untethered. Nothing had changed much in my day-to-day life, and yet somehow everything had changed.

And none of that needed to be unloaded on Zella in that moment.

"I'm really fine. Go. Let the man give you the ride of your life...whatever that may mean."

"Hussy," she said then gave me a sad sort of smile. "If you need me, text me. I'll have Cutter pull over and wait for Flinch to catch up. Promise."

And somehow, I knew that was exactly what she would do if I needed her. "I appreciate it. Now, go."

Zella grabbed my hand for a quick squeeze before turning and striding across the parking lot toward Cutter. Flinch caught my eye, his brow furrowed. The man's gaze held me in the same way his arms did, warmed me without contact. I was safe in that gaze even if it was a questioning one. I had no answers for him or anyone else in that moment, none that made sense, at least. So instead of trying to think of any, instead of trying to sort through the emotional chaos within me, I headed for the man who soothed my soul with his very presence.

"All good?" he asked as soon as I came close enough.

"Of course. Zella's riding with Cutter."

"I saw that." He tucked me under his arm, pulling me in for a hug that I so desperately needed. "You sure you're okay with going back to the clubhouse?"

"Yeah. I would rather be with a group than alone."

"You wouldn't be alone, short stack."

"I know. But I need to be...even less alone tonight. If that makes sense."

He gave me one last squeeze before grabbing my hand and leading me toward his truck. "Baby, nothing in grief makes sense, but I'm here for whatever you need. Let's head out."

Nineteen

Locklyn

We drove onto the clubhouse parking lot an unknown amount of time later. The lot looked packed as everyone else had likely driven straight there. Flinch had taken a detour...and somehow ended up with his face between my thighs under the desert sky. Not that I was complaining. Distractions were necessary, it seemed.

"You ready?" he asked, turning to look right at me as he ran a thumb over his bottom lip. "Or do you need another distraction?"

The implication made me shiver, but I didn't need another distraction. I needed noise and people and Zella.

"I'm ready." I rose onto my knees and leaned across the console to plant a big, greedy kiss on his lips. Still tasting myself on them. "Let's go."

He smacked my ass then slid out of the truck and rushed around to my side to open the door, holding my hand as I exited. He then looped my arm through his and led me inside, keeping his head up, his back straight, and a mean motherfucking glare on his face. The man looked ready to fight.

"You okay?" I asked as we walked inside.

He nodded once, which felt incomplete to me.

"Why do you look so mad?"

"Just reminding these assholes they don't want to mess with me." He leaned down to grab my ass and plant one hell of a kiss on my lips as the shifters around us cheered. "And since you're mine, you deserve that same respect. Anyone fucks with you, tell me. Tell Cutter. Hell, tell Rush. We'll take care of them."

I nodded, my chest tightening with nerves until I spotted Zella across the room. She sat at the bar with Cutter beside her, both talking and smiling. Laughing, even. Outside looking in, that man appeared to be smitten, which wasn't hard to imagine. Zella had a way with people and usually attracted men easily. Keeping them was another story—most of them didn't stick around once they learned how sick she was. Or at least when they learned her illness would directly affect her being able to be the fun, vibrant Zella they wanted. That Zella took energy, and she didn't always have it.

As if he could read my mind, Flinch directed me across the room and to the bar where Zella sat. My friend jumped up and hugged me, whispering something about wondering where I had been, but I couldn't concentrate on her. The largest bouquet of dark red roses sat to the side of the bar, the display nearly as tall as I was.

"Who sent those?"

Cutter glanced toward the roses before giving me a shrug. "Not sure. They were outside when we got back. They're addressed to you, but there wasn't a note to say who they're from."

"They're ginormous."

"Want me to put them outside?" Flinch asked, ever the gentleman.

I shook my head, peeling my eyes away from the massive roses that felt really out of place. Who sent red roses to what was essentially a funeral? A lover, maybe, but Chiggy hadn't been dating. At least, not that he'd told me. I doubted he'd been hanging out with someone who would send such an obviously expensive bouquet, and yet there they sat. Taking up space. And they'd been sent specifically *to me*. I hated them for absolutely no reason that made sense.

"Come on, Lock." Zella grabbed my hand and pulled me to an empty chair at her side. "Have a drink."

I would have loved to, but behind the bar, a tall woman with super-short, platinum-blond hair was trying desperately to keep up with the men hollering their orders at her. I knew her body language, had been that lone bartender in a sea of people without any backup.

"What's up?" Flinch asked, obviously noticing my focus.

"Will there be another bartender tonight to help her?"

Flinch looked up, frowning, then bumped Cutter's arm. "Anyone coming in to relieve Billy?"

Cutter looked across the bar in concern. "Shit. I knew I forgot something."

I shook my head, not able to stand by and watch a woman drown. "I've got this."

Flinch grabbed my arm. "Locklyn, you don't—"

"It's fine. I need the distraction." I rose onto the balls of my feet to give him a kiss then walked behind the bar, smiling at the woman called Billy. "Hey."

"What's up, Flinch Junior?"

The nickname...well, it sort of fit, I guessed. "I'm a bartender. Thought I might hop back here and get you out of the weeds."

She nodded, popping tops off beer bottles and listening to an order from some woman with her tits practically draped across the bar at the same time. "Just don't get in my way."

And with that, I slipped into bartender mode. It didn't take me long to get the lay of the land, though I did stake my claim on the far side of the bar from Billy and rearrange the bottles on the rail. Cutter dropped in beside me, laying out pricing and showing me how to work the computer system that, thankfully, was very much like one I had experience with. Once I had a good understanding of what we stocked, where glasses were stored, and how the POS system worked, I stepped up to the bar.

"What are you having?"

And that was how I spent the evening—focusing on making other people happy and pushing aside the grief I felt over my dad being gone. Every Hellion who approached me offered their condolences the first time, but after a while, even that stopped. And I was thankful. My dad wouldn't have wanted me to be sad. He wouldn't have wanted me to be behind the bar at the clubhouse slinging drinks, either, but at least I wasn't crying in a corner somewhere.

"Lock, gimme five drafts with Jack chasers." Zella slid in behind me, digging out a tray from under the bar. "These fuckers are drinking like fish and clogging the path to the bar. Figured I could deliver a few drinks to break it up."

I poured the beers and the shots, lining them up on the tray. "Got a card?"

"Guy said put it on Zed's tab."

I caught Cutter's attention. "Do we tab for Zed with no card?"

Cutter nodded. "Absolutely. The executive team has that privilege. That's me, Mule, Banger, Zed, Flinch, Preacher, and Ridge. Enter their payment as holding tab and type in their name. The system will do the rest."

"Got it." I did as I'd been instructed, logging the charge to

Zed's tab before moving on to other orders. Billy continued working beside me, both of us powering through the worst of the congestion with Zella's help. Eventually, the front of the bar cleared enough for us to pause and take a breath.

"You're solid," Billy said, giving me a fist bump. "I appreciate the help."

"Anytime." I slipped an arm around Zella and leaned into her shoulder. "Thank you for playing waitress for us."

"Like old times, but without the white tablecloths."

"Very much so." But as she walked away, I noticed a hitch in her gait. A limp that hadn't been there. I caught Flinch's eye and nodded toward her. His gaze slid over my best friend, and he immediately leaned closer to Cutter and whispered something in his ear. Cutter was up and moving in a flash, coming around the bar and offering Zella his hand.

"How about we go sit in the conference room? It's a lot quieter than out here."

"Sure. I could use a little break." She shot me a smile. "Can you grab me a seltzer?"

I pulled a canned seltzer from the fridge at my knees, picking her favorite flavor. "I'll put it on Flinch's—"

"Mine," Cutter said with a growl that had the hairs on the back of my neck standing up. He coughed slightly and shot a glance at Flinch, who had begun to rise to his feet. "Anything for Zella should go on my tab. Always. Flinch, can you give me a hand real quick?"

Flinch didn't look thrilled to leave me, but I had a feeling he understood something was wrong with Zella. He jumped into action, coming to the rescue of my best friend. And me, of course. He wouldn't be Flinch if he didn't.

He grabbed one of the guys in a group at the end of the bar —Rush, my babysitter—and tugged him over. "Cutter and I need a minute. You got this?"

Rush nodded, slipping onto a barstool and spreading his elbows wide as if purposefully taking up as much space as possible. With that, Flinch headed for the back, giving me one last look over his shoulder before disappearing down the hall after Cutter, after an obviously tired and possibly hurt Zella. Taking care of my best friend because I needed him to.

I owed him one.

"Looks like you're babysitting again," I said to Rush with a smile as owing Flinch circled around in my brain. "Want a drink?"

"Got one." He did a chin nod toward Billy, who looked to be paying attention. "You two hungry? Want some pasta?"

Billy glanced at me—big, round eyes screaming surprise—then shrugged. "I could definitely eat."

"Same."

Rush nodded and pulled out his phone. "I'll order. Got any requests?"

"Cacio e pepe," I said. "Can we order for Zella, too? She's vegetarian but eats cheese."

Rush nodded, typing away with his thumbs. "Eggplant parmigiana? Does she like mushrooms? The restaurant has this amazing polenta and mushrooms dish that I think will fit the bill."

"She likes mushrooms."

"Cool." He threw a glance at Billy. "What about you, killer?"

"They got a carbonara sauce?"

Rush grunted. "The best around."

"Sounds good to me. Thanks." She grabbed a towel and began wiping down the bar. A towel with a wolf print on the bottom. Decorative.

Like the ones Zella and I always bought for the apartment.

Like ones most people had—color-coordinated or personal to them in some way.

Unlike Flinch, who had nothing personal in his home.

And that was when my brain latched on to an idea that I knew I needed to make come to fruition.

I moved in closer to Rush, catching his eye as soon as he dropped his phone. Spotting a rare opportunity I didn't want to pass up.

"What's up?" he asked with a head cock that was slightly less than human.

I pursed my lips, my head spinning a bit. Ideas and plans formulating. "I may need your help with something."

His face hardened, his eyes practically glowing as they met mine. "Who's fucking with you?"

"No, no. Not like that. I want to do something nice. For Flinch."

"What are you thinking about?"

"I'm not sure—I have an idea, but I may need some help pulling it off."

"Let's work it out. I'm yours, kid."

TWENTY

FLINCH

Crawling out of bed when I had a warm Locklyn by my side wasn't ever going to be my favorite way to start the day, but I had shit to get done and she needed her rest. I kissed her cheek before heading for the bathroom to get ready. We had an executive team meeting at the clubhouse bright and motherfucking early—likely to begin the process of voting Cutter into the head spot—and no way could I be late.

Once showered and dressed for the day, I made my way through the house. Zella lay asleep on the couch in the living room, so I kept my steps quiet. The girl needed her rest. She and Locklyn had spent a good couple of hours serving drinks at the club, something I appreciated. I liked how both slipped right into club life. Into my life.

Both of them.

Fuck.

A realization slammed into me, one I hadn't seen coming until just then. One that was about to turn my world upside down. I looked around my little house—one bedroom, one-and-a-half baths, pool, tiny living area—and I knew it wouldn't work anymore. I now had two women to take care of—Locklyn and her bestie. They were a package deal, and Zella needed us more than she would likely even admit to. My old house wouldn't work for my new situation.

I sighed and rubbed a hand over my face, murmuring to the empty room, "I'm going to need a bigger house."

"For what?"

I turned, eyeing Zella as she stood in the doorway to the kitchen, wrapped in her blanket. The scent of her sickness preceded her, the deep, earthy scent something I wanted eradicated. Something that had me more worried about her than anything else. She looked so small in that moment—almost like a child. One I had a duty to protect.

"You sleep okay?" I asked, avoiding her question.

She scowled as if she knew what I was doing. "Yeah, fine. I don't think I'm ready to be up yet, though."

"Go back to bed. I have club business this morning and will be gone in a few—I just wanted to set up the coffeepot for you two."

"So, you're leaving?"

"For the day, yeah."

"Perfect. I'm taking your spot." With that, she walked down the hall and into my bedroom, shutting the door softly behind her. My wolf and I had a moment of stunned silence where neither knew whether to rage about someone else being in bed with our mate or to be thankful the two would be together since I couldn't stay.

I finally shook all those thoughts off. "Definitely need a bigger house."

Once I had the coffeepot set to brew, some breakfast pastries laid out, and a note written to the ladies, I locked the women in the house and headed for my bike. Rush rolled up right on time.

"What's good?" he asked before bumping my fist. "They inside?"

"Yeah. Sleeping still."

"Cool. I talked to Mule about Zella. He's going to poke around his contacts to see what he can come up with. Might take some time, though. He says the witches don't like to be poked."

There was a joke in that statement I had no intention of making. Witches were one of the few things that scared me. "Thanks. Keep on him for me, and I'll get Cutter involved, too."

"Sounds like a plan." He took his seat on the porch, sitting back and throwing his legs out in front of him. Getting comfortable. "Oh, by the way. Locklyn mentioned something about wanting to run some errands later, so I may call in one of the brothers to back me up. Two women is a lot of women."

I snorted a laugh. "Tell me about it. I just realized I'm going to need to buy a bigger house."

"So Zella can stay?"

"Yeah. I don't have a second bedroom or bath."

Rush looked over my place. "We could add on. You've got the land for it. Hell, put in one of those tiny home things, but not so tiny for her."

A separate building. Might be nice—Locklyn and I could keep our privacy, but the two would still be able to be together all the time. Zella would be under my protection. "Might work."

"Let me know. I've got family in the construction business."

"Why does that not surprise me?"

Rush sat a little deeper, throwing his arms wide as he grinned at me. "I'm here for you, big guy. Whether it's building on to your house or just getting the best Italian food in the state delivered. Whatever your mate needs."

I stopped short, staring at him. How the fuck...

"You figured that out, huh?"

Rush shrugged, pulling himself together before sitting up. "Anyone with half a brain in their head would have figured it out. Luckily, most of the brothers keep at least two-thirds of their brains in their dicks, so I think your secret is relatively safe. For now."

It was the *for now* that made my skin itch. "Any whispers at the club?"

"Not that I've heard."

"Good. That's good." I offered my fist for one more bump. "Seen Eloise lately?"

His mate. The spirits brewer he had killed a human over. The woman he hadn't claimed yet but definitely wanted to.

His face grew harder, his expression almost unreadable. "Saw her the other night."

"Like a date night?"

"Maybe."

Interesting. "I haven't heard any whispers about her or that human."

"You told me to keep my mouth shut. I've kept my motherfucking mouth shut."

I had. On a night that seemed a lifetime ago but had been less than a week. He'd killed a man, I'd helped dispose of the body, and then Locklyn had shaken up my world like a goddamned snow globe. Not that I would have rather her not have done the shaking—I was just looking forward to things calming the fuck down.

"I've got to hit it," I said, knowing Cutter would be waiting on me so he could ask about Zella. "Keep 'em safe, okay?"

"I'm on it."

With that, I mounted up and walked my bike to the end of the driveway, not wanting the noise of starting it to wake up the women. Within minutes, I had the machine roaring full out toward the clubhouse with my thoughts finally calming. Other than the need for a bigger house—that bitch wasn't going to release her claws from my brain.

Once at the clubhouse, I parked my bike and headed inside. Downloading a realty app along the way to get a feel for the market. Having bought and sold dozens of houses over the decades, I understood the process and had a good sense for when something was a deal or overpriced. The whole credit score bullshit had slowed me down when they'd first come to be needed, but I'd figured a few ways around the banking industry nosing into my business dealings. Mostly, I paid with cash, but I had other options as well. I just needed to get my shit cleaned up before I made any decisions.

"Flinch."

I turned at the door, spotting Cutter coming from behind the building. "What's doing?"

"Got Rush on duty?"

"Yeah. Why?"

"Just making sure the ladies are covered." He looked out across the desert, as if he could see my house in the distance. "Two women to watch over is a lot."

I agreed. "Rush mentioned that. Said he might call in a brother for backup if they left the house."

Cutter pulled out his phone, typing quickly. "I'll send Diesel over as backup."

"We've asked Mule to find a witch for Zella."

Cutter's sharp eyes stabbed into me, his frown intense. "You think that's the best idea?"

"I think those old hags in the hills know more about healing than any human doctor ever born."

He grunted. "Does she know?"

"Fuck no. I don't even think she knows about us, let alone witch healers."

He flipped his phone a few times before pocketing it, his agitation clear. "Every fucking guy in that room last night knew she was sick."

Yeah, they would have. That scent was unmistakable. "Yes."

"They'll see her as weak." He glared at me, the unfuckwithable leader back in place. The man who saw everyone but brothers as blood bags probably realigning his loyalty right there in the parking lot. "If you hear even a word about a brother coming for her—"

My own growl cut him off. "That's my mate's best friend. They're practically sisters, which makes Zella family. No one is fucking with my family."

Cutter held out his fist and took the bump I gave him with a nod. "Same, brother. I've got you covered."

Which meant he had Locklyn's back. Something I already knew but would always bring me at least a little relief hearing from a man like Cutter.

"Our women are going to be the end of us," I said, half joking and half...well, not.

Cutter chuffed, more wolf than man in that moment. "But we'll die fucking happy, won't we."

No doubt.

Conversation done and guidelines set, Cutter led the way into the building. The place reeked of smoke and beer, a sign there'd been a good party the night before. As was the stickiness of the floor. Motherfucker, I hated early morning meetings primarily for that reason. I'd have to wash off my boots before I left.

"Cleaners coming this morning?" I asked.

"About ten. Don't worry—I pulled out the boot cleaner and have it set up at the entrance to the conference room." He looked down, glaring at the floor. "How the fuck does this get so sticky?"

"Some of the brothers are fucking children and can't hold their beers." We made it to the conference room door and, just as he'd said, the boot cleaner sat at the entrance. He sprayed a degreaser on the soles of his boots then rubbed them back and forth over the rolling bristles, stepping inside only once both feet were clean. I followed suit, making sure to get the sides as well. Grunting in satisfaction when I took a few steps in and didn't feel any residual tackiness.

"Ready for this?" I asked once I had settled into my usual seat.

Cutter nodded, dropping into his chair. "Sure the fuck am."

"You've got my vote."

"Appreciate it, brother. Let's hope the others feel the same."

The rest of the executive team filtered into the room, each taking the time to use the boot scrubber under the watchful eye of Cutter. No one needed directions, though this wouldn't have happened with Chiggy. He hadn't given a fuck over such small details. Cutter obviously did, and that scrubber—that need to keep the party debris out of the executive room—was the first sign of a very big change coming up.

Zed walked in last, eyeing the boot scrubber as if it were an alien life-form before spraying the cleaner and getting down to it. He scrubbed his boots well then kicked the device to the side, shutting the door behind him. He gave a simple nod to let us know we were ready to begin before dropping into his chair.

Meeting time.

"I'm going to keep this short and sweet, gentlemen," Cutter said. "Now that Chiggy's been honored appropriately, we need to begin thinking about the future of the Hellions. In that vein, I am informing this team that I will be seeking votes for the president spot."

"You know we, as the executive team, can just assign the role to you, right?" Banger said with a heavy, furrowed brow. "There's no need for a full club vote after the death of an executive member."

"I'm aware, my friend. But I feel like Chiggy got his spot with a vote, and I got mine from him. If I want to lead these men, I need to make sure they want me in the head chair. So we go to a vote." He looked around the room, eyeing the team that had been appointed by Chiggy. The ones who would soon need to follow him. "I want to be sure I have my executive team on board before I take this to the members. Anyone got beef they want to talk about while we've got some privacy?"

I glanced around the room, checking the overall feel of the place. Letting my wolf out to take a peek as well. Nothing off, no one seeming disgruntled or upset. Looked like Cutter had his team...if he wanted it.

A fact I wasn't the only one to consider.

"Reminder that the prez picks the executive team," Zed said, his low voice breaking the silence. "You've got my vote, Cutter, but are you looking to make any changes?"

Banger and Mule—the two older men on the team and Chiggy's crew, for sure—sat a little straighter, jaws tight and feet planted firmly on the floor. Cutter turned his gaze to them specifically, looking each man over.

"We have a solid team here, one I trust. The only changes I would want to make would be to bring on a new VP and add a role."

"What role?" Banger asked, looking a lot more relaxed after being told his job was safe. "What are we lacking?"

Cutter sighed and sat deeper, somehow taking up even more space. "We've got vamps, boys. I know they've always been out there, but they came for us and we took a direct hit with the loss of Chiggy. I don't want to take another one, so I'd like to add another enforcer to the team. Someone to work with Preacher on upping the security around here."

Banger looked toward Preacher. "You good with this idea?"

The ever-stoic club enforcer nodded. "Cutter and I have talked about it and are in line with our thinking. Bringing on a second means we can focus on figuring out the vamp issue while keeping the clubhouse secure. I'm good, boys, but I can't be in two places at once."

A rumbly chuckle circulated around the room. Even Cutter had a slight rise to one corner of his mouth.

"We good?" Cutter asked after everyone had quieted down. "Second enforcer, a position which Preacher agrees with, comes on this week. Preach and I have already discussed options, so let's finalize that today." He paused until he got a nod of approval from the enforcer. "Good. And If I get the vote, I bring on my own second. Everyone else stays the fuck where they are. If you're in, give me an aye."

Every man in the room called aye without delay, including me. Cutter would make a good prez—the man was strong and sure without the reactivity of younger wolves. That was why Chiggy had brought him on as veep. Which left me wondering about who Cutter's second would be.

Once all of the day's business had been covered and the announcement of Cutter's presidential run had been planned, the rest of the men moved on to the bar itself for a drink and chat. I stuck with Cutter and Zed in the conference room for a few.

"What's up, boys?" Cutter asked, obviously aware that we had questions.

Zed cut right through the bullshit. "Who you bringing in as veep?"

"Why? You want the spot?"

Zed coughed a sarcastic-sounding laugh. "That's a big ol' fuck and no, sir. I just want to know who we're going to be spending Sundays with."

Because club business was usually handled on Sundays. Some men called it church. I preferred just to think of it as business meetings.

"You two got opinions on who I should or shouldn't ask?" Cutter asked, his voice a warning.

I shrugged. "Not really. But you pull one domino, and the rest could start to fall. We need to keep our eye on the internal politics bullshit."

"Exactly," Zed agreed. "We're just looking bigger picture."

Cutter sighed and looked up at the ceiling, worrying his lip for a moment before saying, "I think Diesel for veep and Rush for second enforcer."

Zed met my stare, giving nothing away. I could only nod, thinking over everything I knew about both men.

"Rush can be impulsive," I said, knowing that fact wouldn't affect his chance of getting the spot. But the next one...maybe. "He's got a connection to Eloise that you and Preacher need to know about in case he blows up. Otherwise, they're both solid choices."

"What kind of connection?" Zed asked.

No fucking way was I outing another man stuck in my position. "Ask him."

Cutter frowned. "Is that related to what you two were cleaning up the other night? He step over a line?"

I kept my mouth shut, staring right back at the man. Not in disrespect. Just as I would have told anyone who asked—shit only went sideways for two reasons: being unprepared, or being an idiot. Telling Cutter details about the human Rush had murdered would fall under the being an idiot category. Wouldn't be happening.

"I get it," Cutter finally said. "You think he'd be a liability?"

I sat with that. Really gave the idea some thought. The kid was pretty solid—the only issue had come into play when someone had fucked with his mate. Now that I had one of my own, I understood Rush's reaction a bit more. But the kid would need to be talked to, would need to understand the rules. Fuck, he would need to claim his mate and tuck her away someplace safe to get his head out of his ass.

"No, I think he can be impulsive but not in a way that would harm the club on purpose. And he's got connections—he'd be a solid choice."

Cutter nodded. "You in agreement, Zed?"

My taciturn brother nodded. "Absolutely."

"Then the decisions are made. Once I get the vote, I name the two, and we go full bore against the vamps. Until then, we solidify our defenses. I don't want to lose another brother to those lifeless fucks."

That was something I thought we all could agree with.

Once club business had officially been called complete, I hurried to my bike to head home. I usually would have hung around, but I wanted to see my girl more than I wanted to spend additional hours at the clubhouse. I'd already been there all day, our early morning executive meeting turning into an afternoon full club one so Cutter could make his announcement about the vote. Then came the jibber-jabbering—the brothers wanting to talk over all things Cutter as prez and what it would mean. Fucking chatter, man. I hated it, but it was practically a part of the club culture. The brothers had to talk everything through, which meant I was leaving well past dinner time. I needed my girl.

I had made it halfway to my bike before I heard my name being called again. I wanted to ignore it, but that voice—the tone. Zed.

"What's up?" I said as soon as he reached me.

"Heading home?"

"Trying to."

"I won't keep you, but I told you I would let you know if I heard any static about your mate."

I stopped dead in my tracks, turning slowly to face him. Feeling my wolf waking up on the edge of my consciousness. "Yeah?"

"There's chatter. They liked what they saw last night." He stood back, arms crossed, entire body deep in shadow. "A couple have said they want a turn."

There was no controlling my wolf in that moment. The pure fury coursing through my blood at the very idea of another man making a play for my mate had me losing all control. Zed caught my advance with a hard hand on my shoulder, not striking back but standing his ground as he kept me at arm's length. Waiting me out as I half shifted and snarled his way.

Eventually, I was able to wrangle control from my wolf and return to my fully human form. I took a moment to just breathe, making sure my wolf had receded far enough to maintain my composure, before addressing my brother. "I'd say sorry, but—"

"You're not." Zed stayed firm in his stance before me, not giving me an extra inch as he looked me up and down. "So the impassive Flinch does apparently *flinch.*"

"Not hardly."

He smiled slightly, the shadows making the expression seem almost malevolent. An expression that dropped within two seconds. "You can't lose control like that with them."

"I know."

"Until they know she's your mate, they'll talk shit about challenging for her. The dumb ones might continue after they know."

"I know all that, too."

"Claim her. Let the club know. Then take down anyone who dares challenge your claim on her."

I sighed, knowing he was right. Feeling it in my bones.

Wanting the taste of her skin and her blood in my mouth so bad. Needing it.

"I have to make sure she understands it all first."

"So make her understand." He turned and walked away, throwing one last bit of shit over his shoulder. "They talked about Zella, too. Don't think Cutter's going to like that any more than you like them talking about Locklyn."

Fuck me, I hadn't been paying attention to Cutter and Zella the night before, but he did stick awfully close to the bar. He had given her a ride back to the clubhouse and home at the end of the night, all without trying to hide it from the brothers. He had also sent Diesel over to my house to babysit without a moment of hesitation. The man hadn't said a word, and yet I knew. I fucking knew, and obviously Zed did as well.

"Mated wolves are going to be the death of me," I said to the empty parking lot, knowing that fact included myself.

Twenty-One

LOCKLYN

"Ready?"

I took a deep breath and gave the living room one last look. A blanket lay draped across the back of the small couch that matched the handful of pillows I'd bought. Framed images of the desert around us hung under glass on the walls, all giving life to what had been a single-note color scheme. I had even added a rug to ground the space and keep everything from looking too bachelor pad, though I wouldn't say I'd added a feminine touch. More...softened the rough edges.

"Ready." I gave Zella a hug as she and Rush—my two partners in crime—headed out to the porch to meet Flinch. I stood in the room and waited, unsure if he'd like what I'd done or not.

"Short stack?" Flinch peeked inside, likely wondering why things seemed so weird tonight. Why I wasn't outside with the others to greet him.

"Hey." I linked my hands together and crossed my legs at the ankle, knowing my posture screamed how nervous I felt. "Welcome home."

He frowned then looked past me, his eyes going wide. I stared as he took it all in—the rug, the blanket, the pillows, the lamps, and art. All the little details I'd picked up for him, playing completely off his already established color scheme.

"What did you do?" he asked softly.

"Do you like it?"

"I do." He stepped toward me slowly, still looking over the room. Keeping his voice soft as he asked, "How did you do this?"

"Rush took us shopping."

He wrapped his arms around me, pulling me in tight. "He better have paid."

"I paid." I shivered at his answering growl, loving the way the sound seemed to reach through my soul and tug on something deep within me. "Though, technically, I paid with your money."

"How's that?"

"You've been giving me cash all week."

"That was for you." He frowned, his brows pulling tight. "All that money was for you."

"It was too much—I couldn't possibly spend it all, so I bought you a few things."

He sighed but hugged me tighter. "Well, thank you. No one's ever been so thoughtful. And the room—I love it."

"You do?"

"Absolutely. I hope you do, too. It's your space and not just mine."

Stomach butterflies...I had them.

"I do like it—it's still your style but more comfy and personal. But there's more." I grabbed his hand and tugged, leading him down the hall to his bedroom. "Just...keep an open mind."

I let him pass me, watching as he looked around. This was

the space I had spent the most on. Another new rug, soft bedding, new pillows, curtains, an actual headboard. I had completely redecorated this room, even putting in a few touches that were far more my style than his. The space had become an amalgamation of the two of us, and I worried he wouldn't like it.

"Locklyn," he said, that growl coming through plain as day. He closed the door, the quiet snick of the handset engaging like a gunshot in the room. The tension growing between us.

Breathing hard, I answered with a soft, "Yeah?"

"Where's Zella?"

That question stunned me stupid for about three seconds. "Uh...outside with Rush."

"Good." With speed I had no idea he was capable of, he lunged and picked me up by the backs of the thighs, flinging both of us onto the new duvet. I landed with a giggle, clinging to him. Loving the feel of his weight on top of me.

"Flinch, what are you—"

"This is amazing," he said, his voice barely more than a whisper. The moment suddenly heavy with an intimacy I hadn't expected.

I ran my hands through his hair, staring up into those light eyes I had come to care about so much. My heart wanting to beat right out of my chest. "You like it?"

"I love it." He stared down at me, body relaxing. "And I love you for putting in so much effort just to make me happy."

Heart...dead. Body...no longer mine. Those words carried so much weight, so much meaning. He loved me? How had we gotten here? And why wasn't I terrified of any sort of emotional commitment to this man?

Because I wasn't. At all. In fact, there was only one response I could think of in that moment.

"I love you, too. That's why I did this."

With a growl, Flinch pulled away, tugging at my clothes until he had my leggings off and my shirt tugged up around my neck.

"Love you and it. This room is amazing. I fully intend to fuck you on every pillow, blanket, and rug, so feel free to fill the whole damn house with them."

My laugh turned to a groan as he dipped down to take a nipple in his mouth. Flinch wasn't messing around—he was going for maximum response in minimum time, and I appreciated that. I spread my legs as he slid a hand between them, knowing he would have me wet and ready in seconds if I wasn't already. The man knew my buttons and seemed hell-bent on pushing them all right then.

"Flinch." I gripped his shoulders as he kept moving down, arching into the feel of his lips. "We don't have much time."

"How long?"

"Maybe ten minutes." I yanked his shirt over his head, needing to feel his warmth on me. Inside me. "Zella and Rush will wonder where we are."

He growled and crawled between my legs, spreading me and lifting my ass off the mattress when he sat up. While one hand began teasing where I was definitely growing wet for him, the other pulled his phone from his pocket. He typed with his thumb, showing off at being ambidextrous by teasing my clit in slow circles at the same time before tossing the phone across the bed and grabbing my thigh.

"They won't wonder now," he said with a wicked, slow smile spreading across his face.

"What did you do?"

"I texted Rush and told him we're out for the night." He lunged forward, arms wrapping around my thighs. "Fuck, I need a taste of that pussy. Been craving it all damn day."

He dove in, tongue and fingers and growl working together to tease me into a frenzy. I arched and mewled, weaving my fingers through his hair and trying so hard to just ride out the pleasure he imparted. Something felt missing, though. A sensation I chased but couldn't quite get to. Flinch must have figured that out because without warning, he grabbed me around the waist and flipped us both. Lying back and yanking me to straddle his head.

"Here, mate. Ride my tongue. I want to feel you come all over my face."

"Flinch," I moaned, but then my body took over. I worked my hips in small circles over him, chasing the high that seemed so much closer already. Grabbing the headboard I'd only just installed and holding on as his tongue made filthy words fall from my lips. Made me lose all control and come on his face the way he'd wanted.

"There we go," he said once I had pulled away, flipping us over once more so I lay facedown on the bed. "My turn now. Gonna fuck this pussy good and hard. Make sure you know who you belong to."

I wanted to argue—to put my feminist rage on display and remind him that I belonged to no one—but I couldn't. In that moment, with that man nudging his hard cock inside me, I did belong to him. At least like this. At least when he wanted nothing more than to force me to find my pleasure. I would surrender to him for this.

"Deeper." I cried, pushing back once he had his cock wedged inside me. Grabbing on to the pillow as he teased me with short, shallow thrusts. "I need you deeper."

"I've got you, baby." He slammed home, growling deep and low before pulling out once more. Dragging his cock over my tender flesh before pushing back in. He rocked me forward with every thrust, forcing me to brace myself against the headboard and push back into him. Giving me the deeper I'd so craved. And when I came, when my entire body seized around his and I screamed his name in a painful sort of pleasure that wrapped me inside out, I felt it.

A bite.

Teeth embedding themselves into my shoulder.

A burning that set my soul on fire and had me falling into a pit of pleasure unlike any I'd ever experienced. I came longer and harder and more, chanting Flinch's name as I lost all control. As he finally released me and rose onto his knees to pound home.

"Fuck," he groaned, thrusting faster, rocking the entire bed. "Fuck, Locklyn, I didn't mean to. I couldn't... Couldn't stop."

He came with a roar that nearly shook the house, both of us panting and sweat-covered and falling into a tangle of limbs.

And blood.

FLINCH

I bit her. Had completed the claiming on my end. Fuck, I hadn't meant to. I truly hadn't. Not before I had talked to her about it. Explained what it meant. I hadn't meant to, but I refused to regret the action. Especially once I started to feel her more—her emotions, her pleasure, the warmth of her feelings for me. Those were a fucking gift to experience, and I wouldn't be refusing them.

"You bit me," Locklyn said with a little laugh. I chuckled and nuzzled into her neck, licking at the spot where I had, in fact, bitten her. Laving over the blood and teeth marks.

"I did." I bit her again, softer this time. Not breaking skin. "You're fucking delicious."

My mate laughed and held me closer, blissing me out in that moment. I might as well have been high—could have been drunk and stoned for how I felt. The release of tension, the total relaxation I received from claiming my mate. I was floating because of Locklyn.

"How would you like it if I bit you back?" she asked, sounding playful and almost teasing. I rolled us over, ending on my back with her sprawled on top of me. Her hair hung down around our faces, curtaining us in, and her breasts pushed against my chest to make this delicious shelf that I really wanted to fuck at some point. I wanted to do everything with her—spank her, tease her, bathe her, fuck her everywhere, feed her, take care of her. This was my mate, the woman I had been waiting my entire life for. I wanted every moment going forward filled with her.

But I would need to explain how a mating worked at some point.

"You can bite me wherever and whenever." I kissed her nice and deep, tasting every bit of her I could. Tangling our tongues and breathing her breath. Needing more. Breaking away only to ask for that more. "Get your pussy up here. I need another taste."

She laughed and dropped her head to my shoulder. "I'm too sensitive. You'd get one lick in, and I'd be coming all over you."

"I see nothing wrong with this."

"I do." She slid to the side, letting her hand rest on my stomach. Moving it lower as she held my gaze. "I feel like I owe you orgasms."

That statement pulled me up short enough to basically ignore the fact that my mate now had my dick in her hand. "You feel what?"

"I mean, you always make sure I have at least two." She rested her head on my chest, that wicked hand sliding over where I was already so fucking hard for her. Teasing me. "You only get one."

"You don't owe me orgasms, Locklyn."

The pout she threw my way had my balls pulling up tight and my heart practically breaking open. My connection to her meant I knew she was teasing—felt the joy at her little game—so I played along. Letting her jack me off as that bottom lip begged for me to bite it.

"So, you want me to stop?" she asked, ever the temptress.

I growled and reached for her ass, grabbing tight and digging my fingers into the flesh. "Never."

"Good." This woman—my mate—held my gaze as her hand got real fucking serious. Fingers wrapped around my girth with a grip just short of painful and a rhythm that had my toes curling and my inner wolf singing to the moon above. Fuck me, her touch felt good. Better than good—tremendous, life-altering, phenomenal. All the words I couldn't have spoken in that moment to save my life because every bit of blood had left my brain and flooded south to where she continued to stroke up and down my cock.

It felt so good, I was about to embarrass myself.

"Short stack," I groaned, thrusting my hips into her hand and moaning loudly when she did some sort of twisting motion in response. "Fuck, I'm going to come in your hand."

"That's sort of the goal right now, big guy."

I reached between her legs from behind, unable to bend my hand in a way to slip my fingers inside her but knowing she was sensitive enough for a little play. Just a bit. I managed to align two fingers in her pussy folds and slide up so I had her clit clamped between them. Locklyn moaned and writhed at the touch, likely both wanting to avoid the added sensation on her sensitive flesh and needing more of the contact. I knew she could come again. It was my job to convince her she wanted to.

"Feel good, mate?"

She nodded, still hand-fucking me. Not breaking her rhythm one bit. "I wanted to make you come."

"Oh, you will. And soon. But this pussy is too wet for me to ignore. You like jacking me off?"

"Yes," she moaned, the pained sound bringing out another growl in me. A soft one—almost purr-like. One I had never made before.

"Fuck, your hand feels so good. Nowhere near as good as this pussy…" I raised my hand off her and brought it back down, smacking her clit. Chuckling at the way she jumped and mewled. "But it's still so good. So good."

And it was. My girl had a grip on me—strong, unyielding, and absolutely divine. She also twisted and pulled and flicked the head of my cock in ways that sent vibrations shooting up my abdomen. There was no way I could hold back from coming, but I needed to push it off. Just a bit. Just enough to make her come first.

Because yeah, I would never take without giving.

"Come on, baby," I whispered, squeezing my fingers over her clit and rubbing her harder and faster than before. "I want to see you break apart on my hand again. Come for me like the good girl I know you are."

"Flinch." She rocked against me, tucking her head into my side and moving her entire body as she chased her pleasure. Still fucking my cock with her hand like a champion. I kept my eyes on her, kept what little focus I could muster pointed her way. Which really just meant watching her ass move as she writhed against my fingers buried between those thighs. The view was spectacular, I had to admit. All ass and occasional peeks of my cock in her hand.

Fucking amazing.

"Harder," she whispered as her hips began to move a little faster and her grip tightened almost unconsciously. "Oh god, harder."

I obliged like a good mate, squeezing my fingers around her clit and pushing up. Trapping that little pearl of flesh between my hand and her pubic bone. It had to hurt a bit, had to bring so much sensation to her, but she didn't complain. Instead, she groaned long and loud before her entire body seized. The trembling, the erratic pulls of her hand still trying so hard to get me off, the sound she made as she found her release. I came with a snarl, arching off the bed while holding Locklyn to me by her pussy. Both of us breathing heavy and clinging to each other. Her pleasure pushing mine over an edge I hadn't been prepared to hit. Doubling it. I could have come for hours—felt as if I had.

"Fucking fantastic," I whispered once we had both settled onto the bed once more. I yanked my girl into my arms, kissing the top of her head. "You're the fucking dream, short stack."

She smiled up at me, pushing forward to drop the sweetest kiss to my lips. Filling me with a sense of happiness I hadn't been prepared for. This woman. I would do anything for her, kill anyone who threatened her. I would destroy the world just to keep her safe if I had to.

And with vamps around, ones that had murdered her dad, I just might have to. But not tonight. Tonight was about rewarding her kindness and celebrating her love, because somehow, I had managed to make this amazing creature actually love me. Didn't know how and likely never would, but fuck if I wasn't going to honor that emotion every chance I got. Forever.

Twenty-Two

LOCKLYN

I woke up on the verge of what had to be my twentieth orgasm and with Flinch's head between my thighs. In my sleepy, dreamy state, I wasn't sure of reality for a brief moment in time, but then he growled against me, nearly setting my entire body on fire. I gasped and grabbed his head, fisting his hair and tugging him closer. Asking for more without a single word.

I came quietly, my body shaking and my breath escaping in a gasp. No moan, no yell. Thank the gods for that because I had a feeling Zella and Rush had both heard more than enough from us overnight.

"That was a nice way to wake up." I laughed and tugged on Flinch until he acquiesced, leading him up my body so he could lie next to me instead of on top of me.

"Goal accomplished." He hummed and reached for me, tangling us together. "It's late."

I glanced over his shoulder, for the first time noting the

amount of sunlight peeking around the edges of the blinds. "How late?"

"Almost lunchtime."

I groaned and rolled away. "Zella's going to kill me."

"Maybe not. Rush took her to breakfast."

"He did?"

"Yeah. They just got back about ten minutes ago."

"Oh." I stared at the ceiling, my brain spinning. "Are they..."

Flinch laughed. "No. Definitely not."

"How do you know?"

"I just do." He dropped a kiss on my collarbone. "Go take a shower. Let me check in with Rush and see what's up with the club."

"Sounds good." I rose from the bed, groaning through a stretch. Every muscle hurt, every bone ached, and my thighs throbbed from the night before, but I didn't mind a bit of it.

"You keep making noises like that and I'll be trapping you in our bed for the day."

I glanced over my shoulder, nearly sighing at the image of Flinch pulling his jeans over his bare hips. He tucked himself away and fastened them closed, all while looking at me with an expression of so much want. How could he possibly...

"We have to be adults." I wrapped a sheet around myself and rose to my feet, coming around the bed to lay a hand on his bare chest and kiss his chin. "But maybe later."

He growled, eyes sharpening as they devoured me. Not for the first time, I felt the presence of his wolf. Saw the gleam from the beast within. It didn't scare me, though. His presence excited me instead. Something I would need to think over once I had left the sex bubble he'd captured me in.

As soon as I pushed Flinch out the door, I showered and hurried through a pretty basic morning routine, foregoing makeup and letting my hair dry naturally. I had a need to see

Zella, to check in on her. To talk to her. I wanted my best friend, especially after missing her for so long.

When I walked out of the bedroom, she was sitting on the couch. Leg bouncing. Watching the door for my appearance without her usual smile on her face. I had a sudden flashback of my mom sitting that exact same way, with that same expression on her face. Knowing then exactly how much trouble I was in for some rule-breaking I couldn't even remember anymore.

Nothing to do but get through it.

"Hi," I said, knowing exactly how lacking that greeting was.

Zella huffed, looking me up and down. Expression hard. "You're such a whore."

I stood still, letting her words sink in. Eventually sighing and nodding slowly. "Pretty much."

Her smile exploded across her face, every bit of joy practically bursting from her body. "He's outside with Rush—who is really nice, by the way—so you've got probably thirty seconds to tell me everything."

I rushed over and settled myself on the couch next to her, relief making me feel almost giddy. "He's so...giving."

"Yeah, I know. I heard you hollering every time you 'received' last night."

Eek. I had expected that, but still. "Sorry."

"Don't be. At all. I'm happy he makes you happy."

"He does. He really does." I sighed and laid my head on the back of the couch, so damn thrilled to have Zella back in my everyday life. "What's this about Rush and you and breakfast?"

She waved me off. "Girl, no. It's not like that. He's really nice, though."

"What did you two do last night?"

"Nothing. I ended up going for a ride with Cutter."

"Cutter?"

"Yeah. He stopped by, so I talked him into showing me the sights."

I huffed, knowing Zella far too well. "I doubt he had to be talked into anything."

She laughed. "No. Not really. Now, come on—the guys are taking us for coffee, and you need it."

We headed outside to find Flinch and Rush laughing about something by the passenger side of Flinch's truck. When the door opened, both men turned to look. Flinch's eyes raked over my body from head to toe, his smile turning more wicked. The man was able to look at me and make me feel his gaze, a trick I had never seen anyone else accomplish before. I could practically taste his attraction to me.

"Good lord," Zella said. "Stop eye-fucking her and let's go."

Flinch raised an eyebrow but softened his gaze. "Whatever you want, Zella. You ready, short stack?"

"Are we back on that nickname?" I headed right for him, grinning up into his face as he opened the door for me. "I'm not short."

He leaned in for a quick peck of my lips. "Compared to me, you're a tiny little thing."

That sort of made sense—Flinch and his fellow wolves were some of the biggest men I had ever met. Being average around them meant you were the smallest. The nickname suddenly clicked.

"Fine, I'm a short stack next to you. But I'm honestly not short in the human world."

"I am," Zella said as she rounded the front of the truck with Rush following her. "Come on, Locklyn. Get your ass in the truck."

Flinch took that moment to growl right in my ear, to lean close so he could grab my ass and whisper, "Yeah, Locklyn. Get that ass in my truck so I can caffeinate you."

The teasing tone had me giggling, his playful nature something new and quickly becoming a favorite for me.

"Fine, but only because you say the sweetest things." I hopped into the passenger seat of the truck, not needing his hand on my ass to climb in but appreciating it, nonetheless. "Thanks for the help."

"Gotta protect that ass." He squeezed my thigh then shut the door, hurrying around the front of the truck to the driver's side. He quickly opened the crew cab door for Zella. She slipped into the back and took her seat, Flinch helping her just as he'd helped me. Without the ass-grab.

"Thanks," Zella said as she scooted into her place. "So, where are we going?"

"We've got a little mom-and-pop in town that serves good coffee." Flinch sat in the driver's seat and started the engine. "The one the prospect took you to a few days ago."

My heart thumped and my skin went cold. "Yeah, I remember. Sounds good."

But it didn't sound good. All I could think about was the man who had been outside watching me. Staring. Making me feel vulnerable.

Flinch pulled out onto the highway but reached over and squeezed my leg just above my knee. "You okay?"

"Of course."

His frown told me he didn't believe me, but that was okay. I wasn't going to ruin a coffee run with all of us just because some guy had made me uncomfortable. I had Flinch with me this time. He wouldn't let anyone near me.

Flinch parked in a spot on the road, leaving enough room so Rush could back his bike in sideways up against the front of the truck. Rush came to open my door as Flinch helped Zella down, his eyes going wide when he saw my shoulder.

"What?" I asked, suddenly uncomfortable.

"Nice bite mark." He grinned and leaned closer. "The brothers at the club are going to have a field day with that."

I had no idea what he meant, but at that moment, Flinch appeared and grabbed my hand, tugging me into his side as he guided us into the coffee shop. Just like before, the decor felt warm and inviting, if a little on the shabby side. I liked it. Zella apparently did as well because she immediately found a spot on a couch near the front and plopped with her legs folded underneath her.

"This is our kind of place. Right, Lock?"

"Yeah. Absolutely." I tucked myself into a chair that gave me a good view out the window. "But without the snow falling outside the window."

She looked around a bit, a small frown forming. "Does anyone else smell roses?"

I nodded, suddenly very aware of the floral scent, mostly because it seemed out of place in a coffee shop. "For sure."

"Smells like sweet rot to me," Rush said, looking around. "Though it's really subtle."

"I only smell coffee." Flinch leaned closer, obviously looking over at the menu board. "What can I get you two?"

Zella piped up before I could. "I'll have an iced cold brew with a splash of almond milk and Lock will have an iced coffee with cream and two pumps of vanilla." She scrunched her nose my way. "You were here before—it's still two with their regular size?"

"I assume. I got a cappuccino last time."

She sat back, eyebrows raised in an exaggerated fashion. "Drinking a big-girl coffee when I'm not around?"

I shrugged. "The prospect who brought me said they had the best espresso. I had to try it."

"And?"

"It was really good, but I want my regular iced today."

"Iced it is." Rush bumped Flinch with his shoulder. "What're you getting?"

"Cappuccino."

"On it." Rush headed for the counter, talking loudly with the barista. Both of them laughing. Rush had a definite charm about him—a way of interacting with people that made others want to join in. Made them feel comfortable enough to share with him. He may have looked like some sort of Special Forces soldier, but he had a way of putting people at ease that I almost envied.

"He's worked in food service," Zella said, watching him the same way I had. "He's got the vibe."

I nodded, puzzle pieces about the man fitting into place. "Absolutely. Like a waiter or bartender—he knows how to chitchat."

Eventually, Rush came back with our orders and an espresso for himself, then headed outside. Something about keeping an eye out just in case. His being almost a physical wall between me and anyone watching from the street should have made me feel much more relaxed, but it didn't. Instead, I felt anxious and exposed. In danger.

"What's up?" Flinch asked as he leaned forward from where he'd settled. "Why are you stressed?"

Zella looked my way, her brow furrowing.

I shook them both off. "It's nothing. I'm fine."

The two exchanged a look that grated against my nerves.

"I said I'm fine."

"Then you're fine." Flinch sat back, sipping his cappuccino as if he didn't have a care in the world. "What plot are you two going to enact today?"

"Plot?" Zella asked with a cock to her head.

Flinch raised an eyebrow. "The complete redecoration of my

home—that I love, by the way, so thank you—seemed plot-like to me. I'm just wondering what's next for you two."

And so we sat, Zella and Flinch talking about sight-seeing opportunities and local places to visit. I chimed in when I could, but the longer I sat in front of that window, the colder my body became. The more exposed I felt. Watched.

"Locklyn," Zella said, recapturing my attention. "What are you—"

Flinch's phone rang, and he looked down at the screen with a frown. "That's Cutter. Give me five."

Without waiting for a reply, he rose to his feet and strode out the front door, phone already to his ear. I watched him through the window, noting how Rush paid particular attention to the man. How neither looked happy.

"What do you think that's all about?"

Zella huffed. "I'm more worried about what the hell is wrong with you. You've been in a daze this whole time."

I sat a little deeper in my chair and sighed. "This place makes me nervous."

"Why?"

"Last time, there was some creepy guy watching me from across the street. I can't get the picture of him out of my head."

Zella turned to look outside, her eyes tracking back and forth as if memorizing every inch. "I don't see anyone out there now."

"No, that's why it's stupid. I shouldn't feel so uncomfortable."

"You should feel however you feel. There's no morality tied to emotional response."

I sighed. "Quit being smart."

"Wish I could."

Flinch stormed into the coffee shop at that moment, looking completely harried. "We have to go. Now."

"What's wrong?" I asked, immediately hopping to my feet and readying myself to leave.

"I need to get to the club." Flinch took his cup back to the counter. Our iced drinks had been served in plastic, so Zella and I could take them with us. He grabbed my hand and pulled me along behind him, leading Zella and me out of the store. Meeting Rush on the sidewalk.

"Ready?" Rush said, typing on his phone with his thumbs at a speed that took me by surprise.

"What's going on?" I asked.

Flinch responded with a grumbled, "Club business."

That didn't sit right with me. As much as I knew bikers had a loyalty to their club, I didn't like him cutting me off from info like that. Info that likely had to do with the death of my father since that seemed to be the only club business lately.

"Done," Rush said before tucking his phone in his pocket. "Cutter is sending two guys to the house to babysit since he wants me involved."

"You're definitely needed." Flinch glanced my way, obviously distracted. "Let's go."

The ride home was tense and quiet, a long stretch of nothing but the sound of the road under the tires. By the time Flinch pulled into the driveway, two men on bikes had just turned onto the street ahead of us. Our babysitters had arrived.

"Hurry, girls." Flinch hopped out of the truck and rushed around to the passenger side, helping Zella and me out from that side. He hurried us onto the front porch and unlocked the door. "Stay in today, okay? Pool and backyard are fine, but don't leave the house. If these two even look at you wrong, text me."

"Got it," I said, crossing my arms and watching as Rush waited at the end of the driveway on his bike. "Just go."

"Let me get you inside." He followed us in, checking through the room quickly before returning to the living area, his boots just missing the rug I had so meticulously laid the day before. "I have to go."

"Yup."

He froze, looking me over from head to toe as if just now seeing me. "You okay?"

I shrugged, definitely not okay but too damn mad to admit it. "Fine."

He stared at me for a long, quiet moment before approaching slowly. Grabbing me by the upper arms and pulling me closer to him in a slow, calculated movement. As if I were a wild animal he hoped to tame.

"We okay?"

I stayed silent, unable to answer him. My anger growing deeper and brighter within me. Flinch finally sighed and, with his eyes locked on mine, murmured, "Zella, can you leave us alone for a second?"

"Absolutely." My best friend stepped into the kitchen, leaving me with Flinch in the living room.

"Tell me," he said once he had me alone.

"I could say the same to you."

He jerked back, brow furrowed and confusion clear on his face. "This is about the club business?"

I wanted to answer, I really did. But I was mad and couldn't let it go, so I stood in silence. After a while, Flinch growled, his hold on me growing tighter. His pull stronger. He yanked me right against his chest and leaned down to be able to speak directly into my ear in a soft, quiet voice.

"The brothers found Chiggy's truck. It's at some sort of compound and not abandoned, which means whoever moved it likely has a connection to the property." His hold on me tightened, my instinctual desire to step away from him thwarted. "Rush and I are needed to start surveillance on the area so we know what we're up against. We're hunting your dad's killer, Locklyn."

All anger flowed out of my body, quickly being replaced by a rush of fear. "Please be careful."

"I will. But I'll also avenge your dad's death. That's a fucking given." He dropped a huge kiss on me, tangling our tongues and groaning as he grabbed my ass. "For fuck's sake, just stay home so I know you're safe. Got it?"

I nodded, squeezing his arms before pushing him away. "Go. I'll stay here."

He grunted one last time then headed out the door, yelling something to the two bikers at the bottom of the porch that sounded an awful lot like a threat. Zella joined me at the window, both of us watching Flinch and Rush peel out onto the road with their engines roaring.

"You okay?" Zella asked, wrapping an arm around my shoulder and tugging me closer.

I was about to say yes, but I couldn't. The lie wouldn't come, so I answered with a question. One I was terrified to know the answer to. "What if they get to him like they did my dad?"

Zella sighed and shut the curtains on the window, sealing us inside. "I don't know, Locklyn. I really don't know."

Twenty-Three

I hated leaving Locklyn at home, but finding Chiggy's killer had to take priority. Her dad needed to be avenged, and my brothers were the ones craving that justice.

"Where?" I asked the second I walked into the conference room at the clubhouse. Cutter stood in the back of the room looking over a map spread out on the table. Someone had printed photographs as well—aerial shots that likely had been taken by a drone. The pictures showed a dirt lot with a shabby building at one corner. Chiggy's truck—those damned longhorns clear as fucking day on the front—sat in the lee of the building. Hidden from what I had to imagine was the road leading to the property.

There was no hiding from the Hellions.

"Truck's on a dirt patch of property out past the north highway spur. Diesel got aerial shots of the land and access points."

I moved in beside Cutter, looking over the map and the

pictures. Building the full image of the place in my head. "We coming in hot?"

Meaning were we riding up plain as day, engines roaring and guns blazing. Always an option, though rarely the smartest move. Not in this day and age. Humans had gotten camera crazy.

"No," Cutter said with a shake of his head. "There's cover in the hills behind the spot. I say we come in from the north and stake out the place a bit. Make sure we know what we're walking into. The last thing we need is a nest of vamps scattering like fucking roaches into the night."

Diesel grunted his approval and pointed to a spot on the map. "I can get the drone up from that vantage point. Fly it high enough so the bastards won't hear it and get a live feed."

"Live and vampires don't really go together," Rush said as he came striding in.

"Feed and vampires do, though," said Cutter, giving the potential new executive a once-over. "Everything good at Flinch's?"

I avoided the darted look Rush threw my way, the surprise at being asked that question by the prez one I shared. Not that I was going to show it.

"Yeah," Rush said. "Locklyn and Zella are all good. We've got Tex and Gator on their security detail for now."

"Good. That's good." Cutter stared at the table for a long, awkward moment, the energy around him agitated. Finally, he asked, "And Zella's good?"

Rush cocked his head, giving away his surprise again. "Definitely. Caffeinated and fed. I made sure of it."

Cutter nodded once, keeping his gaze on the map. "Good. So let's get ready to fuck up some vamps and bring Chiggy's truck home. Zed...load 'em up."

Zed stalked out of the room and turned toward the prez's office, likely heading for the armory. As the warlord, his job was to make sure we had what we needed should anything like this come up. And anything we needed came down to weaponry. Rifles, handguns, tactical gear, ammunition. All of it fell to Zed. Thank fuck the man had a solid hold on the industry and knew what was quality and what was crap. As a club, we were also lucky Mule understood the cost of quality munitions. There was no cutting corners at the Desert Hellions clubhouse.

I headed out with the rest of the brothers who would be moving into monitoring positions. Cutter stood off to the side staring at his phone, looking far more worried than I would have liked.

"You good, old man?" I settled in beside him, both of us leaning against a truck we didn't own.

He grunted and typed a quick message before returning his phone to his pocket. "Solid. Ready for this?"

"Always." I sighed and kicked my legs out, crossing my ankles and forcing myself to relax into the hard metal at my back. "So... Zella, huh?"

Cutter whipped his head in my direction, a low growl rumbling through his chest. "What about her?"

"Mated or just interested?"

He stood staring straight ahead for a long moment, the silence weighing heavy between us. Telling all his secrets without saying a word.

Finally, I nodded. "That's what I thought."

His sigh was one I understood, one I likely had given as well. The stealing of breath that came with the realization that the fates had just thrown a mate in your path. A perfect female solely for you. The sigh of a man whose life would never be the same.

"Got any advice?" he asked, voice quiet but rough.

"Fuck no," I said with a laugh. "I think I'm messing every-thing up."

"You smell like Locklyn, though. Can't be doing everything wrong."

The mood shifted, the anger I felt at myself growing hot under my skin. My shame growing.

"I bit her." I kept staring ahead as he turned my way once more. Unable to look a man I respected in the eye for the first time in my life. "I haven't told her about the mating, but I bit her."

He didn't yell, didn't remind me of how important a mating bite was. How sacred that moment should have been or how a nonconsensual bite could destroy a mating. He simply kept his voice quiet and low as he asked, "So, you feel her emotions now?"

"Yeah," I admitted. "She didn't bite me back so it's not really strong, but I can feel a shadow of them."

He sighed again, his gaze dropping to his shoes. "Women deserve more control of their lives. She's going to be pissed."

"Probably."

"And you deserve all that ire."

"Definitely."

"What are you going to do?"

I pushed off the truck as Zed approached with two duffels in his hands. "I'm going to fuck up some vampires, avenge her father's death, then come back and explain. Once I do that, I'll probably grovel for a few days."

Cutter huffed a laugh. "I'd give it a solid week. What's up, Zed?"

"Supplies." He handed Cutter one bag and me the second. "Specialized."

"Specialized?" I unzipped the bag and looked inside. "Okay, yeah. Specialized."

Because no human target would require the level of firepower in that bag. Focus being on the *fire*.

"How many flamethrowers did you have hidden in that war

room?" Cutter asked, obviously noting the same thing I did.

"Enough to take on a colony of vamps."

"Solid." Cutter threw the bag over his shoulder and headed for his ride. "Let's light this candle."

I hoisted my bag and turned for my bike, knowing the sooner we got this attack over with, the sooner I could get back to Locklyn.

The sooner I could explain what a fucked-up thing I did.

And the sooner I could beg her for forgiveness.

LOCKLYN

Zella could fall asleep anywhere. Being an autoimmune warrior meant she suffered from some pretty intense fatigue. I knew this —had always recognized it—but there were times when her ability to simply drop into REM shocked me.

Like when I turned around while plating dinner and found her fast asleep with her head on the kitchen table.

"Dinner for one, apparently." I covered her plate and set it in the microwave so she could warm it once she woke up. I also left her alone. The one thing Zella needed the most was sleep, so trying to get her to move to the bed or make her more comfortable was worse than letting her sleep on the table. I had learned that one over the years as her roommate. So long as she had ended up in a safe location, the best thing for me to do was allow her to rest.

I settled on the couch with my own dinner, but I didn't begin to eat. The energy around me buzzed, the worry for Flinch and his brothers burning a hole in my gut. And my neck—the bite mark Flinch had left on me. It practically zinged. I had no idea how to explain the sensation that came from that mark, but it comforted me for sure. Like a reminder that Flinch was alive and safe and coming home eventually.

A knock at the front door had me scrambling to my feet, plate of food immediately forgotten as I set it on the coffee table I'd picked out for the space. I hurried across the soft rug to the front door, peeking outside before unlocking it and pulling it open.

"Yeah?"

One of the wolf shifters on the porch looked me up and down with a bland and yet almost violent expression. "You good in here?"

I had to think about it for a second because his tone—the gruffness—and his worry were so misaligned. "Uh, yeah. We're good."

"Let me see the other one."

"Excuse me?"

He looked past me, frowning. "Cutter's girl. I need to see her."

I stood there stunned, unable to respond. Cutter's what? And who? Thankfully, Zella must have heard the commotion because her soft voice sounded from behind me.

"What's going on?"

The man at the door directed his gaze over my shoulder to where she had to be standing. "You good?"

"I think so. Are we good, Lock?"

"Yeah, we're fine. Everything is fine." I frowned up at him. "Are you two good?"

He huffed and turned, ignoring my question. "Yell if you need us. Otherwise, one of us will be back to check on you both in an hour."

I closed the door once he settled onto the porch step, turning slowly to find Zella looking as surprised and concerned as I felt.

"What was that?" she asked, her brow furrowed deep.

"I have no idea."

"The other guys watching you haven't checked on you like

that?"

"Never."

"Weird."

"Definitely. As was him calling you Cutter's girl."

Zella stared right at me, not flinching in the slightest. Giving nothing away. A sure sign there was *something* going on.

Something she hadn't told me about.

A thought that made my heart lurch a little and my stomach tighten. "Oh."

She shook her head. "Don't go getting all excited here. It's not like that."

"Not worth talking about?"

"There's nothing to talk about...yet." She approached me slowly, holding eye contact, a slow smile spreading across her face. "I think he likes me, though."

And that right there was when the penny dropped. The facts of the situation my presence in Mesa had exposed her to. The... creatures that she had known about since my dad had told her, but maybe not understood. Maybe not realized how many of them were sniffing around. "You know he's...one of them."

"A biker? Yeah. I know."

I was such an idiot—letting her come into this world and not warning her. Not preparing her the way my dad had prepared me. Not protecting her. She knew Chiggy had been a wolf shifter, but did she understand he wasn't the only one? Did she have any clue we'd been hanging around a pack for days?

"He's more than that," I said, that clenching in my stomach growing stronger, making me feel nauseated. The sudden floral aroma infiltrating the house not helping in the least. "They're all more than that."

"More than what? What are you talking about?"

But I didn't get a chance to tell her because at that moment, someone started pounding on the back door.

Twenty-Four

The scent of death and rot practically permeated the ground. It hung heavy in the air and lingered over every bit of brush or desert flower we came upon, confirming our suspicions. There were vampires in our midst.

"I hate dealing with these motherfuckers," Rush mumbled as he picked apart some sort of stick he'd found.

"We aren't dealing with them yet." I crossed my ankles, the shade from the truck behind me growing longer and deeper as the night began to fall. "Anyone green enough to be assuming they're like storybook vamps and only come out at night?"

Cutter huffed what sounded like a sarcastic laugh, looking over the crew with a hard gaze. "If only. They'd be easier to deal with if the fuckers followed their own canon. But no—we get to deal with sun-loving vampires."

"Wonder if they sit around bitching that we don't only turn into wolves on the full moon," Diesel said, sticking close to Cutter like Rush kept close to me. Both men not new to running jobs with us but inexperienced when it came to the walking bloodsuckers we were about to destroy.

"Wrong canon." Cutter grabbed his binoculars and peered toward the barn hiding Chiggy's truck. "Werewolves turn due to the moon phases. We're shifters—different breed."

"No shit, but that doesn't mean they accept the species differentiation." Diesel shot me a quick smirk, knowingly goading our current commander. "They could be pissed we're not all weres."

Cutter nodded once and brought down the binoculars, giving his usual partner a flat-eyed stare. "They could be, though it would be their own damn fault for throwing shifters and weres in the same group. Not like we're out here lumping vampires and incubi together and expecting them to act the same."

Diesel grinned. "Fucking incubi have the life. Sex, chaos, more sex, a little bloodsucking thrown into the mix. Never having to experience fleas."

"You've had fleas?" I stared, unable to even comprehend that possibility. "My brother, bathe thyself."

"You've never had fleas?" Banger asked as he sidled over, the old man looking tough and ready to rumble.

"Not fucking once." And I never would. That shit seemed torturous.

"Could you imagine only shifting once a month and having no control over it?" Rush asked. He rubbed at his chest, his face contorting as if in physical pain. "That would suck."

A growl sounded inside my mind, low and vicious in its intensity. As if even the idea of keeping my inner beast locked up was any sort of option.

"My wolf would rip me apart." That seemed to appease the fucker as he quieted once more. I could still feel him, though. Still sense him watching the world through my eyes. He was a wolf ready for a fight. Craving it. But he was going to have to have some patience. I nodded toward the house in the distance. "How long are we going to wait on them?"

Cutter looked toward Zed and Mule, who had appeared from out of nowhere as if walking away from the house. The two men heading right for us, obviously ready to give us the lowdown from their recon.

"Just waiting on him," Cutter said with a nod toward Zed.

The warlord glanced at me before focusing on the old man. "Truck looks workable to me and Mule. We won't know for sure until we try to start it, but it doesn't look like they tore it apart."

"See a way off the property for it?"

Mule pointed behind us. "Straight through the front gate. That's the only way."

"Who's driving her?" I asked, wanting to make sure I understood the plan.

"I am." Mule crossed his arms over his chest. "I've got the most experience with that truck. I can run it."

Facts—the man had been Chiggy's personal mechanic for a lot of years. He also had a penchant for fast cars, drag racing, and all-around tearing it up with anything that ran with a combustion engine. He'd even taken a few cars to the salt flats over the years. He'd likely outrun anything on the road so long as that truck's engine held on. And being that he'd likely been the last one to work on said engine, he had the most knowledge of how far to push it.

Cutter nodded his approval, his expression strong and fierce but tense. As he should have been. "So you need cover from us."

"Yes."

I shrugged, stretching and cracking my neck for show. "You'll have it. Get the truck back to the clubhouse. No matter what."

Mule gave me a chin nod. "No matter what."

"You ready to go?" Cutter asked, looking more toward me than Zed for some reason.

"Fuck yeah. Let's get this shit done." I whistled low and long for the rest of the guys, jerking my head in the direction of the house once I had their attention. "It's go time."

Everyone rose to their feet and began collecting their weapons. No discussion, no need for further directions. This wouldn't be the first time we'd infiltrated a domicile as a team; it wouldn't even be the first vampire nest some of us had dealt with.

It would be the first time I'd put myself in danger since finding my mate, though.

"You good?" Zed asked in a quiet voice as if he could read my thoughts.

I nodded, my focus torn. Part of me worried about Locklyn and wanting her as far away from the fuckers who had murdered her dad as possible. The low buzz of our connection seemed solid, though. No sharp emotional swings, no big feelings in any direction. I had to assume that meant she was fine, which meant I had time to get some work done. "Let's eradicate this nest."

Cutter stepped in beside me, looking out over the house with a focused expression. His energy a real close match to mine.

"Thinking about Locklyn?"

I ducked my chin once, making my acquiescence subtle. "Thinking about Zella?"

He kept his eyes on the house, but his jaw tightened. "Let's get this shit done. I hate these dead motherfuckers."

Which was about as much of an answer as I could expect from him in that moment.

Our forward crew crept onto the actual vamp lands with weapons drawn, the secondary line following closely. A total of twelve men ready to take down the slightest threat. None came. Even once Cutter and Zed had mounted the porch, the entire compound remained still and silent. Instead of busting in, we surrounded the house in intervals close enough to keep an eye on one another, everyone peeking into windows or looking for access points. Still no movement on the inside, but that didn't mean shit. They could have been lying in wait for us, which meant we kept to the plan.

Once we had the house surrounded, Zed gave the signal to move in. The idea had been to create immediate chaos, every man busting inside by whatever access point he had closest to him. To act quickly and without care for noise or damage. I broke through a window with Rush right on my tail, both of us landing with a roll before jumping to our feet and immediately assessing the room around us.

"Door," Rush yelled as I yanked the door all the way open to look behind the slab.

"Clear." I rushed through the empty space and into the hallway, gun raised and eyes forward. "South bedroom and hallway secure."

Cutter answered from the other side of the house. "North bedroom, bathroom, and hallway secure."

Other men yelled from their positions—kitchen, clear. Utility room, clear. Living room, clear.

All fucking clear.

We met in the middle, all of us converging on the living area. The empty living area.

"What the fuck is this?" I kept looking around, expecting something. Anything. Some sort of proof the vamps had at least lived there at one point. Anger and irritation brewing inside me because we had been ready to kill these fuckers, and they had just...disappeared. Not good.

"They've moved on." Cutter lowered his weapon, his words coming out with a growl that gave away his irritation. "Check every closet and cupboard for things left behind. Once done, we'll move on to the barn."

Four of us tore through the house, opening doors and

cubbies, yanking out drawers and busting out medicine cabinets. We trashed every possible hiding space we could think of, even tearing down the attic access panel to investigate that sweltering space. We found nothing. Not a single shred of evidence that anyone—let alone vampires—had ever resided in the home.

"Clear," I said as soon as we'd finished our final search, growing more agitated by the second. "Let's move out."

We exited in a stream through the front door with Zed in the lead. Once again, we crept across the property with our guns drawn, ready for a fight. Tension growing with every step. No enemy assault came, though, which was almost worse than if someone had opened fire on us. The silence, the lack of activity, the nothingness... We had come ready for a gunfight to what was beginning to look like an abandoned plot of land in the middle of nowhere. Where the fuck had they gone?

Once at the barn doors, Zed threw hand signals to lay out how the breach would go. Two men would open the swinging doors, the rest would stay back out of the way for two seconds then be first over the threshold. So long as they weren't lined up with their own weapons drawn, we would make it in. If they were, well...

"Stay the fuck out of direct fire," Cutter hissed at me as if reading my mind. I signaled that I'd heard him then waited for Zed to start us off.

Without a warning, the warlord had the doors swung out and open, giving us full access to the interior of the barn. The seemingly empty interior.

"*Go! Go! Go!*" Cutter rushed in first, leading the way into the space and immediately searching out every shadow and corner in case the enemy was hiding. Aiming his weapon in sharp, precise movements meant to verify there was no threat around us. Once again, we ended up in an empty building. Not a single vamp.

"Where the fuck are they?" Rush asked as he slammed what

appeared to be an empty plastic barrel to the floor. "I thought we had them here."

Zed shrugged, his voice tight and anger strong as he said, "They were on-site less than twenty-four hours ago."

"They knew we were coming. They had to." I crept through the building, keeping an eye on the hayloft above. My instincts screaming that this was the right place. This was the vampire nest, not the house. The smell, the energy—this building was their command post. We had just gotten to it a little later than we needed to.

Cutter stayed right behind me as if he, too, felt the energy of the place. As if he understood this would have been the site of the battle had we arrived in time. His movements stayed sharp, his eyes constantly sweeping the space—every corner checked, every shadow identified. Our wolves were on high alert even though it sure as fuck seemed as if we didn't need to be.

After clearing the entire main floor, I made eye contact with Cutter and jerked my chin toward the ladder. He nodded once, slinking toward the vertical death trap. There really was no way to climb a straight ladder with your gun drawn, so I mounted the steps only a few feet behind him and hurried up. Both of us moving as quickly and quietly as possible. The shifters below also went silent, watching us with their guns at the ready in case they were needed.

The hayloft had no hay in place, but there were signs of life. Tables, chairs, a chalkboard with shadows of writing on it, and more surge protectors plugged into one another than I had ever seen. They snaked across the floor, linking from one to the next. All with little glowing lights indicating they had power.

"What is this?" Cutter asked in a whisper as he kicked one of the surge protectors. "Ten plugs each, one taken up by the next device, fifteen devices... They were charging 136 phones?"

"Doubtful. No nest is that big." I moved past the devices and toward the chalkboard, moving it out of the way. "Back here."

The footsteps of the other guys joining us in the loft registered as my eyes started putting together the scene before me. Under a low eave of the barn lay a table with documents and pictures strewn about it. No, not strewn. I moved closer, trying to make sense of what at first appeared to be a mess but wasn't. Those pictures and documents were in a pattern, laid out intentionally and with care. This had been a planning room.

"Chiggy," Rush said, pointing to the far corner. He was right —a picture of Chiggy lay with a red X over it. Another printed picture of his truck sat in a circle to the left.

"It's like a fucked-up game of Risk." I crept around the side of the table opposite Chiggy's picture, looking at the rest of the printouts. "Motherfucker."

Zed hurried to my side and growled as he took in the same thing I was. Pictures of the clubhouse, of each member, of our bikes and cages. Our houses. Mostly from above.

"Drone shots," Diesel said, seemingly hitting the same conclusion I had just seconds before me. "They must have had a fuck-ton of drones flying to get all of these. Flying high, too. We would have noticed those cheap-ass drones that buzz like a beehive."

Surge protectors, so many outlets, all the electricity needed. They hadn't been charging their phones—they'd been charging the soldiers in their aerial army.

"They've been monitoring us for a long time." Cutter moved a picture of the clubhouse, his finger pushing the edge along the table. "And we had no fucking clue."

"It's a puzzle." Diesel looked over the pictures again, his brow furrowing. "They wanted us to find this or else they would have taken it all with the rest of their shit. It has to be a puzzle."

We all turned back to the pictures, circling the tables and

frowning at the chalkboards as every man began trying to figure out what the vamps had been doing. Why they had left so much behind for us to find. Why they had ever even started watching our club.

"The set. It's not complete," Zed said, pointing toward the pictures. "Every man's accounted for on here but one. Where's Flinch's shit?"

"He's over here." Banger caught my eye and pointed from the other side of the table. "You got something to tell us, man?"

I moved to his side to look over the section of the puzzle he indicated and felt my breath leave my body. There right next to the pictures of me, my house, and my bike sat a picture of Locklyn. They also had a shot of my truck connected to her, as if they knew she was the one who'd been driving it lately. I recognized the location of Locklyn's pic—the coffee shop we had just gone to in town—but the clothing and her location inside the shop were wrong for our visit.

"Shit." Rush leaned past me, staring at the picture. "Wait, that's not our trip. She went there with the prospect, right? He let some vamp fucker get pictures of her?"

His words made sense, but my brain couldn't process them. All I could see was that picture of my mate, how exposed she had been, how close they had gotten to her. The truck, the house, her... They had been watching, and I'd been too caught up in my mating to her to realize it. I had fucked up so hard.

"What the fuck is with all the roses?" Diesel asked, his words penetrating my haze but not hitting hard enough for me to care. "There are boxes of the things over here."

Roses that had been left around us for days. Roses that had been sent to the clubhouse on the night of Chiggy's burning. Roses that had seemed so out of place and yet innocuous.

Fucking bastards had been sending messages we hadn't picked up on.

Cutter growled low and deep, his claws gripping the table. I met his eyes, recognizing his wolf. Knowing he saw mine as well. Both of us barely hanging on to our control as the house of cards began to fall. I glanced down again at the picture of my beautiful —and very human—mate and noticed a string leading from her pic to one of Zella. A picture with another string leading toward the one of Cutter but not connecting, as if they hadn't yet figured the two out but knew they were together occasionally.

"Holy fuck," Rush growled, shaking his head. "Flinch, they were there..."

He pointed to a picture at the head of the table. This one had been taken at the house. Zella sat in the hammock by my pool with one leg hanging down, while Locklyn floated in the water. Both outside and exposed for anyone with a fucking drone or a long-range lens to see. The fucking vamps had gotten close—far too close—and had identified both women as targets. Which meant they'd been on or near my property within the last two days.

And we had left Locklyn and Zella there together.

"Get to Flinch's, now!" Cutter hollered just before I shifted. Someone else yelled about grabbing my phone and calling Gator, but it didn't matter. No one could save my mate but me, so I had to haul ass.

My wolf took control in a snap, jumping from the hayloft to the dirt floor below then racing for the door. A roar met my ears as I scrambled for purchase on the hard earth outside, but I didn't pay it any mind. All I could think about was Locklyn in that house. What would happen if the vamps showed up. How little she could do to protect herself from them. This wasn't some teenage romance novel where vampires sparkled and turned humans into vigilante heroes. This was the real world—those vampires would suck her blood out of her body, leave her dead and dry without a thought in the world for the loss. They would rip her apart to share her pieces among themselves.

Motherfuckers would destroy her for a goddamned snack.

I ran hell for leather for a good half mile, which gave Mule a chance to catch up to me in Chiggy's truck with Zed in the passenger seat. The warlord didn't try to stop me or slow me down, instead giving me a head nod before Mule slammed his foot down on that gas and took off in a cloud of dust. The truck was fucking fast, but I would beat them because I had no need to stick to actual roads. In fact, as soon as I hit the highway, I veered off the road and headed for the desert, knowing it was a big, open wasteland between my location and my house. Nothing but open land and rocks. Lots of open land and rocks. Miles' worth.

I had made it past the first patch of scrub bushes a few miles off the road when two more wolves caught up to me. I recognized both—Cutter and Rush. They raced at my heels, all three of us beelining it for where we knew the women to be. A pack in its own right heading in to fight for their most vulnerable members.

I could only hope we wouldn't be too late.

But as we hit the slopes of the hills, a tug on the bond to my mate had me almost tripping. Had my steps stumble mid-stride. Motherfucker, the jolt of fear that blasted through to me had me yipping a cry unlike any my wolf had ever made. My mate was in trouble.

I ran faster.

Twenty-Five

"Everything okay?"

I nodded, trying hard to calm the way my heart had started racing when I'd heard the pounding on the door. Thankfully, it hadn't been anyone to really be afraid of. "Yeah, we're fine."

Gator, one of our two guards for the night, looked over Zella then gave a single chin raise. "Things are quiet. If you want to go out back for a swim, you can do that."

"That sounds nice." Zella shrugged my way. "What do you think, Lock?"

"Sure. I could go for some cooling off."

Gator hunkered back outside while Zella and I retreated to separate spaces so we could slip into our swimsuits. Flinch kept the clean pool towels in the back room, so I ended up there first, with Zella following quickly behind me.

"You ready?" I asked. She nodded, so I opened the door.

And then I froze.

Something about stepping outside—about that open sky and endless desert behind the house—felt ominous. It felt oppressive. I could almost hear the laugh from the nightmares that had brought me to the desert. Could almost feel that same negative energy wrapping around me.

And why did the breeze cutting across the patio smell like roses?

"You okay?" Zella laid a hand on my shoulder, pulling me out of the dreamlike state I had found myself in.

I huffed a laugh and shook my head, fighting hard to regulate my breathing because nothing in that moment made sense. We were at Flinch's house with two men watching over us. We were safe.

"Yeah, sorry," I said, shoving down my anxiety. "Just distracted for a second."

In an act of normalcy that felt almost like a mirage, we stepped outside into the hot night air, both of us laying our towels on a chaise before diving into the pool. No slow walk in for us—Zella had water therapy twice a week, and I would rather face the blunt, cold shock quickly instead of dragging it out. Plus, I thought the water might wash away the last of the reservations I felt about being outside since they didn't make sense. Gator stood off to the side—not quite out of sight but definitely not impeding our fun, and certainly not being a creeper and leering at us. I appreciated the effort he took to disappear into the shadows.

"This is nice," Zella said, settling in against the side of the pool and kicking her legs out in a modified sort of float. "I could do this every day."

"Your bones would love it."

"My bones need this water to be about fifteen degrees warmer for love, but the infatuation is real."

I laughed and found my own spot along the side, mimicking her position. "How have you been feeling?"

Zella paused, the small moment of quiet a sign that she needed to put her words together in a palatable way. Her autoimmune arthritis left her tired and hurting more often than not, but she didn't complain. Never laid out all the ways her own body betrayed her on the daily. That pause was as close to a truth about the level of pain she had been feeling than I would ever get in words.

"I'm okay," she finally said, turning her head and giving me a small smile. "Stress is hard on me, and I was stressed when you were out here alone. It's better now that I can see your face and know you're all right."

"I'm sorry I added stress to your life."

"Don't apologize. It's my fault, not yours."

Lies, but no way would she ever tell me different. "I'm really glad you're here."

"Me too." She shivered and looked off into the distance, something in the sudden change of her posture making my heart begin to race. "It's sort of creepy out here with nothing around."

I followed her gaze, eyeing the mountains in the distance. Noting the vast nothingness between us and them. Not truly nothing—there was desert vegetation along the way. Shrubs and cacti and tall grasslike plants that moved in the wind. That anyone could technically hide behind.

"Yeah. It's a bit secluded." But now that Zella had pointed out the creepiness, I had no way to avoid it. Every time the wind blew those grasses, I darted my eyes in that direction. Every bug buzzing and twig snapping, I jumped. And the entire time, I stood in the pool and felt someone else's eyes on me.

"Sorry," Zella said, stealing my attention back and giving me another small smile. "I have a feeling I just completely freaked you out."

"No, I'm just..." I tried to find the words to explain how I felt —tired, anxious, nervous, scared—but none of them quite matched the sensations and instincts running through my body. Something felt off about the night, and that fact led me to feel something more than fear.

I felt like prey being hunted.

"Maybe we should—" Before Zella could finish her sentence, a sound reached my ears that had me frozen in place. It was a laugh, one I had heard a hundred times over. One that had haunted my dreams for weeks. One that had brought me out to Arizona in the first place.

"No," I said almost automatically. "Zella, we need to go."

Without question, she turned and pulled herself up onto the pool edge. Climbing out with much more grace and speed than I would have expected. Once on her feet, she held out a hand and pulled me up behind her, not asking why. Not waiting for more info. A good thing, considering I didn't have anything more than what could have been a trick of the wind.

Gator appeared behind Zella, looking me up and down as I reached for a towel.

"What's wrong?"

Before I could answer, his phone began to ring. From the table under the patio, so did Zella's. Both adding auditory chaos to a moment of pure stress.

Gator turned his back to answer his phone while Zella jogged over to grab hers. She answered on speaker, Cutter's voice an immediate addition to the night.

"Get inside. Right now. No matter what you're doing, get your asses inside and stay there. We're on our way."

Zella's amber eyes caught mine, likely reflecting the fear I felt, and then we were in motion. Gator must have gotten the same message from someone else because he began growling out orders for us to get inside and lock the doors. We rushed in through the back, Zella continuing through the kitchen on her way to presumably make sure the front door was locked. I turned to slam the back one, making the mistake of looking up through the open doorway one more time.

There, just past the pool where Zella and I had been swimming, stood the man from outside the coffee shop. The one who had been staring at me. The one who had made me feel so uncomfortable and out of control. That pale skin and those long fingers suddenly just a few yards from me, emitting that rosy smell that I had caught on the breeze. He stood close enough for me to really see him. To notice the almost waxiness of his skin, to catch the slight gray tone to it. His bony face looked off, his expression one of almost lust. And he still stared seemingly into my soul, but he also wore a smile this time. One that sent ice down my spine. One that meant I had been right—I'd felt like prey, and I was.

He'd been hunting me.

"Lock, close it!" Zella shoved me to the side to slam the door as Gator shifted, leaving her frozen in the doorway just as I had been. This time because of Gator's explosion into wolf form. There was no stripping off of his clothes or pause in his human form. He went from a man standing on the pool deck to a huge, snarling wolf with pieces of fabric falling all around him like some sort of textile confetti in a split second.

Zella screamed and stumbled backward as I rushed forward, the sight of the wolf clearing my head enough for me to act. I finally slammed the door and engaged the lock before grabbing her arm and pulling her so we were face-to-face.

"Wolves, remember?" I gave her a slight shake, both of us breathing hard and clinging to each other. "Are you okay with what you just saw?"

"Yeah, I think so. I just..." She shook her head gently and let out a breath. "That was more. It was so much *more* than I had expected. He was a man and then not. And the fabric. His clothes, like...exploded."

Out of all the things to have your brain lock on to in a moment of pure panic, that might have been the best because it was the most harmless.

"Yeah, they do that. They usually strip if it's a planned shift to their wolf. I think the presence of an enemy had Gator in a rush." I sighed, my brain spinning with everything that had happened in the last two minutes. Nearly laughing at the heaviness of knowing we were under attack and there would soon be lots of wolves fighting for us. What sort of life had I fallen into? "Did you see the guy across the pool?"

"Mr. Tall, Dark, and Looks Like a Literal Corpse? Yeah. Noticed him."

"I think he might be the one who killed my dad. That laugh I heard in the pool—it was the same as in the dreams that brought me out here. Even if he's not the one, the wolves are likely going to fight him. Showing up like this—it's a sign of an attack. They won't let that slide." I waited, wanting her to say something. When I got nothing, I finally cocked my head. "You good?"

"Good is not the word I would use." She spun and strode through the kitchen, calling over her shoulder without even pausing, "Come on. If we're under attack, we should be wearing more than just these wet bikinis. Otherwise, we'll be nothing but typical horror movie side characters."

I wanted to say something back, but she was right—running around in bikinis while paranormal creatures battled outside your door would definitely put us in horror movie side character territory. We couldn't go down like that.

"Yeah, okay. I'm coming."

But as I left my post near the back door, as I crept through the kitchen as if not to awaken someone in the room, growls and snarls and some weird screaming noises enveloped the house. The sounds ugly and chill-inducing. Terrifying.

"Locklyn, hurry up!"

I couldn't argue with her. If the noisemakers were coming inside, we needed to be prepared. And in that moment, prepared meant at the very least wearing pants.

Twenty-Six

Flinch

We raced across the desert, house in sight, listening to what sounded like the vampires singing an off-pitch battle hymn. The screeching wails of a vampire attack were the stuff of nightmares, and the sound coming from my own house—the place where my fated mate likely stood—sent ice straight into my soul. My wolf hated the way the noise vibrated inside his ears, but he ran faster anyway, knowing his mate was also listening to it. Knowing she had to be scared. Knowing we were the only hope she had of survival.

And taking comfort in the low buzz of our connection to her coming to life the closer we got to the house.

I hit the pavement in my backyard before any of my brothers, pounding the two steps to the pool edge before pushing off with my hind legs and leaping. The two vamps on the opposite side of the pool looked up in time to see me flying at them, both hissing as they moved forward as if to stop me. There would be no stopping me.

Cutter and I landed almost at the exact same moment, both of us immediately lunging for the vampires. Mine grabbed me by the pelt and hissed in my ear, the creature close enough to bite but not strong enough to bend my body to his will. I took advantage of his nearness—twisting around and crushing his skull in one quick chomp. A putrid liquid filled my mouth and ran down my throat, but I didn't let up. Not until he stopped fighting. Until he lay even more dead than he had been before. I'd dealt with vampires in the past—there weren't a lot of ways to kill them, being that they were walking around dead already, but beheading seemed to do the trick. So did setting them on fire, but we were in a time crunch and flames would draw attention. Biting the nasty fuckers would have to do, even if it meant filling my gullet with their vile rot.

Once my vamp lay still and no longer in one piece, I swiped his head across the patio like a soccer ball and looked for more prey. Cutter and Gator had their own vamps they were tangling with, both seemingly winning, so I left them to it and edged toward the house. I took out two more vamps as I fought my way toward the door, pinning another motherfucker to the concrete for Rush to chomp out of existence. I didn't hurry—not really, at least. I kept a solid forward motion toward the door. My backyard looked like a bowling alley for all the heads rolling, and I was all for helping my brothers take out as many vamps as I could so long as I kept feeling the connection to Locklyn. That buzz meant she was alive and likely okay inside the house. I had trust in our connection.

I was almost to the door, fighting off the last three vamps between me and where my mate had to be, when a high-pitched yelp from behind me caught my attention. I turned just enough to watch as three vamps ripped the front leg off Tex's wolf before they tossed him into the pool. My growls increased, my absolute rage at these fuckers targeting us exploding within me. They were learning—it was no longer a one-on-one battle. They were attacking in twos and threes, which meant our advantage had lessened. Fuck that.

Before I could even attempt to head for the pool to help Tex, five brothers jumped into the fray. Zed led the way, attracting the attention of the handful of vamps who had all been about to go into the water after our injured brother. That move meant Tex had a moment to get away, which he did as best he could. Cutter and Diesel also pounced, breaking up the last group of vamps to give Gator time to shift and get his human ass into the pool to help Tex.

"C'mon, buddy," Gator called, tugging his best friend across the water. "It's going to hurt like a bitch, but I need you to shift so I can deal with this."

Tex answered with a low mewling noise, something that spoke to the beast inside me. I took two steps toward the pool, fascinated, staring as fur was replaced by skin and my brother began to squeal from the horrible pain of shifting while injured so badly. I was about ready to shift and go help Gator get Tex out of the water, but a thump on my back and the pulling of one of my legs refocused my attention on my own fight and sent a newfound jolt of adrenaline through my system.

The burning sear of claws ripping through my flesh also helped me refocus on staying alive and fighting my way past these fuckers.

I reared back and managed to rip the head off the vamp trying to claw through my midsection as my anger fueled me. As rage pulsed through my body at these bastards thinking they could come in and destroy our club. They had taken Chiggy from us and had tried their damnedest to take Tex, too. They needed to be destroyed so they never got their claws on another brother.

The next vampire dumb enough to try to take me out went

down faster than the ones before, my claws slicing through the rotting flesh of his neck with ease. Two down, I turned toward the third that I had almost lost track of. He had joined in a party trying to overtake Zed, piling four vamps on one wolf. Thankfully, Cutter and Diesel hopped into that fray, and the three took out the vampires without another injury, all fighting as a unit. My brothers had learned right along with the vampires —no one was fighting alone. It was pretty much two wolves to three vampires, and the wolves were winning every fight.

Knowing my brothers would be able to take care of the remaining vamps, I turned back toward the house, catching sight of a huge motherfucker about to crawl through my laundry room window. Going for my mate. I snarled and leaped, knocking him to the ground with my paw. This one fought harder than the rest, his size giving him quite an advantage over his emaciated brethren. I had no idea if this was the bastard who had killed Chiggy—there would be no way to tell unless one of them stopped fucking screeching and used their words—but I fought him as if he was. I battled the creeper hard, taking swipes along the way but never backing down. Another vamp joined in, practically straddling my hind end, but Rush leaped from wherever the fuck he had been and knocked the bastard to the ground before disappearing into the fray around us.

I fought, I growled, I herded that vampire away from my house and my mate, and in the end, I won. The body fell to the concrete pool deck without fanfare, his neck crunching as I used my claws to rip off his head. I took one moment to glance around, to check my team's sixes, to figure out where the next fight would come from, but all seemed almost calm. The chaos had settled because the vampires had begun to retreat, disappearing in the desert night. Cowards.

"Let's get some help here," Gator yelled, obviously also recognizing an ebb in the attack. My brothers began shifting human, Zed jumping into the pool to help Gator pull out Tex. More brothers moved to help, jumping out of the pink water right after him. They rolled Tex's body onto the wet concrete, bringing his dismembered arm to sit right alongside them. My poor brother writhed naked on the ground, biting his lip but managing to scream out his pain anyway. I had a feeling there would be no fixing his injury, but I didn't have time to deal with that. Right at that moment, the bond between Locklyn and me zinged to life. No, zinged was the wrong word.

It set my soul on fire in all the wrong ways, forcing me to shift human in a sudden and painful way.

"Fuck," I cried, body curled almost in half from the shock of the shift. Looking up and staring at the house, unable to move for a second. Fighting off my own wolf as pain consumed me from within. My beast raged inside me, pushing against every bit of willpower my human possessed, demanding I shift back even though that wasn't what I wanted in the moment. But what I wanted didn't matter to him. As he took control, as he wrestled away my free will and my body began to morph without my permission, I screamed for the only person who might be able to help, the single word garbled and rough from the constriction on my vocal cords.

"Cutter!"

The man appeared at my side, face expressionless but eyes nearly glowing with a suppressed rage I assumed we were both feeling. Rage and knowing—Cutter had been in my position before.

"Cutter," I growled, the word more vibration than anything else. My wolf wanting to howl instead of speak.

Without warning, Cutter threw a punch that connected with my cheek and nearly knocked me off my feet.

"Better?"

I shook off the pain of the hit and growled, rising to my full height. Or as full as I could, seeing as how my wolf had begun our shift and I was stuck halfway between human and beast. "What the fuck, old man?"

"Your wolf is an asshole—rein him in." He looked toward the house, obviously distracted. "How's your mate?"

His question refocused me, reminded me of the burn through the connection to my girl. Of the reason I had shifted and why my wolf had wanted to take back control. I took off without answering him, nearly ripping the back door off the hinges with my claw-tipped fingers. Fuck, I needed to get control of my beast, but I couldn't focus on him right then.

"Lock!? Locklyn!"

No answer. The connection vibrated, the burn less but still there. Fur sprouted on my arms as I moved through the kitchen, but I fought against the shift. Sensing that I needed to find her in my human form. My wolf could kick some vampire ass once I knew our girl was okay. Until then, I needed two legs, not four.

"Where are they?" Cutter asked as soon as he came slinking into my kitchen, but I didn't answer him. Couldn't. My house reeked of vampires but also something else. Something familiar and yet completely out of place. I couldn't take the time to figure out what, though, because the overwhelming smell of burned flesh had caught my nose, and my wolf refused to lose focus. I was both furious and terrified—what if we were too late? No, couldn't be. That connection was alive, which meant Locklyn was as well. But that didn't mean she wasn't hurt.

I raced through the rest of the kitchen and into the living room, pounding down the hall to the bedroom door. The closed bedroom door. I kicked the slab of wood open without a thought, snarling and growling with Cutter right by my side. Both of us ready to fight.

But the sight before me had me frozen in place, and the only thought that entered my mind came falling out of my mouth.

"What the fuck are you doing here?"

LOCKLYN

I stood in the house, listening to the horrific screeching coming from the backyard, and I wished for Flinch. Prayed he would make it to us in time. That he would both protect us and be protected from those things outside.

"Are you okay?" Zella stood near the bedroom door, looking far calmer than any person should, considering the situation.

"I'm okay. How are you?"

"So very not okay." She spun as something crashed against the outside wall, her eyes going wide. "What are we going to do?"

I shook my head, feeling really stupid for not having an answer. "We wait for Flinch."

"And if he doesn't show up in time?"

I had no answer for that.

Because if the creatures out there somehow got inside...

We would be dead.

The screeching built, the rumble of growls soon added into the mix. The sound of wolves calmed me somewhat, made my fear more manageable. The louder the growling, the more I believed Flinch had arrived. And when I heard a slam and footsteps through the living room, I was absolutely certain he had come to rescue us.

I had never been so wrong.

The door opened inward, a simple act followed by a not-so-simple visage. A man appeared in the opening, one who didn't belong here. An average yet fit man wearing a bright-red tracksuit and an absolutely terrifying smile.

"Oh, how delightful. I see I found the party."

Zella moved closer to me, both of us reaching for the other as subtly as possible.

"Who are you?" I asked.

His smile grew, the skin around his mouth moving and stretching in ways that were wholly inhuman.

"My name is Adam, and I've been waiting to meet you, daughter of the one known as Wolf Chiggy."

The mention of my dad made my blood run cold. "Are you the one who killed him?"

He shrugged, obviously trying to look casual even as something in his eyes gave away his predatory nature. "No, dear. I am not the villain in his story. From what I understand, Chiggy was in the way. His death was nothing more than clearing the road."

Zella grabbed me by the elbow, holding me in place beside her as my blood ran like fire through my veins.

"Nothing more than..." I huffed a breath, practically pushing my weight into my heels to keep from running up on the guy. "He was loved."

Adam pinned me with his gaze, cooling my ire immediately. His expression filling me with dread.

"There is no love, sweet Locklyn. Only lust and need."

Suddenly, Adam appeared directly before us. So fast it was almost as if he hadn't moved and simply teleported. Not touching, just close. Really close. Close enough that he was able to lean in and sniff us.

That was definitely not something a human would do.

"Amazing energy you have, my sweet. Addictive, really. So much chaos and wreckage. You would be a delicious treat for me." He grinned in that terrifying way of his, taking a step away and giving us back our space. I didn't trust his retreat, though. Neither did Zella, it seemed.

"Why are you here?" she asked him, creeping into my side even more. Turning us into a united front.

Adam shrugged. "I like the energy of supernatural fights. It feeds the demon within me."

So, he was a demon. Zella glanced my way for a fleeting moment then refocused on the man. That flicker of a look gave away her surprise at the fact that demons actually existed, though she hid it well. Had we not been such good friends, I might not have even noticed the look she had shot me.

"You carry a similar energy as Wolf Flinch," Adam said, focusing on me. Creeping closer as his eyes darkened, not even trying to appear human. "What is it? The feeling is delightful."

Before I could stop him, he grabbed my wrist and pulled my hand to his face. His fingers burned as they gripped me, his eyes completely wild and almost glowing as they focused on my hand and thumb. I tried to pull away, but he held me tight, the burn of his hold growing hotter and more painful. Inescapable.

"Such a delight," he murmured against my flesh, his lips grazing against my palm in a way that made me gag.

"Zella." I gasped and yanked as his tongue made contact with my skin, the acid-like touch something I couldn't stand. "Zella, run."

But she didn't run. She never would. Instead, she linked her hand with mine, distracting Adam. Gaining his attention. Those wild eyes met hers for a moment before his entire being seemed to turn toward her. Before his breathing increased and he curled over our hands in a posture that made my insides crawl.

"Ah, there it is. You also carry an energy about you, but not for Wolf Flinch. No. And not as strong. The local wolf pack has been very blessed this season, I do believe." Adam clutched Zella's wrist like mine, both of us resisting but without success. Not that we tried hard. Something about Adam—about whatever spell his demon wove—kept us much more complicit than normal. Had a man at the bar grabbed me this way, I would have punched him in the throat and kept walking. But Adam? He had a presence that almost locked me in place. That had my brain resisting the instinct to leave, even as something inside me screamed to run away from him. The man controlled me with nothing more than his presence, and that terrified me more than whatever it was that seemed to have set my wrist on fire.

"Please," I finally whispered, still trying to pull away, though meekly. "Please stop."

His red, flame-filled eyes met mine, and I froze. Completely under his control as he stared and made it seem like he was cataloging my soul. I may have whimpered, the feeling of losing control of my own body so foreign and terrifying as to garner such a ridiculous response instead of any sort of self-defense. My sense of survival had ceased to exist, apparently. All because of a demon in a tracksuit.

"Of course, dear," Adam finally said, breaking eye contact and giving me a reprieve from whatever the hell sort of magic he had just spun over me. "I wouldn't want to anger my good friend Wolf Flinch."

The demon released us both, giving up his hold on our wrists, and the haze of his control ebbed. I grabbed Zella and shoved her back, both of us trying to put as much space as possible between Adam and ourselves. Something he noticed if the smirk that slid across his face like a snake was any indication.

"The energy is one-sided. That's why I couldn't place it." He cocked his head, looking over me once more but not making eye contact. "How fascinating."

I shook my head, making sure I still had full control of my body. My mind. "What energy?"

"The mating energy, of course." He practically leaped at us, landing inches away. Grabbing my hand and bringing it back to his nose. Freezing me in place with his proximity but not with his magic. Not yet. "You're mated to my good friend Wolf Flinch. His scent is in you, which means he bit you, but you didn't complete the ritual. You have yet to bite him back. The energy is fascinating in its makeup because I can feel the holes. The lack of your side."

My heart sank, the bite on my neck suddenly pulsing, as if simply acknowledging its existence woke it up. "What do you mean? How do you know this?"

Adam leaned in closer and ran his nose from my wrist to my fingertips, keeping his eyes on my neck the entire time. On the bite mark left by Flinch. Licking his lips before finding his words.

"You're mated to your wolf, beautiful. Forever and always, especially now that he's bitten you. He's going to feel you, no matter where you go. He's going to know how to track you, mostly because losing you would mean his own death. Oh yes, losing a mate destroys the inner wolf of those like our good friend Wolf Flinch. You and he are a package deal for all of eternity." His grin turned even more wicked. "Or did he forget to tell you that part before his teeth broke through your tender flesh?"

I couldn't move, could barely breathe. All I could do was stare at the demon before me as my heart tried to beat its way out of my chest. Dear god, what had Flinch done?

But I didn't have time to think about all that—about the way Flinch had likely trapped me in the desert with him. Didn't have the ability to focus on that because as I stood there stunned and reeling, another man walked into the bedroom. One I recognized. One who sent ice straight down my spine.

"No," I whispered, pushing Zella back, wanting to get us both away from him.

From the man who had been watching me.

"Good evening, ladies." He nodded toward Adam. "Demon."

"This is a bad idea," Adam said as his eyes went solid black. As his energy shifted into something that had me ready to jump through a window to get away from. No magic holding me in place this time, even though it seemed the demon had finally entered the chat. Fully. "You're making a mistake coming for this one."

The man gave what once had to have been a smile, but his waxy skin didn't move quite right. His facial structure didn't shift the way one would expect it to. And his eyes. Bright and yet dead, those orbs that seemed to be trying to look into my soul sat dark and dull and yet shiny in a way that didn't make sense in my brain. Terrifying.

"You know not of what you speak, demon."

"I know killing Wolf Chiggy was one thing. You riled a hornet's nest with that move and earned yourself your own grave. Killing the fated mates of two executives of the Desert Hellions?" He choked out a sound that was likely supposed to be a laugh as smoke literally began to drift out of his mouth. "Even I don't want to witness the amount of chaos that move would cause. Those shifters will burn the world to the ground if you fuck with their mates, vampire."

Zella grabbed my hand tighter, tugging us closer. Both of us staying silent and yet listening to all the plurals in Adam's sentences. Not mate, mates. Two. Fuck, what had Flinch *and Cutter* done?

"We want the desert," the vampire said, staring my way without blinking. Ever. He didn't fucking blink. "The dogs have to go."

Dogs. Meaning wolf shifters. Meaning the Hellions.

"This isn't the way to get them to leave," Adam said, inching slightly closer to us. Almost...protecting us. "This is the way to start a supernatural war and get your rotting asses nuked out of existence."

"A pack of dogs is no match for the royal army of the vampire queen." The vampire hissed and bent forward, as if readying himself for a fight. As if about to attack. Adam growled low and deep, a tone not at all like a wolf growl. Those were warm and comforting. Adam's growl sounded like something from my nightmares.

"Today is not the day for this fight," Adam said, growling through every word. A powerful energy building around him with each syllable. "Killing Wolf Chiggy created chaos in the supernatural world. Too much chaos. You won't survive the retribution for that act, but your queen will. You take out the fated mates of two shifter leaders, and the pendulum will swing against her."

For the first time, the vampire blinked. Sort of. More closed his eyes partway for a moment then reopened them. As if he had to think hard for that split second. As if he needed a break for that tiny allotment of time.

"No demon will threaten—"

"This demon will—and did. These women aren't yours to take tonight." Adam moved a step closer, keeping his eyes on the vampire even as he reached in our direction. Even as the smell of burn and rot rose in the room and the smoke practically billowed from his mouth. "Sorry, ladies, but it's the only way."

He moved faster than I could have predicted, turning to face us as his eyes slid from solid black to pure fire as he grabbed Zella and me by the wrists. One second, there was nothing but confusion in my brain—a need to run overridden by outside forces held in those fiery eyes. An unsurety of what was coming or why. And then, there was pain. Searing, soul-shattering pain. And screaming. Whether that was coming from Zella or me, I had no idea, but the sound would be something that haunted my dreams for the rest of my life. As would the memory of the feeling of my entire body going up in flames.

My final thought before the heat seared its way to my very core, the only person who came to mind to think of as my insides burned, was Flinch.

And how this was all his fault.

Twenty-Seven

"What the fuck are you doing here?"

The one thing I hadn't expected to find in my bedroom on the night of a vampire attack was a chaos demon. Adam stood in the corner, looking... Well, he looked out of his fucking mind. His eyes glowed a deep red, and his top lip had pulled back as if he were some sort of animal smelling a female in heat.

But even Adam's presence couldn't fully distract me from my mate.

Locklyn sat on the edge of the bed with Zella beside her, both girls looking haggard and disheveled. Whatever had happened tonight had definitely affected them negatively.

"Lock, baby. You okay?"

She didn't even look up at me, but Zella did. Zella shot me a glare that turned into an almost embarrassed sort of look as she reached to grab Locklyn's hand. A hand that looked red and inflamed. Burned. Motherfucker.

"What is this?" I practically fell at their feet, crouching in front of both women.

"Jesus, Flinch," Zella said, not looking my way at all. "Cover that thing up or something."

It was only then that I came to the realization that Cutter and I were completely naked. Our clothes never shifted with us, and while I was used to being balls out around my brothers—and Locklyn—the presence of Zella added a twist to the moment I had not contemplated.

"Sorry." Keeping my feet planted, I stretched behind me to the dresser and opened the drawer that held my more comfortable clothes. It took two seconds to tug on a pair of baggy gray sweats, another one to toss a pair to Cutter, and then my focus returned to the women before me. "Now, what happened here?"

Cutter growled in a warning from behind me. I had no idea if the growl was intended for me or Adam or fucking Santa Claus, but it didn't matter. I had gotten close enough to smell the burned flesh, to see the damaged skin encircling both women's wrists. To notice the appearance of a perfect line around the one side, as if someone with short, chubby fingers had grabbed them and somehow burned his flesh into theirs.

"Who did this to you?" I asked, my words more growl than voice. My wolf breaking through as the scent of exactly who had done this to them met my senses. My fingertips turned to claws, and I saw my nose lengthen as my snout appeared. There would be no holding him back this time, and yet I tried. Tried for Locklyn because I knew she would be more comfortable with the human version of me than the animal one. I tried to hang on to my control because I knew once my wolf wrested it from me, it was game over for Adam.

I really didn't want to have to kill a fucking demon, but I was about to.

"Cutter." I rose to my feet, knowing I wouldn't be able to

hold off the shift much longer. Turning to face the man who had fucked up royally. "It's him."

Adam didn't move a muscle. Not at first, but when Cutter's snarl joined in with mine, he finally looked our way.

And he grinned.

"Vampires don't like the taste of demon, Wolf Flinch of the Desert Hellions, so you had better be thanking me for that move."

"Thanking you for burning my mate?" I snarled long and low, ready to attack the fucker. "You've got a fucked-up idea of what actions deserve thanks."

"Perhaps, but at least I wasn't the one who left them alone to be vampire snacks." His grin only grew as his words stabbed into my chest. I *had* left them, even though I had thought my brothers could keep them safe. Locklyn and Zella being anywhere close to vampires was my fault. One hundred percent mine. And he knew it.

"That doesn't—"

"We can argue about this later," he said, flames forming in his eyes. "For now, perhaps you should watch your back."

No sooner had the last syllable passed his lips than something big and hissing landed on my back. I allowed more of my wolf to take control out of instinct, flipping and snapping my teeth at whatever had attacked me in my half-human, half-wolf form. A vampire I hadn't seen yet screeched and lunged at me again with his mouth open. I'd gone up against a number of vamps that night, but this one fought differently—harder, swifter, more cunning. He gave me more fight than the others. We crashed through the room, neither of us giving an inch to the other. Bouncing off Cutter more than once as he stood in place, guarding the women like a sentinel. Which was good because I had to focus on the motherfucker trying to bite me.

I yanked my adversary around to face me during a spin,

wanting to grab the son of a bitch by the throat. He rolled with me as I tried to get my hands in position to pop his fucking head off, snapping and lunging in a frenzied sort of way that was easier to block than it should have been. That was when I felt it—something cold and wet on my arm. A lot of cold and wet right under where his mouth hung open.

"Are you drooling?" I pushed off the foot of the bed, ignoring the loud crack as I shoved the fucker against the wall. "You're drooling all over me."

"You'll be bleeding out soon enough and won't care about that."

"Pretty sure I'll always care about unwanted oral secretions, motherfucker."

He hissed, spraying spittle all across my face, and tried to lunge again. Head cocked, mouth open, eyes wide. He truly looked like some sort of movie villain vampire, except he had a weird film over him. Something almost cold that didn't aid in my grip and yet felt oddly...sticky.

"Are you... Is this wax?" I growled and pushed him into the wall again, ignoring the crack of falling drywall dust. "Why are you waxed like an apple?"

"Focus, Flinch," Cutter said. He stood across the room from us, keeping his body in front of Locklyn and Zella. Making sure they stayed safe while I fought the vamp. And apparently riding my ass for no good reason.

"I'm focused." I leaned closer, holding his jaw. Smiling as a glint of fear appeared in his otherwise dead eyes. "What's with the wax?"

"Part of my skincare regimen, dog. You might want to try some yourself."

I snarled and snapped, knowing I had again partially shifted. Seeing the end of my snout where nothing should be. That was likely what had ignited the bit of fear in him. Wolves didn't play well with vamps.

But it was the sound of my mate's voice that stopped me in my tracks.

"They found wax on my dad's body."

Dead. This motherfucker was about to be so much more dead than he already was.

I pressed my weight into his body, letting my claws sink into the flesh of his neck. Pinning him in place as I growled, "Did you kill Chiggy?"

The vamp squirmed at first then settled into an eerie sort of quiet stance, staring back at me with his dead eyes. No fear, no emotion. Just the dark depths of someone without a soul.

"He refused to give me what I needed."

That was as much of a yes as I needed. "You're fucking dead."

But the vampire just grinned in a very strange, almost impossible way. As if his flesh wasn't quite connected to his bones. Son of a... I had a feeling the wax was to help control his decomposition. This bastard had to be old as fuck to have rotted to this level.

"We want this region," he said, dripping black liquid from the corner of his mouth. "Get your dogs out of it, or it'll be more than Chiggy left to rot in the desert." He sniffed, eyes darting to look over my shoulder as a sound similar to a laugh bubbled up out of him. "We know she's your fated mate. I wonder if she'll taste as good as her father. She's human—I wouldn't even have to shoot her first to immobilize her. Hell, I might like it more if she fights back."

I had no thoughts left in my head, no strategies or battle plans. There was nothing but rage. My wolf pushed through my control, turning me into a monster as he twisted my body into more canine than man. As he took over my thoughts and my actions. We slashed the creature before us, growling and snapping as waxy flesh shredded beneath our fingers. The vampire's screech of pain filled the bedroom but fell on deaf ears—I had no sympathy left for the fucker. No worry in his killing. He had murdered my club brother—my president—but the threat to my mate had sealed his fate in the most painful way. I didn't go for the throat—didn't behead the bastard to end things quickly. No, I stripped his flesh from his bones in increments. Wanting it to hurt. Wanting him to feel the fear of dying a slow death at my hands.

I tortured him for being a threat to my mate. And I felt no regret over that decision.

Only when the bed had been broken from my fit of rage and all the pretty details Locklyn had added to the space had been destroyed, when the vampire was nothing more than a skeleton and a puddle of black, gooey ribbons of flesh left on the very rug my beautiful mate had only recently purchased for me, did I stop. Heaving breaths didn't quite calm me, but I knew I needed to regain my composure. To allow the human me to take full control. Locklyn had just watched me shred a sentient being into nothing—I needed control of myself before I turned around and faced her.

But it wasn't going to be quick or easy to do that. "Cutter."

"They're okay."

I took a deep breath, calming my wolf. Letting him settle inside me so I could face my mate in my human form. But fuck, he was worked up and ready to keep fighting. For her.

"I'm sorry, Locklyn," I finally said, turning just enough to face her. My heart dropping when she refused to look at me. "I am so sorry for killing that vampire in front of you. I was an animal, and you didn't need to see that side of me."

She looked up for the most fleeting of moments, eyes darting along my body as if taking stock. I could only imagine what she saw. Her mate, bare chested and wearing low-slung gray sweat pants, covered in a gooey black substance while sporting some bloody slashes on his rib cage and likely still sprouting wolf hair in places. Not something she should have seen. Ever.

Finally, she shrugged a shoulder. "He killed my dad. He deserved it."

Adam hissed a long, low whistle sort of sound, which reminded me of his presence. He looked over the scene of destruction with more glee than I had ever seen on someone's face. Enjoying the visage as only a chaos demon could. The concern in his voice, though, didn't match his expression.

"The other vamps will bring more chaos."

Yeah, that much I knew. Which would put all of us at risk. Especially the humans in our midst.

"Flinch," Cutter finally said, bringing my attention to him. It didn't stay there long—my eyes zeroed in on my mate, who seemed emotionless but pale. And who definitely didn't look my way. Though perhaps she was too busy holding her friend upright. "I think Zella needs to go to the hospital."

"I don't," Zella said. I sniffed long and hard, the scent of her sickness difficult to ascertain over the burn of the demon and the rot of the vampire, but there. Heavy and dark and stronger than usual.

Zella's sickness had somehow gotten worse in just a matter of hours.

Locklyn pursed her lips and frowned at her best friend, apparently not liking the refusal of help. "Are you okay?"

"I'm fine—"

"She's not fine," Cutter interjected, sniffing and frowning. "I can smell the sickness, Zee. It's building."

Zella sighed, keeping her eyes on Locklyn. "It's no big deal. Tonight has just been...a lot."

Locklyn grabbed her friend's hand. "Do you have your pain

meds?"

Zella shook her head, eyes on the floor. Appearing almost defeated.

"Then you do need to go to the hospital. Let's get you out of this pain cycle before it becomes overwhelming." Locklyn glanced up at me, just a quick and cursory overview as if taking inventory of my person, before refocusing on her friend. "For me. Go for me."

The green eyes I loved so much had met mine for a fleeting moment, all care and concern disappearing in that second. Our connection cold and quiet. Distant. I had fucked up somehow. Big-time. Whether it was the vampire attack or the demon or just the fuckedupness that the evening had turned into, something had caused my mate to turn cold to me. A fact that had my wolf mewling in my mind.

Adam sighed and shook himself like a dog, breaking my concentration and demanding all the attention in the room.

"I'm so glad I popped over tonight. This was an amazing show. I look forward to the chaos these women continue to bring us." He grinned, his face stretching in unnatural ways, moving as if to pass me but never breaking eye contact. "The burns are surface-level and were done to protect the women. No vampire soldier would go up against a chaos demon for funsies."

I nodded, understanding but still not liking it.

But Adam wasn't finished. He held that uncomfortable eye contact, letting me see the fires burning within the depths of his eyes. Letting me know the demon was speaking for the man. "You owe me, Wolf Flinch of the Desert Hellions. For saving your fated mate, you owe me."

I froze, knowing owing a demon was not something I wanted on my record. But there was no way around it—he had shown up to enjoy the chaos but ended up helping my mate. I *did* owe him. So I nodded once. Sealing my fate.

And immediately moving into cleanup mode. "Let's get the women to the hospital."

Twenty-Eight

Locklyn

I couldn't even look at Flinch, and yet the sight of him naked before me, bleeding from gashes on his ribs and streaked with the black blood of the vampires he'd fought to get to me, refused to leave my brain. As did the pure animalistic attack I had witnessed from him. The way he had cut that vampire into ribbons would be something that haunted me...but more because he had done it to avenge my dad and protect me. He had lost all control, for me. Why that was so appealing and yet so horrifying in the same breath was not something I was ready to comprehend. So I pushed that aside and focused on another emotion of mine—anger.

I darted a glance his way every few seconds, afraid he would somehow disappear but wanting him to be gone at the same time. Loving and hating him in the same breath.

Why had he done something so stupid? And why hadn't he told me anything about the bite and what it meant?

But the mess he had made was secondary to helping Zella.

We ended up in the emergency room. All of us, which meant me, Zella, and what looked like every member of the Desert Hellions. I doubted the place had ever seen that much leather and testosterone.

"Just hold on," I whispered to my best friend, hanging on to her hand like a lifeline. She moaned and curled toward me, though I had a feeling the action was more in response to the pain crushing her than my voice. The pain that had gone from zero to a hundred in the time it had taken us to arrive.

"What do we do?" Cutter asked, looking harried and desperate. "How do we get this to stop?"

"We don't," I said, still focusing on Zella. "We wait for the doctor to give her some good pain medicine and hope it kicks in fast. Then she sleeps for a day or two."

I ran my hand over her head, hating the way she trembled under my touch. I had seen Zella in pain before—seen her curled up on the couch, crying with it. Seen her limping into the bathroom in the hope that a hot shower would help. Seen her laid out for a day or so, unable to function without heavy doses of prescribed medicine to quiet the pain—or not-prescribed medicine to help her forget about it.

I had *seen* her pain, but I hadn't ever seen her this bad—this lost to the screaming within her own body—or seen it take over this fast. My best friend looked as if she were dying, and that terrified me more than the vampires had.

Cutter slipped into my view from the other side of Zella's bed, looking just as worried as I felt. He had donned a pair of Flinch's sweats and acquired a flannel shirt from somewhere to cover his post-shift body. Neither of which looked right on him. But he was there, refusing to leave Zella's side. Something I appreciated because carrying the load of concern for Zella had always been solely my job.

"How do you live like this?" Cutter asked as he leaned over her bed and softly touched her forehead. "You're so strong."

Zella didn't answer him, and I couldn't because how Zella lived with the amount of pain I knew her to be in on the daily was a mystery to me. But as we stood there watching her, as Cutter whispered words I couldn't hear over her and ran his fingers along her skin, she began to unroll herself. To loosen her muscles and relax her body. Cutter softly soothing her also slowed down her breathing. The short, stubby gasps turned into almost normal inhalations, and her exhales quieted. That was a good sign.

Thankfully, a doctor came in at that moment, knocking on the edge of the opening into the room where we had been left then appearing through the privacy curtain.

"So, what's happening here?" she asked, glancing over her tablet and tapping on the screen before giving Zella a soft, tired smile. "Looks like we're in a lot of pain."

The "no shit" I wanted to say stayed inside my head, though from the look on Cutter's face, he was thinking the same thing.

"Hi, Doctor," Zella croaked, moving slightly in the bed as if to flatten herself out. "I have psoriatic arthritis and ankylosing spondylitis. I've been trying to handle my pain levels, but with stress and stuff lately, it's gotten to be too much."

The doctor nodded, tapping a note into her tablet. "You listed some pain medications on your intake form. Are they not working?"

"I'm traveling, and I don't have any of my pain medicine with me."

"Zella," I hissed.

She pursed her lips. "I was in a hurry to catch a flight out here. Things were forgotten."

Guilt sucked the wind out of me, making any sort of argument I might have had die inside me. She had been in a hurry because of me. Because I had needed her. Because she had known I was in trouble and refused to allow me to suffer alone.

Flinch laid a hand on my leg as if to ease me, but all his touch did was make me angrier. At myself, at him, at Zella's illness. Hell, at my dad for not figuring out how to escape a vampire. My guilt may have withered, but my anger grew strong and tall. I pulled away from his touch.

"Well," the doctor said, still typing on the tablet even as she moved closer to where Zella lay. "Let's see what we can do here."

The doctor moved in to give Zella a quick once-over, checking her heart rate and breathing before having Zella perform a few simple mobility tests as best she could. Zella's pain made it difficult on her to move around much, but luckily, Cutter was able to step in and assist as needed—lifting, supporting, easing her body back down. He made sure she didn't exert a single extra drop of effort.

It was when the doctor saw the burn on Zella's wrist that I knew things were about to go sideways.

"What happened here?"

Zella looked my way, eyes wide and expression giving away too much, before pasting on a subtle smile that did nothing to hide her nervousness. "We were working on some jewelry pieces and got stupid. Hot metal is hot."

The doctor did not look convinced, though I couldn't blame her. The perfect circle of burned flesh around Zella's wrist—the one that turned the skin maroon halfway down her palms and matched mine—was definitely not the norm. And a hot bracelet wouldn't have made it look as if we were wearing red fingerless gloves, the color an ombre of damage to our skin that started at the wrist. But what could we say? A demon had marked us to keep a vampire away? That would go over well.

"And you?" the doctor asked, looking my way. Intentionally eyeing the mark on my own wrist. "Working with metal?"

"Yeah," I said, fighting to keep my expression as flat and neutral as possible. "It really was hotter than we expected."

The doctor nodded, looking completely unconvinced. "Let me work with the pharmacy to see what we can do about your pain. Meanwhile, I'm going to order some burn ointment for the two of you." She nodded to Zella. "I'll take care of your friend first."

"Oh no." I waved her off. "I'm good. I don't—"

"It'll take a few for the pharmacy to release anything strong enough for your friend. Let me make sure that burn won't get infected."

Which likely meant "let me get you alone to ask you questions in case I need to call the police." I sighed and rose to my feet, ignoring the low growl Flinch released. I had gotten good at ignoring him over the last few hours.

The doctor took me to an exam room down the hall, closing the door behind us before offering me a seat. She settled in across from me after grabbing something from a cart she had to type a code into to open up, looking serious and concerned.

"We can get you help," she said as she put on a glove, keeping her eyes averted from mine. She opened a small tub of something white and creamy-looking, slipping a gloved finger inside before reaching for my hands. "We can get you away from these men if they're hurting you."

It took me a full ten seconds to react, the last week playing out behind my eyes. The good, the bad, the fantastic, the terrifying.

Good lord, I had only known Flinch *for a week*.

And I knew—deep down—that I didn't need anyone protecting me from him.

I laughed, the sound not joyous but sarcastic. My anger bubbling up right along with my grief and sadness. "No offense, Doc, but the men with us are the least of our problems. We don't need help getting away from them. We need Zella to function with as little pain as possible."

She finished rubbing the salve into my damaged skin and nodded. "Okay. I couldn't let you two walk out of here without at least offering."

"Don't lose sleep over it—just because they're bikers doesn't mean they would hurt us." Because they wouldn't. No way, no how. Not intentionally. "They'd die to protect us, to be honest."

And they would. Flinch would die and kill to protect me. Had fought vampires for me. Had slaughtered them. I knew I was safe with him, and yet I still couldn't stand to look at him. Not after finding out what he'd done. What he had neglected to tell me.

But I didn't have time to deal with that. I needed Zella better.

The doctor and I made the trek back to Zella's room, neither of us talking along the way. She did type a lot on her tablet, though, so hopefully she had done something to get the medicine Zella needed. Once back in the room, she grabbed a new pair of gloves and her little tub of burn ointment before heading for the bed.

"Let's start with the wrist while we wait for your pain medicine, okay?"

Zella nodded, glancing my way. "You good?"

Always looking out for me first. "Of course. How about you?"

"I'd be great if someone could just yank my spine out and give me a new one."

"How long have you had autoimmune issues?" the doctor asked, focusing on Zella's wrist. Zella glanced up at Flinch, then me, eyes hard and emotionless. Lips pressed together in a tight line. Cutter stood at the head of her bed so there was no way she could look at him, but her message was clear. She did not want to have this conversation with the guys in the room.

Before I could even think about how to get them to leave, Zella jumped and hissed, yanking her arm away from the doctor. That set off a chain reaction where Cutter then Flinch both basically exploded into angry men. Cutter lurched forward, towering over the doctor and Zella's bed in one go, while Flinch jumped to his feet. Both looking ready to fight. To kill. Again.

"Enough," the doctor said, rising to her feet with a grace that seemed almost inhuman as Cutter leaned over the bed and glared at her. "Get out. I need time with my patient, and you two are impeding that."

Cutter didn't like her demand. "Lady, if you think—"

"Go," Zella said, interrupting him with her calm but firm voice. "I can't get better without her, so go. Lock and I will be fine."

Cutter didn't look happy. He stood in place staring at the doctor for a good five seconds, probably waiting for Zella to rescind her banishment. But Zella had made her decision—she wanted the men gone from the room, which meant they needed to go. And oddly enough, the doctor didn't back down from his animallike stare. She stood with her head up and her eyes locked on his. Looking ready to fight him.

"She said get out." I crossed my arms and glared, refusing to give either man an inch when it came to Zella. "Go."

Cutter growled but finally broke his stance, nodding to Flinch before the two sulked out of the room.

The doctor kept her eyes on Cutter until both men had left, then shook her head as she reclaimed her seat. "You sure you don't need any help?" She looked my way before refocusing on Zella's wrist. "You wouldn't be the first women who came in here needing more than wound care. Especially from..."

She looked up at me, sentence left unfinished. Implication floating in a sea of possibilities. Especially from...bikers? Big men?

Shifters?

Paranormal creatures?

What did the doctor know?

"We're good," I said, not taking her bait. "Just take care of Zella's pain."

The doctor sat back, finished with the burn ointment, and shook her head. "There's not a lot I can do other than write a script for pain meds."

"I know." Zella sighed and moved, stretching slightly. "It was a stressful night, and now my pain is super high. If I can just get out of this pain cycle, I'll be fine."

The doctor nodded. "I can give you OxyContin tonight and a script for some steroids to try to knock out this inflammation. But if the pain persists, you're going to need to make an appointment with your regular doctor. Do you have a primary care physician or no?"

Zella looked my way, reality hitting us. "I have a full team—rheumatologist, pain management doctor, PCP, everything. They're just all in Detroit."

The doctor nodded. "Looks like it might be time to take a trip."

Or go home. Because that was what was going to have to happen—we were going to have to go home to help Zella.

But Flinch had made going home more difficult than it should have been.

The reality of which infuriated me even more.

And made me want to leave simply out of spite.

"We're going home." I gave Zella a single nod, the decision solidified in my mind. "This week. We're going back to Detroit."

Twenty-Nine

Being kept away from my mate was torture. Pure, unadulterated torture.

"This hospital is filled with fucking sadists," Cutter said, locking my opinion into my head.

"Agreed." I took a sip of the horrible coffee being offered in the waiting area then paced the length of the room. I needed to do something. Needed to see or feel or, *fuck*, even smell Locklyn. Keeping her away from me, especially after the total fucking mess of the past few hours, made my wolf one agitated motherfucker.

And Cutter wasn't doing much better.

"You think Zella is going to be okay?" he asked for what had to be the hundredth time.

Zed caught my gaze, both of us frowning deep.

"I don't know," I said, my voice a low growl. A warning. One my club prez didn't heed.

"I think that doctor's a quack. Maybe we should go in there and tell her to fuck off. Take the girls to another hospital."

Zed huffed. "Or maybe we should all calm the fuck down and let the professionals do what they've been trained to do."

Cutter could only shake his head, mumbling under his breath about pain. Likely about Zella's pain, which was certainly something to be concerned about. That little human had gone from bright and full to near helpless in a matter of a few hours, the scent of sick she always carried with her increasing until it had filled the room. She had seemed to fold under the weight of whatever had started hurting within her, her entire body collapsing into itself until all that was left was the physical representation of her pain. I'd never seen Cutter so panicked or Locklyn so worried.

Locklyn.

Our connection zinged to life, the sensations flowing toward me thin and fiery. Pain but not her own. Fear but not terror. My mate felt unsettled. I needed to get to her. To help her. Support her. Fucking see that everything was all right with her. I needed to be in that exam room with her to make sure she was safe and cared for.

But instead, I got the hospital waiting area, Zed, and an obsessed Cutter.

"Zella had better be fucking okay."

I was going to punch him.

Finally, the woman who had banished us to the waiting room appeared. We surrounded her within a single breath, three hulking shifters ready to fight the human. Not that we needed to.

"She's comfortable," the doctor said, looking from me to Cutter to Zed before focusing on her tablet. "We'll be releasing her within the next thirty minutes—I just need to get her paperwork in order. Then you can take her home."

"How's her pain?" Cutter asked, inching forward. "Is there anything more we can do for her? Anything we should be watching out for?"

The doctor shook her head. "Discussing her case with you would be a HIPAA violation. All I can say is she's comfortable and being released. If Zella chooses to talk to you about her medical situation, that's up to her. She didn't give me permission."

And with that, the woman turned on her heel and walked away, leaving Cutter looking absolutely shell-shocked.

"Maybe she just forgot to sign those papers." Zed placed a hand on Cutter's shoulder. "It was a bit chaotic when we got here. Easy to miss."

"Yeah. Right." Cutter shot me a glare. Love-sick pup gone, biker club vice president in full effect. "Pull up the truck so we can get both girls out of here as quick as possible."

"I've got it," Zed said before disappearing down the hallway, presumably to retrieve the truck. I stood with Cutter, both of us antsy. Anxious. Unable to resist much longer.

Finally, I broke. "I'm going in."

He followed me immediately, both of us storming into Zella's room with little more than a knock on the frame of the opening. No door between us, just a curtain. And a big, bad wall of energy that made my wolf whimper.

"You okay?" Cutter asked as he approached Zella. She reached for him, and all of his angst from the last few hours almost seemed to melt away. The two began whispering, their heads together as Cutter bent himself in half to move closer. I understood his desire for proximity. Felt it myself. Unable to resist another second, I beelined it to Locklyn, taking in her messy hair and defeated posture. The burns around her wrist covered by bandages and the way she refused to look at me. Really noticing just how sad and dejected she appeared. Fuck, things were bad.

"You okay, short stack?"

I got nothing more than a nod. My wolf went still and silent, his world zeroing in on his mate. His confusion over what to do next rattling both of us.

A nurse entered at that moment—the noise startling—and handed Zella some paperwork, saying the wheelchair was right outside whenever she was ready to go. Zella gave me a blank stare then turned her focus to Locklyn, the blankness evaporating. Concern and care shining through.

"You ready, Lock?"

"Yeah." Locklyn rose to her feet, shooing me away when I moved as if to help her up. Still not looking at me. "Let's go home."

Something in her voice didn't sit well with me, but I helped her out the door and to my truck. My brothers lined the hallways and poured out into the parking lot, most of them looking a little worse for wear. We hadn't gotten to debrief yet, to go over what had happened with the vamps. Every second of my time had been spent dealing with Locklyn and Zella, which had left my club to deal with the end of the fight without me. Without Cutter, too. We were failing as leaders.

Or at least I was, because as soon as we made it to my truck that Zed had pulled into the ambulance bay, Cutter jumped into the bed of it and stood over our brothers, looking regal and filled with rage.

"Tonight was a rough night for all of us, but especially for our brother Tex. The last update I received from his blood brother stated that he was alive and stable. They have a witch coming tonight to check over his shoulder and see if the damage can in any way be repaired. Know that even as we sat in that hospital room for the humans in our midst, our thoughts stayed with Tex. With all of you." He made a point to meet the eyes of every shifter in attendance, keeping his head up. Leading. "I am so proud of each and every one of you for how hard you fought.

Flinch was able to destroy the one who took out our revered Chiggy, but we will be going on the attack soon to get our revenge for him. To make sure the entire nest is annihilated. No one fucks with a Hellion and lives to tell the tale."

The men all cheered, the night filling with the sounds of yips and growls. Locklyn watched but didn't react, didn't respond as I would have expected. Instead, she held on to the handles of Zella's wheelchair and kept her eyes on the crowd. Not on me.

"Thank you all for sticking around to watch over our humans," Cutter continued, shooting a small, sad smile Zella's way. "They're on the mend and going home, and I want to give every one of you that same chance. Head home. Get some rest. Heal up. Tomorrow, we start hunting vamps."

The howls that came after that sentence rose into the night sky like a song, serenading the moon above. I didn't howl. I couldn't. My entire world rested on the shoulders of a tiny human who looked so damn lost, and I had no way to reach her.

"Come," I finally said, directing her with a hand on her back toward the truck. "Let's get you two home."

I did not receive an answer. Instead, Locklyn pushed Zella's wheelchair to the passenger side of the truck then stepped back as Cutter lifted the frail human into the front seat. My mate followed, climbing into the back seat to be close to her friend.

Heartbroken but on task, I hurried around and hopped into the driver's spot, immediately starting the engine. Cutter jumped back into the truck bed, giving me two slaps to the roof when he was ready to go.

"You good?" I asked, my words directed to Zella but my eyes stuck on Locklyn in the rearview.

It was Zella who chose to answer. "Yeah. Let's go."

I pulled out of the parking lot with at least twenty motorcycles behind me, all following us home. Making sure we would be safe on the drive as they had been the entire evening. From the house to the hospital and now the drive home, the Desert Hellions had protected the two humans in our midst as if they were family because of the women's connections to Chiggy, Cutter, and me. No questions asked, no other option than to step into the protective role. True brothers in every sense of the word.

And yet, my mind could only focus on my mate.

We arrived to my house without issue, though once in the driveway, I realized my mistake. The house looked as if a war had happened there, likely because it had. Deep grooves were carved into the ground in front, and my favorite cactus looked about ready to fall over. I had no idea what the backyard would look like or even the inside, but I knew there was no way we would be staying there.

"We'll get you two inside to pack, and then I'll take us to a hotel or something." I sighed and climbed out of the truck, ending up beside Cutter, who was already opening the door for Zella.

"They can stay at my place," he said before reaching up to carefully lift his girl out of the truck. "I've got a spare room they can share."

I glanced at Locklyn to see if she liked that idea, but she was once again not looking at me. Fuck.

"Yeah, that might work." We got the girls inside and headed through the absolute mess of my house to the bedroom. The black goo left over where a vampire had once stood had me halting everything and redirecting the girls to the living room to set up shop. I even grabbed their bags and set them on the couch to get them started. The girls immediately started packing, both bringing clothes and toiletries to the living room and filling their bags with a speed that surprised me. As did the amount of stuff Locklyn loaded into hers. That wasn't for an overnight trip.

"What's happening here?" I asked, watching as my mate emptied the dresser that had housed her clothes completely.

Locklyn didn't look at me, so her words hit even harder as she said, "Zella needs to go home."

Home. As in Detroit. As in not here with me.

I nodded, my stomach turning and my brain spinning as I tried to work out the logistics of a trip to Detroit. Tried to figure out how I could handle that without leaving my brothers unprotected during a vampire invasion. "Okay, so we'll need a few hours to get the brothers at the club aligned on what to do before we leave. I'll get Cutter and—"

"No. Zella needs to go home for medical care." Locklyn finally stopped and stared right at me, eyes dead. Anger leading the charge. "And I'm going with her. Just us."

The world stood still, the heavy brick of Locklyn's declaration shattering my mind and heart straight into a million fucking pieces. My mate was leaving. Ending everything. Walking away from me. From us.

"Lock, you have to—"

"I have to *nothing*." She turned away from me, back straight and head up. Hardened. "I'm not happy right now. With you, with this...with finding out from a goddamned demon that when you bit my neck, you tied us together for life. Without you ever saying a word to me."

Fuck. Fucking fuckety fuck. I wanted to kill Adam, and yet I couldn't because her anger was more than justified. I had bitten her without explaining what it meant. I had chosen not to tell her about the link I had created.

I had fucked everything up.

"Lock, baby—"

"No. Don't baby me, especially not right now." She inched closer, looking fierce and ready for battle. "You bit me but didn't bother to tell me what that meant. You tied us together—forever

—without my consent, and left me to find out from a demon on what just might have been the most terrifying night of my life. It's all too much to deal with, so I'm leaving. I'm taking Zella home. End of story."

I had no idea what to do or how to argue with her. How to apologize enough for failing her and letting the vampires claw their way into our world. How to beg enough for her to stay. No clue how to convince her to give me another chance to make things right with her. I had failed my mate, and she was letting me know that by walking away from our bond. There was no instruction manual on how to fix that. No way to put pieces of a puzzle never finished in the first place back together.

End of story...end of *our* story.

In her mind.

"That's fine," I said, backing away. Wanting so badly to grab her and shake her, to make her stay with me. Knowing that would only make things worse. "You need a break, you take one. I'll buy you the fucking ticket to leave me. But there is no fucking end to this story. Not today, not tomorrow. You'll always be mine."

Those green eyes stabbed into me, hard and dark and filled with a rage I could not understand. "But what if I don't want you to be mine?"

Shots fired, hits taken. Blows fatal.

Fated mating over.

"You don't mean that."

But she did. She must have because she didn't even bother to respond. Locklyn turned her back to me and continued packing. Leaving me. Destroying us.

As a man, I didn't know what to do with the sudden collapse of my entire world, so I handed over my consciousness to my wolf. We shifted on the spot, howling a sad song as we turned and ran from the room. As we pounded through the living room with the pieces of our broken heart rattling inside us. We couldn't fix this, so we left. Out the front door. Into the desert beyond. Away from the pain and dejection.

My mate had rejected me, and there was nothing we could do about it. So, we ran.

Thirty

LOCKLYN

The chaos of the airport first thing in the morning didn't help my mood. Neither did seeing Zella snuggling into Cutter's side while we waited to go through security. I stood alone—just how I had arrived. Flinch had run off into the desert, and the rest of the Hellions had either gone home or stayed at Flinch's house to begin cleanup, which had felt both like the right thing and so very wrong. Especially in regard to Flinch. I had no idea what I wanted from him long-term—if anything—but in that moment, I wanted him at my side. I wanted to know he at least cared enough to show up. Even though I had been the one to push him away.

Anger and disappointment were strange bedfellows to have to contend with.

I took a deep breath, closing my eyes and dropping my head back to stare up at the ceiling before letting it out.

"You okay?" Zella asked. I let my chin fall, trying hard to paint on a smile. She and Cutter had turned their full attention to me, two sets of eyes focused on mine and adding to the pressure of the moment.

"Fine." I took another deep breath, ignoring the dual expressions of disbelief. "I just hate flying."

A lie, but one I hoped would at least tell my best friend to give me a little space.

The two went back to their quiet whispering, Zella once again snuggled into the side of the shifter. Leaving me to suffer in the solitude of my own making.

Solitude of my...for fuck's sake.

I had fallen for a wolf shifter biker who also happened to fight vampires, and this had somehow turned me into a morose poet who thought things like *solitude of my own making*. What a mess.

"I think we're about at the end," Cutter said, glaring at the few people still left in line in front of us. "You going to be okay?"

Zella nodded, looking pale and tired. "I'll be fine."

Another woman lying, but I couldn't blame her. She would be fine because she was used to being in pain, but that fact didn't negate the suffering this flight would cause. As with everything in life, fine was relative.

"You sure you want to come with me?" Zella asked. Her question shook me because my initial, almost instinctual, response was no. No, I wasn't sure. No, I didn't want to go. Just no. But I knew it was the right thing to do. She needed me to help her until she could get her flare under control, and I needed space to give my situation with Flinch some thought. I needed time to recover from the whirlwind of the past seven days.

I had only met the man *seven days* ago. It already felt like a lifetime.

"Of course I do. You need me."

"I need more good drugs." She gave me a weak smile, leaning into Cutter. "You don't have to leave here."

But I did. I knew I did. I needed to leave to give myself time and space to think. I needed to get away from Flinch to be able to evaluate everything that had happened with a little distance. I needed...

I needed to tell him how mad I was, but that he still held my heart in his hands. No matter how much it would hurt to give him hope when I felt...hopeless. When I was missing the comfort I felt obliged to offer. Making sure he knew I wanted to come back to him, even though I wouldn't. Not until I was sure about him. About me. About us.

Because there was an us. And maybe there would be an us again in the future.

"Hey," I said, knowing my time with Cutter was coming to an end but suddenly filled with a desire to communicate to Flinch. Not wanting to call him in case his voice was enough to change my mind and make me stay, but knowing he needed to receive words from me. So I chose the coward's way out. "Can you give Flinch a message for me?"

"Sure." Cutter glanced behind me before jerking his chin in a sort of nod. "But I think you should give it to him yourself."

I spun, already knowing what I would see but still floored by the sight. Flinch had arrived, every tall, powerful inch of him heading right for me. His clothes looked fresh and clean, but the deep shadow on his face made him appear gritty and dark. Tired but not letting up on the gas of life. And his expression—he looked like a man on a mission. And finding me was definitely that mission.

I didn't even have time to say a word to him before he reached me. Before he bypassed everyone in the line and stood before me. Without preamble, he herded me out of line. Forcing me to move until my back hit the wall. Even then, he kept coming, caging me in with his big body. Covering me with it.

Creating an air of privacy that definitely didn't actually exist in the security line of the airport.

"I'm sorry," he said, those two words carrying a weight that created huge cracks in the wall around my heart. "I should have told you everything from the start. Should have explained that you were my fated mate and what that meant." He ran a thumb over the mark on my neck. The one he had left on me. The one that was causing me so much angst. "I would have told you about the mating bite, but I hadn't planned on biting you that day. I hadn't started this thinking it would be okay to do that without your consent. Losing control like that threw me."

"Flinch—"

"Hang on. We've only got a few minutes." He took a deep breath, leaning even closer. Invading my space even more. "I've been battling my wolf since that day because he doesn't care how it happened—he wanted you and would have taken you however he could have you—but as a man, I know what I did was wrong. I did you wrong."

That admission, those words, took away so much of the hurt I had been carrying. So much of the anger. But not all of it. "You did."

"I did. But I love you, Lock. So much." He ran a finger down the side of my face, his huge hand uncharacteristically gentle. "Not just because you're my fated mate, but because you're *you.* Because you're fucking amazing and beautiful and kind and... Everything. You're everything. And I love you enough to let you walk away from me right now. To give you the freedom I owe you. My feelings won't change, though. My love won't stop. You say the word, and I'm coming to you."

I swallowed hard, my heart pounding hard enough in my chest that I knew he had to feel it. Maybe even hear it.

"You would leave the club and just move up to Detroit?"

"For you? A thousand times yes. Without a question or a doubt."

Pretty words—even the ones I wanted to hear—couldn't fix everything. Had my dad made my mom the same promises? I doubted it. Chiggy had always been club first. But Flinch had said he would leave Arizona. Had chosen me over the club.

But did I trust him enough to believe him?

"Flinch—"

"I hate to do this," Cutter said, interrupting our moment and stealing every bit of our attention. "Their flight is boarding, so they need to get through security and to the gate."

Flinch growled low and deep but took a step back. Giving me my space. Releasing me. And damn it if that wasn't the last thing I wanted him to do.

Without a second thought, I leaped at him, wrapping my arms around his thick shoulders and hanging on. He pinned me against him, arms around my waist, and pulled me right off the floor. Whispering how much he loved me and how sorry he was for fucking things up. Promising to come the second I wanted him there.

But then he let me go, and he took a step back. And another. Expressionless Flinch face on lock. Cutter leaned into him and said something I couldn't hear. Flinch nodded once, keeping his eyes on me as I turned toward the counter where the TSA agent stood waiting for us. Cutter gave Zella one more hug then sent her in my direction, both of us making it through security without issue. The two shifters waiting on the other side of the barrier and watching us go.

"Be safe, girls," Cutter said once we made it through the metal detectors, his voice carrying over the noise of the airport. "Take care of each other."

Which wouldn't be an issue. I grabbed Zella's carry-on bag and waited for her, ready to hurry us to the gate once she slipped her shoes back on. Ready to help her suffer through the flight home. Ready to suffer in my own way as well.

Just before we walked off for the gate, Zella turned and yelled out, "Thanks for flying me out here, Flinch."

The man in question caught my eye, nodding once as if in acceptance of her thanks. Still looking so hard and mean and ready to snatch me out of the airport if I gave him the signal that I wanted to stay.

I broke the stare and looked toward the gates instead.

Zella's words ate at me, though. They swirled around in my head, making sense and yet surprising me. I waited until we had made it through the throng of people outside security, let her words sink in for a full minute before I asked the question dancing through my head.

"What did you mean by that?"

She shrugged as if she hadn't just rocked my world. "He loved you. He didn't want you to be alone for your dad's wake, so he made sure I was here. He bought my ticket, set up my ride to the airport, and had one of the guys pick me up to take me to his house. All I had to do was show up."

Words were hard. I hadn't actually thought about how Zella had gotten to Arizona. I'd assumed she had flown there but had also assumed she'd paid her way. It made sense for Flinch to tell her when the events for my dad had been happening, but to fly her out? To set up her transportation to even get to the airport? That was a lot.

"How?" I asked, answers still not fully formed in my head. The picture growing clearer but not quite in focus. Pressure building in my chest as the reality of what he had done for me came to light.

"How what?"

"How did he know to get *you* here?"

"I asked him the same question when he reached out." She

looked away, a weird almost-scowl on her face, before sighing. "He knew who I was because of the phone call. That day you were scared in the mountains and he came to find you—he knew my name and that I was your best friend. He admitted that he went through your phone to find my info so he could get me here for the wake."

I...didn't know how to respond to that other than to say, "That's so invasive."

"It is, but his heart was in the right place. And one of the first things he said to me was he only looked for my info—he never opened any apps or went digging for stuff he shouldn't have." She shrugged, tugging me with her as we edged our way around a group of travelers spilling out into the walkway. "He snooped, but not too much. Plus, his snooping brought me here."

"So the end justifies the means?"

"No. But love makes you stupid, and sometimes that stupidity needs to be forgiven because the intentions behind it were so good. Now come on, they'll shut the doors on us if we don't hurry."

My best friend grabbed my hand and pulled me behind her, leading the way to the plane that would take us to Detroit. The place we should have thought of as home but I didn't know if I ever would again.

I had a feeling my heart knew that home was in the desert.

Or wherever my taciturn wolf shifter happened to be.

But Zella needed medical attention from people who could help her, which meant that had to be my priority.

THIRTY-ONE

FLINCH

My world became a very dark place without Locklyn in it. Everything kept moving on, but I didn't have a single fuck to give about any of it. Even my brothers—my fellow Desert Hellions— couldn't pull me out of my misery. Though they tried.

"Yo, Flinch."

I turned on my seat at the bar to look over at Ridge, our road captain and all-around asshole of the club. "Yeah?"

"If you're going to pout like a baby, at least do it while getting some titty milk. Come suck on these." Ridge grabbed one of the women who hung around and pulled her top down, baring her breasts as she laughed at his antics. I scowled and turned my back to them, not at all interested. I wouldn't even have been at the clubhouse had it not been mandatory. Cutter was being voted in today. Finally and officially. And the man had the votes—there was no worry to be had with that. After how he had handled the vamp attack and knowing Chiggy's murderer had been destroyed, the entire club stood solidly behind him. Everything at this point was a formality.

"Hey, man." Rush slid onto the seat beside me, motioning to Billy for a beer. "How you doing?"

I raised my own beer to my lips, pausing before slugging it back to say, "Life is fucking perfect, my dude."

A lie and he knew it, but what was I supposed to say?

Rush whispered a thanks to Billy when he received his beer then sat silent for far longer than I had expected. His energy wasn't calm, though. The man almost seemed to be hyping himself up for something. I had a feeling I knew what it was, too.

"Ask me," I said, turning in my seat just enough to face him. "Whatever it is, just fucking ask me."

Rush frowned then sighed. "I liked her too, you know? Not how you did, but I thought of her as a friend. I just wanted to know if you've talked to her and how she's doing." He picked at the label on his beer, refusing to look me in the face as he quietly said, "I've been worried."

Yeah, everyone had. Locklyn had somehow infiltrated our little club with her wit and her heart. People had stopped asking me about her after I'd kicked Zed in the chest for doing it on week two of her being gone, so it shouldn't have been a surprise that anyone was still wondering. Rush had taken a risk asking me about her. The least I could do was respond.

"I don't actually know how she's doing."

"You haven't talked to her?"

"Talked, no. Texted, yes." I sighed and stared down at the bar top. "She won't answer my calls."

Rush grunted, acknowledging my statement. He then sat quietly again, his energy calmer but still putting me on edge.

Finally, he slammed his beer down and nodded as if having decided.

"Look, I'm a fucking idiot when it comes to women. I am

fully aware of that. But it seems to me that she loved you. No, not past tense—she *loves* you. You hit a bump in the road, but the love was there. It's like you had a good bike. A great one, really. But something happened and you had to lay it down. Are you going to never ride the bike again just because it got a few scratches? Fucking no. You're going to throw money and time at the problem to fix it the best you can because it's surface shit. The good ride is deeper and is still there. You hear me?"

Oh, I had heard every word. I didn't fucking understand it, really, but I had heard it. "Yeah. I hear you."

"So there you go." He threw a twenty on the counter for Billy and rose from his seat. "Go get your girl. Fuck this whole needing-space thing. Space is overrated."

I didn't want to say he was wrong, but I also couldn't fully accept that he was right. Not yet. But his words had filled me with something so close to hope, I couldn't turn away from it.

"We'll see about that."

Mule opened the door to the meeting room where the vote count had been happening, slipping through the space with Cutter and Banger following. It was time for the official announcement—time to pay attention to the club business happening. But before I left Rush's side, I wanted to return the favor with a little advice of my own.

"Be smart," I said, grabbing his shoulder with one hand as I moved past him. "Be really smart and maybe apply all of what you just said to yourself. Eloise might also be a good ride."

And then I headed across the room to stand with the executive members. Thoughts swirling from club to Locklyn and back. Unable to focus but standing tall and unflinching in the moment.

"The vote has been counted and certified," Mule hollered, waiting for every single man in the room to grow silent. "Cutter has received a unanimous approval vote to become President of the Desert Hellions."

The cheer that erupted from the men in the room shook the foundation of the building, everyone happy and proud to have Cutter in control. I whooped right along with them, knowing this was the right decision for the club.

"Thanks," Cutter said after everyone quieted down. "Thank you all so much for trusting me to lead this brotherhood. The loss of our esteemed Chiggy will scar us forever, so we will continue to avenge that death. We will forever right the wrong brought upon our house. And we will annihilate the threat any vampire colony poses to our friends and family."

Another cheer rose from the crowd, barks and howls adding to the cacophony. Cutter nodded along, biding his time. Waiting for the boys to grow silent once more.

"Moving on to official business—I'm leaving my executive team intact with two additions. As is customary, the president gets to name his VP, and I'm bringing on Diesel to be my right-hand man."

Another cheer went up as Diesel strode across the room to join the execs. He was a good guy, and Cutter had a strong relationship with him. A friendship of sorts filled with enough respect to call each other out on their bullshit when necessary. They would be a good leading team.

"And finally," Cutter said. "With the attack of the vampires and the death of Chiggy, I have made the decision that we need a second official enforcer. Someone to step in if a brother needs help. Someone to help Preacher keep the club as safe as possible."

The guys went silent, everyone likely wondering who would be promoted. Being on the executive team was a big deal and an honor, but it was also a responsibility a lot of these guys wouldn't have wanted. I had a feeling we had made the right decision, though.

"I would like to offer the new enforcer position to Rush."

Another cheer went up, though not as loud. That was to be expected—there would be some feelings hurt by the decision. Nothing Cutter and the team couldn't squash, but the sting would hit in the moment.

Rush sidled his way to Cutter, who had his hand out in offering. The new enforcer didn't even pause—just grabbed that hand and shook it, bringing Cutter in for a good backslap as well. Title accepted.

"There we go," Cutter said as Rush took his spot next to Preacher. "It was a tough decision—we have a lot of great men in this club—but I think our team will be stronger with the addition. I want to thank Rush for being willing to take on the challenge and all of you for giving me the opportunity to lead you. I don't take the responsibility lightly." He gave the crowd another once-over, hesitating when he met my stare for the slightest moment before moving on. "Now that the formalities are over, let's get shit-faced and fuck around."

Another cheer—louder than any before—rose up, and the music immediately started pounding through the speakers. Men mostly headed for the bar, likely to grab more beers and shots to celebrate the new team. Or just to get stone-faced drunk so they could pass out in the parking lot later.

Nothing I was interested in. I wanted to talk to the man in charge.

I locked my gaze on my target and followed him down the back hallway. He should have gone out on the floor and mingled with the guys as the new prez of the club, and he likely would, but not yet. He was headed to his office, so I followed.

"Cutter," I called before he could shut the door. "Got a minute?"

He looked over his shoulder, glaring my way. Up close, I could see the bags under his eyes, the tiredness bleeding through the expression of anger. The man looked a mess. Zella being gone must have hit him harder than I had thought, though I doubted it hit as hard as my loss of Locklyn. Which was what I needed him for.

"What do you want?" he asked once I entered his office.

"Have you heard from Zella?"

The look I received would have caused a weaker man to crumble. "That's none of your fucking business."

I nearly lunged at his throat in response to the anger in his voice. "I don't know what crawled up your ass—"

"Shut your fucking mouth." He snarled violently, the noise making the hair on my arms stand on end. "Your stupidity caused Locklyn to leave, and now Zella is in another state, dealing with your mess instead of being here where I could take care of her." Cutter stalked closer, words more growl than language. Rage fueling the warning in his voice. "It's been fucking weeks. If you weren't a Hellion, I would have skinned you alive already."

The growl I released had nothing to do with his words and everything to do with my wolf not liking the feel of being threatened. I clenched my fists at my sides, fighting not to shift. Not wanting to go up against Cutter, especially not on Desert Hellions property. Thankfully, Zed and Rush came storming through the door at that moment and jumped between the two of us, Zed holding me back and Rush blocking Cutter once he had slammed the door closed.

"Stop, now," Zed ordered. "The crew will revolt if they see you two fighting on the night of the fucking vote. You need to stop thinking about these fucking women and start thinking about keeping our club alive."

And fuck if he wasn't right. Still, I waited for Cutter to make the first move. He'd been the one to threaten me—it would be his job to set things right.

Cutter nodded once, obviously still furious but in control. "You're right. We have to work together, and my anger is more at the situation than at you, Flinch." He held out a fist to bump. "I don't actually want to skin you alive."

"As if you could." I gave him the bump he had initiated. "The shit with Locklyn is my fault, and I'm sorry it bled into other areas."

Rush stepped away from Cutter, looking from his prez to me and back again. "You two could work together to fix this, you know. If the girls are best friends, they'll stick together. You should, too."

"Fucking right," Zed chimed in. "Plus, working together to retrieve these women would likely keep you two from killing each other in front of the whole club."

He wasn't wrong. Cutter gave me a chin raise, for sure a sign of being willing to work together. I nodded once in response, acquiescing. Especially since the last couple of weeks of working on the Locklyn situation on my own had led to absolutely fucking nothing.

"Let's bring them home," I said. The need to fight had wilted, the desire to go up against my brother dissipating into the ether. What remained in my emotional bank was a sadness—a loneliness—that exhausted me and left me wanting to do nothing but sleep to make the time pass faster. And as much as I knew it was probably best to fight through that feeling, I was done for the day in every possible way. "I'm going to head out. Let's connect tomorrow to start figuring out how to get the women back here."

Cutter nodded. "Sounds good."

"Don't go through the bar." Zed stepped in front of me, brow furrowed as he blocked my way out. "The brothers will know something's up and start squawking. Cutter doesn't need the heat."

He wasn't wrong about that. Plus, I had no interest in interacting with anyone else. It was time to retreat. "Understood."

Zed let me go, giving me a hard stare as I left the office. Likely making sure I turned in the correct direction. But he had nothing to worry about—I slipped out the back door into the parking lot, needing the fresh air and the quiet to calm my nerves. Needing the escape. Fuck, I had messed up my life so badly. Messed up Cutter's, too. And I didn't know how to fix any of it.

My phone rang at that moment, and I fumbled to answer it, disappointment hitting me hard when I saw the call was not from Locklyn but from an old friend.

"What's doing, Flinch?" Were the first words I heard when I swiped to accept the call.

"Rebel. How's it hanging out there in the Dirty D?"

Rebel was the leader of the Detroit club of the Feral Breed and an old, old friend. I had called on him for a little help when Locklyn had left with Zella. As a mated wolf, Rebel had understood my plight and taken up the challenge, no questions asked.

"It's good, man. All good. I've still got my team on your girl and her friend as requested. I know the saying is no news is good news, but if Charlotte were out of my sight and I didn't hear shit from whoever had their eyes on her, I'd be climbing the fucking walls, so I figured I'd give you a non-update."

"I appreciate it, brother. Hopefully we can get this figured out soon and let your guys go back to fucking club pussy and taking Sunday rides out there."

"My guys need the job to remind them this shit ain't all sunshine, roses, and Jack Daniel's."

That need fit just about every shifter club I'd ever heard of. "I hear that."

"I'll let you get back to your night, but just as a reminder, we've got plenty of room to put you up in Detroit. If you need to head out this way for anything, you just let me know."

He likely meant long-term—like if I needed to move to Michigan to be with my mate. I looked out over the desert behind the club, the shadows of the mountains in the distance just a little more black than the night sky, and I breathed in the hot, dry air. Fuck, I loved the Southwest. Loved the desert life. I had fought to find a home like the one I had and a club like the one I was honored to help lead.

But I missed my mate something fierce.

"I appreciate that," I said, breathing out a sigh. "Just got one question for you."

"What's that?"

"How bad is the fucking winter up there?"

THIRTY-TWO

I was beginning to hate Detroit.

The vibe of the place had remained the same as before I had traveled to the desert, but something about the noise had suddenly begun to get on my nerves. Or perhaps a particular noise. One I hadn't noticed being as prevalent before.

Because everywhere I went in the city, I heard motorcycles.

Everywhere I drove, I *saw* motorcycles.

It was as if the city had suddenly been inundated by large men on expensive bikes, and that reminded me of Flinch. I was not in the mood to be reminded of Flinch at every turn. He already took up too much space in my head.

With the rumble of engines practically chasing me down the street, I headed to the coffee shop on the corner. Zella still hadn't been feeling well so I figured she needed a pick-me-up, and I needed caffeine as sleep had simply not been happening.

"Good morning," I said with a smile to the woman at the counter. "Can I get one large iced cold brew with a splash of almond milk and one large iced coffee with cream and two pumps of vanilla, please?"

"Coming right up."

I paid the woman who sat at a register then moved down past the bakery case, looking at and drooling over the pastries and treats but not adding any to my order. Zella was on a strict no-sugar, no-gluten diet, which meant I was as well for moral support. I missed gluten, but not nearly as much as I missed my friend being able to move without wincing.

The familiar rumble of motorcycles interrupted my browsing, and I scowled as I looked outside. Three bikes sat parked out front—not the source of the noise, but there, nonetheless. Each one had a man in black leather astride, and they all seemed to be chatting. I could easily picture them as Flinch and Cutter and Rush, hanging out on their bikes. In a different situation, they could have been out there waiting for me. Ready to help me take care of Zella. In a different situation, I could have been thrilled to see them instead of irritated.

I needed to get the Hellions off my mind.

"Ooh, someone doesn't like motorcycles." A tall, ridiculously beautiful blond woman smiled my way, her gaze stabbing right through me. "Or is it just men you're not partial to?"

I looked out the window once more before turning to refocus on the woman, hoping the barista would be done with my drinks quickly so I could just go home. "The noise has been getting to me."

"Of the bikes? I can see that. It has seemed awfully busy with motorcycles in the city lately." She stepped around me as the barista called out a drink—Americano, sweet—but turned back and gave me a smile once she had her coffee. "You should feel safe when you hear the sound, though. Especially in the city."

Something in her expression sent ice down my spine. There

was a quality to it I couldn't place. An animalistic edge that was both familiar and completely out of place.

"I don't know," I said, keeping my chin up but definitely feeling like a rabbit in the face of a lion. "My dad was a biker. I know enough not to believe that line wholeheartedly."

"Clubs without women tend to become a little wild, or so I'm told." The woman nodded once, glancing over my shoulder before pinning me in place with her steely blue gaze once more. Looking even more predator-like as she leaned in closer. "I'm Kaija, and if you ever need anything at all, find a biker with a Feral Breed patch. They'll know how to reach me."

With that, she strode out of the building, hips swinging right along with her long blond hair. She slipped into place behind one of the men on the bikes, a huge, dark-haired man with sunglasses on. All three men and Kaija looked my way, staring longer than was probably appropriate before starting their engines and rolling out of their spots. As the man with Kaija wrapped around him turned my way at the last minute, he pulled the sunglasses off his face, his light eyes locking on mine. And in that moment, I knew. I felt it. They were wolf shifters. I didn't know how or why or what group they were with, but I had no doubt. They were shifters.

And I suddenly missed Flinch even more than before.

Coffees acquired, I headed home, my mind firmly on the shifters in Arizona. Even the sound of motorcycles in the distance didn't irritate me as much as they had before meeting Kaija. Now, they made me sad.

"I should not be missing the desert," I said to myself before opening the door to our apartment. I didn't call out to Zella just in case, which was a good thing. I found her lying sideways on her mattress, sound asleep. I grabbed a blanket from the end of her bed and laid it over her gently, hoping she could get a good nap. Zella hadn't been doing great since we'd been home. She'd restarted some physical therapy to help with a new pain situation and was trying a new medication, but the autoimmune fatigue had been higher than usual. She had been struggling to make it through each day and often found herself confused or distracted when she should have been wide awake. She'd even extended her FMLA leave at work to give herself time to work through the flare without needing to deal with her job. I worried so much for her but was constantly at a loss as to what I could do to help, other than work to help cover her part of the bills.

Distracted and so very tired, I poured Zella's iced coffee into an insulated tumbler so the ice wouldn't melt, set it on her night-stand, and closed the bedroom door behind me so the woman could rest. I decided to do something similar and moved to my room, sitting up on my bed and taking a sip of my own coffee as I pulled out my phone. I had a question about today that needed to be answered, and only one man could give me what I wanted.

> I met a Feral Breed MC member named Kaija today. A woman. Did you send her to me?

His reply came faster than I had expected. A simple one-word message.

No.

> Did you ask that club to watch me or something?

Yes.

His simple responses made my blood boil, and yet I couldn't blame him. I had been refusing his calls and keeping him at arm's length since I'd gotten home. A little taste of my own medicine was likely exactly what I deserved.

> You realize how overbearing it is to have an
> MC following me around?

You realize how dangerous that city is?

I wanted to throw my phone across the room, but I didn't. I took a deep breath, and I tried really hard to be an adult who communicated.

> This is the problem. You refuse to respect me
> as an independent person. I've lived in this
> city on my own for a long time. I'm fine
> without protection.

My phone stayed silent, no reply from Flinch. I waited a good three minutes with the phone in my hand, almost hoping for an alert. A message. Something.

I got nothing.

At least not until the screen lit up with an incoming video call.

I didn't want to answer. I didn't want to fall back down into the hole of loving the man who would be on the other end, but I had to. I missed him too much to decline the call that time.

With a swipe of my thumb, he appeared on my screen, looking just as breathtaking as ever.

"Hi."

"My god, you're beautiful."

The smile that crept across my face could not have been stopped. "You look tired."

"Can't sleep without you." He sighed and ran a hand over his head, looking away before meeting my gaze once more, determination on his handsome face. "I'm sorry if making sure you and Zella are safe oversteps, but I couldn't send you out there without backup."

"I've been without backup my entire life."

"Nah, girl. You've just never noticed. You think the Detroit Feral Breed hasn't been keeping an eye on you for years? Chiggy was a better dad than that."

My heart sank, and my eyes immediately burned. "Don't lie to me."

"Baby, I'm not lying. I've known that club for decades. When I called in a favor to have them keep an eye out, they already knew everything about the two of you. That was your dad, making sure you were okay even when you were out there living your own life."

Tears burned their way down my cheeks, and I rolled over, cuddling my pillow and staring at the man who still had my heart.

"I never noticed," I said.

Flinch gave me a sad smile. "It's okay. He didn't do it so you would notice. He did it because he loved you. And I'm doing the same—making sure you're safe, even if from a distance. Because I love you, too, short stack. And I miss you so fucking much."

My heart thawed a little. Just enough to let a tiny ray of hope glimmer in my mind. My truth slipping out even though I wasn't fully ready to admit it yet. "I miss you, too."

"You do?"

"Yeah."

He sighed, his expression relaxing. His voice growing deeper as he said, "I want you happy, baby. No matter what—I want your safety and happiness to be the top priorities. I'll keep doing whatever it takes to make that happen."

"I want the same for you."

"You mean that?"

"Of course."

He leaned closer, his face growing larger on the screen. His eyes locked on mine and filled with an intensity that had me trembling where I lay. "You *really* mean that? That you want me to be happy?"

In for a penny... "Yeah. I really mean that."

His slow smile sent a shot of heat through my body. "Good. Then I'm going to make myself happy."

I had one last glimpse of him—of his smile turning absolutely wicked—before the phone went dead. Call disconnected.

Flinch, gone.

Thirty-Three

There was just something so demoralizing about being hollered at while trying to do something as mundane as pump gas.

"Yo, baby. You gonna give me that number?"

"Oh, for fuck's sake." I grabbed the pump and pressed the button for the lowest grade, needing gas badly enough to have to put up with him. Not wanting to, though. I squeezed the pump handle hard enough to hurt, as if that would make the gas enter my tank faster. I could get away with just a couple of gallons—I could always fill up another day when it wasn't already dark outside or I wasn't alone. I just needed enough to get home from the bar.

"Hey, baby. I'm talking to you."

"You are never allowed to fall into the trap of 'I'll fill up after work' again," I whispered to myself. I kept my eye on the screen, ready to run at any moment. Ready to swing as well, just in case he decided to make his move. Thankfully, I could still see the guy yelling at me from the corner of my eye and definitely noticed when he started walking my way. That was my cue to GTFO.

I moved as if to put the nozzle away but froze when the sound of motorcycles rolling in caught my attention. Two bikes came roaring onto the lot, both headed right at my car. One far too familiar for me not to recognize.

"Flinch," I whispered, unable not to. Finding it impossible to hold back the name of the man who had not left my thoughts in weeks.

The man in question swung his leg over his bike, eyes meeting mine for one hot second before he turned an inferno of a glare on the guy who had made the mistake of continuing his approach toward me.

"Yo, baby—"

"She's not your baby." Flinch stepped right in front of him, blocking me from view. "You've got three seconds to turn around and head back the way you came before I lose my temper."

"Don't want that," the other biker—still sitting on his bike and looking as if this were some sort of entertaining spectacle— said with a huffed laugh. "Old boy here has a huge temper. Explosive, really. You don't want to see him lose it."

The catcaller slowed but did not look convinced. "I was just trying to talk to the female."

"She doesn't want to talk to you," Flinch said, a definite growl to his words. A dangerous tone to his voice. "Now, go."

I wanted to warn the poor human—to tell him how violent Flinch could be. How I had watched him shred a vampire until there was nothing but some sort of bodily fluid in a puddle at my feet. Wanted to tell him the man before him was as ruthless as they came.

I wanted to say all that in warning, but also to brag. My mate wouldn't allow anyone else to hurt me. And he was there—right in front of me—ready to go to war again.

Why was that so...delightful?

The catcaller froze for a second then made the right decision, turning on his heel and walking away. Muttering under his breath but being smart enough not to say anything too loud. Once he was gone, Flinch turned my way, the look in his eyes one that stole my breath. That sent a spear of ice skirling down my spine. He approached me slowly, cautiously, then reached out and took the gas nozzle from my hand before leaning closer. Invading my space and drowning me in his sage and leather scent.

"Get your ass in the car."

The brashness of his words—the anger in his voice—shocked me right out of my stupor.

"I...what?"

"I said get your ass in the car." He paused, the moment filled with enough tension to steal my breath. "Please."

The added please did not soften his demand.

"I was just filling up with gas."

"I know, but that's my job. So, get in the car."

This time, I followed his demand, stumbling my way to the driver's side and climbing inside. Flinch closed out my order then inserted his own credit card, putting the nozzle back in to fill up my tank the rest of the way. I watched him move, unable to see his head or even his shoulders but still enthralled by the view. Enraptured by the vision before me. Flinch had come to Detroit. He was there, pumping my gas and making demands. I had no idea how or why, but he had come to me.

I wasn't sure how to feel about that. Or rather, wasn't sure what the *right way* was to feel about that. Because what I felt was utter joy at being in his presence again.

When the tank was full, Flinch returned the nozzle to the pump and gave me two loud thumps on the trunk, not saying a word before he returned to his bike. I started my car, assuming I was free to leave, heartbroken that he hadn't wanted to have a conversation. But as I left the gas station, the two bikes followed me. In fact, they followed me all the way home, not letting silly things like traffic or red lights dissuade them from riding so close, I worried they might crash into me. I drove slowly, splitting my time between watching the road ahead and watching them in the rearview. Obsessed.

I pulled toward a parking spot on a street I liked about two blocks from my apartment, but Flinch rode up beside me and motioned for me to follow him. I did, one motorcycle leading and one following. He led me to the surface lot next to my apartment building and stopped on the side of the driveway, again motioning me as if to go inside. I rolled down my window and stopped beside him.

"I don't park here."

"You're going to start."

"Flinch, no. It's twenty dollars a day." Which was money I couldn't spare. Never had been able to, and I had always been okay with that fact. Some things were more important than a convenient parking space. "I'm not paying for something so silly."

"You're right—*you're* not paying for it because I bought you a monthly pass. Now park that piece of shit and get inside. It's late, and I've got you."

My temper flared, the warmth of seeing Flinch again replaced by the heat of anger directed at him.

"You don't get to tell me what to do."

He leaned closer, still on his bike. Light eyes locking on mine. "I said I've got you, which means *I've got you*. It's safest for you to park here, so drive that car in, find a well-lit spot, then get your ass inside to Zella."

Using Zella against me wasn't fair, but I was tired of arguing. Really, I was just plain tired. Working, taking care of Zella, and avoiding his calls while missing him so desperately had consumed me for the weeks we'd been apart. As had the loneliness of not having him with me. I had made the mess and forced myself to suffer while wallowing in it, but Flinch had just shown me a way out of my misery. He'd made a move—a huge one—by showing up in Detroit. The least I could do was see how his plan played out.

I did as I'd been told. I found an empty spot under a light and parked, locking the door behind me when I left the car. I headed straight for Flinch, who now stood beside his bike. Another bike had rolled up, the three machines blocking the drive into the lot. I recognized Kaija on one of them, the pretty blonde throwing a smile my way as my eyes met hers. But none of them mattered—I needed to deal with Flinch.

"What are you doing here?" I asked, stopping a good five feet from him. Keeping space between us so I didn't do something stupid like fall right into his arms and cry on his shoulder. That would be bad.

He shrugged, completely casual. "You told me to do what makes me happy, and taking care of you is the only thing that makes me happy. So, I'm here."

My brain stuttered, the words from our last conversation— the only one I had allowed us to have not over text—running through my mind. "That's not what I meant."

"Too fucking bad. It's what you said."

His smugness irritated me more than anything else. I couldn't even find my words, couldn't figure out how to vocalize my emotions past my anger and irritation. Once again, the man had ignored my wishes and did just what he wanted. No consideration for anyone else. No including me in the decisions being made that affected me. I hated him for it.

Or at least, I wanted to hate him for it.

Because truth be told, I had never been so glad to see someone. Not ever. I had meant what I said—I wanted him happy. I just hadn't been prepared for what made him happy to be me. But I was so glad for it.

And somehow, he knew that.

"Go inside, short stack," Flinch said, his voice a low rumble of pure care and concern. His tone one that made me want to curl up in his arms and bask in the warmth and safety he provided. His eyes darkened as they ran up and down my body, his jaw tightening as if working to hold something back. "You're safe. We'll make sure of it."

We. It was the we that broke through and reminded me we weren't alone. I glanced past him at the bikes lined up, pursing my lips. "You called in backup?"

"Yes." He shrugged one shoulder, eyes locked on mine. "I've got a precious commodity to keep an eye on. Backup is required."

I sighed. "Flinch—"

"Inside. It's late, and I know you just left work." He reached out and touched my hand. A light brushing of his fingers against mine that somehow took a gigantic weight off my shoulders and set the world to rights once more. "Go rest—we can talk tomorrow."

I didn't want to listen, but I knew he was right. I was too tired for the conversation we needed to have and too shocked at his sudden appearance to make sense of my emotions. I needed time to process—more than just overnight. "Not tomorrow, but I'll call you once I…"

Figure things out. Know how I feel. Am ready to give in.

"Go," he said, his voice strong but tinged in sadness. As if he could hear my inner monologue of confusion. "I'll be here whenever you're ready for me."

So I went. Only turning around once to make sure he was actually there and this night hadn't been some sort of fever dream. Shivering as I felt his gaze on me before I disappeared into the building.

Thirty-Four

Flinch

The Feral Breed clubhouse in Detroit was a hell of a lot different from the Hellions one. First off, there were women there. Not club pussy—mates. More than a handful of them. There were also children running around. I'd never seen anything like it.

"Are all the standard Feral Breed clubhouses like this?"

Rebel looked around, frowning. "Like what?"

That would be a no. "The women. The kids."

"You don't have women in your clubhouse?"

"Club pussy, sure. Staff, definitely. Not mates."

"Too bad. It's a lot of fun watching mated pairs navigate club life." He took a sip of his beer, sitting deeper in his chair and offering me a smile. "How's your mate doing?"

"Fine. Good. Not talking to me much, but living life."

Living a life I could only watch play out. I missed her so much, and my fucking wolf wouldn't stop whining for her. Rebel probably knew all of that, seeing as how he'd been by my side—watching Locklyn right along with me—from the moment I had driven into town.

A little girl came barreling through the doors as we sat there, screaming for Uncle Gates in a voice that seemed far too loud for such a tiny being. Fifteen heads turned in her direction, every wolf on alert. Every man ready to get up and solve whatever problem that little girl had. But then Gates appeared, and the only problem seemed to be that she needed a hug. A man who looked like a bigger, more grizzled Gates followed her into the clubhouse, grabbing arms and greeting everyone as he moved. A scene of a reunited family playing out in a place where I would have expected more X-rated displays.

"Seriously," I said, amazed at how the men in the room bent down to greet the little girl as if she were one of their own. "What the fuck is up with this place?"

Rebel sighed and tilted his chair back, balancing on the back two legs. "I found my mate first—a human, like yours—then Gates, then Phoenix, then Beast—Gates' brother. The dominoes just kept falling for us. Gates' mate, Kaija, wanted to ride with us, which opened the clubhouse up to the women in our lives. Beast's mate was pregnant when she popped into the picture—"

"With his baby?"

"Nope," he said, popping that P before pointing the top of his beer bottle in my direction. "But that little girl is Beast's through and through. Don't ever make the mistake of thinking otherwise."

"Understood."

"Phoenix's mate is a witch, so that brought a whole other set of drama into the mix, especially when her sister mated to our Shadow. Then we got a necromancer mated to Jameson—you probably know him, seeing as how he's from your region."

I did know him. I also knew his mate. The woman was creepy as fuck, but she seemed nice enough, and Jameson definitely didn't seem to mind that she tended to smell like death. A lot. "Yeah, I do."

"The Fates just kept fucking rolling. My mate's brother even found his mate in one of the female shifters around us. Pure fucking chaos for a handful of years. But in the end, we all wanted to ride, we all wanted to live the life of mated wolves, and we all wanted our families to know us and our brotherhood. We wanted to build those connections." He shrugged before taking a long gulp of his beer, dropping back down to set his chair on four legs before leaning across the table. "You could have this, you know."

I looked around, taking in the smiling faces. The comfortable energy of the room. The women looking happy whether cuddling with their men or chatting with others. It was like a scene from a goddamned rom-com, one I didn't quite fit into. "I don't think my mate wants me right now, let alone any sort of connection to club life."

"Maybe not, but we've all been there. Especially those of us mated to humans—that learning curve when it comes to shifters and humans being in a mated pair is fucking steep." He looked around, catching eyes with his pretty mate, Charlotte, who had been sitting at the bar with what appeared to be two shifters she knew. "Totally worth it, though. Every second of strife is worth it in the end."

"I don't think the Hellions would be willing to accept mates and kids the way you guys have."

"So, come here." He turned his ice-blue gaze on me, his face a mask of seriousness. "You're technically a Feral Breed outpost, so it's not like you'd be changing clubs. Just making a move to a different city."

That thought had already been rolling through my head for days—moving to Detroit permanently for Locklyn. I'd do it in a heartbeat if she asked, but she *would* have to ask. This being half in and half out of her life wouldn't work for me in the long run, and every decision on our future needed to be led by her. I'd fucked us up enough—I couldn't be trusted to take the reins again just yet.

So I admitted the one thing truly holding me back from making any sort of decision. "She'd have to actually want me with her."

"Yeah, her refusing to talk to you is sort of a problem." He smiled at his mate again. "I don't know what the fuck the fates were thinking, mating us old men to these modern human women. I feel outranked on the daily, but she's so fucking good at being mine."

I sighed and ran a hand over my head, torn. Not having a definite path and needing Locklyn to help guide me to the right decision. For her. For us. Because the days of making decisions for just me were over. I had known that before the vampire attack, before the wake for her father, before I'd ever kissed her. The days of being just me ended that first night when I looked into her eyes. I wanted us to be an *us*, which meant making decisions that were best for the two of us. I'd failed at that by biting her without laying out what that would mean. I would not make a similar mistake again.

"At least I wouldn't be fighting vampires up here," I said, leaning back in my chair and giving the clubhouse another once-over.

"Yeah, they don't really cause too much trouble in the Midwest." He frowned. "I'm real sorry about Chiggy. I know I've said it, but the words will never be enough. He was a good man. Always full of laughs and energy when he came up this way. He will be missed."

Yeah, he would be. By Locklyn and the brothers he left behind back in the desert. That was a given.

"I need to track down the rest of the fuckers who participated in his murder. Get my girl the payback she deserves by annihilating their entire fucking nest."

Rebel nodded, tipping his beer in my direction. "You need backup, you let us know."

And that right there was the sign of a good club president—willing to go to war for a brother, whether one of his own or one from another house. Willing to pull up when needed. I would probably enjoy being a Feral Breed Detroit member with Rebel at the helm.

And I would definitely enjoy moving my entire life if it meant having Locklyn in it.

If she wanted me.

LOCKLYN

Lunch out with my bestie had not been the norm since we'd come back to Detroit, but when the restaurant Zella had once worked for had a new menu launching and needed taste testers, we took advantage of the opportunity.

"This is really good," Zella said, gracefully stirring the soup she had chosen. "Did you like your salad?"

"I did. I would eat a whole other one if there weren't five more courses coming." I wrote a note on the pad the chef had given me, jotting down my thoughts on the salad. He wanted to know everything—immediate thoughts when it arrived at the table, presentation impressions, did the ingredients seem well proportioned and balanced. And of course, taste. It was a lot of work on our end to supply them with the info, but I otherwise wouldn't have been able to afford to eat in such a place.

I caught sight of Zella glancing to the side, obviously looking out the window.

"Don't," I said with a shake of my head. "Don't mention it."

"How can I not? He's *right there*." She motioned with her spoon. "He's so smitten."

"Shut up." My face grew warm as I, too, stole a glance through the large front window. Flinch leaned against his motorcycle out front along with two other riders. They seemed to be having a conversation, one that made Flinch smile a bit. As I watched, he brought a hand to his head and ran it over his hair. I loved when he did that.

"You are also so smitten," Zella said, stealing my attention back.

"Shut it."

I sat back as two servers came to take our plates and a man in chef's whites brought us another dish. This time, we had each gotten some sort of pasta. Which struck me as odd.

"Is that gluten free?" I asked, knowing Zella's dietary restrictions meant she rarely got to eat pasta.

"It is. Gluten-free sweet potato ravioli—they have a separate kitchen area in the back for allergy orders."

"I bet your situation inspired them to do that."

"Maybe." She took a small bite, brow furrowed as she obviously gave the taste and texture a lot of thought. Then she looked up and grinned at me. "That's perfect."

I couldn't hold back my own smile. "Good. Maybe I should get a job tending bar here so I can bring it home to you at the end of the night."

"I somehow doubt you'll be needing to get a job in this city anytime soon."

My chest tightened, truth and denial and the whisper of acceptance fighting for dominance in my gut. "Why do you say that?"

She looked outside and shrugged a shoulder, likely knowing my words were nothing but a front. A place to hide behind. Knowing it but ignoring it like any good friend would do. "If you're not ready to see it, then there's nothing I can say."

That felt like a scolding of sorts. "Zella, I—"

"Have you talked to him?"

I sat back, picking at the beautiful pasta before me that I no longer had much of an appetite for due to the brick of guilt that had settled on my stomach. "Not really."

"Why not?"

That answer took me a lot longer to come up with, mostly because I *wanted* to talk to him. There was so much to talk about, yet I couldn't make that move. Couldn't be the one to initiate the conversation for some reason. The need to be next to him, to feel his body against mine, ate at me, but I refused to make that happen. And the reason for my refusal made me feel even worse.

"Lock," Zella said, her voice much softer, her gaze filled with understanding. "Talk to me."

I set down my fork, knowing this course was a wash for me. "I'm waiting for him to make the first move."

Zella blinked, her stare solid and sure. "Why?"

"I don't know." I glanced out the window, catching Flinch's eye. His gaze warming me from top to bottom even through a window. "I feel like I need him to take the first step in fixing us."

"He flew all the way to Detroit just to keep an eye on you. That's a hell of a first step."

She wasn't wrong, and yet it wasn't quite enough. And man, did I feel like a jerk even thinking that. I wanted Flinch back in my life, but he had messed up. Big-time. My dad had always said to never trust a shifter. Well, I had tried to, and he had failed me. That fact had broken my heart. He would need to show me he could glue it back together before I would show a moment of weakness. He would need to regain my trust.

"He has to be the one to clean up the mess he made," I finally said, picking my fork back up and shoving down all the emotions the conversation had stirred up. "I wish they had added cacio e pepe to the menu. That's my favorite."

Zella didn't say anything, just stared at me for a long moment before nodding. "Yeah, that would have been a good add. You should write that down."

I shrugged but did as she recommended, catching her on her phone when I finished. "Everything okay?"

She set her phone down, looking far too pleased with herself. "Yup. Absolutely. Let's get back to the food."

We ate more than we should have, both of us laughing and enjoying our time at the restaurant. The head chef came and thanked us when we were finished, giving Zella a hug and reminding her that she was welcome for family dinner anytime. He also invited me to come along, which had me hoping we might actually accept his hospitality at some point.

Once finished at the restaurant, I drove us home, watching the motorcycle headlights in the rearview. The two motorcycle headlights—Flinch had not been outside when we'd left. A knot had formed in my stomach when I'd noticed, and a surprising sadness had moved into my soul. Our relationship was a mess— an absolute mess. I loved him, missed him, and wanted to fix things but couldn't because for some reason my brain was demanding that he do the work. All of the work, no matter how selfish that seemed at times. He had messed up big-time, and he needed to repair it for me to be willing to give him another chance. I just didn't know if he would be willing to do that.

We made it back to our building without issue, me pulling onto the surface lot that Flinch paid for to park for the night. The knowledge that he cared, that he was taking care of me even when I was giving him absolutely nothing in return, hit me hard. Made me feel guilty. I missed him so much, and not telling him what I needed wasn't fair, but I couldn't get past my own shit to move us forward. Couldn't stop thinking the man needed to fix his mistakes to prove he cared enough about me to try. I needed him to work for our connection, not just rely on what the fates had thrown in his way.

That realization unlocked something inside me I hadn't even begun to recognize. I wanted Flinch to put in the work because a fated connection seemed like a cheat code. Like an easy button. Relationships needed a foundation stronger than that.

I was halfway to the front door of the building, still stewing over my view of relationships versus matings, when I spotted him. Flinch, in all his biker glory, stood on my stoop with flowers in his hands, looking more nervous than I had ever seen him before. His anxious eyes met mine, and heat exploded inside me. He was making his move, and I had a feeling I knew what had given him the confidence to do so.

"What did you do?" I asked Zella, still gazing at Flinch. Unable to break our stare.

"I pulled your head out of your own ass." She walked past me, smiling at the shifter with the bouquet. "Hi, Flinch. Good to see you."

"Zella," he said, giving her a slight nod while still staring at me. "Hey there, short stack."

My god, I loved him. "Hi. Are those for me?"

"Yeah." He handed me the flowers. They were a mix of oranges and deep reds that reminded me of the desert back in Arizona. And thankfully, the bouquet was rose-free. I doubted I would ever be able to enjoy those again without the smell reminding me of the vampires who had killed my dad.

I brought the bouquet to my nose, sniffing softly. Smiling at the delicate scent floating around the flowers. "They're beautiful."

"So are you." He stepped closer, his eyes locked on mine, the tension between us growing with every second that passed. "You're so fucking beautiful, my love."

I gasped, nearly trembling before him. Wanting so much to touch him, kiss him, feel his warmth against me. Wanting to stop fighting the need to be with him.

Thankfully, Zella made sure my internal battle was a quick one.

"Okay, you two," Zella said, slipping past us to unlock the door. "Let's head on upstairs so we don't get some sort of obscene behavior charge. The sexual energy between you two is enough to turn everyone on this block into a cornball."

Yup, battle forgotten.

We climbed the stairs to our apartment, all three of us silent. I didn't know what to say—my emotions were running through me too violently to find words to match their energy. And Flinch, he just watched me with a hungry look in his eyes. One I could feel.

"Don't start anything yet." Zella disappeared as soon as we entered the apartment, coming back from her room with a small duffel bag thrown over her shoulder. "I'm out. Now you can go for it."

"Where are you going?" I asked, feeling more than a little dumbfounded by the last five minutes.

"Your mate rented me a little escape for the night, so he could —what did you say earlier? Clean up his mess." She smiled at Flinch. "Try not to fuck this up."

"I'll do my best." He shot me a quick look, his expression almost shy all of a sudden. As if being alone with me worried him. "I got you a hot tub room—Cutter said the tub would help with any joint pain you might be having."

Zella bit back her own smile, a flush deepening the color of her neck. "Cutter told you that?"

"He did. He also said you should be protected at all costs, so the Feral Breed are taking you to the hotel. You won't need them after you get there, though."

Wouldn't need them...as in for protection. I had a feeling Flinch hadn't been the only shifter to make the drive from Mesa to Detroit, but I wasn't about to get Zella's hopes up just in case I was wrong.

Though I had a distinct suspicion that Zella knew her man was in town if the look of absolute joy on her face was any indication. "Take care of Lock for me."

Flinch growled, coughing slightly as if to cover up the noise. "You have my word."

Zella squealed before giving me a hug. She then jumped right at Flinch, practically hanging from his neck as she said, "You know you're my favorite, right?"

"Don't tell Cutter that." He huffed a laugh as he patted her on the back. "Kaija's downstairs to take you to the hotel and do the handoff."

"Cool. I'm out." She stopped long enough to drop her smile and look at me with a serious expression. "Don't be an idiot."

And with that, she walked out the door, leaving me alone with Flinch. With the man I had fallen in love with so quickly. The one who had made me promises he hadn't been able to keep.

The one who had driven from Mesa to Detroit to make up for his mistakes.

The one I was absolutely so ready to forgive.

We stood in silence for a long few seconds, the tension between us growing. The mood darkening.

Finally, Flinch sighed.

"I know I really fucked up, Lock, and I am so sorry."

And with that, I was in motion.

THIRTY-FIVE

FLINCH

"I am so sorry." Out of all the words I had said or would ever say, those four carried the most weight, and I meant them. I was endlessly sorry for so much in regard to how I had handled being mated. And if Locklyn had chosen to kick me out and not accept my apology, I would have deserved that shunning because of what I'd done.

But she didn't kick me out.

Instead, she ran right at me. Directly into my arms.

"Oh, Locklyn," I growled, pulling her close and lifting her off the floor. My little mate wrapped herself around me, and I felt whole for the first time since those fucking vampires had attacked us. Since everything had gone completely sideways in my life. I finally felt like the world was solid again. This was it for me. *She* was it for me.

"You're such an idiot." She pulled me in tighter, burying her face in my neck. "You messed up so badly."

"I know, baby. I know I did. I don't deserve your forgiveness, but if you give me another chance, I promise you that I'll never be so stupid again. I will never leave you out of the decisions or hold back information from you." I leaned my forehead against hers, my entire body on high alert. Ready for rejection but praying for forgiveness. "If you can give me another chance, I'll honor you the way a good man and mate should honor the woman he loves."

She choked out what sounded like a sob, a smile forming on her lips. "You'd better, because I've missed you."

My entire body went liquid, all my bones melting at her words. I dropped to the floor, still holding her. Cuddling her in my lap so I could be surrounded by her warmth and smell and energy. So I could be a part of her. And then I opened my mouth.

"I am an idiot, and I'm so sorry for that. I'm just a man who loves his woman but made a big fucking mistake along the way. I'm also a wolf shifter who adores his fated mate, and we would do anything for you." I pulled back, making sure I had her attention. Gazing into those green eyes I had fallen so deeply in love with. "My real name is Finnegan. I'm really fucking old, short stack. Well over three hundred years old, and I sure as fuck hope that doesn't matter to you. I grew up in a shifter community, but my club brothers became my family and were all I really cared about until you. Finding my mate overwhelmed me, and I definitely didn't do things the right way, but I'm going to try. I'm going to fix what I messed up. Ask me anything—I'm an open book for you."

She looked up, smiling. Teary-eyed but happy. "What's your wolf like?"

"He's an annoying, egotistical pain in my ass. He sheds like a motherfucker once a year and makes me miserable. He's also smart as fuck and keeps me alive. And he's been the biggest pouty baby since you left us. Pretty sure he'd hump your leg right now if I let him out."

She looked up at me through those lashes, naughtiness sparkling in her eyes. "Just my leg?"

Done. Over. Dead. I picked her up with me as I rose to my feet, not willing to miss a single opportunity to be with my mate. Hump just her leg? Nope. Not today. It had been weeks since I'd been allowed access to her sexy body, and her leg wouldn't be enough.

I walked us into her bedroom and collapsed on the bed, wrapping my body around hers even as I groaned and pressed my rock-hard cock against her stomach.

"Fuck, baby. Everything in here smells like you."

"It should—it's my room."

It was, but the scent. By the Fates, the scent rocked me. I was drowning in her and loving every breathless second of it.

"We can't stay here," I said, groaning as I flexed my hips against her. Wanting to feel her weight on my dick. "I would never get soft if I had access to this bed. You would be so annoyed with me and my dick trying to get into your pants every second of every day." I inhaled, my face pressed into her mattress, rocking my hips against her again as her scent filled me. "Seriously, short stack. I'm going to come just lying here in this scent. Ask me anything while I'm still in control of my brain because the blood is flowing out at this point."

She laughed and rolled us over, ending up straddling my hips and rising above me. Dropping her weight on me and making me clench up at the pure pleasure of the feel of her. I stared at her in wonder, unable to believe she had forgiven me. Or maybe not— she could still be upset—but we were definitely heading in the right direction. And the right direction at that moment was me inside her.

"Be with me," she said, her voice soft but strong. "I don't need to ask anything more right now. Just be with me—I've missed you." She dropped her gaze, her smile softening. Her expression turning almost shy. "I still love you, Flinch. I never stopped."

Done. Over. Death by my mate's sweet words. Nothing else mattered in that moment, just her and me and reviving the connection we both needed.

I grabbed her hips and lifted her onto my thighs, unfastening my pants and ripping the undies off from under her little skirt before letting her slide back down. And then there she was—all warm and wet and soft, pressing up against my cock. Ready to cradle him and welcome him home. I groaned and thrust upward, so fucking ready to be back inside her. Needing it. But I was nothing if not a gentleman in bed—and I had made her a promise. Two for one.

"Hang on," I said, grabbing her hips and yanking her up the length of my body. "Let me get you good and ready to take me."

"I am ready." But the groan she released when I licked her rudely right between her legs told me she could be even more ready. I settled her on my face and went to town, licking, sucking, teasing that pussy until I had her dripping down my chin. She rode me like a rock star, making sure I hit every part she wanted. Gasping and shaking as I sucked her clit between my lips and growled to give her a little extra stimulation. My girl lost her fucking mind at that point, rolling her hips and making all these adorable mewing noises. I couldn't see her face, though. Her skirt kept me hidden away between her thighs, which I actually didn't mind. The setup made everything feel just that much more naughty. A little dirty. Like we were sneaking. A thought that had me ready to blow.

"Flinch, I'm..." She didn't finish her sentence, but her body went stiff and she groaned this deep, guttural sound. I knew that one—had heard it before—so I grabbed her thighs and got more aggressive with her clit. Sliding two fingers inside her soaking wet cunt so I could feel her come. And come she did, all over me.

Shaking, chanting my name, jerking her hips. I loved every fucking second of it, but no way could I last after that. No way could I hold back.

I flipped my mate and immediately sank my cock deep inside her, both of us groaning in concert as I filled her. I needed her to get one more, though, so I pulled one of her legs over my shoulder to expose more of her pussy to me, and I made sure her clit got the attention it needed with every thrust. Fucking her good and hard. Dying as every move made her scent grow around us.

"That pussy's so good," I said, growling as I tried to hold back my own orgasm. "You're just swallowing me up right now. Letting me go so deep. Fuck, baby. How can I resist it? You're just so fucking hot and wet." I adjusted my angle and came at her harder, grabbing one ass cheek in a tight hold and slamming her body into mine with every thrust. Grinning as she practically screamed my name. "Oh, you like that, don't you? Like when your mate fucks you rough and mean. Gimme another one, baby. Come on your mate's cock so I can feel it. I want you to soak my dick with your heat."

She groaned and arched her back, digging her fingers into my shoulders. So close. I knew she was close. Knew she just needed a little push over the edge. I had to make her come before I did, so I slipped a hand between us and pressed my thumb against her clit, knowing the pressure would be too much. That we would likely cross the line between pleasure and pain. I kept my eyes on her face and thrust as I pushed, not wanting to hurt her.

And when she came, she was more beautiful than anything I had ever seen in my life. Head back, hair a mess, makeup smeared, mouth open on a cry that went silent halfway through. Her body clenched against mine, her pussy growing impossibly hotter and wetter as it locked me into place. I followed right behind her, unable to hold back. Dying as that pussy gripped me.

"Fuck, baby. You're so fucking tight around me. Perfect fucking pussy." I leaned down and kissed her lips softly, still coming. Still feeling her trembles. "Perfect for me every time. I'm going to ruin that fucking pussy so it only ever wants me."

LOCKLYN

Hours later, after more orgasms than I could count, we lay cuddled together in my bed. My back to his chest, his arms wrapped around me, and one leg thrown over my hips. Surrounding me. I couldn't rest, though. My brain refused to turn off and instead kept circling a subject we hadn't talked about yet. Which meant I was going to have to bring it up.

"Hey, Flinch?"

"Yeah, baby?"

"Tell me about the bite."

His entire body went stiff, the anxiety rolling off him in waves for a solid ten seconds. But then he relaxed, drawing me close and running a finger over the mark on my neck.

"I was wondering when we'd get to this." He leaned in and planted a soft, wet kiss to the mark, making me shiver. "It's a mating bite, my love. A mated pair will bite each other to complete their bond, usually during sex. It's the ultimate act of possession and passion."

"But...why?"

"So many reasons. It ties us together as a mated pair, so whenever you're around another shifter, they will smell me on you. Since you're human, it will slow your aging so we can spend more time together."

I spun around, unable *not* to be looking into his eyes for that one. "It will *slow* my *aging*?"

He nodded, looking almost chagrined. "Yeah. Significantly."

I wasn't sure how I felt about that. I didn't have family to watch die, and my only real friend was Zella, whose end I truly didn't want to even begin thinking about. It would likely be just me and Flinch, together for years and years and...

"How slow?"

"I've met a mated human who was over three hundred years old."

All the air left my body in a single exhale. "Wow."

"Yeah."

"So, we are *really* going to get to know each other."

He huffed a laugh, pressing his forehead against mine. "Yes, short stack. We are. You ready for that?"

Staring into his eyes, wrapped up in his arms, and warmed by his skin, I really only had one answer for him.

"Yeah, I am. Just don't keep things from me again."

He pulled me close and kissed me, his tongue sweeping into my mouth. His cock hardening against me. I should have been too tired or sore for another round, but there was no way to resist him. I had missed his touch so much, and I was certainly addicted to it. I couldn't get enough.

"In the spirit of not keeping things from you, there's more," he said, breaking apart from our kiss but still rocking his hips into mine. "The bites link us emotionally, too."

I grabbed his hand and dragged it between my legs. Needing his touch. Wanting so much to stop talking already. "What does that mean?"

He groaned as he slipped a finger inside me, both of us sighing at the contact. "Fuck, baby. I can't think and finger-fuck you at the same time."

"Try."

He growled deep and low, filling me with another finger and rocking his hand against me until he had me panting and clinging to his arms.

"Like now—right now—I can feel your pleasure. Your happiness. That bite left a little bit of me inside you—"

"Fuck." I arched into him, my muscles clenching at the pleasure running through me. My pussy feeling so wet and stretched by his hand. "I want a big bit of you inside me."

He nipped at my lips, growling. "Naughty girl. You asked the question, let me answer. Then you can have every inch of me."

I sighed, spreading my legs wider so he could have better access to me even as I said, "Fine. Emotions—linked by them."

"Right, linked. I can feel yours. Not as strongly as if we had completed the bites, but enough to know your emotional extremes." He leaned closer, kissing the bite on my neck again as he pressed his palm against my clit. Slowing his movements as he whispered, "It broke my heart knowing how sad you've been and not being able to fix it."

I threw my leg over his hip, pulling him on top of me. Needing to feel his weight. He pulled his hand from between my legs and notched his hips to mine. So close to filling me. So ready to bring us both together.

"I needed you to make the first move," I said, my voice hoarse and soft. Weak.

He nodded against my forehead. "I know. Zella told Cutter, who told me. I had been trying to give you the space you'd asked for."

"I know, but I didn't actually want space. I'm just an idiot who couldn't pull my own head out of my ass."

"Don't talk about my mate that way." He slid inside me, pressing deep with a groan that I felt all the way through me. Filling me and joining us just how I wanted. The slow slide of him pulling out caused my nerve endings to sing, and the harsh thrusts forward made them scream in something close to agony. I was sitting on the razor's edge between pleasure and pain, unsure which way I wanted to fall. Knowing both brought so much to my already exhausted body. But I still wasn't done. I wasn't ready to end the conversation, even though his cock sitting so deep inside me made words hard to find. We had one more aspect to discuss.

"Wait," I said, bringing a hand to Flinch's face when he froze. Trying to soothe the look of fear and confusion that appeared there. "So, do I get to bite you now?"

His hips jerked almost as if in reflex, as if he had no control over them, and a low growl bubbled up from within him that he had to cough away.

"I would be honored if you did, but that would tie us together forever. Permanently. My only biting you is an incomplete link, and it would fade over time. You would never have to deal with the loss of it. But if you bite me..."

"It's us forever."

"Yeah." Forehead on mine, he began a slow dance of in and out. Forward and back. Leaning down to kiss me deep, thrusting slower than ever. As if savoring the connection between us. Something in the way his entire body seemed to be wrapped around mine, about him being around and inside me at the same time, left me feeling so attached to him. Needy for him. In love with him.

I had to.

Without asking, without even thinking too much about it, I bit him right where his neck joined his shoulder. He jerked and slammed into me, his growl deep and loud. His body tensing as sparks shot off along every inch of me.

"You have to break the skin," he said through gritted teeth. "Fuck, baby. To complete the mating, you have to bite harder."

I took a deep breath through my nose, preparing myself for what was to come. Knowing this would be it—we would be bonded forever. Accepting that, falling in love with the idea of it, I bit harder. The metallic tang of his blood hit my tongue, and my world flipped upside down. Or rather, he flipped me to the side so that he could completely encapsulate me in his arms. It didn't matter, though. I was lost to the most erotic sensations coursing through my body. Pleasure unlike any I had ever known tossed me right over the edge, throwing me into an orgasm the likes of which I hadn't known existed. I came with a scream, my entire body tense and alive as every single nerve ending possible sang with pleasure.

"My mate. My fucking mate. You're all mine," Flinch said, hissing through his words as he growled and arched and locked me in his grasp until I could barely breathe. And then he fucked me, so hard and fast and out of control. Pumping, thrusting, growling the entire time as he held my head in place with one hand and used the other to grab my ass right up to the point of pain. My headboard pounded into the wall as he used his entire body to bring pleasure to mine, as he gave himself over to the need to fill me relentlessly.

I came again with my teeth still embedded in his neck, only letting go to be able to breathe, but that wasn't the end. The emotions swirling through me—the feeling of intense love and connection and ecstasy that weren't my own—dragged me over the edge again. And again. And again. Five orgasms later, I clung to Flinch as he roared through his own release, as his happiness raced through the bond and smoothed all the jagged edges. As we became a true mated pair.

"My love," he whispered, still inside me. Clinging to me like a life raft in rough seas. "You're everything to me, and I'll forever put you first. I swear it. You will never question where you are in my priorities. And I will never—not ever—neglect to tell you something as important as what this moment means to us. I swear it."

And I believed him. Truly. Not even the club would come before me.

Because his honesty bled through our bond. His surety locking in that promise.

He loved me. No doubt.

And in that moment, I knew for a fact that I could actually trust *my* shifter. My fated mate.

EPILOGUE

FLINCH

Life with my mate in Detroit didn't last long. Not because I'd fucked up again—that wouldn't be happening—but because a few weeks in, Locklyn and Zella both started talking about missing the desert. I had those two packed up and on a plane in under a week. Both of them. Moved them immediately in to my little house.

Of course, that hadn't lasted long, either.

"Are we taking Zella to the clubhouse tonight?" My beautiful mate smiled over her shoulder at me, lipstick in her hand. She had been getting ready for us to go out, though why, I had no idea. Don't get me wrong—that smoky eye makeup and shiny lip stuff looked fucking amazing on her. But she also looked fucking amazing with nothing on her skin at all except some sweet-smelling sunscreen she claimed she had to have. I preferred her bare and in my bed, but I loved her in whatever made her comfortable. Tonight, that meant lots of eye makeup.

"Nah. Cutter's picking her up. I offered, but it's his birthday party, and he wanted to walk in with her on his arm." Which shouldn't have been a surprise. No announcement had been made yet, but my new prez was certainly happy to have Miss Zella back in the desert. His bike always tended to end up in my driveway on the nights when Zella stayed home. In her home, because mine had gotten too small, too fast. And by home, I meant the tiny house I had set up in my backyard. I'd even added a composting toilet so the girl could be fully independent, though she spent most of her time with Locklyn. Her daytimes, at least. Locklyn's nights were mine, and Zella's certainly seemed to belong to Cutter.

I sat down to wait for Locklyn to finish getting ready, loving the sound of her singing along to the music coming from her phone. Enjoying the soft buzz of happiness tingling along our connection. Growing hard as I watched those hips sway. Goddamn, the girl was amazing and perfect. She could have asked me for the moon, and I would have figured out a way to snag it for her. Hell, she *had* asked me to put a heater in my pool —in the desert, where pool coolers were a thing—so Zella could do hot water therapy, and I'd complied. Never seen a pool guy so confused in my life, but we'd made it happen. My girl would have anything she wanted. Thankfully, she mostly just wanted me and Zella. I could handle that.

"I'm ready." Locklyn came out of the bathroom looking like sin. Dark blue jeans, torn-up black top that wrapped around her neck and showed off her shoulders, and that fucking makeup drawing attention to those green eyes I couldn't get enough of. She was ready to go, and I was ready to tear every stitch from her body and make her scream.

"You sure you want to leave?" I tugged her closer by her belt loop, biting into my bottom lip as she smiled down at me. "We could have a lot of fun right here, you know."

She leaned over and dropped a soft kiss on my lips, leaving

behind the taste of fruity sweetness. She also ran her thumb over my lips, likely wiping away whatever shininess had been left behind. I didn't much care—that sticky stuff just proved she was mine and I was hers. A man should be so lucky as to be covered in such a woman's lip gloss.

"We can have fun here later," she said, her eyes sparking with promise. "Let's go be social first."

I sighed but rose to my feet, pulling her into my arms for a second. Getting two good handfuls of that ass before smacking it. "All right, then. Load up. We're taking the truck."

The drive to the clubhouse was as uneventful as always, though I kept looking side to side occasionally. We may have taken out the vamp who had led the attack on our club, but that didn't mean they were all gone. The threat was still out there, the vamps who had joined up with Chiggy's murderer still hanging around. For the moment. Because we were making plans to eradicate those motherfuckers, and we would. No doubt about it.

The clubhouse was packed with people and too loud to even think by the time we arrived, all the brothers feeling boisterous about Cutter's birthday, it seemed. I headed to the bar, knowing Locklyn would eventually slip behind it to help serve drinks, wanting to keep my eye on her as she did. The woman liked to be helpful and we certainly appreciated it, but my brothers could be assholes. I made sure none of them decided to turn that part of their personality on my mate.

"You two finally made it," Tex said, giving me a pat on the back with his remaining arm. "I was wondering when you and Cutter would get here."

"He's not here yet?"

Tex shook his head. "Haven't seen him or his girl."

That surprised me. I had expected them to have left before us. I would have asked Lock if she'd spoken to Zella, but, as expected, she had jumped behind the bar and was in full bartender mode. I'd have to wait. Zella tended to break plans if she was feeling under the weather, which happened a lot. Maybe they had decided to hole up at home for the night.

"How's the pool?" Tex asked, as he always seemed to do. Losing his arm and about a quarter of his blood supply in my pool tended to come up in conversation, what with him still being armless. The fucker wouldn't grow back, but he had adjusted well enough to the loss. Tex still rode with us on every trip, and we all knew driving a big bike one-handed was a bitch and really worked a man's shoulder. Even his wolf had figured out how to tripod it across the desert at top speed. I had to admit, the man impressed me.

"Clean as a whistle. How's the not-arm?"

"Still not there but not slowing me down." He nodded over my shoulder. "Looks like someone wants to talk to you."

I turned to find Rush sauntering my way, a big smile on his face. "What did you do?"

"Nothing," he said, putting his hands up and grinning even wider. "Though I think Mule might be trying to steal your girl."

I spun around to find that old coot leaning across the bar, talking to Locklyn. He looked animated and intense, while she had a small smile on her face and seemed almost distracted. I growled low, bringing my fingers to the bite mark on my neck that she'd left me. Her eyes met mine almost instantly, our connection strong. She gave me a cheeky grin then refocused on Mule, nodding to something he was saying.

"Never gonna happen," I said, giving Rush a fist bump. "Old man ain't got nothing on me."

Rush hung around for a bit, busting my balls endlessly. Not that I minded. The boys could think I was whipped all they wanted—I was. I had been blessed with a mate who loved me good and strong. Fuck yeah, I was whipped. She treated me like a king and looked like a fucking goddess. Any asshole in the room would have gotten down on their knees and begged for such a woman in their life. And deep down, they all knew it.

Needing to touch Locklyn, wanting so badly to feel her against me again, I slipped in behind the bar. She turned my way and smiled, the look in her eyes a curious one.

"Hey," she said, tossing her towel on the rail and stepping closer. "What's up?"

"Nothing. Just missed you." I wrapped her in my arms, holding her tight against me. Curling my body over hers so I could rest my cheek on her head. She chuckled softly before running her hands down my back to slip them into the pockets of my jeans.

"Are you thinking about what we did here last time we got some time alone behind the bar?"

My dick sucked every ounce of blood from my brain in an instant, standing up straight and tall at the memory she had brought up. True, I had once said I wouldn't do anything with Lock in the clubhouse because I hadn't wanted any of my brothers to see her getting off. But when we had found ourselves alone in the club, she had taken advantage of the privacy to live out a certain fantasy. And I had been more than happy to participate.

"Fuck, I hadn't been, but now I am." I tugged her tighter, bringing my face to her neck so I could whisper into her skin. "Very little has ever felt as good as the feeling of your lips wrapped around my dick."

She giggled and gripped me tighter, a teasing energy bouncing between us. "You know you could have that more often, right?"

I shook my head, swaying with her. Smiling down at the woman who had brought me so much happiness. "I'm still a two-for-one guy, short stack."

She smirked, rising onto the balls of her feet and lowering her voice as she said, "Two-for-one doesn't specify order. I can get down on my knees for you first, then you can let me ride your face afterward. You'll be ready to fill me up with that thick cock by the time I come on your tongue."

Fucking vixen, my mate. The idea of that, the logic she had put into her plan to suck me off, broke every bit of restraint I had. I grabbed her tight and dropped a heavy, deep kiss on her lips. Growling through the act as my dick grew harder and heavier in my pants. As it came alive and begged for attention.

Fuck this party. Cutter would understand.

"Come," I said once I had broken away. I grabbed her hand and tugged her behind me, heading for the back door. "Come with me."

"Where are we going?"

I dragged her out the door and into the parking lot, too wired to give her more of an answer than, "Home."

"But we just got here."

I spun her around and pressed her up against the side of my truck, slipping a hand into her pants and diving deep for that pussy as I kissed her again. Tongues tangling, breaths mingling, I finally reached my goal and nearly collapsed at the heat and squeeze of her.

"You're already wet." I tugged my hand out and brought my fingers to my lips, licking her juices from them while staring into her green eyes. "You've been ready to go since before we got here."

She nodded, still smiling. Looking completely love drunk. "Yeah, I have. But mostly because I've felt how much you've been wanting me. The mirroring of emotions makes everything that much sweeter."

"So let's go home and feel each other. You, me, and a night of synced-up orgasms. What do you say?"

She gave me a quick kiss then turned her back to me, rubbing that thick ass against where I was so damn hard for her. "Take me home, mate, so I can love all up on you while you make me scream your name."

Sounded like a dream to me.

THE END

Did you catch the little tease there at the end? The "Are you thinking about what we did here last time we got some time alone behind the bar" line? If you want to read the scene this line inspired that line, head to ellisleigh.com/flinch for a bonus scene!

About the Author

A storyteller from the time she could talk, Ellis grew up among family legends of hauntings, psychics, and love spanning decades. Those stories didn't always have the happiest of endings, so they inspired her to write about real life, real love, and the difficulties therein. From farmers to werewolves, store clerks to witches—if there's love to be found, she'll write about it. Ellis lives in the Chicago area with her two daughters and a German Shepherd that never leaves her side.

Ellis can also be found writing tropey, erotic shorts with her bestie Brighton Walsh as London Hale, slipping into the contemporary world as Kristin Harte, or taking her signature style into the mystery realm as Millie Thorne.

Let's be social!
www.ellisleigh.com
ellis@ellisleigh.com

www.ingramcontent.com/pod-product-compliance
Lightning Source LLC
Chambersburg PA
CBHW030958190726
48285CB00004BB/1368